Praises for Pine Cone Motel

Pine Cone Motel is the kind of novel you want to snuggle into for inspiration and romance. True to her style, Gallagher creates an inviting cast of characters who are searching for healing—aided by each other, their faith and of course by a loyal canine. Perfect vacation read!

Maureen Lang, RITA and Cristy Award Finalist

In *Pine Cone Motel*, Author Sherri Gallagher doesn't take it easy on any of her characters but creates conflict and tension in every decision they make, every step they take, and in every relationship they have. No aspect of their lives is immune. Her resolutions to these conflicts are not pat, but satisfying, creative, and rooted in Scripture. Gallagher has won her readers over with this romance.

~ Clarice G. James, award-winning author of Party of One, Double-header, and Manhattan Grace

The Adirondacks come to life in this heartwarming story of struggle against all the odds. Can a traumatized combat veteran and a young, ambitious, feisty entrepreneur pull together to beat the clock and the prejudices of others? The answer is contained in a tale that is so much more than romance—it will keep you engaged and interested as Shellie and Ronan use every ounce of determination, hard work, and faith to keep a roof over their heads and build a future for the neglected Pine Cone Motel. Add in a highly intelligent ex-combat dog with a slight mischievous streak and the realistic backdrop of a tourist community and you've got a story that will keep you guessing from the first page to the last. Highly recommended.

~ Jane Steen, award-winning ————— *House of Closed Doors series and the Scott-De Quin*

Pine Cone Motel

Book 3 of Search the North Country

Sherri S. Gallagher

Pas Auf Publishing

coming along when she did. If I could have gotten an advanced degree, we wouldn't be in this position."

"It's not Shellie's fault I got pregnant. I didn't realize antibiotics would interfere with the pill. If I had, we could have refrained until my preventive measures were working so don't blame her."

"Great! So I suppose having a surprise baby is all my fault, now, too."

"No, I'm not saying that, but Shellie isn't to blame. Besides, I don't understand why it's so important to you to teach college. Your mother did a fine job supporting the two of you on a teacher's salary."

"Because professors are treated with respect. They have nice houses and intellectual discussions. I want to finish my thesis comparing *Legend of the Ages* to *Beowulf* and have someone I can discuss my ideas with instead of having to listen to discussions about football teams. The last five high school teacher's jobs I've applied for required me to coach a sport to get anywhere. I hate sports. When my dad died, I was able to leave all of that behind. I'm not going back to that world ever again."

"Why can't you finish your degree in the evenings? That would give you a reasonable excuse not to coach."

Her dad's voice was almost a snarl. "How am I supposed to concentrate with all the noise the children make, and you expect me to go watch their stupid soccer games? No, my chance at a better life was over the instant Shellie was born. All that's left to me is to work. It might as well be a job I can enjoy."

"Fine. Then I'll get a part-time job to make up the difference and you can turn down the coaching.

Shellie and Matt are in school most of the day and she's old enough to watch her brother and baby sister."

"Daycare for Leslie would take everything you might make."

The sound of the closet door opening and closing drifted up the stairs. Shellie scooted them back even further. No way did she want her dad to spot them.

"Where are you going?"

"Out I'll be back when I can find a professor's job that will take me. I'm done with teaching in high schools."

The front door slammed, and they could hear their mom crying and then the sound of broken china being cleaned up.

Matt whispered into the darkness. "Do you think he'll be back, or has he left us for good this time?"

"He'll come back. He always does." Shellie stood, dragging her brother with her. "We better get to bed so we don't get caught and make things worse."

Once Shellie had tucked her brother in, she slipped back between the now cold sheets of her bed. It hurt knowing she was the cause of all their problems. Shellie thought about running away, but that wouldn't help her dad finish his Masters degrees. No, the only answer was to be super good, get good grades, and not cause any more trouble than she already had by being born.

The King will reply, 'Truly I tell you, whatever you did for one of the least of these brothers and sisters of mine, you did for me.' Matthew 25:40

Chapter 1

"What is it, boy?"

The dog's silent alert had Ronan Flanagan wide awake and straining to identify any danger lurking in the Adirondack darkness. Blue might be small for a German Shepherd, but his hearing worked as well as a bigger dog's.

The rain combined with sleet rattled down on the roof in waves. Add the acrid smell of gunpowder and Ronan would have thought it was bursts of fire from an automatic weapon. Thankfully, it was water, not lead, pounding the roof of his cabin.

Ronan signaled Blue to his side and slipped out the cabin's back door. He left his bright yellow rain poncho behind, invisibility more important than being dry. His dark fleece and jeans soaked through before he had gone twenty feet.

Droplets of rain and ice ran down his neck and under his collar, chilling his skin. He ignored the discomfort the same way he had ignored the oppressive heat of the desert. It was not currently life threatening. His focus was on identifying what brought Blue to full alert.

He spotted her on the porch of the *Manager's Cabin*. She gave a final yank and the recalcitrant sliding door opened. Ronan shook his head. He had seen some drenched people, but she looked like she had dived head first into the Au Sable River.

He stood ten feet away in the darkness watching her. Most people would have felt his stare and turned to look over their shoulder, but she was either too innocent or too high.

Which was it?

A match flared in the dark interior and flames grew in the fireplace.

"*Fuss.*" Ronan hissed the heel command.

He backed up a few feet and turned slightly so the light wouldn't reflect off his and Blue's eyes. The fact she lit a fire made it more likely she intended to stay a while, so he could rule out her reason as vandalism. Someone looking to spray paint graffiti or smash up the place wouldn't have wasted the time. But that still left the question, was she there to do drugs or find shelter?

When she started to take off her clothes, Ronan spun, facing away from the view. His face warmed at the thought she might spot him and think he was a peeping Tom. He'd never understood voyeurs.

"Thanks, bunches, Alice." Shellie Morgan muttered to the empty room, shivering. "Promise to pick me up and let me crash on your couch for the night, then pull a no show."

Her face warmed at the memory of standing in the downpour of ice and rain for over an hour. The guy in the mini-mart charged her five dollars to use the phone only to get no answer, and he had refused to return the money.

Wrapped in a serviceable wool blanket she'd found on a nearby chair, Shellie approached the musty old mattress suspiciously. There was no telling how many mice were living in that thing. Still, there was no other place to sleep except the cold and dusty floor.

Stretching out on the cotton ticking, she stared into the flames in the fireplace. Shellie spared a moment to wonder if the door had been locked or glued shut by years of spider webs, dust, and pine sap.

It wouldn't matter unless the police came. At least if they arrested her, she would be locked in a warm, dry cell and maybe even given something to eat.

Tears clogged her throat. Was it really only two weeks since the expulsion hearing?

Easter had been the culmination of the dreadful months after Christmas while her life languished in limbo. The school suspension had prevented her from signing up for classes. It didn't really matter as the hearings ended in her expulsion and her grades would have been eighteen hours of Fs. She had tried so hard to be good and get good grades so her dad would be proud of her.

Tears hadn't helped then: they had just served to anger her father as he had shouted and ordered her out of the house. No, tears weren't the answer. If she was going to survive, she had to make it happen and tears only served to sap her strength. It was all up to her.

She fished one of the after-dinner mints she had filched from the restaurant reception stand out of her pocket and popped it in her mouth. Her stomach still complained.

It wasn't really stealing since they were set out for patrons to take.

Okay, technically she wasn't a patron. She had stepped in, asked to see a menu, and waited until the hostess was busy seating people to drop the menu, grab a handful of candy, and go.

A wave of guilt washed through her, but she squashed it. When you were down to your last seventeen dollars and thirty-four cents, guilt was a luxury you couldn't afford.

Tomorrow she would walk the rest of the way into town and get that job Grandma had asked an old friend to give her. He had reluctantly agreed to set up an interview and Shellie had used her last two hundred dollars on a bus ticket.

She usually managed a good impression and would work as hard as she could to do that tomorrow. If she got the job, she could walk to the youth hostel Gram told her about and stay there until she saved enough money to rent an apartment.

She'd have made it to the hostel if she hadn't wasted a couple of hours waiting for Alice to pick her up. After it was too late to check in, she'd started walking in hopes they'd bend the rules a little. A close call with an SUV's bumper forced her to dive into the abandoned motel's driveway and pointed out the foolishness of trying to get to the hostel tonight.

There was nothing left to do but hide from the hunger gnawing at her belly in sleep. As she closed her eyes, another tear managed to escape. She vowed it would be the last.

When he glanced over his shoulder, he didn't see her at first. He moved closer and finally found her stretched out on the old mattress.

The firelight sparkled in a tear on her cheek and compassion filled his heart. The intruder needed nothing more than a place to get in out of the rain. He offered a small prayer for the Lord's love to fall on the poor girl and returned to his own cabin, leaving her to a night of rest.

Dawn was starting to wash the sky from black to gray when Ronan awoke. He dressed quietly, his stomach aching a little from hunger, but that was nothing new. The fishing had been poor the day before due to the strange weather and all he had caught was one small sunfish. He had given it to Blue and contented himself with a salad from his glass-house garden.

The manager at the local McDonald's was a nice guy and always seemed to have some work Ronan could do in return for a meal. He made a slight detour to the *Manager's Cabin* to see what his visitor was doing. He smiled when he saw her wielding a broom. A new fire had been laid on the hearth. Nope, no need for him to say anything unless she was still there when he came back later. He headed out with the hope in his heart of earning a meal and the prospect of a better day of fishing.

Shellie suspected her clothes smelled of wood smoke, but there wasn't much she could do about it. The mirror in the ladies' room at Mickey D's showed she was clean, and she'd used the facilities to brush her teeth. Her subtle cosmetics emphasized her brown eyes and high cheekbones. She had brushed her long auburn hair and rolled it into an old-fashioned French twist in the hopes of making herself look older. A last inspection of her nylons told her the run near the top hadn't spread below her hem — yet.

She stepped in line behind a man with a bushy, red beard and long hair pulled back into a ponytail. He somehow managed to appear composed and shy all at the same time. His clothes were ragged and mismatched, the plaid shirt a total fashion "no" with his Camo pants. Clearly, he was homeless. She kept a safe distance; afraid the bum might have a fit or something.

The man stepped forward and addressed the kid at the counter. "Jerry promised to give me one of the old breakfasts for cleaning up outside and taking out the trash."

The server gave him a disgusted once over look. "Go talk to Jerry. I'm taking care of paying customers."

The man gave the kid a look that commanded attention. "Jerry had to leave. He said to come up to the counter and ask for a meal when I was done."

The server smirked. "Guess it sucks to be you."

The man shook his head and walked away.

"What can I get you, miss?" He winked and smiled at her, like she approved of his cruel treatment. The smile reminded her of Chad's expression at the expulsion hearing and moved her temper to throw caution away.

"T-two of the dollar breakfast muffins and-and a cup of coffee with a double cup. To go." She hesitated; the thought of how little money was left making her stutter.

Shellie didn't like coffee, but most men seemed to and if she put enough cream and sugar into it, she could manage to drink it. The server handed her the white paper sack and hot cup. She hurried to doctor the drink and rushed out the door. She spotted him walking up the parking lot, his head turned to the side while he seemed to be speaking to the skinny dog walking beside him.

"Hey, Mister." Shellie hurried toward him as fast as her wheeled suitcase and encumbered hands would let her go. The man turned at the sound of her voice and waiting.

"I – here." Shellie thrust one of the sandwiches toward him. Once he took it, she unstacked the cups and poured half of the liquid into the empty container.

"I hope you don't mind cream and sugar in your coffee."

He simply stood there staring at her. Shellie put one of the cups in his empty hand and turned away, walking to one of the outside tables in hopes the clear mountain air would remove some of the smell from her clothes. She could barely wait to chomp on her sandwich.

"May I join you?" He stood quietly beside one of the plastic benches. Shellie nodded her agreement warily, a little afraid of his mental state and the potential to acquire vermin. All she needed was a case of lice to make her misery complete. As he sat the only scent wafting her way was wood smoke and soap. The dog plopped beside him.

He set the food on the table. "Thank you."

Shellie nodded and set to work unwrapping her sausage biscuit. The man bowed his head and folded his hands in his lap, eyes closed and lips moving silently.

Shellie felt the blood creep up her face. She had been so angry and hurt she hadn't wanted to talk to God lately. After all, He let this happen when she was innocent. She hadn't stopped believing in Him but, she was too angry to talk to Him.

The man finished his prayer, whipped out a big pocket knife and cut his sandwich in half. He wiped the blade on his pant leg before folding it one-handed and stowing it in his pocket. He placed half of the sandwich on the ground between his dog's paws.

Shellie noticed the fur on the dog's lower legs was mottled and missing in patches and some of the nails were missing or disfigured. A neighbor had been a German Shepherd breeder and Shellie had learned enough to know this was a good quality, purebred dog apart from his deformed feet. She shrugged; maybe a breeder had given the homeless man the dog because the canine was born imperfect.

The dog watched the man with an intense focus, the tip of its tail tapping out a steady marching rhythm. The man gave a hand gesture and the dog set to work. Shellie had expected the animal to gulp down the food in one big bite. Instead, it separated the bread and meat, chewing each piece extensively before swallowing.

The man turned back to his own half and picked it up for his first bite. Shellie swooped up her greasy sandwich, ready to wolf it down.

"If it's been a while since you last ate, take small bites and chew slowly."

His voice rolled over her like a rich, chocolate sauce. It took a moment for his words to register in her brain, then the heat of a blush flooded her face. "How did you know?"

He remained focused on his own food as he took a neat bite, chewed and swallowed. He finally looked her in the eyes, and she was struck with the notion she had never seen anything so beautiful. They were an intense blue-gray with slivers of silver and small black flecks. The irises were outlined with a thin black line.

"Been there, done that. It makes it easy to see in others."

"Why does it matter how fast or slow I eat?" she asked meeting his gaze. "Other than manners, I mean."

"Well, first, small bites let you relish the taste. Second, it gives your stomach time to adjust so you keep it down, and third, it gives you time to learn when you are full instead of thinking you are still hungry."

Shellie took a small bite and chewed slowly, savoring the spices in the sausage patty. Her grumbling stomach quieted, and an imp of humor sparked to life. "There is some question as to whether this is really food or if we would get more nutrition from the packaging."

He threw back his head and laughed. "You've got sand, girl." He took a swallow of coffee. "But if you had money to buy food, why did you go hungry?"

Shellie ducked her head. She knew her face would give her away.

He waited. When it was clear she wasn't going to answer, he asked, "Did you steal it?"

Outrage poured through Shellie's veins that this bum would think she was a thief. This was the punishment she got for being nice; once again, falsely accused. She carefully enunciated her words to make sure he understood her. "No, I did not steal it. Not that it is any of your business."

"Since I am enjoying the fruits of your labor, if you had stolen it that would make me your accomplice, so it is my business."

"And why would that bother someone like you?" She regretted the words the instant they were out of her mouth.

The man did not react to her insult. "I don't steal. Whatever Blue here and I need we work for. If we can't work, hunt or fish for it, we do without. And yes, sometimes that means going hungry."

Shellie closed her eyes. By this time, she should know enough to hold her tongue.

"It does bring us back to the point of why you were saving the money?"

Shellie did her best to look down her nose at him. It was difficult to do since he was a good foot taller than her. "If you must know, I am down to my last seventeen dollars. I was trying to make it last until I got a job."

"But you used part of it to feed a complete stranger?"

She reached for her coffee, hoping the cup would hide her face. "I didn't like the way that guy treated you. You had a deal and he cheated you."

"It wasn't your responsibility to feed me."

"No, but I knew I would have had a hard time eating, knowing you were going hungry."

He shook his head. "Someone raised you right, Angel."

Pain lanced through her with the memory of her last argument with her parents. "If they had I wouldn't be here, so listen up: I'm nobody's angel."

Shellie stood, crumpling the wrapper and turning to hand the remaining bite of her food to the dog.

"Stop."

Shellie froze and met his eyes. Why wouldn't he let her give the dog a little more food?

"Blue and I have been in some places where people might try and poison him, so I taught him to go into protection mode if someone tried to feed him incorrectly."

She straightened and shuddered, imagining the damage Blue's teeth could have done to her hand. "Can I give it to you for him?"

He smiled. "Set it on the ground between his paws with your left hand."

"I have to know left from, right?" Shellie quipped to hide her nerves. Her hand shook as she placed the morsel on the ground. Once again Blue watched his handler intensely. A quick hand signal and the dog practically inhaled the tidbit.

Shellie put her trash in the receptacle and started rolling her suitcase up the parking lot. One last glance over her shoulder told her he watched her go.

Chapter 2

Shellie waited in the cheerful lobby of the *Lakeside Resort and Hotel*. She breathed a sigh of relief that a fire burned in the big central fireplace and would mask the smell of wood smoke on her clothing. She thought the interview had gone well so far and Mr. Grady seemed to have gone from wary to impressed. Most hotels had empty rooms except on special occasions, maybe she could live in one of them until she got paid.

He returned from a short interchange with a discreetly uniformed staff member. "Miss Morgan, I am a little concerned that a night desk position here is not the safest job for someone of your age and gender. Are you sure you want the second shift position? Something else will open up in a month or two."

Shellie stopped herself from saying, "Uh, duh," and settled for, "I don't believe that will be an issue."

"Are you sure you want to start your training today? You can take a couple of days to get settled, get your local address for HR and that sort of thing, instead of using your grandmother's information."

The sooner she started working, the sooner she had a paycheck, but no point in letting the man know how desperate she was. Her dad insisted she get a degree in literature, even though she had wanted a degree in business. The compromise was all her electives were from the business school. Shellie utilized a sales method from one of those courses. "Mr. Grady, the sooner I am trained, the sooner my co-workers can go back to their normal schedules and the hotel can stop paying overtime.

I can find a place to live after work, I already have some ideas."

Grady smiled, and Shellie had the fleeting thought that it was too bad she wouldn't be able to complete her degree. Now that she was on her own, she could switch her major to business. Shellie pushed the idea aside and concentrated on the rest of the facilities tour.

"There are a few odd perks of this job. First, if the laundry facilities are not being used the staff can use them for their personal garments, but no taking in laundry or the privilege will be withdrawn. Second, we have a very discerning clientele and they get upset if they see the same special on the menu two days in a row, so we allow our employees to take the unused cooked food home. Again, for themselves and their families only."

Shellie nodded. Free food? Yes!

Grady turned to face her. "There is one point that we are very strict about. Under no circumstances are staff to utilize empty rooms unless they pay the full nightly fee. Your predecessor ignored that, which is why the position is now open. Are we clear?"

"Yes, sir."

The hope of living in the beautiful surroundings fizzled up and died. No way was she risking losing this job. Shellie focused on the fact that being able to do laundry for free would save her fifteen or twenty dollars a week and right now that was the equivalent of her entire fortune.

By five o'clock her hand was cramping from taking notes and she was dizzy from hunger. She headed out the door straight for the hostel. Knowing she was employed, and in a month or two and she would have saved a security deposit and first month's rent was the first positive she'd had in a long time. Surely, she had turned the corner and her life would improve.

The hostel was quite a bit further out of town than Gram had said. At night, the country road would be dark. Without street lights or sidewalks, it would be treacherous walking home from work at midnight when she got out. Still, it would only be for a month or two.

Dragging the suitcase became impossible the last mile. By the time she got there and could set the beastly thing by the desk, her hand was sore and blistered and her shoulder ached. No one was around so she rang the small bell on the counter. A girl her own age appeared, chewing part of her dinner with an open mouth. "Can I help you?" she asked around what appeared to be a mouthful of corn.

"Yes. I'd like a room for a month, please."

The girl laughed, and a speck of corn flew from her teeth. "First off, you get a bed in the dormitory, if there is one available, which there isn't. Second, the most we rent by is a week and it is thirty dollars a night, paid in advance. Third, no one is allowed to stay for more than a week. "She looked Shellie up and down with that disgusted expression that had become familiar lately. "We aren't a flop house for bums and indigents."

Shellie knew instantly she would never be allowed to stay here. Even if every single bed was available, this girl would use her authority to keep Shellie out. She was just one of those kinds of people who take an instant dislike and stick with it.

Decision made, Shellie drew herself up and deliberately looked around the place, making sure her disapproval showed. "You could have fooled me; this place is a shamble. The manager should be ashamed."

She spun on her heel and stalked out the door. Thankfully, her suitcase waited until she was on the road to hit a pebble, flip over and drag Shellie into the ditch. Setting her jaw, she collapsed the roller handle and picked up the bag for the long walk back to town. As she passed by a laundromat, she saw a free weekly advertiser in a rack by the door and took a seat on a bench. The perfume smell of laundry soap hung heavily in the mountain air. The more she read, the more depressing reality became. No wonder her predecessor tried to sneak free nights at the hotel.

Rents were exorbitant as befitted a resort area in high season. The ads for a roommate wanted more than she would make a month. The only places she could afford were well outside walking range and no buses were available during her normal working hours.

Shellie stared at a small clump of crystallized snow without seeing as she tried to figure out a solution. Now that she had a job, if she could survive a few months, she could save for a cheap car which would open her housing options. Clouds covered the sun. Her light jacket and skirt offered little protection against the damp air.

Stepping inside the laundromat, she spotted a pay phone at the back. Dropping the change in, she dialed Alice's number. By the fifth ring, Shellie was ready to give up and disconnect before it switched over to voice mail and she lost more money.

"Hello?"

How could Alice sound so sleepy at five in the evening?

"Hey, this is Shellie. I'm here."

Silence.

"Here where?"

"Saranac Lake. You know, you said I could stay on the couch at your timeshare for a few days."

"Yeah, I forgot." Alice yawned. "Sorry, we were out clubbing until almost five this morning."

Heat flushed through Shellie and her vision blurred. Her body shook as she struggled to keep her voice level and she fought not to scream angry words. Somehow, she managed to say relatively calmly, "That couldn't have been much fun with how bad the storm was."

"What storm?"

"I stood in a freezing downpour outside the bus stop, for over an hour."

"Sorry."

Alice didn't sound sorry.

Shellie reined in her rioting emotions. "That's okay. I understand. So, I'm not too far from Main Street. Is your place in walking distance? I can bring you up to date once I get there."

"Look, Shel. Since I'm twenty-one, I really wanted a chance to see all the clubs and stuff, so I talked to my parents and we switched to a time share place in New York City."

Shellie heard a top of a can pop, but whether her friend had opened a beer or a soda, she had no way to tell.

"I'm a couple of hundred miles away, definitely not in walking distance."

"Why didn't you tell me that when I called?"

"I didn't think it was a big deal. I figured you'd get tired of waiting and find a place to crash for the night."

Shellie squeezed the plastic receiver until her fingers went numb, fighting angry tears. For one irrational moment she wanted to shriek mean names and stomp her feet like a two-year-old. Alice was more of an acquaintance then a friend, but Shellie thought she'd be more dependable than this. "It would have been better if you'd been honest in the first place."

"Okay. Sorry. Maybe next year. Gotta run."

Shellie was left listening to silence. She carefully replaced the handset wrestling to control her emotions and slid to a sitting position on the floor, her head resting against the wall. How could Alice have done this to her?

The flash of lightning and crack of thunder brought her present situation front and center. She needed a roof over her head. Now.

A vision of the abandoned motel rolled up from her memory, but could she get away with it? Was it trespassing or stealing, or both? Resolutely, Shellie stood and started wheeling her suitcase along the quickly emptying main street. She eyed the black clouds overhead and figured it was even money, whether she would be inside before the downpour began or not. Well, if she wasn't, she could dry her clothes by the big fireplace again tonight. Surely the heavy rain would hide the smoke from passersby.

She was passed McDonalds when she saw the man from this morning. Blue ran up to her, tail wagging before she spotted his owner emerging from the trees holding a string of fish. Shellie looked at him warily, conscious of their lonely setting. They were only a few hundred yards out of town, but the surrounding forest made it seem like they were miles from anywhere.

He smiled and waved. "Hi, Angel."

"My name is not Angel."

"Since we haven't been properly introduced, I've been thinking of you as Angel."

"You've been thinking of me?" She cringed as soon as the words escaped her lips. She sounded like a breathless school girl with a crush.

He seemed surprised. "You were generous and non-judgmental, showing a kindness I haven't been given in a long time. Of course, I was thinking about you."

She wasn't so sure about the non-judgmental part. Thunder rumbled, and Shellie watched the clouds scuttle before the strong wind. She was almost to the motel but didn't want this strange man knowing where she planned to spend the night.

"Well, thank you for your generous thoughts, but I imagine you will want to get home before the rain starts."

"Actually, I'm going to the same place you are."

Alarm bells sounded in Shellie's head and she took a step back toward town only to trip over her suitcase. When she regained her balance, she asked, "What do you mean?"

"You're going back to the motel, right?"

Shellie's mind went blank. She didn't know what to say and lies never came easily to her. Apparently, her expression gave her away.

"Mrs. McClelland lets me stay there to keep away vandals and vagrants."

The heat of a blush climbed her cheeks. "You were there last night?"

"Yup. End cabin."

"Why didn't you throw me out?"

"You weren't hurting anything. You just needed someplace to get dry and sleep. As a matter of fact, you not only left a new fire set, you swept the place. That was a lot of work."

"You were watching me?" Outrage combined with fear to raise Shellie's voice several octaves. "The entire time?"

Now his expression was offended. "Of course not. But next time if you don't want someone with less integrity than me to take in the peep show, draw the curtains."

Shellie tipped her head back and closed her eyes. He was right.

"I figure anyone down to their last few dollars would have to come back." He held up the string of fish and smiled. "I thought I could treat you to dinner since you treated me to breakfast."

Shellie opened her mouth to politely decline, but the rain chose that moment to slash down, the cold bath stole her breath.

The man grabbed her hand and dragged her forward. "Come on."

Shellie ran behind him as fast as her recalcitrant suitcase would let her. Water ran from her soggy bangs into her eyes. Blue seemed to think the whole thing was a great game and ran circles around them, barking. The man's laughter at the dog's antics had a nice sound and somehow relieved some of Shellie's anxiety.

By the time they made it to the porch, she was soaked, and her teeth were chattering.

"Wait here a minute."

The man turned and sprinted to the end cabin, Blue matching his strides. Before Shellie had much time to stand around shivering, he was back with a cheap, yellow plastic rain poncho in a pouch with a local lumber company logo. "Here you go, you can keep this. Go ahead and change and I'll meet you in the *Dining Cabin*. First one there has to light the cook stove."

He ducked between two buildings at a trot, the stringer of fish in one hand and pulling his knife from his pocket with the other.

Shellie looked at the front door of the cabin and saw the small plaque *Manager*. Turning, she could make out a similar sign on the larger cabin next in line which read *Dining*. She debated for about fifteen seconds on whether to stay or return to town, until her teeth began to chatter.

The man seemed to have no physical interest in her, although she had the same impression about Chad until it was too late. That unhappy thought had her picking up her suitcase and taking a step toward the road. But if she did head back into town there was no place to go. She couldn't wander the streets in the rain all night and have any hope of working in the morning.

Besides, he offered food. There were no leftovers from lunch and the only freebie she had been able to score was cold French fries which were probably water logged by now. Fresh fish was a definite step up. The lock on this cabin seemed sturdy and she could find something to block the sliding door from opening. Decision made; she tried the front door of the cabin. It opened easily. Had he done that?

Stepping inside, she saw the old-fashioned key in the lock and turned it. She put her suitcase on the table. Going to the sliding glass doors, she noticed a stick propped against the wall. She was sure it hadn't been there this morning when she swept. Shellie picked it up and dropped it into the track. It was a perfect fit and would prevent the doors from being opened more than a few inches. She drew the curtains and stepped back.

The air was cold and damp. She hurried to unzip her suitcase and pulled out dry jeans and an old fleece.

Just to be on the safe side, she changed in the bathroom. Moisture condensed on the tile floor, making her running shoes squeak as she walked. Shellie grabbed the poncho and left her new sanctuary.

She took a minute to pull the poncho over her head and dashed around the growing puddles to the dining cabin. Shellie opened the old-fashioned wooden screen door and pushed wide the heavy plank door behind. Big windows on the back wall showed a vista of a fast running stream, the banks dotted with tall maples and pines and a large, well-tended vegetable garden and glass-house.

A fireplace dominated one end of the room, a large, soft, hand woven rug with a Native American design placed strategically in front. Several tables that would seat four or five people at each were arranged randomly across the remainder of the room.

A half-wall separated the dining area from the kitchen. Shellie stepped through the doorway. An original 1800's wood-burning cook stove had a place of prominence along with all the appliances of a restaurant kitchen. There were a few staples like flour, shortening, and salt in the tin-lined cupboards.

The refrigerator stood empty; the door held a-jar with a couple of clothespins. She tried a wall light, but other than the click of the switch, nothing happened. The electricity was definitely off.

The fish were filleted and laying out on a plate on the sink drain board. Beside them were fresh gathered greens still wet from the rain. A couple of buckets of water sat in the sink. They'd probably been gathered from the river since they were stained with tannins. A plastic jug looked like it held drinking water.

Hoping hers was the only cabin without running water, she tried the faucet handles. Nothing happened. Apparently, there was no running water in the entire place. A sigh slipped between her lips, so much for a long hot shower.

The man chose that moment to enter. Even in the gloomy light, Shellie could see his eyes twinkling. "Never used a woodstove before?"

She shook her head.

"It's a lost art." He said with a smile. "Tell you what, watch me this time and you can try it next time."

Cooking was more her element, so Shellie seasoned flour mixed with cornmeal and dipped the fish, rolling them in the coating, while the man coaxed the fire to life. He added a lump of shortening, which quickly melted into a thin layer of grease. When Shellie dropped the fish in the hot oil they sizzled and smelled divine.

She reheated the fries in another pan while the man prepared a salad. A kettle steamed on the back of the stove and the man poured it in the stoppered sink along with some dish soap.

A small work table with two chairs had been placed against the half wall within the warm circle created by the stove. As Shellie turned from setting the table, the man placed a percolator near the back of the stove and dropped the pans in the sink to soak. He set the salad on the table and pulled a chair out for her. "Care to join me, —"

He stopped, "You don't like Angel, so I won't use it, except in my thoughts, but since we are to be neighbors, what would you like me to call you?"

Shellie stepped forward, taking her seat and spreading her napkin in her lap. "I'm Michelle Morgan, but please call me Shellie, Mister...?"

He walked around to his own chair, "Flanagan, but I would like it if you called me Ronan."

Ronan couldn't remember the last time he had relaxed and enjoyed the sight of a beautiful woman over a good meal. Shellie's easy laughter throughout the simple meal demonstrated a good sense of humor and she hadn't pried into why he lived the way he did. Sooner or later he would have to bring it up and warn her, but for tonight he wanted to pretend he was normal, and their candlelight dinner was a nice first date. A flicker of his last date with Andrea flashed acrossed his mind, but he firmly pushed it aside. Andrea deserved better than the shell of the man he had become.

His nose told him the coffee had perked enough so he rose, moving the sugar bowl and a small saucer with the handful of creamers collected from fast food places to the table then poured coffee for both of them. He reached out to pick up both cups and placed one in front of Shellie.

"No. I'll get my own, thanks." The shrill in her voice warned him the lady might have some triggers of her own. Ronan deliberately controlled his body language to give non-threatening cues and took his seat again.

Shellie stood, poured the coffee he'd served down the drain and got a clean cup. She hesitated for an instant, then reached for the pot and poured herself fresh hot java. When she returned to the table, she refused to meet his eyes. He could ignore her distress or try to bring it into the open. Decision made; he took a deliberate sip from his cup before setting it down.

"Did you think I would slip something into your cup?"

The direct approach worked. She made eye contact. He watched her chew on her lip for a moment and he almost wished he hadn't spoken.

"It happened once. I will *not* make that mistake again." Her hands shook as she raised the cup to her lips.

Ronan wanted to reach out and hold her and promise he would never hurt her that way, but judging from her expression, physical contact would undoubtedly frighten her right now. The only way to get her to talk would be to expose a part of his own history.

"You know, when I was in the service after some of the really tough battles, we didn't want to talk about it. It stayed inside and hurt until we wanted to explode and smash something, but once we got it into the open, it was easier to put it behind us." He took another slow sip of coffee. "I've done some amazingly stupid things in my life, so I promise not to judge if you want to talk about it."

He waited, letting the air grow thick with tension. He stifled the impulse to chance the subject. She needed to let it out. If he let it go, the whole thing would be ignored and continue to fester in her like an infected cut.

She cradled the warm cup in her hands and spoke in a soft voice. "It was after finals, before Christmas. My friend talked me into going to a frat house that was having a big party to celebrate another semester finished."

Her voice cracked, and she stopped to take a sip. "I had been taking eighteen to twenty-one hours a semester, so I was technically a senior, but too young to drink alcohol. Chadwick Meyer the third, son of the chancellor, brought me a can of soda since I refused to drink the beer and wine and punch, they had."

Ronan waited, letting her set the pace and flow of information.

She looked over at Blue sleeping in the corner, then back down at her cup. "That's the last thing I remember until I woke up next to Chad feeling completely exhausted and my vision messed up and distorted."

Ronan hadn't expected to have her confession affect him as much as it did. He wanted to go find this Chadwick fellow and pour some drugs down his throat then drop the guy off in a very bad section of town. He drew a slow breath and released it just as slowly to quiet his heart rate. "Did you report it?"

Her brittle laugh made him wince and brought Blue awake and on his feet in sentry mode.

"That was an even bigger mistake. Several of Chad's frat brothers swore I had been guzzling the wine and I practically dragged Chad upstairs. I was the one who ended up expelled for lying, underage drinking, drunken behavior, and - you know, sleeping with a guy."

Ronan wondered at the strict rules that seemed to be something from a generation ago or more, but he knew of a few educational institutions that still tried to implement those standards. He wanted to ask why the frat house hadn't been punished for providing the alcohol, but those were questions for another time when she was less fragile.

Ronan sipped his coffee, pretending a calm he was far from feeling. "Did you get tested for the drugs that must have been slipped in the soda?"

"Chad followed me to the security office trying to talk me out of filing a report. He said if I did, he would make sure I was sorry. When I got there, he claimed I had thrown myself at him and called his dad, the chancellor. They kept me at the security office asking over and over if I was trying to force Chad into a relationship or wanted money. By the time they let me go and I went to the clinic I was told it was too late to test for any date-rape drugs."

Blue came over to her and plopped his big head in her lap. She immediately started to pet him. Ronan was glad the dog had acted to provide comfort that he knew was too soon from a man.

Her voice dropped to a whisper. "That wasn't the worst part."

It got worse than that? Was she pregnant? A desperate series of thoughts flashed through his mind on how to help her. Actions any normal man could do without a second thought, but that had been outside his ability. Still, he would not abandon an innocent baby and desperate young woman. He would have to find a way; no infant starved on his watch. Ronan reined in his runaway thoughts and steeled himself not to show any of his emotions. "What was the worst part?"

"My dad is a professor at the college and part of his salary came in the form of our house. The Chancellor told my parents either they had to send me away or the whole family had to move off campus. I have a younger brother and sister and Dad had a hard time finding a job this good at a college with only a bachelor's degree, so Mom gave me some money and put me on a bus. I can't even go home and see them, and I'm worried about my brother and sister."

Ronan slowly stretched his hand across the table, palm up. "I'm not much, Angel, but I promise never to abandon you like that or send you away."

Shellie placed her hand in his and he gave a gentle squeeze. Her trust gave him both strength and trepidation. He would work his hardest to keep that promise. He may have failed everyone else in his life, but he wouldn't fail her, even if he was half the man he had been before going to war.

Ronan was back in a Humvee, but instead of Martin across from him it was Shellie. Her glorious hair was tucked up under her helmet, but her eyes twinkled with humor. Her arm rested on the weapon clipped to her body armor.

Blue sat between his legs, panting in the oppressive heat.

"Hey lieutenant." Joey shouted over the rumble or wheels and engine.

"Yeah?" Ronan answered.

"Knock-knock." Joey grinned.

"Who's there?" Shellie yelled with a smile.

White light and flames ripped through the belly of the Humvee and Ronan was thrown backwards and pinned in the debris. The explosion was followed by a muffled roar, as if he were hearing it under water. Then the sound came back, and he wished it hadn't. He could hear screams as flames flooded around the soldiers.

A wall of fire separated him from Shellie. He could see the agony in her eyes. He tried to reach her, but he couldn't move.

He struggled against the metal pinning him in place. He had to get to her. He had promised he wouldn't abandon her but couldn't move. Something was pinning him down.

From out of nowhere Blue appeared, stretching his furry body across Ronan's chest and frantically licking his face. Slowly the blinding flames and brutal desert sun disappeared. Ronan was no longer in a heap of burning metal and sand, but in a bed in a dark room where the crisp smell of pines rode the cool air.

He was tangled in the flannel sheets and Blue was still on his chest washing his face with dog kisses. Ronan drew in a deep breath, savoring this scent of home as the last vestige of the nightmare left him.

Hugging Blue tight to his chest, he rolled to a sitting position. Settling the dog in his lap, Ronan ran a shaky hand through his sweat soaked hair and down his face.

Where had that dream come from? It had been months since he had relived the bombing that took out his entire patrol. And what was Shellie doing in the dream? Thank God, she had never been in that place.

Ronan shifted Blue to the bed, turned on a flashlight then padded barefoot to the bathroom. The kettle of hot water, he had brought from the dining cabin had cooled and he poured some into his hand and splashed it on his face.

The dim reflection in the mirror showed a man he didn't like. The expression of defeat, fear and unworthiness was one that haunted his mirror since he returned. He closed his eyes to shut out the sight of himself. No wonder Andrea had tossed his ring at him and left. He was a shadow of the strong, confident man who went to war. She deserved better.

Ronan returned to the bedroom and pulled on jeans. There would be no more sleep for him tonight. He stepped out onto the porch and listened to the rain tapping down on the roof. The cool air caressed his bare, sweaty chest like the gentle touch of a lover. The rain settled into a typical soft, steady rhythm Adirondack residents recognized. The breeze brought him a whiff of wood smoke.

Shellie must have lit the fire again tonight.

The thought brought him front and center to his problem. For the first time since his military life had ended, there was someone other than Blue depending on him. A human someone with nowhere else to turn. Someone he had promised to help and protect. Ronan dropped to his knees, crying out to God with his mind, *don't let me fail her like I did everyone else.*

The sun was starting to turn the sky from black to gray when Ronan struggled to his feet and went back into the cabin.

Chapter 3

Thankfully the poncho Ronan gave Shellie kept her dry on the walk into work. Her feet were still damp, but it was nice not to have to shiver through the day in wet clothes and pretend nothing was wrong.

Shellie glanced at the clock. She had half an hour before she needed to clock in.

"Mr. Grady, may I use the office phone to make a long-distance call? I need to finalize my living arrangements with an out of town owner."

"Since you asked permission, fine. But get a phone service of your own set up as soon as you can."

"Thank you."

Ronan had given her Mrs. McClelland's phone number and encouraged her to call and ask permission to stay at the motel.

An elderly woman answered on the seventh ring; her voice creaky with age. "Hello?"

"Mrs. McClelland? My name is Shellie Morgan. Ronan Flanagan gave me your number."

"Did he? Why was that, dear?"

"I was calling about the motel."

"Oh dear, is it starting to fall down? If you were injured, I can look up my insurance company."

Shellie thought about the peeling paint, moss covered roofs and lack of utilities. The comparison to the pristine hotel employing her was not a good one. If the lady still had insurance, she would probably be better off to burn the place down and collect a check if it weren't illegal. Of course, that wouldn't help Ronan or Shellie.

"No, nothing like that. It does need work, but it isn't dangerous."

"You know my grandson does most of my finances and I told him to have the place fixed up. Not everyone wants to stay in those big chains. Some people would appreciate the personal touch of a family operated place. But he said my expenses use up my money and the only value of the place is the land."

Shellie looked around her at the elegantly appointed room and tasteful flower arrangements and was inclined to agree with Mrs. McClelland's grandson. Still, bed and breakfasts were popping up all around so maybe she wasn't completely out of touch. "I was wondering if maybe I could rent a cabin. I just started working and I can only pay six hundred a month, but I'm willing to work and clean and paint the place and fix some stuff that I know how to do for the difference."

The silence stretched so long Shellie was pretty sure the answer was no, and this nice old lady was trying to figure out how to tell her.

The sound of a sniff came through the phone. "You know, I think you are the answer to my prayers. I loved that old place and raised a family there. It has a lot of good memories. It's bothered me that it was probably falling apart from neglect. I bet between you and Ronan you could fix it up good as new."

Hope filled Shellie. "Do you think you could get your grandson to maybe pay a little for materials each month? Paint isn't really expensive and that would make a big difference in the place."

"I'm afraid part of Henry's problem is he doesn't want anything to do with the motel. He's a financial planner and likes investing people's money in stocks and such."

Shellie's heart sank, but she could scrub the place anyway and do her best to earn the rent.

"You know, I wasn't counting on any income from the *Pine Cone*, but if you sent me a check, my grandson would put the money into stocks and not where I want it to go. So, you take the rent money and buy materials to fix it up and send me receipts and pictures once a month instead."

Shellie wanted to do a happy dance. This was the best deal of all. "You've got a deal, Mrs. McClelland. I promise you won't regret this."

"You've made an old woman's day. Make sure you send plenty of pictures. I miss the place and now I can rest easier that it won't fall apart. So, tell me, how is Ronan doing? It was so sad what the war did to him."

Warning bells went off in Shellie's head. Was she as wrong about Ronan as she had been about Chad?

"He seems to be doing fine. As a matter of fact, I didn't even realize he had a disability. Could you tell me what happened?"

The old woman sniffed, and her voice was clogged with tears. " About a week before he was to come home, his truck or whatever they use nowadays, hit a bomb. Everyone, but Ronan was killed, and he would have been too, if his dog hadn't dragged him out of the flames. The poor creature's feet were so badly burned they were going to euthanize him. Ronan somehow managed to smuggle him home and the local vet treated the dog for free."

She paused for a moment. "To get the dog home Ronan refused treatment. Ronan's own burns healed eventually, but he was so upset that he drank a lot and got into fights over nothing, smashed things up, that sort of thing."

It sounded to Shellie like Ronan had PTSD. "Did he ever get violent with women?"

"Oh no. Some of the fights started when Ronan thought a fellow had treated a girl rudely. If ever he'd had a reason to hit a woman, it would have been that selfish chit he was engaged to."

"Ronan was engaged?"

"Yes, and she broke it off saying his injuries had made it impossible to marry him. He could have been violent, instead he told her to sell the engagement ring and he walked away."

Shellie felt an irrational spurt of anger at the unknown woman but tamped it down. Mrs. McClelland's words gave Shellie a better understanding of Ronan. "Is that why he's living at the motel?"

"No, the fights got worse and worse until things got so bad his parents were afraid to have him around and asked him to leave. It was the middle of winter."

No wonder he'd been so sympathetic. Ronan had been abandoned by his parents, too. At least it was Spring when her parents sent her away. "What did he do?"

"I think he would have let himself freeze to death, but he wouldn't allow that to happen to the dog. He called and asked me how much I wanted for rent. I told him he had to stop drinking and go to church on Sunday. He could keep an eye on the place instead of paying rent."

"I didn't see any alcohol at the motel or smell it on him." The memory of Ronan's soap fragrance floated through her mind. He had been so understanding, listening to her side of that disastrous night. His story was certainly more traumatic than hers, but instead of demanding sympathy he had given it to her.

"Well of course not, dear. When Ronan gives his word, he keeps it. Please tell him I keep him in my prayers."

Chapter 4

Ronan awoke, exhausted, but at least he was aware of his surroundings and not having the kind of panic attacks the nightmares usually brought on.

He glanced at his watch and realized it was still morning. With Shellie living and eating at the motel, his stash of staples wouldn't last long. He needed to find some work that would pay more than a single meal for one person.

Sitting up, Ronan scrubbed his face with his hands. His eyes felt sandy and his mouth tasted like the bottom of the La Brea tar pits. Time to wash up. He was tempted to shave for the first time in almost a year, but the memory of the scars hidden by his beard stopped him.

Thirty minutes later, he was on the road to town wearing his best jeans and a pressed, long sleeved shirt covering the burn scars on his arms. As he rounded the curve, he could see the dock area of the local grocery store. He counted at least five people rushing back and forth carrying things. That was a good sign. Maybe they could use some temporary help.

Ronan put Blue in a down stay in the shade of a tree and marched inside. He approached the customer service desk with a confidence he was far from feeling. This was a big step back for someone with an accounting degree and a big step up for a bum who couldn't seem to hold a job. There weren't any customers around to slow his approach. "I'd like to speak to the manager on duty."

Credit the girl at the window, she gave him a smile with her response instead of a sneer. "Is there a problem, sir? I might be able to help."

Ronan returned the smile. "No problem. I was wondering if they might need a little help on a temporary basis. You know - moving stuff and cleaning up."

She nodded. "We're getting ready for inventory. Tom Carter, the manager on duty, is back on the dock trying to get things organized, so I think you might be in luck." She pointed toward the back. "You can't miss him; he's wearing a blue polo shirt with *Manager* stitched on the front."

Ronan nodded. "Thanks."

Instead of going through the store, he went back out the front and moved Blue to a tree near the back of the store. The dog would be able to see him if he was working back there, but no one was likely to notice the dog.

Ronan sized up the dock area as he approached. It was covered, but open to the pine scented air, although the nearby dumpster added its own kind of fragrance when the wind changed. "Mr. Carter, sir. Do you have a moment?"

Carter was about forty with thinning dark blond hair and fair complexion. His athletic build and calm demeanor gave Ronan a modicum of hope.

Carter gave Ronan an assessing look and extended his hand. "What can I do for you?"

Ronan shook hands. "I was wondering if you had any temporary work? I'm not afraid of getting dirty or heavy lifting."

Cater paused and stared at Ronan. Ronan automatically dropped into inspection stance, chin up, shoulders back, eyes focused straight ahead.

"You former military?"

"Yes, sir. I've dug my share of latrines so I'm willing to take the dirtiest job you've got."

"I was in the Corp, myself. Welcome aboard, son."

Ronan allowed himself to relax his stance and smiled. "What do you want me to do first?"

Carter turned and pointed to a set of pallet racks buried in boxes and broken up corrugated. "Clean up that mess and get some order in it so we can inventory what is there and decide what needs to be thrown out and what can still be returned."

"Yes, sir."

Carter smiled at Ronan. "Son?"

Ronan turned to look over his shoulder.

"My name is Tom, so don't sir me. When I was in the Corp, I was a Gunny and worked for a living."

Ronan smiled back. "You've got it, Tom."

Shellie had trouble concentrating for the rest of the day. Ideas and plans buzzed through her mind. It was a relief to return to the motel. A gentle breeze had blown the early morning drizzle over the mountains, leaving the afternoon air crystal clear.

She unlocked the *Manager's Cabin* and passed the musty check-in desk to the bedroom she had claimed as her own. The bed was still wrapped in the flannel sheets and a cheery red and green plaid quilt she found in the linen closet. The scent of pine and oil soap drifted in a soft undercurrent of scent. The linens had been stored with sprigs of lavender in the folds and they added a hint of sweet floral to the tangy air.

Her suitcase was where she had left it and she could see her toothbrush and cosmetics on the bathroom vanity. She had her own place.

The thought left her light-headed and Shellie slipped into a nearby chair to look around. This was her home now. No more wandering and wondering where she would spend the night or where her next meal was coming from.

No more restless nights protecting her few belongings in a homeless shelter or sleeping on Gram's couch while the management harangued the older woman about Shellie's presence. She felt like a kid on Christmas morning after unwrapping that impossibly special gift she'd dreamed of but didn't expect.

Looking down, she realized her fingers had left an abstract pattern in the dust on the table beside her and motes danced in the sunlight struggling through the dirty sliding glass door. Since this was her place it was time to get to work and clean.

She added a little Murphy's Oil Soap to water from the stream and started scrubbing. It didn't take long to clean her bedroom and she opened the sliding glass door to let in some fresh air. The bathroom took more time and she looked longingly at the shower.

Ronan had explained how without electricity the water would not run, but by using buckets she could fill the tank of the toilet and he promised they could heat enough water on the wood stove to take baths. By the time the bathroom was gleaming and smelled distinctly of bleach she knew a basin wash up wasn't going to cut it tonight.

Maybe she could put a little shampoo in the water and turn it into a bubble bath.

Shellie decided to leave the other two bedrooms in the cabin for a later day, but noticed the dirt was tracking from the front door into her clean domain. That would never do.

The reception area was an easy job, though. It was kind of cool to go through the paperwork and ledger left on the desk. It really looked like one day Mrs. McClelland had locked the door and walked away.

Some vinegar from the dining hall and old newspapers left the windows sparkling and the bright yellow pine desk and walls needed a good dusting. The slate floor glowed in jeweled shades of green and blue after a quick mopping. She mopped her way out onto the porch and stopped in the doorway to admire her handy work.

"Hey, Angel, are we neighbors?"

Shellie spun to see Ronan standing in the driveway, a bag of flour on his shoulder and a box at his feet. A pickup truck accelerated passed the empty in-ground pool and pulled out of the motel driveway. The driver beeped his horn. Ronan turned and waved, before turning back to her with a huge grin.

Shellie decided to give up on getting him to stop with the angel nickname; she would have to come up with something good for him. "Yup, you're stuck with me, Red."

Ronan's grin said he didn't mind. "Open the *Dining Cabin* door and take a look at what I got for us."

Shellie hurried to open the screen and heavy wood door while Ronan hefted the box under one arm and balanced the flour on his shoulder with the other. Once inside, he shrugged his shoulder to drop the bag on the counter with a thud and a small cloud of escaping flour. Shellie quickly investigated the box to find eggs, powdered milk, sugar, some dented cans of vegetables and soup, and even a bag of chocolate chips.

"This is awesome!" She quickly moved the eggs to a safer location and started unloading the box.

"The grocery store is getting ready for inventory. Not only did they pay me, they gave me all the broken, cut, or dented goods I could carry."

Shellie found a meaty soup bone in the bottom of the box, which explained why Blue's nose had been glued to the cardboard container. She held it up and gave him a questioning look.

Was Ronan actually blushing? It was hard to tell behind that bush of a beard. He shoved his hands in his pockets and scuffed the toe of his boot in the dust on the floor. "Yeah, that's for Blue since he did a world class long down while I worked. He couldn't come into the store, so he stayed by the loading dock all day."

Shellie smiled at his little boy's actions; they reminded her of her brother. "Why don't you take him outside and play to burn off his energy while I make dinner, then he can have his bone while we eat?"

Ronan nodded and called to Blue. The dog paced a few steps after Ronan and then back to Shellie, or more accurately the treat she held. It wasn't until Ronan pulled a hard rubber ball on a string from his pocket that he got Blue's full attention. The dog raced after him and out the back door of the cabin. Shellie watched them go for a few seconds before turning to light the stove. The lunch special had been roast beef au jus, and it had not sold well on the warm day. She had been able to score two large portions along with leftover potatoes and vegetables. She quickly created a nice stew that would last them a couple of days.

Glancing down, Shellie noticed a white dial on the oven door. Looking closely, she realized it measured the temperature in the oven and indicated a perfect temperature for cookies.

If she substituted shortening for butter, she had all the ingredients for chocolate chip cookies. She hesitated to risk their limited food supply on an experiment, but what else could they do with the chocolate chips? Besides, both she and Ronan would have some cash in a few days, so maybe a disaster in the kitchen wouldn't be such a big deal.

Stirring the ingredients together without an electric mixer had her shoulder aching, but the results made it worthwhile. It took more attention to feed the small pieces of wood in and keep the oven temperature up, but before long the cabin smelled of the divine mixture of vanilla, warm chocolate, and brown sugar.

Blue slammed through the door in front of Ronan, the ball clenched in his teeth, the string hanging out and his chest heaving like a bellows. He trotted to the corner and slumped onto his blanket with a thud. Shellie pulled the second batch of golden cookies from the oven as Ronan came through the door, nose sniffing like a bloodhound on a scent. "You made cookies?"

"Yeah, it was easier than I thought it would be." Shellie lifted the cookies to the cooling rack with a spatula. "I figured we could have them with coffee."

Ronan washed up from the bucket in the sink and set the coffee pot to perk.

"You should have seen the store dock. It was a mess. Tom, the manager, had me clean up and sort the stuff that couldn't be sold. It took almost forty-five minutes to dig through the pile of dirty corrugated to get to the rack."

"That sounds yucky."

"I've cleaned up worse. Anyway, I labeled the racks for expired and damaged and started sorting."

"So that's how we got this windfall?"

Ronan smiled. "Yup. But I wasn't the one falling?"

"What do you mean?"

"Eddy is one of the stock boys and he's about your size, but he must think he's bigger. Anyway, he always carries more stuff than he should to the dumpster. With each trip his shoelaces untied a little more. I warned him twice, then he told me to mind my own business. A few loads later, the laces got him, and he landed head first in the dumpster."

Laughter bubbled out of Shellie at the visual Ronan's words painted. "He must have been really angry."

"You have no idea. The produce department had just finished dumping the spoiled vegetables, so he landed in rotten tomatoes and soggy lettuce, among other things."

"Poor man."

"With him being so short he couldn't reach the top of the dumpster and every time he tried to jump his feet would slip out from under him and he'd land back in the slop."

"You did help him out, didn't you?"

"Eventually, but I was so weak from laughing, I dropped him once or twice." Ronan winked and grinned.

Shellie tried to make her expression reproachful, but her giggles spoiled the effect. As they settled in with coffee and cookies Shellie shared her news.

"Mrs. McClelland is an absolute sweetheart."

Ronan smiled. "She's been a life saver."

"She wants me to spend the rent money on fixing up the motel and send her pictures and receipts. I figure I can do the scrubbing and cleaning this month and get the electric turned on with my first paycheck. I think having running water is the first step to making repairs. What do you think?"

"It makes a lot of sense. With lights we can keep working after dark. We'll need to turn the water on to each cabin individually and make sure no pipes froze and burst."

Shellie's heart took a nosedive; plumbers were expensive. Her salary wouldn't cover much work.

Ronan apparently read her expression. "Don't worry, my dad is a contractor. I learned how to do a lot of repairs working for him, including plumbing."

Hope restored; Shellie tried to figure out how to broach a much more personal subject. Drawing in a fortifying breath, she decided to plunge in before she lost her nerve. "Mrs. McClelland asked how you were doing. From what she said I got the impression you had some PTSD when you came home."

Ronan's face went from smiling to shuttered and the life seemed to leave his eyes. Much as it scared her to touch a man, she knew instinctively it was what Ronan needed. She stretched out a tentative hand and rested it lightly on his.

Ronan sat for a full minute staring at her slender fingers touching his scarred hand, drawing air swiftly in and out of his lungs. Blue left his bone and sat, his chin resting on Ronan's thigh. With a last hard exhale, he closed his eyes and flipped his hand over to clasp Shellie's like a drowning man grabbing a life line.

"Had and have PTSD. You need to be careful around me, Angel. I don't think I could forgive myself if I hurt you. I know I promised not to abandon you, but --- if things get too dangerous, I'll have to leave."

Shellie's heart beat frantically in her chest. She shivered at the dangers surrounding a lone woman living in as isolated a place as this motel. How was it she had come to trust Ronan so quickly and completely? But that was a thought for later, alone in her cabin. Right now, she needed to offer Ronan the kind of support and understanding he had given her.

She kept her voice soft and soothing, using the tone she had reserved for comforting her siblings after a nightmare. "What should I know?"

Ronan thought for a moment. "The worst time is when I'm asleep. I have a lot of nightmares and I'm really disoriented when I first wake up. I think I'm still in Iraq and under attack, so I defend myself. My dad tried to wake me up once and I accidentally broke his nose."

"Got it, stay out of arm's reach if I hear you having a nightmare. Should I shout from the doorway or poke you with a stick?" One look at Ronan's face told her the joke didn't work.

"Send in Blue. Sometimes shouting can set me off if I'm not ready for it, and the stick will feel like a weapon, so I will attack."

Shellie tilted her head. "You don't hurt Blue?"

Ronan gave her a ghost of a smile. "No, he sits on my chest and licks my face. It works every time."

"Since we aren't even in the same building, I don't think it will be a problem. It seems unlikely I will hear you and licking someone's face just isn't my thing."

Ronan wore a strange expression for an instant and then it was gone.

He looked down at their clasped hands and quickly released his death-grip on her fingers. As if realizing what he had done, Ronan gently stroked and massaged her tingling hand. "It isn't just at night. Sometimes, during the day something will set me off and I'm right back in the middle of a fire-fight."

"Do you know it's coming or what triggers it?" With the feeling back in her fingers, she returned the favor and went to work on his wide appendage. As she rubbed, she could feel the scars ridging across the back and made out the faint differences in skin tone caused by burns.

"Sometimes it's straightforward. Like the nail guns going off on the job sites. Other times it isn't. I can ride in a vehicle one time and have no problems. Other times I go into a panic attack riding in the same vehicle and I don't know why."

"Does it matter what the vehicle is, like the difference between a car and a truck?"

"No, it's happened in both."

Shellie thought out loud. "I wonder if it is a smell or going over a pothole that rocks the vehicle?"

Ronan stilled. "Potholes."

"Excuse me?"

Ronan focused on her and grinned. "The times it's happened, we've hit a pothole or been on an off-camber surface, so it felt like the vehicle was going to flip as it did that day in the explosion."

He scrambled to his feet so quickly his chair squealed on the wood floor. He snatched Shellie out of her seat and whirled her around the close space. "You're a genius, Angel. You spotted a trigger I couldn't find."

Ronan drew her close in a hug. Shellie's arms naturally went around his waist and she tipped her head up to smile back at his glowing eyes. His head started to come down and for an instant she thought he was going to kiss her. Excitement and fear mingled in her blood shaking her whole body. She wanted to have him claim her lips, but at the same time she wanted to draw away and hide. As his beard brushed her skin, Ronan drew back. Instead, he gently disengaged her arms and lowered her back into her seat.

He spun toward the stove and lifted the coffee pot with one hand while shoving his hair out of his eyes with the other. She noted that his hands weren't any steadier than hers.

"More coffee?"

Shellie nodded and reached for a cookie. She didn't want either, but they kept her hands busy. By the time Ronan joined her, he was back in control of himself.

Pretending a nonchalance, she didn't feel, Shellie asked, "Do you think it will rain tomorrow or not?"

After all, the weather was such a safe subject.

Chapter 5

Shellie straightened her uniform jacket with a shrug and stepped up to the desk. The sun shone through the big entry windows for the first time since she had arrived in Saranac Lake and the automatic doors whooshed open and closed repeatedly as people hurried into the lobby and directly to the desk. It was unusual to have this much traffic so early in the day. The queue built up as her harried coworkers spoke with guests at the head of the line. None of them had time to spare her a glance. If the red faces, tense expressions, and rapid hand movements of the guests were any clue, most of them were irate.

Shellie pasted a smile on her face and moved to an open computer. She nodded to the next guest in line, a thirties something couple that looked like they could model for a magazine.

"May I help you?"

The man spoke. "We'd like a room for tonight."

"Let me see what we have available." Shellie clicked away on the keyboard. The screen came up a red *no availability*. That didn't make sense. She refreshed the screen only to get the same result. She glanced at her coworkers' screens; all were showing the same message.

"Is this going to take long? We're tired and want to rest before tonight's concert." The female guest complained.

Shellie looked up, making eye contact first with the woman and then the man. "I'm sorry. It looks like we are sold out for tonight."

The woman began to pout and tugged at her companion's arm. He patted her hand and reached for his wallet. "Here, this may help. I'm a diamond member. There are supposed to be rooms held for us that are unavailable to other guests."

Shellie released the breath she had been holding and brought up the diamond club screen, quickly typing in the man's membership id. The screen once again came back *unavailable*. She looked at the man and his cranky companion, mentally preparing for the temper tantrum about to ensue. "I'm sorry, but even the diamond club rooms have been taken for tonight."

"Bobby, do something." The woman's voice rose and drew out the last syllable.

The man reached into his pocket and pulled out a crisp hundred-dollar bill and waved it at Shellie. "Are you sure there isn't a room available?"

Shellie took a step back. No way was she going to get mixed up in the type of trouble a bribe would cause. "Let me get my manager."

She spun quickly away and crashed into Mr. Grady. He steadied her, a stern expression on his face. Shellie motioned with her head for them to step out of hearing range of the guests. She spoke softly, just to be on the safe side. "Mr. Grady, that man is a diamond member and there are no rooms available, but he doesn't want to take no for an answer."

"So, I noticed." Grady looked over at the couple and then back at Shellie. "I don't like upsetting someone who is such a frequent customer, but there's nothing we can do. Even the repair rooms are full."

Shellie tilted her head toward the woman. "I don't think his companion would put up with a repair room anyway."

"Do you want me to take care of them?" Grady asked with an understanding smile. "I saw him try and bribe you. You handled that well, by the way. The shocked expression was perfect."

He believed that was an act? Shellie shook her head as she tried to organize her thoughts. "Before you send them away, I have an idea. There are several bed and breakfasts over near the elementary school. What if I give them a call and see if they have any availability? That way we aren't telling Mr. Pushy no even though we don't have rooms or sending him to a true competitor."

Grady waved a sheet of paper. "You have excellent instincts, Miss Morgan. Here is a list of approved B&B's. Things have been so hectic; I haven't had time to make sure we have the most current information."

Grady glanced over at the couple waiting impatiently at Shellie's station. "I'll comp them a meal and continue to handle the difficult situations. I want you to call all of these places and confirm their availability and pricing."

Shellie nodded and hurried to a phone in the office beyond the hearing range of guests at the check in desk. She dialed the first number on the list.

"Good morning, the *Blue Spruce Bed and Breakfast*."

Shellie turned on her most professional manner. "Good morning, this is the *Lakeside Resort and Hotel*. We are experiencing an overflow of clients. Before we send them away, we wanted to check your availability and pricing."

"Why, thank you for thinking of us. Yes, we do have several rooms available. Our cost is two hundred and fifty dollars a night."

Shellie had been sipping a diet soda and almost choked. She glanced at the date on Mr. Grady's sheet. It had been updated two weeks ago. "Excuse me, but that is double the rate we recently were quoted."

"You know the law of supply and demand. A wise business person makes a profit whenever they can and with the concert tonight, conditions are ripe for profit."

"That may be, but potential clients have to find you first. Under the circumstances, we will have to remove you from our recommended list, perhaps permanently. We can't risk our reputation with a facility that tries to gouge their guests."

Silence.

Shellie counted to ten and reached for a pen to change the room price.

"Under the circumstances, we would normally increase prices. However, in order to maintain our long running relationship with *Lakeside Resort and Hotel*, we will charge our standard pricing for guests you send us."

Shellie grinned. "Thank you. Expect our registration staff to be calling you shortly with the names of guests we are sending your way."

It took about fifteen minutes to contact the remaining B&B's, all of whom happily agreed to take the overflow customers at their standard pricing. Only a couple needed a little coaxing about their place on the referral list.

Shellie gave Mr. Grady the sheet. He scanned it quickly and nodded. "I'm surprised they didn't raise their prices though."

Shellie squirmed, wondering if she overstepped her authority. "Um, several raised their prices, but I was able to convince them to charge our guests their standard rates."

Grady looked Shellie up and down. "How did you manage that feat?"

"I told them we'd take them off our list."

Grady threw back his head and laughed. "Well done."

The reception staff turned toward them drawn by the unusual sound of Mr. Grady's laughter. More than a few wearing looks of confusion and surprise.

He turned to them and waved the paper in his hand. "Here is a list of alternative accommodations I am authorizing you to offer the guests without reservations. If they agree, call and secure them a room, provide directions and overall help them to have an enjoyable stay."

Grady turned to walk away but stopped and looked over his shoulder. "And you have Miss Morgan to thank for providing a reasonable alternative."

Shellie moved to her screen.

Mr. Grady smiled. "Good job."

Butterflies filled her stomach. The world was definitely looking up.

By lunch Shellie felt as limp as an over-boiled noodle. She sat in the employee dining room, dipping French fries in catsup and drinking iced tea, her back against the wall as she watched some of the maids and porters talking. Kelly James, one of the other reception desk clerks, walked over with a plate of salad. "Okay, if I sit with you?"

"Sure."

Kelly plunked down across the table and settled her plate on the wooden surface. She wrinkled her nose before stabbing a piece of lettuce with her fork and dipping it in dressing.

"That looks healthy."

Kelly swallowed. "I'm trying to lose weight, but I'd rather have fries."

Shellie laughed and pushed the plate between them. "We can share."

Kelly nailed one of the potato pieces with her fork. "That idea you had about the B&B's was brilliant. I wasn't sure I could survive much more hostility from the walk-ins without going ballistic."

"Mr. Grady had the list. All I did was make sure our guests would have a pleasant stay."

"Still, it's the kind of thing we talked about last semester in one of my classes."

Shellie dipped another fry. "What's your degree in?"

Kelly finished chewing salad before answering. "I don't have it yet. I'm going to Williams College for hospitality management. I'm thinking about switching to nights here part-time, so I can go to classes during the day. You're going to be on nights starting in a couple of weeks, right? Are you interested in signing up for some classes? Maybe we could carpool."

Shellie's heart gave a lurch and she drew in a fast, shallow breath. What she wouldn't give to finish her degree. She only needed a couple of courses. Reality crashed in, drowning her hope and leaving her slightly numb. She couldn't afford to even think about college. Still, it would be satisfying to write to her dad if she got a degree. After all, his parting comment when she left was how disappointed she had made him at blowing an opportunity for an education with foolish partying; but he wasn't surprised, she had been spoiling things since the day she was born. Shellie buried the thought. That was the past. She had to focus on her present situation.

"Right now, I'm working to put a roof over my head and food on the table."

Kelly nodded. "Yeah, if I couldn't live at home, I wouldn't be going to school. Still, they have a pretty good tuition reimbursement program here. Talk to Mr. Grady, especially after your move today; he might get creative to help out."

Shellie stood. "I've got to get back to work."

Kelly waved and turned her concentration to her lunch. The thought of getting her degree was tempting, but where would Shellie come up with the money? Maybe someday. Right now, she needed her first paycheck to get running water and a hundred other things before a luxury item like a college education. Survival first.

By the time Shellie made it to the motel, all she wanted was to curl up in bed and sleep, but if she was going to keep her bargain with Mrs. McClelland, she needed to keep on cleaning. She was surprised at the silence when she arrived.

"Blue? Come' ere, boy."

No loud barks or rambunctiously bouncing dog greeted her.

"Hey, Ronan? Are you here?"

Panic washed over her and chilled her skin. She rubbed her arms reflexively and hurried into the *Dining Cabin*. What had happened? Had her presence driven Ronan away? Had he had an episode, and someone had locked him up and sent Blue to Animal Control?

Shellie glanced around wildly. If only she had a phone. But who would she call? The police? She didn't even know how to get in contact with Ronan's family.

She dumped the Reuben sandwiches she had brought home on the table and spun in the circle of warmth. Warmth?

The fire in the stove had been banked but had burned down to coals. Ronan had to have been there in the last few hours. Was he in his cabin, disoriented and frightened?

Heart pounding, she stood in the *Dining Cabin* trying to decide what to do. Should she knock on his cabin door? Was she better to stay away or offer food and pretend everything was normal?

"Stop it. You're no good to Ronan in a tizzy. Think."

Her voice sounded hollow in the big room, but the effort of speaking helped her break the panic spiral. She concentrated on breathing normally until her hands stopped shaking.

Shellie turned to the stove and added a big log to the fire. It smoldered before catching in a puff of flames, quickly generating a steady wave of heat.

"Good. That will hold for a while and give me time to change clothes and think."

She stepped out into the cool spring breeze and headed for her cabin. Approaching the door, she saw a white envelope pinned there, her name neatly printed on the front. Her chills returned. She told herself it was from the breeze, not worry. She took solace there was no official return address on the envelope, so it most likely wasn't some government agency telling her Ronan was incarcerated. She slipped inside and settled in a chair, drawing out the single sheet of paper with shaking fingers.

Hi Angel, I am going to be working until 3 AM unloading trucks at the grocery store. I left the fire banked, so hopefully the dining cabin will still be warm when you get there. See you tomorrow. Ronan

Breathing a sigh of relief, Shellie tucked the missive back into the envelope and felt like melting off the chair seat and onto the floor.

Refusing to think about why she had been upset over a man she had known for a very short week, Shellie concentrated on changing and developing a plan of action.

Since Ronan wasn't around, she would finish cleaning her cabin. Funny how they had tacitly given each other privacy. She had not entered his cabin and since she had arrived Ronan had avoided entering the *Manager's Cabin.*

The other two rooms didn't take much time. Both looked to have been bedrooms, one painted pink with a floral border and the other green with a wildlife motif. The pink room had been converted into a sewing and craft area, complete with a shelf of scrapbooks. Taking one down, she looked at pictures of a child as she grew from infant to womanhood with a baby in her arms. It was interesting to see the changes the motel had gone through in the background. Other volumes appeared to be family vacations and the last a little boy's life. He had grown into a young man, handsome in his Marine uniform. The last page jarred Shellie and tears filled her eyes as she looked at the death certificate. He had been her age when he died of battle wounds.

Shellie returned the books to their shelves, letting her tears fall freely for all that was lost. How could she be such a whiner over her poor life simply because she had to go to work and support herself? She was alive. She was strong and healthy and that was a lot more than could be said for a lot of others who had reached her age.

She would ask Mrs. McClelland if she wanted the scrapbooks shipped to her. Certainly, the memories might be too bittersweet, and the photos had been left behind for a reason. Only Mrs. McClelland would know. She thought about asking Ronan but decided against it. He had lived through the agony of losing his friends and comrades and that scrap book would surely bring up his own painful memories.

For now, all she wanted was something to eat and a good night's sleep.

Ronan stood on the brightly lit dock, letting the cool night breeze caress him and waited as the second truck approached with a steady beep warning it was in reverse. Tom Carter walked over and handed him a bottle of cold water.

"I gotta say, having you walk up to my dock was a stroke of good luck. You're doing the work of two men."

Ronan uncapped the drink and took a big swallow. "Thanks. It feels good to be useful."

"What branch did you serve in?"

"Army. Stationed mostly in Kandahar."

Tom shook his head clearly pretending to be disappointed. "How is it an Army guy works as hard as a Marine?"

Ronan grinned back. "It's worse than that. I was a lieutenant."

"No. An officer and a grunt? Can't be."

The truck stopped with a whoosh of air brakes and both men capped their water bottles. As Ronan moved forward, Carter motioned him to wait.

"Really Ronan, I like your work-ethic. If you want a full-time job, let me know."

A lump, clogged Ronan's throat. It had been a long time since someone had wanted him around. He nodded and swallowed hard. "I'll think about it."

Chapter 6

"You're doing rather well with the accounting program, Miss Morgan. Have you used it before?" Mrs. Anderson asked.

"The program in one of my college courses was very similar."

The head of accounting looked over the top of her reading glasses. "I didn't see a college degree on your application."

"No, ma'am, I wasn't able to finish."

"Well, if you decide to go back, investigate an accounting degree. You have a real aptitude for the subject."

Shellie nodded and headed over to clock out. She was more interested in getting home and going to work on the *Dining Cabin*.

It was another warm day, so she opened the windows and doors on both sides and closed only the screens. She started from their spotless cooking area working into the dining space, sweeping and mopping as she went. It didn't take long to clean around the tables. Mostly it was tumbleweeds of Blue's fur.

The varnished surfaces of the yellow pine tables and chairs cleaned easily and dried even quicker. She had gotten to the living area at the far end when Ronan arrived.

"What are you up to, Angel?"

She pointed to the sofa area. "I thought it would be nice to have a place to sit and read or play games after supper."

Ronan nodded. "Sounds like a plan. Let's roll up the rug and I can take it outside to beat some of the dust out of it."

Normally, Shellie would have vacuumed the sofa cushions. Since that wasn't an option, she collected them and walked out the back door. It was her first visit to the patio. She dropped the cushions on a picnic table and looked around with delight.

"This is gorgeous."

Ronan wiped sweat from his forehead with his sleeve. "Yes, I think the slate is the same as the entry to the manager's cabin. They did a good job setting it, there isn't a crack in sight."

The area behind the kitchen was indeed flagstone set in cement with several wooden picnic benches scattered over the surface. A low stone wall made of loose stacked river rocks created a formal edge and a small gate led into the large vegetable garden, partially enclosed with windows trapping sunlight and heat. Now she understood how Ronan had fresh greens so early in the year. Another small gate opened onto a path down to the dock on the river.

Shellie smiled. "Okay, as soon as the weather warms up, we're eating outside."

Ronan swatted a mosquito on his neck. "Eating outside or being eaten?"

Shellie laughed. "Probably both."

She finished the cushions about the same time Ronan rerolled the rug. A quick wipe of furniture polish on the rocker and Shellie moved on to the bookshelf while Ronan inspected the fireplace.

"I love how many books are here, and they're almost all hard copies. You don't see that anymore."

Ronan poked at some mortar at the back of the firebox. "Yeah. Mrs. McClelland wanted kids to read so she would buy all the Hardy Boys and Nancy Drew books as soon as they came out and then loan them out to guests and local kids. She was better than the library since she didn't charge late fees and if you lost or damaged a book or really wanted to keep it you could work around the place to pay for it."

"So you grew up around here?"

"Yes. My parents live over in Wilmington now."

Shellie turned back to the bookshelves. "There's even Trixie Belden books here. I read a few of those and they were good, but they're hard to find." Shellie moved to the next shelf. "I don't recognize these authors. From the description they are for adults, though."

Ronan glanced over her shoulder. "Those are Christian fiction. I'm surprised they're still here. They were Mrs. McClelland's favorites. The science fiction was Mr. McClelland's."

Shellie opened the drawers at the bottom of the bookcase and drew in an excited breath. "Look at the games and puzzles. You up for a round of monopoly after dinner?"

Ronan groaned and shook his head, but his smile gave him away. "As long as I get to be the race car I guess you can get me to play."

Shellie shook her head and moved to the other side occupied by a large wooden desk topped with a secretary. She opened a drawer to find stationary and envelopes all embossed with a single pine cone beside *Pine Cone Motel, Saranac Lake, NY.* Longing washed through her.

"What's wrong, Angel?"

"I was thinking of Mrs. McClelland and all she left behind. It looks like she was planning on coming back."

Ronan sat on the sofa and motioned for her to do the same.

"The motel had gradually been losing money and her daughter moved away. Mr. McClelland died, and she tried to carry on, but when she had a stroke, her daughter moved Mrs. McClelland into an independent living facility nearer to family. I think without her husband here, she didn't have the will to try and keep the place open anymore."

Shellie nodded. "That desk is a wonderful place to write letters. Let's try and make each cabin look exactly how she liked it and send her the pictures and write the updates on her stationary."

"That way she gets a little piece of the life she enjoyed each month and can relive the memories?" Ronan asked.

Shellie nodded. She should have known he would understand.

Chapter 7

Shellie gripped her purse tight to her side and smiled. Tucked inside was cash from her first paycheck. Thankfully it hadn't taken long to open an account at the bank. Since her employer used the same bank they were willing to give her cash right away instead of making her wait for the check to clear.

She stopped on the walk home and signed up for cell phone service. She picked out the least expensive phone with a built-in camera to take the pictures for Mrs. McClelland and moved to the checkout counter. It wasn't the smart phone her Dad took away from her, but it was a start at being in the twenty-first century and moving out of the Stone Age. Now she would be able to text and maybe get back in contact with her friends. Although if they treated her the way Alice had, she was probably better off without them.

The clerk reached for the box. "All righty, let's get you taken care of. Do you want the second phone, hon?"

"What second phone?" Shellie asked.

"Well, for ten dollars more a month, you get a free phone that shares your data plan and gives you a fifty percent increase in usage."

Shellie chewed her lip and debated with herself. Ten dollars a month was a lot, especially since the plan had almost no minutes of usage.

Then a vision of Ronan came to mind from a few nights ago. He had been so happy working and being normal and had looked so devastated and depressed after telling her about his PTSD. If having a phone made her feel so much better, maybe it would do the same for him. Her heart pounded in her ears at her reckless decision and she could barely inhale enough to talk.

"Yes. I'll take it. Put it in the name of Ronan Flanagan, same address."

The clerk smiled. "A surprise for your boy-friend?"

Shellie could feel the heat of a blush suffuse her face. "He's just a friend."

She stopped in front of the store and texted her mom, *have a job and a place to live will write Shellie* before walking to the *Pine Cone.*

Walking home her phone vibrated with an incom-ing call. One glance and she recognized her brother's cell phone number. "Matt, how did you get this number already?"

"Mom left her phone in the charger on the coun-ter. I was having a sandwich when your message came in. Are you really okay?"

A wave of homesickness washed over Shellie. "I'm getting things together. I have a job and a place to live. How are you and Leslie doing?"

"I'm okay, but I'm worried about Leslie."

Shellie's heart started to pound. Her baby sister was only fifteen. "What's wrong?"

"She's crying at night and she's really jumpy. She almost acts like an emotionless robot, trying to be super perfect and please Mom and Dad."

"She always tried to please them."

"This is worse than before. I finally got her to talk to me and she's afraid Dad will throw her out like he did you. She doesn't understand why Dad made you leave."

Leslie had been the shyest and quietest of the three siblings. Shellie and Matt had done their best to shelter their sensitive little sister from Dad's anger. Not being able to help her siblings took Shellie's breath away. She stalked toward the motel with long, angry strides. "Look, Matt, tell Leslie if she has to leave, she's not alone. She can come live with me."

"I got a job at the corner coffee place and I'm saving everything I can. I told her I'd find a way to take care of us if that happened, but she pointed out I was underage and we might end up in foster care."

The unspoken message came through loud and clear. Matt was as scared of being kicked out as Leslie. If something actually went wrong, Shellie wasn't sure how she would support three people, but they stuck together like the three musketeers. "Listen. Give her this number and remind her I'm not underage. I've got your backs and you can live with me if anything happens."

The relief in Matt's voice soothed Shellie's agitation. "Thanks, Sis."

She disconnected the call and headed for the motel, letting the fresh scents, bird songs and gentle breeze calm her further. Frustration and anger at her father warred with worry over her brother and sister.

It wasn't fair to blame him. When she refused to change her story and say she had chased Chad, the chancellor was furious and wanted her gone from campus. Shellie remembered all the moves they had made in her life, almost never staying in one place for more than a couple of years. Her dad had been working at this college for almost four years, the longest she could remember them ever being in one place. They had a nice house on campus and her parents had developed friendships, putting down roots. She couldn't blame them for not wanting to uproot the whole family to protect her.

They had to make a choice between supporting her and keeping a roof over Matt and Leslie's heads. She would not blame them for sending her away. Her one wish was they had told her they believed her, that would have taken away so much of the hurt. They didn't. She would have to live with the hurt and put it in the past where it belonged. Shellie had to concentrate on making her future secure, especially if her brother and sister might become her responsibility.

Sunlight trickled out of the sky when Shellie stopped on the street to look at the *Pine Cone Motel*. The row of cabins had log siding stained a dark brown and the roofs were made of a dark green metal. Both were heavily coated with yellow pine pollen, pine needles, and spider webs. The wood trim had once been a similar green to the roofs, but had faded to a sickly, blotchy, peeling avocado. Small porches ran across the front of each building, their steps in varying degrees of disrepair.

Instead of numbers the cabins had small signs labeled with animals and birds. A small ceramic sculpture hung on each wall showing the animal in its natural habitat. At least the porch roofs had protected those. Shellie figured a good scrubbing would return them to their original beauty.

She noticed Ronan had taken the end cabin, *Loon*, and wondered if it was because he, like loons, enjoyed being a little apart.

The place was pretty and really did have potential. The biggest detraction was the in-ground pool out in front. It was faded, and weeds had grown up through the cracks in the walkways, twining themselves into the chain link fence that surrounded the pool. The way the road curved, the first thing visible was the motel sign and abandoned pool, not the pretty cabins.

She walked to the *Manager's Cabin*. Behind the check-in counter, a set of hooks held palm size wooden carvings attached to keys. Each carving matched the animal for a cabin. Now she understood why.

Raccoon Cabin was the closest to the *Dining Cabin*, so she collected that key. The front porch of the *Manager's Cabin* aligned with the porches of the guest cabins. It was two steps down to the sandy ground and then two steps up to each porch. The steps sagged under her weight, but how hard would it be to replace a few boards?

Shellie opened the screen door. She held it open with her heel while she fiddled with the lock. It took almost a minute of twisting and jiggling before she was able to push the heavy door open and enter the cabin.

The tiny entry was crowded with two rockers and a small table that belonged on the porch. It gave her a place to start.

She took a few pictures to show Mrs. McClelland the "before" and went to work.

Shellie grabbed a broom and mop and quickly cleaned the porch. Without the cobwebs and yellow pine pollen, it was an inviting place. It would be relaxing to sit with a cup of coffee or a glass of lemonade watching the cars pass by.

It didn't take long to drag the rockers back outside, just some banged elbows and ankles maneuvering them through the screen door. Ronan arrived as she dragged the last one out, letting the screen slam shut behind her.

"Hey Angel, what are you up to?"

Shellie rubbed her banged elbow. "I thought we could start with *Raccoon Cabin* and work our way down the line. Can you check this screen door?"

Ronan leapt onto the porch, skipping the steps. He swung the wooden frame and examined the hinges. "What am I looking for?"

"Why is the screen that funny blue-green color in the corner?"

He looked down and let out a soft whistle. "Wow."

Shellie fisted her hands on her hips and squinted at him. "Is it a big problem? Will we have to replace the screening or the whole door?"

"Neither. These old cabins were made with the finest materials. That screen is made of copper and is probably older than our parents."

"How do you know?"

"I grew up on construction sites. Snow collects in that corner and the discoloration is the copper equivalent of rust."

"So, no replacing it?"

"Angel, with the cost of copper right now, it's a wonder someone didn't come and gut these out to sell for scrap. You could buy a cheap car for what you could get in salvage money."

"Good thing you were here or that might have happened."

Ronan shook his head, his eyes unfocused as if he could see the distant past. "This place is like a time capsule from the 1960's -- and early in the decade at that."

Shellie hefted her broom and passed him. "Well, this time capsule is giving up its collection of dust."

"I'll grab fresh mop water and be right behind you."

The screen slammed, and Shellie examined the layout of the cabin. There was a bathroom to the right and two bedrooms on the left and a larger one in back on the right. The larger one held the fireplace, had a queen-size bed and its own entry into the bathroom. The smaller ones held two twin beds each. All the rooms had a double hung window that faced out toward the stream or the garden.

Ronan arrived back, easing the screen door shut behind him. "Do you want to work in the same room or separately?"

"Let's work together in each room." Shellie turned to a small door on her right off the entry. "What's in here?" The metal lined closet held blankets, pillows and soft flannel sheets. A whiff of lavender greeted Shellie. She found sprigs of the stuff tucked between each neatly folded linen.

Ronan glanced over her shoulder. "It looks like Mrs. McClelland put lavender in all the linen closets. I guess she wanted the sheets to smell nice for the guests."

Shellie nodded. "And moths and mice don't like it."

She closed the closet door. "Let's start in the master bedroom."

The dusty curtains were closed tight. A pattern of pine cones attached to a branch with green pine needles repeated across the fabric. She grabbed the edge of the first one and clouds of dust shook free clogging the air. It set her off in a sneezing fit.

Ronan patted her back and looked on anxiously. "Are you okay?"

Shellie nodded and wiped at her streaming eyes. "Let me get these outside so we can breathe."

She folded and stuffed them in a backpack accompanied by more sneezing. "Time to take advantage of my laundry perk."

Sunlight flooded through the windows, transforming the once dim rooms. A good cleaning and the yellow pine floor and white walls would gleam even on a rainy day. Ronan finished flipping the mattress as she walked in.

"Look at this twig bed. I can't believe they left expensive furniture like this behind." She ran a lemon oil rag down each twisted branch in the head and foot boards.

Ronan started to work on the windows with a soapy sponge and squidgy. "It wasn't expensive at the time. Mr. McClelland made the beds and a lot of the other furniture from the trees cleared to build the *Pine Cone*."

The bathroom was an easy clean up and a good mopping of the floors had the interior of *Raccoon Cabin* back to its original glory.

"Let's make the beds and put out the towels so Mrs. McClelland will get the full effect of the transformation. "

Blue gave a plaintive yip from outside the screen door.

"Okay, but after that I have to take Blue down to the river for a swim. If he gets too bored, he'll become destructive."

Shellie smiled at the dog through the screen. "Don't make him wait any longer. I'll have the beds made in a jiffy."

She had finished snapping the last picture when Blue raced to greet her, trailing a wavy path of water with each wag of his tail. She quickly closed the screen door so he wouldn't track mud on her clean floor, catching the dog as he bounced around her. She hugged him, releasing him quickly when he tried to slurp her face. Shellie tugged at her soggy fleece and grimaced. Water was already soaking through her jeans.

"I'm going to change. I left the stew warming at the back of the stove. Can you make sure the fire doesn't go out?"

Ronan was replacing the stove lid when she entered the *Dining Cabin* and asked, "Do you want to set up the coffee pot or pick the salad?"

"I'll get the salad." Shellie walked outside and through the twig gate of the vegetable garden. Short rows of bright green lettuce lifted lacy leaves toward the sky. They made a pretty square. Across the path more rows of a dark purple lettuce mirrored their green brothers. Next came young tomato plants dwarfed by the wire cages surrounding them. Potato plants took up the area across from the tomatoes with plenty of room to hill the plants as they grew. The vines of melons and what looked like pumpkin plants were carefully placed with easy access to the back gate. A bucket sat nearby, and Shellie realized it would be easy to collect water from the stream for the plants, but certainly back breaking work if the Adirondacks didn't get so much rain. All around the edges lavender, basil, chives, cilantro, mint and marjoram grew in raised, stonewalled beds. She smiled and thought no one could look at this pristine garden and accuse Ronan of being lazy.

It took only a few minutes to collect the tender greens and turn them into a fresh crisp salad. Shellie dished up some rich smelling stew and took her place at the table. As darkness slowly seeped though the sky the air chilled and the warmth from the wood stove wrapped around her and Ronan like a cocoon.

Ronan bowed his head and closed his eyes to say a silent grace. Shellie squirmed in her chair. She had been angry at God and had skipped saying grace when there was little or nothing to eat, but looking at the abundant spread of food she knew those excuses didn't apply anymore. She bowed her head and silently started to parrot the words she had learned at her parents' table. Remembered hunger made her stop and she simply gave a heartfelt thanks instead. When she raised her head, it was to look straight into Ronan's smiling eyes. Was that approval she saw? She wasn't ready to talk about the subject and cast around for something else to discuss.

"I talked to the power company. They'll turn the service on Monday morning if they don't get called to solve problems from that big concert tonight or the one scheduled for next week."

Ronan nodded. "I worked over at the lumber yard and the traffic in town was worse than usual. I'm glad I wasn't the one trying to drive an eighteen-wheeler of logs through Main Street."

" I didn't know there were so many concerts held here. The hotel was booked solid and we had a ton of walk-ins. Again. Kelly said it's the same for the big summer events and ski season." Shellie dipped a slice of bread in the gravy. "You would think people coming to a small town for a concert would call for a reservation first."

"I bet Grady wasn't happy about turning away people."

Shellie swallowed the bite of bread. "No, but I had the routine down from the last time and since I was in early, I did the confirmations on the B&B's again. By the time Mr. Grady got there I had all the information out at the individual stations and things were running smoothly."

"He's going to miss you on days when you switch to nights."

"He said something like that, but he would have fewer worries about the place at night when he wasn't there. He changed my training and added a bunch of stuff about accounting and managing the concierge staff even though my job is night receptionist."

"That's a really good sign. Let me know if you need help with any of the accounting, I have a BS in it." Ronan nodded and helped himself to more stew.

Shellie stopped her spoon halfway to her mouth. "You have a degree? As in a Bachelor of Science degree?"

Ronan nodded. "Yup. Courtesy of Uncle Sam and the ROTC program."

"Why don't you use it?"

Ronan set his flatware aside and stared at his plate. Shellie had the feeling he was seeing something other than stew, something like a painful memory.

"When I first got back, I tried. Really, I did. But my PTSD was bad, and they wouldn't let me bring Blue along. If someone startled me, I came up swinging. They let it go a couple of times and then I connected and broke a guy's jaw. That was strike three, I was out. They said I was, and I quote, a danger to the workplace and until I got help they could not allow me to be part of the staff."

Shellie shuddered. "How awful for you."

"No, the awful part was they were right. My dad gave me a laborer's job, but even that was a problem. So here I am. I know the technical stuff, but being around people doesn't work for me." He picked up his fork signaling the end of the subject. "Anyway, if you need help, let me know."

Shellie went back to eating while the silence congealed around them like cold gravy. When they finished, she dropped their plates into the hot water in the sink.

Ronan poured coffee. "I'll stay here on Monday for the power crew. It will be nice to have running water. I don't know which will be better, running water or a working refrigerator."

He placed a cup in front of her and sat back down. "Tomorrow is Sunday and you have it off, don't you?"

Warily, Shellie hesitated to answer. She hoped Ronan didn't want her to go fishing. She'd never liked sticking a hook through a squirming worm.

"Yes," she said, drawing out the word.

"Would you do me the honor of allowing me to escort you to church?"

Heat rushed into her face. Just because she had said grace didn't mean she was ready to forgive God or the parents, He gave her for all that happened. No way was she going to His house until she got over her funk. "No thank you. I intend to enjoy sleeping late and relaxing. No church for me."

Ronan shook his head. "House rules. Mrs. McClelland insisted I go to church and I'm pretty sure she expects the same from you."

Shellie sipped her coffee to delay responding to him. Funny, when had she learned to like the stuff? She didn't want to explain her feelings to Ronan. She knew in the back of her mind, she was being childish, but wasn't that one of the perks of being independent, deciding when and how to spend your time? There were certainly enough drawbacks. She cast around in her mind and finally came up with an answer she hoped would be enough to get him to leave her alone, or at least talk about something else.

"I don't know anything about the local churches and customs. All I need to do is show up late or in the wrong outfit and I've alienated a whole congregation in a very small town. Let me do some research and I'll think about it the next time I have a Sunday off." Shellie was quite pleased with her answer, it sounded very adult and reasonable.

Ronan didn't seem as impressed as she was. "Come with me. My congregation is non-denominational and very forgiving. After all, they welcomed Blue and me, didn't they?"

She really didn't have an answer for that.

Ronan took her silence as capitulation. "Good. We need to leave here around quarter to nine to make the first service."

Shellie groaned.

Ronan laughed. "If you really want to sleep in we could go to the later service, that starts at eleven."

Shellie rolled her eyes and did her best drama queen imitation. "Early service it is. But I'm taking a nap when we get back and you get to do all the cooking."

Ronan held out his hand for her to shake. "Okay, spaghetti it is with a homemade sauce simmered all day on the stove. I'll call you when it's ready."

Shellie laughed and shook his hand. "Who needs a crock pot when you have a wood stove."

This was Shellie's opening. She wiped her suddenly damp palms on the napkin in her lap and pulled a box off the half wall. "Speaking of calling... when I signed up for my telephone, I got a second one for free." She held it out to him. "I put it in your name. We've got like almost no minutes, but tons of data. I figured it would be easier to stay in touch if we could text back and forth."

Ronan looked at the box and then at her suspiciously. "Are you sure this is free, Angel? I don't want charity. I may be the dregs of humanity, but I still have a little pride."

"It isn't charity. The phone was free. The extra line is $10 a month, so you can kick in that amount and if we go over on data we can split it. I couldn't see turning down a freebie. Think of it as payment for the poncho. They were both free, so they're a trade of equal value."

Ronan shook his head and laughed. "How can I argue with that logic?"

Shellie smiled back. Who would have thought hearing that scary homeless guy from McDonalds laughing would make her feel so warm and tingly?

Chapter 8

Shellie wasn't feeling quite as charitable the next morning. Ronan said jeans were okay, but she wore a pair of slacks, just in case the church ladies were less forgiving than Ronan thought.

Ronan had on a clean, pressed shirt with a collar. She would have to find out how he managed that trick without electricity. His boots were buffed to a shine, making her very aware of how scuffed her shoes were, though at least she had a pair of heels tucked in her bag to change into when they got there.

He had washed his hair and pulled it back into a braid and it looked like he had trimmed his beard. It was the most polished, she had ever seen him, and it made her feel more self-conscious. It also made her curious to see his face. She had a feeling under all that fur was a very handsome man.

Ronan stood there staring at her so long she almost ran back into the cabin to hide. She knew she looked all wrong and he was trying to find the words to tell her.

Ronan finally inhaled like a man who had held his breath too long. "Angel, you look so beautiful I'm going to have to fight off all the single men just to get to sit next to you."

His silly comment made her laugh. Maybe things would be okay after all. She closed and locked the cabin door and slipped an arm around the elbow he offered her. Cars whizzed by as they strolled along the shoulder of the road. Their vacuum sucked at Shellie's clothes and tainted the clean mountain air with exhaust fumes.

Ronan pointed to a small trail running off to the side. "Down there is a great fishing spot."

Shellie nodded, wondering if there might be some wiggly worms in her future after all.

A short distance farther a farm supply store was under construction. Ronan stopped, surveying the progress and seemed more pensive than usual.

Shellie squeezed his arm and he looked down at her with a sad smile.

"What's making you unhappy?"

Ronan looked up at the sign and started walking again. "That's being built by my dad's construction company."

Shellie stumbled. The company was large and well known. She had thought his dad's company was a small, one or two-man operation. "You're kidding."

"No."

They walked on. "From observing you, I think you've come a long way. Do you want to try and get in touch with your family?"

For the first time since she'd known him Ronan showed his anger. He stopped and jerked his arm out of her grasp. "No. My family doesn't understand I have no control over my reactions. They don't get that one minute I'm fine and then a noise or a smell and I'm back in the desert with a lot of people trying to kill me and my men."

Blue bumped up against Ronan's pant leg and while Shellie wanted to run away, she reached out and hugged his arm instead. Ronan visibly reined in his emotions and started walking again, patting her hand. "My dad told me to man up and get over myself, and until I could act like a decent human being, I wasn't to contact them. I suppose I can't blame him for being upset, I had broken his nose and was swearing at him and mom in Arabic."

Fury heated Shellie's blood and flashed through her body. "How stupid and out of touch can they be? They're the ones that need to learn about being decent human beings."

She glared back over her shoulder at the sign and started to memorize the telephone number to reach Ronan's dad. The man needed to be taken down a peg or two and she was ready to be the one to do it. How dare they treat Ronan that way? The more she thought about it the angrier she became, striding swiftly down the road and almost dragging Ronan with her.

He slowed and tugged her to a stop. "Angel?"

Shellie snapped at him. "Any possibility I will see your parents at church and have the opportunity to tell them what five-star idiots they are?"

Ronan threw his head back and laughed. Not little chuckles, but belly-deep, joyful laughter.

Shellie stopped and put her fists on her hips. "What?"

He scooped her into a gentle hug. "Oh, Angel, you look like you're ready to take a chunk out of my dad. It's been a long, long time since someone was willing to fight for me."

"So, what if I am?" Ronan's laughter and hug had taken the starch out of her anger.

Ronan released her, and they started to walk again. "I'm thinking he should thank his lucky stars you don't carry a weapon, or he'd be in real trouble."

He continued to snicker as they walked. Shellie blushed and ducked her head. Maybe she had overdone it a little, but if someone had given Ronan even a small bit of the understanding and support he had shown her, his

life could have been a lot different. Then again, he
wouldn't have been there to rescue her.

Glancing around, she realized their conversation
had occupied them all the way to the church. Shellie
chewed her lip as she looked at the old building. The
church was constructed of gray granite, the rough surfaces made her think of a medieval castle. The walls
were punctuated with beautiful old stained glass windows; the entrance was only a couple of steps up from
the sidewalk. Clearly the building had been there for
more than a century. Would the congregation be open
and accepting or so steeped in traditions, they would
whisper behind their hands?

Ronan gave a gentle tug on her arm. "Come on.
We don't want to be late and make an entrance."

The very thought gave her chills and put a catch
in her breathing. "Wait a minute."

She clung to Ronan's arm, ostensibly for balance
while she changed shoes, but in reality, she needed the
moral support his solid presence gave her. Finally ready,
she pushed her shoulders back and raised her chin. Let
them challenge her right to be there. She'd stare them
down. This was God's house, not theirs, and He always
welcomed lost lambs. If anyone fit that category, she certainly did.

Shellie wasn't quite sure when she had gone from
being too angry with God to pray to wanting to investigate this church, but somehow it had happened. Score
another one for Ronan's good influence.

A pleasant, white-haired gentleman in a dark suit
greeted Ronan warmly by name, giving Shellie a firm
handshake, a smile, and kind, welcoming words. Others
smiled and waved at Ronan and Blue. He waved back
before guiding Shellie to the outside of the back row.

She looked at him questioningly, wondering why he selected this seat when there were so many places to sit
closer to the pulpit.

He whispered, "This way Blue isn't in the way
and he can be close to me."

Sure enough, Blue sat, leaning against the arm-
rest of the pew and focused alertly on Ronan. As parish-
ioners began filling the pews, the minister entered from a
door near the choir box. Glancing around, he locked onto
Ronan and Shellie and moved deliberately toward them.
Holding out his hand, he greeted her with a smile. "I'm
Pastor Clark and I'm so glad you joined us today."

Shellie smiled back and shook his hand, even
though she felt like hiding behind Ronan like a two-year-
old. "Hi, I'm Shellie Morgan."

The Pastor looked over at Ronan, but his stance
clearly included Shellie in the conversation. "Did you
hear about the bass, that Joe Mitchell pulled out of
Oseetah Lake?"

Ronan nodded. "I heard it fed two families."

Clark laughed. " I guess that will either give
plenty of witnesses or the truth about a big fish story."

Shellie relaxed enough to laugh with them. Who
could be afraid of a Pastor that talked about fishing and
laughed at the idea a parishioner had exaggerated the
truth?

The Pastor addressed her. "Are you a visitor to
our area or a resident?"

"I moved here a few weeks ago."

"Well, I hope you will feel free to come back and
worship with us anytime you want. All are welcome
here."

A pretty blonde woman in a choir robe peeked
though a door and motioned to the pastor.

Pastor Clark nodded to the woman then turned back to them. "If you'll excuse me, my wife, Ruby, is calling."

Shellie whispered to Ronan, "The pastor and his wife seem really young. Is this their first church?"

Ronan's voice carried no further than Shellie's ear. "Sort of, he was the youth pastor and when the previous minister retired Pastor Clark was hired in his place. Ruby's dad is the minister of one of the churches in Lake Placid and she wanted to stay local so it worked out for them."

After services as they waited in line to approach the Pastor, his wife greeted Shellie with a warm smile. "I hope you enjoyed the sermon and will come back. We need more young people in the congregation."

"I will, thank you." Shellie smiled back.

Pastor Clark gently grasped Shellie's hand in both of his and gave her a wink. "You're a very nice young lady. You didn't fall asleep or yawn once in the whole sermon."

Shellie laughed with him. "Thank you. I enjoyed it very much."

"Come back soon. You're always welcome here."

"I will." Shellie smiled realizing she'd found a spiritual home.

Chapter 9

The sun was just making itself known over the trees when the power truck pulled to a stop. Ronan heard the crunch of truck tires on the gravel driveway as he gave the refrigerator a last swipe to rinse away the bleach he used to clean it. He stepped out onto the dining cabin porch, coffee cup in hand, hoping the crew didn't include someone from his bar fighting days.

A quick glance brought a warm feeling to his stomach, his muscles relaxed, coming off battle ready. The guy driving the truck was an old high school football buddy who had stood back-to-back with Ronan after his postwar return when his PTSD made him want to lash out and smash everyone and everything.

George hadn't asked any questions, just stepped up to keep Ronan from getting himself killed. Now they saw each other regularly at church. George always found a reason to chit chat with him after services no matter how scruffy or unapproachable Ronan tried to appear. Ronan realized he had made some good friends over his lifetime, so why did he keep pushing them away?

Ronan raised his cup into the air. "Want some coffee?"

George came up the steps and shook Ronan's hand. "Maybe after I get the power on and if I'm ahead of schedule. Man, what smells so good?"

"Cinnamon rolls."

Shellie had taken to baking in the wood stove like she had been doing it all her life. Now, instead of working for breakfast at McDonald's, he met her in the *Dining Cabin* for coffee and food before she left for work.

The restful time, delicious smells, and her laughter always started his day out right. No matter how difficult his dreams the night before, her smile in the morning, washed away his tension and depression. Since she had moved in, he felt like there was a place for him around other people more often. Her presence crowded out the need to retreat and find a safe place to protect them from him, as much as him from them.

"When did you learn to cook?"

"Hey, necessity and all that mother of invention thing, you know."

Ronan wasn't about to tell George Shellie lived here. Saranac Lake was a small place and he didn't want people getting the wrong impression about her. His reputation was too shot to matter, but she was a different story.

"Okay, says here the meter is around the back of the *Manager's Cabin*. Point the way."

He showed George the hook up and then went to the shed in back to get some lumber and power tools. If he fixed the steps and painted the porch, *Raccoon* would be good as new, and they could move on to *Chipmunk*.

Within a few minutes the motel sign flickered to life. Ronan grinned. They would need to figure out how to turn it off to keep the bills down, but for now he would leave it for Shellie to see as she walked home.

George ambled up to the *Dining Cabin*. "I'll take that coffee now."

Ronan had poured him a cup of the strong brew and set out the rolls when Blue dropped his bone and went into silent sentry mode.

George looked noticeably paler and froze as he looked at Blue's rapidly chattering, long, white teeth and curled lips, all the more intimidating for his lack of barking or growling.

Ronan rose to his feet; his heart rate more than doubled, his breathing fast and shallow while everything around him moved like it was fighting its way through gelatin and he was at full speed. Blue responded to Ronan's threat reaction and moved between Ronan's legs. In this position they could move as one without breaking eye contact on the dangers around them.

Ronan turned toward the entry when a sharp rapping sounded on the screen door. He forced himself to slow and deepen his breathing. He wasn't back in Kandahar. This was the Adirondacks, no threat stood at the door.

"Fuss."

The dog moved to the heel position and sat, panting, but still alertly watching the stranger at the door.

Ronan tried to make his voice pleasantly professional despite the adrenaline flowing in his blood stream. "Can I help you?"

A man in a suit with a stern expression walked in and thrust a business card in Ronan's direction. Ronan flinched, and Blue rose to a crouch, once again showing his teeth, a growl rumbling in his chest.

The man jerked his arm back. "What in the world? How dangerous is that dog?"

Ronan opened his stance and crossed his arms over his chest. Blue slowly lowered himself back into a sit.

"That depends on what level of danger you present."

Mr. Suit kept a wary eye on Blue and slowly extended his business card to Ronan. "I'm Edgar Williams, the health inspector. I saw your sign lit up and my records show you are past due for inspection - way past due."

Would nothing ever be easy?

Ronan reached out and took the card. He pretended to read it to buy himself time to calm his pounding heart. "I'm sorry, we aren't open for business. We just got the power turned on and I still have to find the switch for the sign."

The man had skepticism written across his face. "We've had nothing but problems in the area with unlicensed facilities springing up left and right; do you really expect me to believe that?"

Ronan looked the man up and down, wondering at his aggressive attitude. Blue inched forward. The smallest hand motion would send the dog on attack mode.

Shaking from the conflicting emotions, Ronan fought with his instinctive need to go back into battle ready mode. He needed to diffuse the situation or Blue would go for William's throat. That would end up with his dog in Animal Control quarantine and a whole bunch of questions he couldn't or wouldn't answer, not to mention the need to find a way to pay some serious doctor bills for a torn-up inspector. Deliberately relaxing his stance, Ronan casually took a firm hold of Blue's collar.

"I'm sorry. I was hired on as caretaker and to clean the place. I'm out of the loop as far as what is going on with motels in the area. I didn't know there was a problem."

George stood up from the table, gulping some coffee to wash away the roll he had finished. He presented himself as an "aw shucks" kind of easy going hick oblivious to the tensions around him, but George's actions brought him in position behind Ronan. Ronan smiled. George still had his back. It helped release the tension Ronan had been fighting to keep under control.

"Believe him," George said, "I turned on the power less than two minutes ago."

The inspector took in George's tool belt and hard hat with the power company logo and glanced out the screen at the power truck. He sniffed, but relaxed a little, too. "Okay, but as long as I'm here, either I get to do the inspection, or I fine you for operating a facility with an expired license."

Ronan shook his head. There wasn't much choice in the situation. The only question was how high the fines would be for the closed-up cabins. "Where do you want to start?"

Williams marched into the kitchen like he owned the place. "Right here. What kind of restaurant will you be operating?"

Ronan turned to watch, Blue spun to stay in the heel position. "The kitchen is for our private use and we will not be selling food."

"If you say so."

The man did a detailed inspection of the kitchen, opening cabinets and appliances, picking up cups and dishes, twisting and turning them as if looking for the smallest speck of food. George whispered, "What a jerk. Bet his wife kicked him out of bed early this morning."

Ronan snorted. Williams glanced his way, then hrmphed and opened the refrigerator. The inspector broke into a spasm of coughing as a wave of chlorine engulfed him. Ronan choked on his laughter and started to cough, too. He could feel heat suffuse his face.

Williams cranked the sink faucet on. The pipes in the kitchen thundered and spit air and rust, but quickly settled into a stream of crystal-clear water. The inspector frowned and harrumphed again, but didn't say anything.

He made some notes on his clipboard and then looked at Ronan. "Show me a sample rental unit."

Ronan took him to *Raccoon*. He skirted around the pile of lumber and tools. Blue trotted along beside Ronan. The dog had come off battle ready the moment Ronan had laughed.

"Watch your step. I was getting ready to replace several boards."

The inspector made a note and surveyed the exterior. He circled the cabin, poking at the mortar of the chimney with his pen before walking up the steps and into the cabin.

The smell of oil soap, lemon oil, and lavender wafted around them. Ronan hadn't seen the inside of *Raccoon* since Shellie made up the beds. The difference from the gloomy rental unit brought a smile to his lips. His Angel had made the place a rustic oasis. Everything sparkled, and the old pine floor shone in the morning sunlight. He wanted to lounge in one of the rockers by the fire with a book. Peace flowed over and through him. Just being there made him feel as if Shellie was stroking his back and promising everything would be all right.

The inspector poked around, lifting the mattress and checking behind the headboard.

"What are you looking for?"

The man didn't even look up from his papers as he wrote. "Evidence of bed bugs."

Ronan stifled the urge to punch the guy as his calm flashed into fighting fire in his blood. After all their hard work, this jerk was looking for infestations? They weren't even planning on renting the place. It was just to send pictures to Mrs. McClelland.

Blue bumped Ronan's hand and leaned against his leg, widening the distance between Ronan and the inspector. Ronan drew a calming breath and moved to the bathroom behind Williams. He caught a glimpse of the man's papers and spotted the note "excellent" in the blank for cleanliness. So, they were okay so far.

The inspector took a quick look around at the sparkling fixtures and turned to Ronan. "I am assuming you haven't turned on the water in this unit yet."

The challenging manner of the inspector drew his warrior's need to fight to the surface, but that wouldn't help him or Shellie. For once fighting wouldn't protect the person who most depended on him. Ronan drew on his military training, shifted into the at-ease position and answered reflexively. "No, sir."

The man observed Ronan for a moment. "Can you turn it on?"

Ronan opened the sink and tub faucets, so the air trapped in the pipes wouldn't compress and explode them. "You may want to back up. If a pipe bursts, everyone in here is in for a cold shower."

Williams shuffled swiftly backwards toward the door, half tripping over Blue. Blue sat there, tongue lolling out of the side of his mouth as if laughing. The inspector quickly stepped around the dog and nodded to Ronan.

Ronan twisted the shutoff valves under the sink and toilet. Air hissed and splattered rusty water, making a mess of the pristine sink and tub. The toilet made a bubbling sound that ended when the tank was full. Once the clean water flowed in the sink and tub, Ronan directed it with his hand to rinse away the rust residue.

The inspector moved back into the room, flushed the toilet and made another note, while Ronan turned off the faucets and used paper towels to dry the enameled surfaces.

Williams tucked his pen in an inside pocket of his suit jacket. "Alright. I'm done here."

Ronan relaxed, now that he knew no pipes were going to explode he could breathe again. He moved to Blue's side and gave the dog the hand command to heel, heading out the door. They weren't out of the woods, yet. The rest of the cabins hadn't been opened in years. There was no telling what Williams would find and no way to gauge his reaction. The inspector seemed to be a real stickler.

"Are you former military, son?"

"Yes, sir."

The man pointed to Blue. "Is that your K9 part-ner?"

"Yes, sir. Captain Blue Devil. Best explosives and patrol dog ever."

Williams stopped and looked down the line of cabins. "The rest of the cabins look like they are still closed up."

Ronan turned to face him. "They are. The owner asked us to get them cleaned up and we've been working on it gradually for the last month. We thought things would go faster with the help of power tools. Our pur-pose is to show the owner the place is back to the level she remembered and to maintain it that way."

The inspector cracked a smile and put a hand on Ronan's shoulder. Ronan saw the movement and barely kept from ducking while motioning Blue to stand down.

"I'm not going to look at them, then. Make sure they are in this kind of shape before you rent them out. I need to go deal with a lot worse problems from people without your obvious standards."

The man scrawled his signature on the form he had been using and tore off a copy, handing it to Ronan.

"Congratulations, you passed the health inspection. The certificate will be mailed to the owner," Williams glanced at his papers, "Mrs. Myrtle McClelland in about six weeks. Here is a copy of the report for your files."

Ronan nodded and swallowed past the lump in his throat. "Thank you, sir."

Williams walked toward his car, only to pause and turn toward Ronan. "Of course, this doesn't include the fire inspection. They'll be by when they're notified of my report or if you're in a hurry to open, you can call them and make an appointment."

As Ronan returned to the *Dining Cabin* his fingers were shaking so bad the sheet of paper fluttered.

He stood beside George on the porch and watched the inspector leave.

George kept his eyes focused on the road in front of the motel, coffee cup in hand. "You all right?"

"Yeah."

"How bad did you get dinged?"

"Nothing."

George spun and watched Ronan suspiciously. "Would you tell me if there was a problem?"

Ronan smiled. George had him there.

Ronan handed over the inspection report. "Probably not. But in this case, see for yourself."

George glanced through the report. He nodded and set his coffee cup on the railing before heading to his truck. He stopped with the driver's door open, one foot on the running board and grinned up at Ronan. "Tell Ms. Morgan thanks for the roll, or better yet, bring her to church so I can thank her myself. I'm sorry I missed her yesterday."

Ronan shook his head. So much for protecting Shellie. He should have known the bill would be in her name.

She had worked miracles in the cabin, now it was his turn to do the same on the outside. But first he had to send her a text.

He almost felt normal.

Shellie rounded the bend and stopped in her tracks. The bright green neon *Pine Cone Motel* blazed even in full daylight. How cool would it look in the dark? She hurried forward, the high-pitched whine of a power saw igniting her curiosity.

She arrived in time to see Ronan position a board on the steps of *Loon Cabin* a mouth full of nails and a hammer in his hand. The graceful power of his movements reminded her of a lion. Watching him made shivers run down her spine.

Steps and porches on every cabin were peppered with the bright yellow of the replacement boards. Every cabin, except *Raccoon*. There the porch glistened with a fresh coat of forest green paint. The entire place had been hosed off. Every. Single. Cabin. Without the pine needle and pollen frosting the motel looked fresh and ready for guests.

"Wow."

Ronan turned to face her and grinned. Sweat and sawdust coated his hair and clothes and a smudge of green paint decorated his nose. Her stomach did a little flip flop.

"You like it?"

"It looks amazing. I thought all of this would take months to accomplish."

Ronan's grin widened. He pulled off his glove and took her backpack only to frown as he hefted the bag up and down. The brush of his warm fingers against her shoulder made her tingle, like she had encountered static electricity.

"What have you got in here? This thing weighs a ton."

"It's not that bad. I have the curtains I washed."

Ronan shook his head. "Okay, but from now on when you're carrying laundry, I'm going with you to do the tote and fetch."

She was about to refuse; after all, she could take care of herself. But next week she would start the night shift and she wasn't looking forward to walking home alone. Having Ronan along now and then would make her feel a whole lot safer and she really enjoyed his company.

"Have you had a chance to see if the plumbing works along with all this other stuff?"

Ronan opened the *Dining Cabin* door for her and followed her in. "I got it running here, in your cabin, mine and *Raccoon.* It's easier to do if there are two people instead of one, so I figured as we work through the cabins we can turn it on then."

Shellie stopped removing food from the pack. "You mean we can take showers?"

"Yup. Speaking of which, I need one - big time."

She stomped down an imaginary vision of Ronan in the shower, water and soap sluicing down his body. Good girls didn't have those kinds of thoughts.

"I can't wait."

Ronan stood, arms crossed and grinned at her. "Me either."

The look on his face made Shellie's heart race. What was he thinking? "I mean about taking a shower."

"Of course, that's what we were talking about. Showers." Ronan continued to grin. The sparkle in his eyes warned her he was in a teasing mood.

Was he reading her thoughts? Shellie felt a blush creep up her face.

She returned to the bags of food on the table and started to load the refrigerator, hoping the cool air would lower the heat in her face. Shellie cast around her mind to find a neutral topic. She picked up a carton of milk. Eureka.

"I stopped on the way home and got real milk. I'm glad to see the refrigerator is working; otherwise we would have had to drink this up in a hurry."

"Mm mm, I can't tell you the last time I had a glass of cold milk. We may end up drinking all of that tonight anyway. I've definitely worked up an appetite."

Shellie glanced sharply over at Ronan. He looked a little too angelic. What was the man thinking? Deciding to stay with the innocuous, she continued. "At work we have a soda fountain for the employees. I like soda, but all I've wanted for the past few days is a glass of milk. It makes me laugh at the times when I was a kid, I pouted because I couldn't have soda with supper while Mom insisted I needed more dairy in my diet."

The memory brought a longing to talk to her mom, but she could never discuss with Mom what she really wanted to know.

Shellie finally looked over at Ronan and their eyes locked. There was something about the way he looked at her that had her hands starting to reach for him.

She curled her fingers into fists and turned away, hoping he hadn't read her feelings in her eyes.

Ronan spun toward the door. "I'm going to clean up the tools and shower really quick. Meet you back here in thirty?"

"Take your time and enjoy your shower. You earned it."

Ronan waved and left the room. Shellie watched him go then slumped into a chair. She could see his head bobbing past the windows as he carried tools and materials back to the shed. Where had these feelings come from? Did he share them? Of course, that begged the question which was worse - if Ronan did share them, or didn't?

Chapter 10

Ronan dipped an Oreo into his glass of milk and then shoved the whole cookie into his mouth. The dipped chocolate wafer dissolved on his tongue followed by the sweet frosting center. He crunched the remainder and took a gulp of milk to wash it down as he watched Shellie remove two of her pieces from the backgammon board.

"Your turn. I've got you this time. The only way out is to roll back to back double sixes." Shellie glowed. Obviously, she was sure of her victory. He hoped she did win. He had never seen her so happy and relaxed.

The commercial dishwasher rumbled in the background. They hadn't filled even a quarter of the thing, but both of them wanted to see if it still worked so they had started it up and moved to the living area. Ronan lit a fire while Shellie turned on the lights and picked out a game. The fire wasn't necessary, but it added to the relaxing atmosphere.

The yellow light from the old incandescent bulbs reflected off Shellie's glossy hair, bringing up the cinnamon highlights in the dark chocolate tresses. She'd left it loose and he wished he could stroke the cool, satiny length. She had changed into sweats, the loose clothing doing much to mask her figure, a figure that could make his palms sweat. Ronan couldn't keep his eyes off her when she wore those mile-high heels, but she looked adorable even in her running shoes and baggy casuals.

Ronan grinned and shook the cup holding his dice before dumping them on the backgammon board.

Both were sixes. Shellie leaned forward as he gathered the dice and dropped them into the cup.

"I warned you I'm lucky with dice."

A quick twist of his wrist emptied the plastic cubes onto the soft surface again. He didn't look. Shellie's face told him all he needed to know.

"How did you do that?"

"Dice like me."

"No way," she laughed, "I'll get the answer out of you."

Shellie reached over and tickled his side, much like she had probably done to her younger siblings. Ronan joined in the laughter and pretended to shrink away until she leaned even further toward him. With a quick move he slipped closer and scooped her into his lap, stilling her hands by hugging her close to his body.

She was so warm and soft in all the right places and it had been a long time since he'd held a woman in his arms. She threw her head back and laughed harder as she squirmed in his lap. His blood heated, and he stopped thinking, lowering his head to claim those soft pink lips with his own. At the last second, he controlled himself, gentling the pressure. He would have released her, but her shy response drove all thoughts from his mind except absorbing the woman he held. He switched the kiss from asking to demanding, his hands kneading her back and drawing her even closer.

Electricity sparked between them, then suddenly she was struggling to get away. She turned her head to free her mouth.

"No. Leave me alone, Chad."

The words were more effective than a bucket of ice water. He released his grip and she scrambled away to sit huddled in the easy chair at right angles to him. Her face was hidden by her hair, but Ronan could see her shoulders shaking and heard the soft sobs.

He slipped to his knees on the floor beside her and stroked her arm. He had thought nothing could hurt more than his burns until she jerked away from his attempt to comfort her.

"Angel, I'm so sorry. Please, please forgive me. I never meant to hurt you." His voice cracked with emotion and he stopped speaking.

She raised her tear streaked face to look at him, stared for a moment and then shook her head. "I'm sorry. I shouldn't have touched you. I forgot to be careful, so this is all my fault."

She thought this was her fault? He couldn't let her think that.

"I am a fully, grown man. You did nothing forward. This is not on you, Angel. I should not have lost control."

"No? Chad said I teased him to a point he couldn't help himself. And stupid me, I did the same thing to you. Dad was right, I'm not fit to be around civilized people."

"If you think I'm civilized, I'd hate to think what you consider rough. Chad was a weasel who drugged you rather than treat you like the exceptional woman you are. And I'm a beast. There is a reason I live out here on the fringes; I'm the one not fit for civilized company. And you, sweet innocent, are the very epitome of what is best and brightest in the world."

He wanted to stalk out of the room, to run from what he had become, but to run was to abandon Shellie and that he would not do. She had called him Chad. That set off warning bells in his head. She needed help getting over what had happened to her. Ronan wasn't much, but unfortunately, he was all she had. Resting his head against the chair cushion, he closed his eyes and prayed for guidance.

Her voice trembled, barely above a whisper. "We are quite a pair, aren't we?"

He raised his eyes to her pale, tear-streaked face and the travesty of a smile. She was so brave.

He slowly reached for her, moving the same way he would around a frightened wild animal and captured her hand in a loose grip. Ronan kissed her fingers before releasing them and moving away to his place on the sofa.

"I'm sorry. I won't let it happen again," Ronan promised.

"I'll work on not teasing you."

They sat in silence, the only sounds the crackle of the fire and Blue's soft snores.

Exhaling, Ronan dove into the question he hated to ask. "When you turned away, you called me Chad. Did I bring back your memory of what happened?"

Shellie's unhappy expression made him grit his teeth. For her sake this had to come into the open, but it was as uncomfortable for Ronan as debriding a wound. Not doing it could be life threatening, but doing it caused serious pain to a woman he cared about. He'd take every ounce of the hurt if he could, but he couldn't, and it wouldn't help her to ignore the elephant in the room.

Her voice was so soft it was almost a whisper. "When I couldn't move I got flashes of memories. I felt so trapped and I think that's what brought them to the surface."

"Do you want to talk about the memories?"

"No! I wish I'd never remembered." Shellie scrambled to her feet and fled, the door closing with a decisive click.

Ronan watched her go with a sick knot in his stomach. He had to find a way to help his Angel.

Shellie stood under the pounding shower spray. Shudders and chills ranged up and down her body as flashes of memory and the feeling of total helplessness hammered her mind. She turned the water hotter, but still she couldn't get warm. Wrenching the knob to off, she grabbed a fluffy towel from the rack.

She bundled herself back into heavy sweats and woolly socks before toweling dry her hair. Too tired to bother with the hair dryer, she braided the long tresses and opened the bathroom door. A cloud of steam followed her into the bedroom. Still chilled, she grabbed the ugly green blanket she'd found the first night and curled up in a chair to stare out the sliding glass door. The cabins were all dark. Ronan must have gone to bed, if he hadn't run away into the night to escape the trouble she had brought with her.

Shellie spoke softly, trying to bring calm to her chaotic thoughts. "No. He wouldn't do that. He said he wouldn't abandon me. The question is, how much am I willing to hurt him with my selfishness? How do I face him in the morning after acting so forward and making him think I was offering something I wasn't?"

The walls didn't answer.

She should have known it would all fall apart. Things had been going too well. The clues were there, she hadn't wanted to see them. Had she subconsciously gone out to sabotage all that she had gained because she knew she didn't deserve it?

Fixing up the motel and getting the power on had been too easy.

Finding a friend like Ronan, someone she could trust, had been just short of a miracle. She shared more with him than she'd been able to do with her mom or even her closest friends. She'd even been dreaming that she could finish her degree; how foolish was she? Was that what God was trying to tell her, not to return to college? Maybe.

Once it was cleaned up the motel wouldn't need two caretakers. She couldn't afford what would be a reasonable rent to stay here and even if Mrs. McClelland was willing to accept less, her grandson would surely step in and demand full value. And he should. It was his job to protect his grandmother.

How foolish could she be? Where would she go?

Shellie shifted position in the chair and closed her eyes. The absolute worst part, the most awful thing of all, was she would have to cut her ties to Ronan. She knew he would make sure she had a roof over her head, even if it meant giving up his own. What kind of a friend would she be to allow him to do that? Then again, she was so embarrassed after what happened, how could she face him? If she had an ounce of dignity she would leave right now. Tonight. But where could she go?

How had they become so close in a matter of weeks? And who would have thought that scruffy bum would come to mean so much to her?

"Why, God? What do you want from me?"

Silence.

Well, at least this time she hadn't turned from Him, but then that was another lesson Ronan had taught her.

How would she face him in the morning?

Exhaling, Shellie dragged herself out of her blanket cocoon and shuffled over to the bed. Tomorrow she needed to go to work and be welcoming, bright and chipper. All she needed was to make a mistake and get fired to make this disaster complete.

As she crawled under the covers she could hear Ronan's voice in the echoes of her mind, "Don't worry about tomorrow, for tomorrow will bring worries of its own. Today's trouble is enough for today."

"Okay, I'll leave tomorrow for tomorrow. I just want today to be over."

Chapter 11

A loud buzzing followed by a knocking on the door, dragged Shellie up from her exhausted slumber. What in the world was going on? The buzz came again.

"Hello? Anyone there?"

Shellie didn't recognize the voice. Who was at the door?

She slipped on her shoes and hurried toward the entry, turning on lights as she went. She latched the security chain before opening the door a crack. A man in his sixties, with a significant paunch and thinning gray hair, stood under the porch light. An expression of relief washed over him when she opened the door.

Shellie leaned her shoulder against the door, ready to slam it shut. "Can I help you?"

The man offered her a weary smile. "I'd like to rent a room for the night."

"I'm sorry, we're not open for business."

"Then why is your sign lit and says vacancies?"

Shellie stifled a groan. She had been so upset she forgot to find a way to turn off the sign.

"I'm sorry we just got the electricity turned on and we haven't figured out how to turn off the sign."

The man scrubbed a hand down his tired face and shifted his weight to lean against one of the porch support posts. "Please, I don't need anything fancy. Heck, I don't even care if the electricity is on. I've been trying to find a place for the night since I got off the Burlington ferry four hours ago. I'll take anything."

"The lady said no." Ronan stepped from the cabin's shadow; Blue at his side, lips curling while his teeth clicked together as if impatient to taste the man's blood. They looked like dark avenging angels.

The man took a step back, his hands up, shaking his head. "Okay. Fine. You're not open. Look, I fell asleep at the wheel twice already. Can I park here and grab a couple of hours sleep in my car? I'm really out of options."

Shellie got a good look at the man's rumpled clothes. He looked like the kind of businessmen who frequented the resort where she worked. The suit was good quality and the shirt had his initials embroidered on the cuff. His shoes still had a shine and the light reflected off his manicured nails.

He also looked exhausted and about at the end of his rope.

Shellie unlocked the door and stepped out onto the porch, sidling close to the wall so she could reach Ronan. Much as the stranger appeared non-threatening, she'd learned the hard way looks could be deceiving.

"Can we talk a minute?" she asked in a hushed voice.

He glanced down at her for an instant, his expression hard as granite, before returning his stare to the stranger. Ronan radiated suspicion and danger. Where was the gentle, easy-going man with the friendly eyes and ready smile? This man was a soldier trained to wariness and ready to address violence.

He reached out an arm, pushing her behind him and Blue and then took a step back moving them all into the darkness. Shellie saw the movement coming and forced herself not to flinch when he touched her.

"*Blue. Pass auf.*"

The dog moved between them and the stranger, crouching, watching.

Ronan turned his concentration to her, his expression softening. "What are you thinking, Angel?"

"When I came here, I was looking for a safe, dry place to sleep for the night and you left me alone."

"So?"

"How is this man any different?"

"It's not raining and he's a man."

"But his need is just as great as ours was. I can't in good conscience tell him to leave when he might end up in a car accident. Neither one of us needs to be responsible for that."

"So, you want to let him sleep in his car?"

"No. I want to open *Raccoon Cabin* and let him get a good night's rest, or at least what's left of the night. And in the morning, I want to call Mrs. McClelland and see if she is up for us reopening the motel."

Ronan stared at her for a moment, his eyes blank and his mouth hanging slightly open. Shellie was tempted to pat herself to see if she had grown a second head.

She elaborated. "We can't charge this man tonight. But think about it. With all the concerts, everything for miles around is booked on a regular basis. Even if we only have occasional customers, it will help pay the taxes and maybe we can run it in return for living here."

"You're right and we did already pass the health inspection. I thought God was pushing me about my PTSD when the inspector showed up, but all along He was setting us up for this."

"So, you're good with the idea of opening the motel?"

"I'm still not sure about that; we need to hear what Mrs. McClelland thinks first. I do agree we can let this man stay here tonight. Tomorrow, I'll look at the motel books and see if I can figure out what we should charge. If we can open the place."

"I'll find out what it will take to accept credit cards and what other inspections will be needed to open."

Ronan stepped back into the light and gave Blue a hand signal. The dog immediately relaxed, letting his tongue loll out the side of his mouth.

"We're sorry to make you wait, but I think you'll like what we have to say," Ronan said.

The man glanced at Blue and back to Ronan, gradually relaxing his rigid stance. "What is that?"

"We are going to give you the use of a cabin for tonight."

"Thank you." He reached into his pocket. Blue charged forward barking and snarling close enough for saliva to pepper the man's suit. He froze.

"*Hier Fuss*," Ronan commanded. Blue quieted immediately and backed into the heel position, never taking his eyes off the stranger.

Very slowly the man pulled out a money clip. His voice was subdued. "What do I owe you?"

Shellie stepped around the men, entering the office and went into business mode. "Nothing for tonight. But thanks to you, we're going to verify with the owner of the property if she would like us to re-open the business."

Shellie grabbed the key off the rack behind the check-in desk. "You'll be in R*accoon Cabin*, which is the first one after the *Dining Cabin*. As we said, we just got the electricity on. We do know the hot and cold water is working, but if you have any problems, please come ring the buzzer and we'll try and help. I'm afraid we don't have wifi or telephones yet."

The man smiled first at Shellie and then at Ronan. "You have no idea how much I appreciate this."

Ronan relaxed enough to smile back. "I'll give you a hand with your luggage and make sure you get settled."

Shellie waved and smiled. "Have a nice night."

Their guest gave Blue a wide berth as he walked out the door. Ronan and the dog followed.

Shellie watched them through the office window. Once the door was open and the lights on, the men shook hands. The rectangle of light disappeared with the closing of the door. Ronan and Blue immediately disappeared into the darkness.

She turned out the office lights and climbed back into bed. Her stomach did flip-flops, and she turned from one side to the other trying to get comfortable.

Had she done the right thing? If Mrs. McClelland would let them open the motel it would certainly solve a lot of Shellie's problems. But what would the woman's grandson say? Still, Shellie had a feeling the older woman would find a level of peace knowing the motel had come back to life after so many years of abandonment.

Rolling to her side, Shellie punched her pillow. Enough. Time to sleep.

Shellie was amazed, first that she had slept and second that she felt so good. She had left the curtain on the sliding glass door open, so the first beams of sunlight awakened her. She dressed quickly and headed to the *Dining Cabin.* After firing up the woodstove, she set the coffee to perk. By the time Ronan arrived, she had the bacon done and in the warming oven along with a stack

of pancakes. Sparing him a smile and a quick glance as
Shellie flipped the last flapjack. Funny how today she
didn't feel shy around him.

"Would you grab the syrup and butter?"

Ronan set the table and poured coffee. He hesitated over her cup. "Would you rather pour your own
coffee?"

Shellie turned to him, spatula in hand. His serious
expression and willingness to understand her fears
warmed her as no fire could. "No, you can pour it. I
know you aren't anything like Chad."

Ronan nodded, swallowing visibly, and she
turned back to the stove and smoking pan. Shellie had
poured the excess bacon drippings on Blue's food and
Ronan took the bowl to the corner Blue had claimed as
his own. The dog trotted over and downed on the old
blanket Shellie had placed there for him. Ronan gave the
hand signal and Blue consumed his breakfast in huge
gobbling bites.

Ronan shook his head. "I guess he was hungry;
he sure didn't wait to say grace."

Shellie laughed and took her seat. "When do you
think we can call Mrs. McClelland? I have to leave for
work soon."

"As soon as we finish eating." A companionable
silence reigned in the cabin broken only by the scrape of
a fork on china or the splash of coffee added to a cup.

Ronan cleared the plates. Shellie pulled out her
cell phone and dialed.

"Hi, Mrs. McClelland, this is Shellie Morgan. I
have you on speaker phone because Ronan is here too."

"Well, how are you two young people doing?"

"Just fine. Wait until you see the pictures. The
place looks great! Ronan fixed all the steps and has the

water running. And we have finished with the *Manager's, Dining,* and *Raccoon* cabins already."

"That's wonderful news. I can't wait to see the pictures."

Shellie looked at Ronan questioning him with her eyes and he motioned for her to continue.

"Now that the electricity is on, the sign out front is starting to draw people looking for rooms. So we were wondering if you would mind if we re-opened the motel?"

"It's open and people are coming?" The excitement vibrated in Mrs. McClelland voice.

Ronan answered. "Yes, ma'am. As a matter of fact, we ended up with our first guest last night, so we thought we should call you."

"I can't begin to tell you what this means to me. It always made me a little sad knowing that the place we struggled to build was slowly falling to pieces and no one wanted to stay there anymore. You've got my heart pounding, I'm so excited."

Ronan looked at Shellie. She continued.

"We passed the health inspection yesterday and I'm going to check on what it will take to accept credit cards, but first we need to know if you closed the business permanently."

"As a matter of fact, we didn't. My grandson said it made more sense to use it as a write off and keep it open. We were going to have to close it next year though, because we'd gone so long without a profit."

Shellie high fived with Ronan.

"I'll call to get the motel phone turned back on and start looking into making a website and getting us on the travel sites. Can you pass on Ronan's cell phone number to your grandson, so we can figure out how he wants us to handle the paperwork?"

"Certainly. And thank you. This makes me feel as good as Christmas."

Chapter 12

After Shellie left, Ronan poured himself another cup of coffee and added a log to the fire. They had left the wooden door open and the sharp tang of pine mingled with the smell of bacon and coffee. The heat from the wood fire wrapped around him like a blanket while the cool spring air nipped at his nose. Birds twittered outside in their rush to find mates and food. All in all, *Pine Cone Motel* hugged him like a safe cocoon against the world. Unfortunately, the world wasn't safe, especially for gentle souls like Shellie.

She had been better this morning, but he'd seen the lines of tension around her eyes. Unless he missed his guess, she was starting to have memories of what happened to her with Chad. Not good. The question was what could he do about it? He didn't like the answer, not much.

He had an accounting degree, not psychology. While he could be supportive, she needed professional help, or she risked staying emotionally crippled. His Angel deserved a loving husband to protect and support her, but if she was unable to even kiss a man without going into a panic attack that wouldn't be possible. For an instant the vision of Shellie in a wedding dress coming down a church aisle toward him brought a spurt of joy. The intensity stunned him.

Ronan sipped his coffee and squashed the vision. He was too broken himself to be a fit mate for anyone, much less a sweet woman like Shellie. He tried to visualize her on the arm of another man, but the jolt of pain came swift and hard. His mind said finding her the right guy was the right thing to do. His heart said, "Mine."

When had she come to mean so much to him? It had been years since anyone other than Blue really mattered. Before Shellie, Ronan could have packed his few possessions and been gone in minutes. Now he was tied in one place, with a human being depending on him for protection. It should scare him to death, but instead he was starting to find excitement and interest in the world around him. Life no longer seemed a grudging effort to survive. For the first time since returning from the war, he wanted to get up in the morning. He looked forward to seeing what the day would bring, and all because of a half-drowned vagrant he didn't chase off into the night.

The screen door on the *Dining Cabin* opened and their overnight guest stuck his head in. "Okay, if I come in?"

Ronan waved him inside. "Sure. Would you like some coffee?"

"Yes, it smells great. I slept like a log and this fresh air has me hungry as a bear after hibernating. Any suggestions on a place to get breakfast?"

"There are some pancakes and bacon here if you like."

When the man nodded, Ronan rose and pulled the food from the warming oven and grabbed a plate and flatware. He placed the platter on the table and motioned to the syrup and butter. "Help yourself."

The man sat in Shellie's chair and took a single pancake and a strip of bacon. "Aren't you going to eat?"

"Shellie and I ate earlier. Eat up so it doesn't go to waste."

The man smiled and piled food on his plate. "I take it Shellie is the young lady I met last night."

Ronan nodded. "Yes. I'm Ronan Flanagan."

"I'm Thomas Witherspoon. I was so tired last night, I guess I forgot to introduce myself."

Ronan sat back down and picked up his coffee. "I don't think we came across as all that friendly last night, either. I'm sorry."

Thomas laughed. "I think your dog scared ten years off my life. I have to say, I had no worries about security around here after meeting him."

Ronan smiled at Blue relaxing on his blanket. "He has that effect on most people."

Thomas sipped some of his coffee. "So, did you get permission to open the motel?"

"Yes. We have some work to figure out the books and get started, but it looks like we have a go."

"This may be premature, but I would like to see if I could rent the place at the end of August for a week."

"You mean you want to rent a cabin?"

"No, I want to rent all the cabins. I've been talking to my staff about a company getaway. My people work hard and usually are like a family. Lately there has been some friction between members. I think there has been too much pressure and work and not enough socializing."

Ronan rose and returned with the coffee pot, warming up their cups. "Don't you think this may be too rustic?"

"I think this is perfect. Each family could have their own cabin, so they could get some down time together, but we would all be a group without outsiders influencing or judging what we do. There is a lot to see and do. It would be easy to arrange tours of the Olympic venues, and fishing, and hiking outings. We could contract with you for breakfast and dinner and have lunch out. This place is the perfect size for us, bigger than a

B&B and smaller than the resorts." Thomas relaxed back in his chair.

Ronan tried to think about what Shellie would say to this proposal. It brought a smile to his lips. Angel would jump at the idea and probably be going a mile a minute with thoughts on how to build it into a marketing angle. The woman threw herself into projects 110%. "I like the idea, but I need to talk it over with Shellie, and we need to get up and running. You don't even know what we will be charging."

Thomas' expression became intense. "I'm not worried, you're both too honest to take advantage of anyone; and frankly, I owe you. I think you saved my life last night."

Ronan met Thomas' gaze, recognizing the depth of the man's feelings. Score another one for Shellie: the woman had a way of making the life of everyone she encountered a little better. It was time someone did the same for her.

Ronan broke eye contact. "Why don't you leave us your business card and as soon as we have things organized we can call and see if this is still an option for you."

Thomas pulled a card from his pocket and rose. "I'd best get going. Thank you again for everything."

Ronan stood, and they shook hands. A few minutes later he heard a car pull out of the driveway.

Ronan washed the dishes, closed the cabins, and went to change into his best clothes.

An easy walk into town brought him to Pastor Clark's house. Ronan drew in a fortifying breath and knocked.

The door opened quickly, and Pastor Clark greeted him with a big smile. "Ronan, come in, come in."

Pastor showed Ronan to a seat in his study. The pleasant room helped him to relax a little. Books and knickknacks filled the shelves and childish drawings were pinned to the walls. Clark resumed his seat behind his desk, pushing an open Bible to one side.

"How are you doing this morning?"

Ronan found it hard to breathe. It felt as if his tie was a noose choking him. He pulled at his collar a little. It suddenly occurred to him, he would be violating Shellie's privacy to talk to the Pastor. Maybe he shouldn't have come. Realizing the Pastor waited for him to answer, Ronan croaked, "Fine."

Pastor Clark smiled as if Ronan had said something brilliant and rose to get a glass of water. He handed it to Ronan and perched on the front of his desk. "So how is the shy young lady you brought to services?"

It was now or never. "She needs help and I don't know how to get it for her, so I came to you."

Clark's expression turned serious and he slipped into the chair beside Ronan. "What kind of help?"

Ronan leaned forward, playing with the glass. "I need to know you will keep this in the strictest confidence and you won't let Shellie know we talked about this." Pastor Clark nodded, and Ronan continued. "She was date raped."

Clark inhaled sharply. "I'm so sorry. That's an evil abuse no woman should go through. Because it happens all too frequently on a date, the victims, and unfortunately society, often blame them for something completely outside of their control."

"That's the case here. She was drugged and at first didn't remember what happened, but I'm pretty sure the memories are coming back and she's making negative comments about herself. She needs help, so this doesn't destroy her."

"I wish I could be more help, but this is outside my education and skill set. If I tried to help I could cause more problems than I might solve. There is a Dr. Parish here in Saranac Lake who the police recommend to rape victims. Unfortunately, she is not cheap, and she won't do pro bono work. If you like I can contact her and see if she can recommend any free resources."

"Will they be as good as Dr. Parish?"

"Probably not."

Ronan nodded. "Can you give me Dr. Parish's contact information?"

A few minutes later Ronan was back out in the sunshine, but the chill remained in his bones. Every time he thought about what Shellie had been through, he swung from wanting to find Chad and beat him to a pulp to the desire to grab Shellie and run until they were so far from civilization no one would ever find them.

Neither reaction would help Shellie. Ronan reached up to make sure the doctor's business card was safe in his pocket. The best thing he could do was get Shellie the professional help she needed, and they would have to pay for that help. They needed a bigger income. Time for him to soldier up and get a real job. It had been weeks since he had an episode in public; maybe he could start to function on the fringes of society. Hopefully the position at the grocery store was still open. If not, he would find something, anything. He would not fail his Angel.

As he walked up the road through Saranac Lake, Ronan dialed the number for Dr. Parish. A car whizzed past, drowning out the ringing. As he strode by *Origin Coffee* the rich smell of the brew was tempting, but the cost of one of those designer drinks was beyond his means. The owners were nice people and a couple of miserable, cold mornings had given him a lavender latte, so he could warm up. They claimed the drinks were forgotten or not up to their standards, but he had known they were being generous. Ronan shrugged; he'd had a good cup before he left the *Pine Cone* and there were more important things to think about. Someday, he'd have the funds to buy coffee and he'd be back because on top of good hearts they made really good coffee.

"Dr. Parish's office, how may I help you?" asked an artificially pleasant voice.

"I was thinking of bringing a friend to see Dr. Parish. Can you tell me her rates, hours, and appointment availability?" Ronan rubbed at an itch under his hat rim.

"Certainly, her billing rate is three hundred and fifty dollars an hour. Normally I am scheduling appointments six months out, but I had a cancellation. The doctor is available Wednesday, the eighth at eleven-thirty in the morning. Can I add you to her schedule?"

Ronan almost dropped the phone. That was a lot of money, about what he'd made in the last month. His breathing became difficult. He didn't have a job to pay for it and he hadn't talked to Shellie. Was he doing the right thing? Ronan almost hit the disconnect right then and there, but the vision of Shellie sobbing stilled his hand. For Angel he would get the funds, no matter what he had to do.

"Are you still there?"

"Yes. Please put Shellie Morgan in for that appointment." If he didn't have the money or Shellie refused to go, he could always call and cancel. The strictures on his lungs eased, allowing him to inhale.

"Certainly, Ms. Morgan. May I call you back at this number in the event of an earlier opening?"

Ronan stared at the phone and grinned, talk about being politically correct. His voice hadn't been high enough to be mistaken for a woman's in close to twenty years. The last of his tension melted at the humor of the conversation. "Sorry, my name is Ronan Flanagan. I'm making the appointment for a friend."

There was a slight pause. "I see, Mr. Flanagan. Will you be joining Ms. Morgan?"

"No. I'll be working."

"Dr. Parish would like to speak to you for a moment."

Ronan heard a few seconds of muffled conversation and then a soft-spoken woman came on the phone. "Thank you for calling Mr. Flanagan. I understand you want to make an appointment for a friend of yours, Ms. Morgan. Does she know you are doing this?"

"No."

" I see. Could you give me a brief understanding of why she should see me?"

"I think she is starting to remember being raped." Ronan waited for the shocked reaction.

Instead Dr. Parish spoke in the same calm, friendly voice. "That is something I can help her with, but may I ask how you fit into her life?"

That was a loaded question. "She's an angel who deserves a heck of a lot better than me, but I'm all she's got and I'm going to do everything I can to make sure she's happy and safe."

"Thank you, Mr. Flanagan. I look forward to meeting Ms. Morgan and perhaps, someday, you, too."

He had reached the parking lot of the Price Rite Grocery store and viewed the familiar structure. The sturdy block building had been around for close to sixty years, but while the style was dated, it was clean and the parking lot crowded. He ran through the potential questions he might have to address and said a quick prayer that PTSD would not be mentioned. Ronan put Blue in a down and walked inside to the customer service desk with a show of confidence he was far from feeling. "Is Tom Carter available?"

"He's out for lunch, can I help you?"

Ronan forced a smile. He could do this. He would do this. "He mentioned there might be an open position here and I'm interested in work."

The girl's grin, unlike Ronan's, looked genuine. "I don't know for sure what Tom had in mind, but we can always use another set of hands." She reached in a filing cabinet and drew out a printed form. "Tom should be back soon so why don't you fill out this application while you wait?"

Ronan took the paper, moved to a side of the customer service counter, and set to work completing the information. He hesitated on the education section; would listing his degree be an advantage or raise a lot of questions he didn't want to answer? Deciding honesty was the best policy, he quickly completed the form. As he gave it a final check, he saw Tom walk in. The girl at the counter moved to open the door and motioned Ronan's way, but Ronan couldn't hear what was said over the clatter of shopping carts and canned music.

Tom grasped the knob and waved Ronan in with a smile. "It's Ronan, isn't it?"

"Yes, sir, " he replied as they shook hands.

"Tom, remember? Don't sir me."

Ronan smiled. "Wouldn't dream of it, Gunny."

Tom sat behind a cluttered desk and motioned for Ronan to sit across from him in the cramped space. "I was hoping you would come back. I can always use a hard-working employee. So, what have you been doing lately?"

Ronan swallowed. He'd been expecting the question, but his hands still shook. "I've been helping to re-open one of the old motels on the way into town."

"Which one?"

"*The Pine Cone Motel.*" Saying the name brought a vision of the old place to mind and a measure of calm descended on him.

Tom nodded. "I saw the sign lit up when I drove passed last night. I was glad to see someone working on it. The McClelland's were good people and I was sorry to see Myrtle closed the place after Angus died."

"She lives in Florida near her daughter now. She gave us permission to re-open it."

"That'll be a full-time job in itself. Why are you looking for work here?"

"A friend and I are splitting the motel work. Running the work will give us a place to live, but no salary and we still must eat. She works nights and will be there during the day. I thought if I could get a day job it would go a long way toward covering our other expenses."

Tom nodded. "I already know you aren't afraid of hard work or getting your hands dirty." He looked down at the application. "You have a degree in accounting. Is this going to be a stop gap salary while you look for a better job?"

Ronan looked the man in the eye. "No, Gunny, I wouldn't do that to you."

Tom stared at him for a minute. Sweat rolled down Ronan's spine and it wasn't due to the temperature of the room. He needed this job.

The store manager stood. "Two of my register operators called in so I'm shorthanded at the checkout. Are you willing to give it a try?"

Ronan nodded and gave a silent prayer of thanks as Tom guided him out the office door and over to checkout.

It didn't take Ronan long to get the hang of the cash register. He had the aisle nearest the office, so no one came up behind him and the carts and people were so noisy he wasn't in danger of being startled. The head cashier, Sally, stood by him for a while, helping to answer his questions. She had been a little peeved that he had started as a cashier until he mentioned having worked on the dock to clean up before inventory. That had mollified her a little.

Tom stopped by after an hour. "So, lieutenant how are things going? It's a bit noisy over here."

Ronan grinned. "It's still quieter than a humvee, Gunny."

Tom laughed. "You can say that again."

After the man walked away Sally gave Ronan a strange look. "You were in the military?"

"Yes, ma'am."

Sally contemplated the floor and then looked up at Ronan with a serious expression. "You know, cashier is a job people work up to, proving themselves before they get here so I was annoyed when Tom started you here even though we needed the help. But you've proved yourself in ways most of us will never experience. Thank you for your service to our country." She walked away and opened the next register over. "Just give a shout if you need help."

Ronan saw a frazzled mom with two cranky toddlers, one in the cart the other with a tight grip on her mom's pant leg, maneuver her cart into his aisle. The walking towheaded toddler immediately grabbed a candy bar and started to cry when it was taken away. Taking advantage of her mother's distraction, the one in the cart grabbed a package of mints. The mom looked about ready to burst into tears herself.

Ronan grabbed a sticker from the sheet Sally had given him for kids and waved it at the closest child. "Do you like elephants?"

A vigorous nod and a finger in the mouth answered him.

Ronan held out the sticker. "How about we trade?"

The little girl thought for a minute and then handed off the mints. Ronan gave her a big smile and gently placed the sticker on her shirt. The child grabbed at the garment, pulling it up from her rounded tummy, so she could look at her prize.

A tiny voice closer to the floor floated up to him. "I like stickers, too."

Ronan leaned over, to see her. "You do?"

She nodded.

"How about you help your mom put the groceries on the belt and then you can get close enough for me to give you a sticker?"

A big grin greeted him, and the lost candy bar was forgotten. She climbed up the side of the cart while her mother unloaded enough groceries for the child to fit in the basket. She was more hindrance than help, but the tears were gone and both children settled into giggles when Ronan wiggled his eyebrows at them. True to his word, the second child got her sticker.

The mom scanned a credit card and looked up at Ronan with a tentative smile. "Thank you."

He grinned and handed her the receipt. "Anytime."

Sally closed her register and came over to him. "Time to take a break."

Ronan nodded and passed his "closed" sign to the last customer in line. As soon as he finished, he removed the apron.

"Do you need me to show you to the break room?" Sally asked.

Ronan shook his head. "No thanks. I think I'll step outside for a minute."

Sally shook her head. "I wouldn't have taken you for a smoker. Your health insurance here will be lower if you can quit."

Ronan froze. He hadn't discussed benefits with Tom and had assumed all he was working for was a salary. "I get healthcare?"

Sally shook her head and looked at him curiously. "Of course, it's the law. If you can stick out the job for a month the company pays half of your group health insurance."

She glanced over her shoulder at the office and lowered her booming voice a bit. "There are really only a few doctors and one hospital in the area unless things are really bad, and you have to get transported to Plattsburgh, but we have three levels of plan. Pick the cheapest one. The others are more expensive because they don't require you to be in a network of approved providers, but all the local doctors are in the network."

Ronan nodded. "There must be a difference between the two more expensive plans. Do you know what that is?"

"The really expensive one adds dental and mental health benefits, but I don't see where you would need either of those." Sally winked and hurried away. If he had health insurance here, wouldn't Shellie have to have it from her employer?

Ronan went out and took Blue around back to play fetch for ten minutes, gave him a drink of water, then moved him to a shady spot in the cool grass. On his way back to his position, he swung by the office.

Tom glanced up from his computer and smiled. "How's it going?"

"Great so far." Ronan wiped his palm on his pant leg. "Sally mentioned that the position has healthcare benefits?"

Tom smacked himself in the forehead with the heel of his hand. "I was in such a hurry to get another cash register open I didn't go over any of that with you. So, you think you're going to stay more than a day or two?"

Ronan nodded.

Tom opened a file draw and pulled out some pamphlets. "Read through these, take your time, you don't qualify for any benefits until you've been here a month. Think about it carefully and remember to take advantage of your VA benefits so you don't waste money on duplicate coverage." He held the glossy papers out to Ronan. "About a week before the month is up, you'll have to fill out some forms as to which plan you want and how much money you want put into your 401 K."

Ronan struggled to breathe. "I get a retirement, too?"

Tom grinned. "Welcome to full-time employment."

Chapter 13

Laughter bubbled up inside Shellie and she knew she wore a big grin as she moved to her station. She made eye contact with a guest entering through the revolving door.

"How can I help you today, sir?"

"I have a reservation under Peter Markham."

Shellie entered Peter and thought of the perfect banner for the *Pine Cone* website, one that excluded the decrepit pool. She shook her head and focused on her screen. She hadn't entered his last name and she couldn't remember it. A chill made her fingers clumsy. "I'm sorry, what is your last name again?"

Concern written on his face, the man answered, "Markham. Is there a problem?"

Shellie tapped in the name. The screen filled with information. Mr. Markham was a diamond club member.

Heat filled her face. "Oh, no sir. My entry error."

She flashed him her most charming smile and quickly processed a key. "Housekeeping indicated the extra pillows you requested are already in your room, but if you need anything else, please call down so we can help."

The man seemed mollified and headed to the elevator. Shellie sighed and drew a total blank on her brilliant idea for the *Pine Cone Motel* website.

A few minutes later a woman dressed in a swimsuit cover-up and carrying a bag full of beach toys walked up to Shellie's station with two young children in tow. "Where's the complimentary breakfast served?"

Shellie stood on tiptoe to lean over the desk and point. "Right over there in the Mount Marcy Room."

As the woman walked away, someone brushed against Shellie's backside and she caught a glimpse of a dark-haired man out of the corner of her eye. Shellie's brain screamed, "Not again." She jerked. In her precarious position that was all it took to tumble her sideways. She would have landed on her rear-end if one of her co-workers hadn't caught her. She jerked away from his strong hands, her breath coming in short gasps and an involuntary squeal escaped her.

Panic threaded the man's voice. "Are you okay?"

Shellie fought to control her breathing as alternating waves of heat and chills washed over her. It hadn't been an attacker. She nodded and offered a weak smile. "I guess next time I'll walk around the desk when I give directions to a guest. Less chance of falling that way."

He apologized profusely for knocking her over as he backed away. Shellie turned to the woman next to her and excused herself before rushing to the restroom. Once inside the stall she half collapsed onto the lid. Alternating waves of numbness, chills, and heat shook her. Shellie fought back the nausea and tears, gulping in deep swaths of air. It took several minutes to get her body under control. Washing her hands allowed herself a few more minutes to collect her shredded nerves. Shellie returned to her station with forced composure. She signed back on and waved to the next guest in line.

Plans for the motel continued to pop into her head all morning wrecking her concentration. But it was certainly better than the times when memories of Chad would bushwhack her, leaving her shaking.

When she had to ask a guest the same question three times, she realized the distraction was interfering with her work. Washed in guilt, she firmly placed the

Pine Cone Motel out of her mind, but half an hour later another thought scrambled her focus.

She didn't want Mr. Grundy to think she was texting with friends, so she didn't use her phone. Instead, she grabbed a pad and jotted quick notes to help her remember the ideas and focus her attention on the job. She hoped Grundy didn't ask to see her scribbles.

She ate lunch quickly, wanting to run through her notes and added details. Instead she found she was debating herself on the incident this morning. A little voice whispered she needed professional help while a second one scoffed that it was a one-time thing, and even if it wasn't there were more important things to take care of first.

Her cell phone rang. She pulled it out wondering why Ronan would call instead of texting. The contact listing sent chills up her spine. Shellie didn't even attempt to keep the anxiety out of her voice. "Mom, is everything okay?"

"Yes, dear. I wanted to let you know that I gave out your phone number to a nice detective, a Sergeant Evans."

Had Chad's father found a way to set the police on her? Wasn't kicking her out of school and driving her away from home punishment enough for standing up for herself?

"What does the Sergeant want with me?" Fear shook Shellie's voice.

"He wants to talk to you about what happened with Chad."

Flashes of memories scrolled across Shellie's mind, including the one where tears slipped from her eyes, but she was unable to speak or stop Chad from touching her. Shellie's stomach knotted and sharpened her tone. "What if I don't want to talk to him?"

"He seems like a nice man, sweetie. Maybe he can do something to clear your name, then you can come home and finish your degree."

"Like Dad would let me in the door. I can't forget what he called me or the fact he believed Chad over me. You know he blames me for his inability to get his masters and doctorate degrees. He told me more than once if I hadn't come along, he could have gotten an education that would open more doors to better jobs. The fact he was limited to small private colleges was all my fault. Everything is my fault with him, and I won't live like that anymore."

"Sweetie, that isn't true. I'm the one who accidentally got pregnant. Dad gets angry and doesn't know how to handle that emotion, so he says things he really doesn't mean."

"If he only said it once or apologized, I might believe that. No, I'm not going back. Besides, I have a job here, and -- and I'm signed up to take courses next semester." That last statement was an outright lie, but she wanted her father to know she wasn't a failure.

"I'm sorry about the things he said. He was hurt and angry and he didn't mean them."

"I'll believe that when he calls and apologizes."

"Give him time, sweetie. I'm sure the two of you can make peace if you're willing to compromise a little. If you told him you were sorry, and you wouldn't do it again, I'm sure he could find it in his heart to forgive you."

Hot tears and angry words burned through Shellie's control. "Forgive me? He owes me an apology

for not believing in me, I didn't do anything wrong and
—"

A burst of laughter nearby reminded her she was
in the employee cafeteria. If she didn't want her past to
poison her present, she needed to control herself. "Mom,
I am at work and I can't talk about this. Please don't give
out my number anymore and call this person and tell him
I don't want to talk to him."

"But, Shellie —"

Shellie hit the end call button, ignoring the plea
in her mom's voice and dropping the phone on the table.
Her hands shook. She could feel her heart pounding in
her chest. All she wanted to do was scream and run until
she got to her cabin and hide under the covers. Then a vision of the *Pine Cone Motel* danced across her mind. The
desire to scream subsided.

Slowly she built a picture of the place, deliberately calling up every detail from the log structures to
Ronan. He was an inseparable part of the image she sum-
moned. She visualized him kneeling on the porch steps, a
hammer in one hand and a fist full of nails in the other.
He had a grin on his face and Blue danced between the
two of them, spinning and barking and jumping as if it
had been months not hours since the dog had seen her.
Her heartbeat slowed to normal or at least to the point
where she couldn't feel it pounding.

That smile of Ronan's -- just the thought of it
made her want to smile, too. Shellie relaxed back against
her chair and looked down at the phone resting on her
pad of notes. A little of her tension returned. She had
never been a liar, so why had she lied to her mother
about going back to school? Dad would quickly find out
the truth and that would make everything worse, unless
she signed up for a course or two. Could she do it?

"Hey, Shellie," Kelly called out. She wore civvies instead of her uniform and hurried over to where Shellie sat.

Shellie did her best to compose her expression, was this a hint from God? "What's up? I thought you had already switched to nights and started classes."

"Classes haven't started yet. I stopped in to pick up my transfer papers to part-time and Mrs. Anderson asked me to find you before I left. You need to fill out some paperwork, get signed up for insurance and that stuff." Kelly struck a stiff pose. It reminded Shellie of a general awarding medals to a soldier. "So, congratulations, you're off probation and are now a full-time employee." Kelly pretended to salute.

Shellie couldn't help giggling. She stood and collected her things. "I was thinking about what you said, about taking college courses. Do you know, is it too late to sign up?"

"Registration closes on Friday. Are you in?"

"I'd really like to, but I'm not sure I can afford it or even what course I should take."

"Talk to Mrs. Anderson. The college reimbursement program here is really good. Since this is the first summer session, we have classes Monday through Thursday mornings and we can carpool."

"What do you mean, the first summer session?"

"The college splits the summer in half that way students can take both semesters of a sequential course and not get goofed up and having to wait a semester to take the second class in a series."

"So, I could take two semesters of a course over the summer?" Shellie had never heard of anything like that.

"Yup. The college wants to serve students who make the commitment to stay for the summer." Kelly scribbled a name on the margin of Shellie's pad. "Call and ask for Mr. Pataki. He's my counselor, he can help you out."

Mrs. Anderson was focused on her computer monitor. Shellie knocked on the open door. The woman looked up and smiled. "Come in, Shellie. We need to complete your benefits package forms."

Shellie perched on the edge of a chair. This was perfect. "I was thinking that I would really like to try and finish my degree and Kelly said the reimbursement program here is good. Is that one of the benefits we'll talk about?"

The older woman smiled and pulled some papers from a file drawer. "After I saw how good you were at accounting, I was hoping you would decide to finish your degree. But first I need you to complete the health insurance forms." She handed the papers to Shellie and motioned to a chair near her. Shellie glanced at the forms while Mrs. Anderson clicked some keys. She pointed at the screen. "We have two plans. The basic plan covers only catastrophic illness or accidents, with no preventative coverage. While the company pays the entire premium for that plan, I don't recommend it."

Shellie chewed her lip. She had always been under her parents' insurance, so this was all new. "Why not?"

"I want our employees to get checkups and have dental coverage. All of that is an out of pocket expense. If you get a flu or need a doctor visit, you must pay for it. That leads a lot of people to avoid going to the doctor until they're really ill and in major trouble."

"What's the other plan?"

"It's something of the gold standard in health insurance. It covers doctor visits including chiropractors, alternative care providers, and a significant annual dental coverage." Mrs. Anderson used the mouse to point to the information on her screen.

"It sounds like a simple decision. Why don't people select it?"

"Cost." She brought up the payment plan.

The numbers made Shellie dizzy. Even covering just herself, and the company paying part of the premium, the monthly cost was almost half her take home pay. No way could she swing that. Right now, she needed every penny. "Much as I would like to take your advice, I can't afford to spend half my income on health insurance."

Mrs. Anderson nodded. Her expression was sympathetic. "If things change you can switch programs at a later time."

Shellie quickly completed the basic plan form and handed it back to Mrs. Anderson.

Mrs. Anderson changed to a different screen. "Now about college. We reimburse tuition based on the student's grade. Full for an A, ninety percent for a B, eighty percent for a C. We don't reimburse for anything less than a C."

Shellie thought about her bank account. After paying the electric deposit there wasn't much left, certainly not enough to pay for even one course. So much for enrolling this semester. She tried to swallow her disappointment and stood.

The woman dropped the insurance form into one of the baskets on her desk. " Are you going to sign up for college this semester?"

Shellie nodded. "I'm probably rushing things, what with moving and getting settled, it will take a while to save up the tuition and with registration closing this week, I guess I'll have to wait."

Mrs. Anderson patted her hand. "Don't give up, yet. "She changed to a stern expression, but a smile hovered on her lips and let Shellie know she was putting on an act. "I don't do this for everyone, but I'm calling in a favor for you."

She picked up the phone and dialed. "Aldo, I'm so glad I caught you. I need a favor. I have a young employee with a lot of potential who would like to finish her degree. She was thinking of enrolling this semester, but there are a few roadblocks. Would you see if you can help her?"

The person on the other end spoke for a few minutes. Mrs. Anderson smiled. "I'll put her on. Her name is Shellie Morgan."

She handed the phone to Shellie, switched her screen to the internet and retrieved her purse from a desk drawer. "I'm going to the restaurant for some lunch. Go ahead and use my computer. The gentleman you are talking to is Mr. Pataki."

Shellie took the receiver as Mrs. Anderson left. "Mr. Pataki?"

"Hi, Shellie. Is this your first-time signing up for college courses?"

"No sir. I was less than a semester away from graduating when I had to leave and find work."

"Excellent. Let's start by getting you on our registration website."

Shellie chewed her lip. "I don't think I have the money right now to pay tuition."

"Okay. Do you think you would have it in a month?"

Shellie did a mental run through of her expenses. If she could keep feeding them from work leftovers and barring any major plumbing issues with the cabins, she should have enough cash in a month to pay for three credit hours. "I could swing one course by then."

"Let's see what we can do. First, let me pull up your transcripts. Where did you go to school?"

Shellie hesitated. Would there be anything in the records about why she left? Still, she didn't want to take all those courses over. "Melody College."

She gave him her student sign-in information and heard keys tapping.

"Excellent. You have all your core courses so now it's a matter of selecting a major here. If we roll the other course that don't apply in as the electives, you'll only need twelve hours to complete your degree in hospitality resort and tourism management. Does that work for you?"

That sounded like a better choice for her current life than the English degree she'd been working on and she'd been taking business courses as electives because she found them more interesting. "Yes."

"Good, there's room in Mr. Edward's class on Hospitality Futures so you should start there. Do you think you can get mornings off for class?"

This was perfect. She could carpool with Kelly. "I'm starting on nights tomorrow, but don't I have to pay when I register?"

"I've set you up to be billed so you'll have about a month before the bill comes due. In addition, your work at the hotel will count toward your field studies. Keep saving after you pay the bill, so we can register you for that course next semester. It's a nine-hour course, it will cost more. Finish that and you'll have your degree."

It took another half hour to finish everything on-line. Shellie stumbled out of the office and headed for her station; her brain felt numb. She was back in college and less than a year from a degree.

Ronan was bone tired and his feet ached from standing all day, but he'd done it. It wasn't bad working the register, especially when they put him on the one nearest the office. Thankfully he had done enough self-service checkouts to be able to work the scanners and his accounting background helped in cashing out his drawer. The rest was smile and joke with the customers.

Tomorrow he would take the course on selling alcohol and how to check IDs, so minors were protected and the store didn't lose their license.

Blue bounced along beside Ronan, occasionally grabbing his pants cuff and tugging or jumping up to try and steal Ronan's baseball cap. "Knock it off. I'll play with you as soon as we get home and I've changed."

His dog exhaled a very human huff. Ronan had to smile; Blue really was a good dog. Tomorrow he would leave Blue with Shellie. She was switching to nights and would be at the motel all day.

The thought made his stomach queasy. It would be the first time he would be separated from Blue since returning stateside, but he couldn't expect Blue to do a down stay, all day, every day outside the store. That wasn't fair and when the weather turned bad it would be plain mean to ask that of him. Besides, he could count on

Blue to keep Shellie safe and she would probably spoil the dog rotten. The thought was enough to brighten his outlook and he picked up his pace, to tell Angel the good news and start trying to talk her into seeing Dr. Parish.

Shellie had the grill going and had set the picnic table on the patio for them. He ducked in through the screen doors of the dining cabin, calling a greeting.

She turned, a smile on her face, and tongs in her hand. "If you went fishing, tuck them in the fridge. I scored some pork chops and —." She stopped mid-sentence and looked him up and down. "Wow, you look great. What inspired you to wear your Sunday best?"

"A job interview. Can you entertain Blue for a few minutes while I change? I'll tell you all about it over dinner."

Shellie nodded, set the tongs aside and grabbed up Blue's ball on a string. "Blue, *hier*."

The dog glanced over his shoulder at Shellie and then up at Ronan, as if asking what he should do.

Ronan smiled at his canine. "Free."

Blue spun and raced to a sliding sit in front of Shellie, tail wagging a cloud of dust from the ground. Shellie half laughed, half coughed, and tossed the ball. Blue charged after it.

Ronan heard her command, "*bring*" as he stepped out onto the porch headed for his own accommodations.

By the time he returned, Blue was stretched out on the cool stone patio and Shellie was removing the chops and corn from the grill. Blue's dinner sat beside the glowing charcoal.

Ronan reached for the dog bowl and turned to Shellie. "It's time Blue learns he can take food from you, too."

Shellie started and almost dropped the platter. "Really?"

Ronan nodded. "You give him his food."

Shellie placed the platter on the table and nervously wiped her hands on her jeans before taking hold of the stainless-steel container. She stood still for a second and Ronan suppressed a grin as he watched her confirm the bowl was in her left hand. She placed it between Blue's front paws and glanced at Ronan.

"Okay, give him the signal."

Shellie's hand movement was perfect. Blue glanced at Ronan. Instead of giving the hand signal, Ronan spoke, "Free."

Blue reached down and lapped up some food, then stopped and looked at Ronan. "Good boy. Dinner."

That was all it took for Blue to settle in and wolf down his meal. Ronan held Shellie's chair for her then seated himself. As soon as they said grace Ronan began dishing up food. "Boy, this looks really good."

Shellie smiled at him and buttered her corn. "So, tell me about this job interview. What's it for? How did it go?"

Ronan started cutting his meat. "I went to the grocery store and was hired on as a cashier. I started today and am now employed full time. In a month, if I can stick it out, I'll have health insurance and even a 401k."

Shellie clapped her hands. "I'm proud of you. That took a lot of courage. What made you decide to do this now? With us opening the *Pine Cone Motel* there'll be a lot more work around here and a lot more demands on your time."

Ronan set aside his cutlery. The time had come to really talk to Shellie. He had to convince her to see Dr. Parish. "I did it for you."

Shellie sat back in her chair. "I don't understand."

"Angel, do you have any idea how important you have become to me? You bring out the best in me. I want to do the same for you."

"I- I don't expect you to support me. I have a job and I can take care of myself. "

Ronan focused on her face, hoping his expression would help her to understand. "Not with me as an anchor dragging you down, you can't. I know exactly what you are spending on materials, so we can open this place. You're paying the utility bills and supplying feasts like this one. If you didn't have to carry me financially you could get help to deal with what Chad did to you."

Shellie had twisted her napkin until it resembled a rope. Her white knuckles attested to the strain his words created in her. "I'm fine. I don't need help from a shrink remembering what happened. I can remember it too well. All I want to do is forget it."

Ronan exhaled. "That's the problem, the more you try and forget it the more it will come out in strange and difficult ways, until you can't function. Take it from one who knows firsthand what that's like."

"I am looking at you. And you've found a way to get a full-time job and put your difficulties behind you. Why should I be any different?"

"Yay, I worked for half a day as a cashier and didn't have an episode. And that's a huge step up from what I have been doing. Let's see if I can get through a week before you start pinning medals on my chest." Ronan ran his hand through his hair and concentrated on obtaining the calm he needed to get through to Shellie. "I have an accounting degree, but all I can handle is the lowest paying, menial jobs no one else wants. And I haven't been able to keep one of those for more than a week. I want better than that for you."

"And you think going to a therapist will help me? In case you haven't noticed, I'm functioning rather well in my job. I even signed up to go back to school and finish my degree, and the hotel will reimburse my tuition. Maybe you need to see the therapist."

Her words stung. She had a point. "Dr. Parish is expensive. Maybe if I can stay long enough to get insurance, I will go see her, but right now we're talking about you."

Ronan shifted his chair. "Angel, look me in the eye and tell me memories aren't coming at the oddest times and disrupting your thoughts and causing you to make mistakes. Tell me you're sleeping okay and not having nightmares. Tell me if I were to take you into my arms and kiss you, you wouldn't want to run away."

Why had he said that last? The memory of her soft lips pressed to his, heated his blood just when he needed to be his calmest and most collected. Shellie's downcast expression tore at his heart.

"You really think it will get worse?" she whispered.

"I have it on the best authority."

She threw her napkin on the table. "I guess I'll think about it."

Ronan stretched out his hand, palm up. "That's all I ask."

Shellie grasped his hand with her chilled fingers, seeming to draw strength from him. He could tell her about the appointment later. For now, all Ronan wanted was to coax the smile back to her lips. "So how did it happen that you signed up for college?"

"I lost my temper."

Chapter 14

After dinner, they turned on the lights in the dining area and shoved the tables to one side. Ronan walked Shellie through Blue's commands, demonstrating them as he taught her the words. The dog looked affronted when Ronan slipped the training collar in place and attached a leash. At first Blue tried to jerk the leash away and return to Ronan. Shellie held tight and quickly got the timing of corrections and rewards. She was a natural with the right amount of pressure, if maybe a tad too generous on the rewards. She was going to spoil Blue. Shellie practiced while Ronan rinsed the dishes and loaded the dishwasher and called out pointers to her.

Finished, he wiped his hands on a towel and they headed over to the *Manager's Cabin*. Ronan cruised behind the desk and picked up the last ledger while the old computer slowly opened. "When I first moved in here, I was bound and determined to get another accounting job, so I practiced by reviewing and auditing the old books. I think if we can get about twenty-five percent occupancy year-round at the old rate, we can cover what I estimate is the fixed expenses with the five cabins. We'll need better than that to cover the variable stuff, and we're almost a third of the way through the year, so we need closer to fifty percent for the rest of the year."

Shellie looked at the figures. "That's a little less than the B&B's are charging and that's for a bedroom and shared bath. With the individual cabins, I think we can ask a bit more, maybe half again as much and not have a problem getting it."

"So that takes us to the equivalent of thirty-five percent occupancy."

Ronan's cell phone rang. He didn't recognize the number, but the area code was the same as Mrs. McClelland's, so he answered and put it on speaker.

A man's voice hammered through the phone. "Who do you think you are, telling my grandmother you're opening that dump of a motel and getting her all worked up?"

Ronan wanted to squirm in his chair. He exchanged a look with Shellie. She looked uncomfortable, too. "Hi, Henry. Look, we didn't mean to upset Mrs. McClelland. As a matter of fact, she sounded really happy to hear this place might re-open."

"Do you have any idea what it's going to cost to fix it up? She doesn't have that kind of money and if she did, I wouldn't let her waste it that way. She'd be better off if it was bulldozed, which is exactly what I was going to do this fall after we close the books. Now you've got her thinking the impossible will happen. Do you have any idea how crushed she's going to be when this falls apart? I almost had her to the point of agreeing to put the land up for sale. I've even been talking to a couple of developers and here you come ruining all my hard work."

Ronan got a glimmer of what was really bothering Mrs. McClelland's grandson. Money. "We aren't looking for you or your grandmother to pay for the repairs, which I have to say, would have been a lot worse if the place hadn't been closed up so carefully. You did that, didn't you?"

Silence. Henry sounded a little calmer. "Yeah. It was mostly my dad; I was a college kid helping. Gram was in rehab but issuing very specific directions over the phone."

"You did a great job. A few boards, some paint and a good scrubbing and we got the *Manager's, Dining, Raccoon,* and *Loon* cabins open."

"What about the rest of it?"

"We're working one cabin at a time opening, cleaning, making repairs. We got the electricity turned on and the sign is lit and drawing attention. You wouldn't know how to turn it off, would you?"

Henry chuckled. "You can't. Gramps wanted that thing lit 24/7 so he had it hardwired to always be on. The *no vacancy* switch is on the manager's desk. It really upset the sign guys when they had to repair it. Don't tell me people are actually stopping."

"Yes. There are a lot of concerts in the area and everything for miles around gets booked up at exorbitant prices. We thought if we could take in the overflow, we could cover the electricity and the insurance and taxes."

"You really think you can do that?"

Ronan glanced at Shellie. She was chewing her lip in that adorable way she did when she was worried but gave him an exuberant nod. He looked at the phone. "Yes. We were going over the old books. Can you text me the actual current amounts, so we have an idea of the size nut we must crack? We're working with estimates. But it really seems doable."

"Alright. I guess I don't have much choice, after the dressing down Gram gave me, but I'm not going to mess around with this. You have until September to come up with the funds for the school tax bill besides covering the electricity and insurance. If you don't, I'm going to insist we close, tear down, and sell the land."

Ronan spoke softly. "Henry, you can't do that to her. You know that will rip her heart out. I know we can make this work; I don't know if it can be done in five months."

"You're stalling so you can live rent free. You can't really turn a profit on that old place and you're playing me. I'm giving you the high season and you don't think you can do it. You have until September thirtieth to pay the taxes. Make it happen or I knock it down."

Ronan closed the phone, covering it with his hand and resting his forehead against his other palm. He didn't want to look at Shellie's face. Once again, the world was crashing in on them. If this didn't work, they'd both be out looking for a place to live. He hated the thought of putting Shellie at that kind of risk.

He felt her warm hand come to rest on top of his on the desk. Inhaling, he turned to look at her, expecting disappointment, or worse – fear — to be written across her face. Instead she gave him a luminous smile.

"We can do this." She pulled out a note pad. "I already talked to the two horse show organizers. This place has plenty of parking for the trucks and they can catch the bypass around Lake Placid and go directly to the fairgrounds. They were excited and are putting us in their brochure. They even had an old picture of the place from before it closed and are running that online and in their info packets. So, we can be full for two weeks right there."

"You're right. Then there's the rugby and lacrosse tournaments and the ironman."

"Okay, I can follow up with those organizers. That would give us four more weeks at full house."

Ronan ran the figures in his head. "That leaves us with too many weeks empty between now and September."

"We do have the winter and the snowmobiler traffic. The *Pine Cone Motel* is a lot better fit for those guests than places like *Lakeside Resort and Hotel*."

"That will get us through the county taxes due in January, but the school taxes are due in September and that's what Henry is using along with the insurance and other utilities."

He snapped his fingers and dug into his pocket for the business card. "You know that guy we helped last night?"

Shellie nodded.

He twisted in his chair to look at her. "He wants to rent the whole place for a week for a company re-treat."

"That's awesome." She closed her eyes, then opened them and blinked. "Now how do I market that on the website?"

Ronan hated to bring her down, but they had to be realistic. "I don't think I want to count on more than the one company until we see how things go."

"That gives us six weeks full in the next twelve. We're halfway there." Shellie looked over his shoulder.

Ronan's phone signaled a text and he recognized Henry's number. Opening the text, Ronan looked at the amount. It was a good thing he was sitting down. The taxes and insurance had to have increased significantly. "This can't be right. The expenses have tripled in the five years the place was closed?"

"Let me see." Shellie tipped his hand and read the figure. "It doesn't make any sense. That means the *Pine Cone Motel* is being taxed more than *Lakeside Resort and Hotel*. I saw the bill when Mrs. Anderson trained me. Would they do that to a small local business versus a big out of town chain?"

Ronan shook his head. "No. I think Henry is trying to trick us. He knows I was homeless, and he equates that to stupid and lazy."

Ronan hit redial.

"Henry here."

"This is Ronan and Shellie. We got your figures and they don't make sense. Are you honestly saying the expenses for this little cabin motel are almost triple a hundred room resort?"

A long pause filled the air. Finally a sigh rattled through the speaker. "Those are my estimates. They might be a little less in reality. I'm estimating the increase in insurance for the place to be open. And you aren't getting to live there for free just for watching the place. I'm charging each of you a thousand dollars a month to live there."

"Henry, you should be paying us a salary for running the place and that's a lot closer to five thousand dollars a month even at minimum wage. In lieu of two full-time salaries, we're willing to accept free rent. Consider it a win. Instead of getting paid two thousand a month you are saving three thousand in salaries, the five thousand you should be paying minus the two thousand you want from us. Please give us firm numbers as soon as you can. Until you do, we're planning on paying you half that amount." Ronan hit the disconnect button his heart pounding. It was a risk pushing Henry, but with Mrs. McClelland in their corner, he figured Henry would back down. There was no point in agreeing to Henry's figures, they'd never bring in that amount with the whole motel rented everyday until the end of September.

"Okay, assuming the real numbers are closer to our estimate, we still have a problem unless —" Shellie became statue still.

"Unless what, Angel?"

She stared at him, silent for a moment, then spoke in a soft, hesitant manner. "Unless you take one of the other rooms in this cabin and we rent out *Loon.* That's the same as a twenty percent increase in occupancy.*"*

Ronan now understood the old saying about being knocked over with a feather. Shellie wanted him to live in the same cabin as her? Didn't she understand the way she affected him? He had tasted only one of her kisses and yet they were invading his dreams at night and making his palms sweat when he thought of them during the day. And what about her? Surely with her own issues, living night and day with a man always around would only make things worse. Yet the pragmatist in him told him she was right.

Shellie looked down at the floor and shook her head. "I'm sorry. I know I'm not the kind of person you would want around on a full-time basis. I know I'm damaged goods. It seems like this is the easiest way out of the financial hole and I figured you were too much of a gentleman to suggest it."

Ronan had to chuckle at the thought of himself as a gentleman. And she was right; it was the financial answer. It would also give him a better opportunity to make sure she was safe once they started renting cabins. He hadn't liked being at the opposite end of the property from her with their guest last night. How would he feel with the place full of a younger, rowdier crowd? "It's a financial answer, but are you going to be able to sleep knowing a man is in the next room, hearing me walk around and undress?"

"I trust you." Her shudder told him a lot more than her bright words.

° *156* °

Chapter 15

Shellie shooed Ronan off to bed, so he would be rested for work. She spent the next three hours designing a website and creating a "to do" list for the next day. She needed internet service ASAP, not only for promoting the motel, but also for school. Shellie shut down the computer, but sleep eluded her. She wandered through the *Manager's Cabin*, lit only by the moonlight streaming in through the windows. Shellie checked the boy's room to make sure it was clean and the closet empty. She was glad the pink room had been converted to a craft area instead of this one. Picturing Ronan standing next to the frilly pink curtains made her giggle.

Still, a deep level of sadness filled her, and she couldn't put her finger on why. Yes, their future was precariously balanced on making the motel profitable, but they were both much better off than a month ago. She shook her head and marched into the bathroom to wash up.

Tomorrow Ronan would drop off Blue and head out to work. He'd warned Shellie to keep Blue on lead for the next few days or the dog would track him to the store. Knowing Blue, he would probably be so worked up she wouldn't get to sleep in. If that happened, she'd take a nap before work.

Early morning light crept in through the sliding glass door when Shellie heard a soft knock. They'd agreed he would open the sliding glass door as far as the stick would allow, send Blue in, and swiftly close the door. She groggily recognized Ronan's voice before the door opened and Blue exploded into the room. It took the dog two strides and he was on the bed, his cold nose burrowing under the covers to find and lick her face. Shellie ducked under the pillow and yanked the blankets over her head to no avail. Blue dug and shoved until he was under the covers and stretched out beside her, his warm, pink tongue slurping first her ear and neck and then her mouth.

Shellie sat bolt upright, shrieking, "Blue!"

A rapid thumping of a furry tail and hot, panting breath accompanied a bright stare. The dog's happy expression stole Shellie's annoyance and turned it into laughter. Deciding two could play, Shellie wrapped her arms around Blue's chest and dropped back on the mattress. Blue squirmed free and whacked her with a paw before spinning in a circle and pouncing back on her chest. Shellie returned the favor and pushed and shoved until they both fell off the bed in a heap of blankets. Blue took off to explore the cabin, dragging the bed clothes with his tail.

Shellie hurried into the bathroom snickering. There were worse ways to wake up. She was in the middle of brushing her teeth when Blue slammed the door against the wall and rushed in to drink from the toilet. Screaming around her toothbrush she garbled the command, "*Platz.*"

Blue slowly lowered his body to the floor, hovering with his elbows up an inch or two. Shellie threw him the 'you're messing up' look and he downed. She changed and headed to the *Dining Cabin*, Blue firmly attached to a leash. It was a good thing, too. He hit Ronan's path and went nose down, digging into the sandy soil with his front paws and dragged Shellie a couple of steps before she reined him in.

Ronan had left several large logs burning so the place and the coffee were warm, but the silence ate at Shellie's comfort. She had gotten used to Ronan's quick wit to keep her laughing. Giving herself a stern scolding, Shellie picked up her phone. The commercial phone line came with a website and guidance on obtaining a domain name.

The sports organizers were quick to add the *Pine Cone Motel* to available rentals, so she had to give them her cell phone. Her first task was to up the minutes on the plan. Her next call was to the telephone/internet provider. The old motel phone number happened to be available. Shellie smiled, thinking that would please Mrs. McClelland.

Ronan had left cooked bacon in the warming oven, so Shellie made a quick sandwich. Blue immediately took up a sit in front of her and begged unashamedly. His expression made her giggle.

She broke off a corner and carefully placed it as Ronan had shown her. She barely gave the signal before Blue had swallowed the morsel whole. "So much for not taking food from strangers."

Breakfast done; she dusted her hands. "Let's get to work on *Chipmunk Cabin,* shall we?"

Armed with a key, she entered a cabin the twin to *Raccoon*. Shellie had to tie Blue to the railing while she dragged the rockers onto the porch. Blue tried to jerk free twice, making Shellie glance at the support posts out of fear they'd snap. She glanced back at the dog as he grabbed a mouthful of the leash. She dropped the chair which scraped down her shin and lunged for his collar. "*No! Aus! Platz.*"

Giving a hard correction finally got the dog to obey and Blue subsided onto the sandy ground with a soft grumble.

Shellie pointed to her scraped leg. "Don't give me that. Look what you made me do."

Blue looked appropriately sheepish and gave a gentle slurp to the slowly welling blood.

"Now that's antiseptic," she laughed. Shrugging off the injury Shellie grabbed Blue's leash and hurried him into the cabin. She removed the curtains with their years of dust, dropping them by the door. After a quick circuit of the place, Blue flopped on the curtains with a thump and lay there panting. When she had cleaned the other cabins, Shellie felt energized. *Chipmunk* was quickly sprucing up, but for some unknown reason, tears rolled down Shellie's face and she couldn't stop them. Snippets of negative comments rolled through her brain. Her mom commenting on her weight and poor eating habits accompanied Chad's voice saying he usually preferred blondes; but he'd take what he could get. Memories of her dad telling her she ruined everything, and no man would want her slowed her movements and she slid to a heap on the floor sobbing.

Instantly Blue was there, licking her face and bumping her with his nose as if trying to lift her to her feet. Shellie wrapped her arms around the dog's chest and gave in, soaking Blue's coat with her tears.

"I want Ronan," she whispered. Blue nudged her again and she gave him a watery smile. "I know, you want him, too."

She used the nearby bedframe to drag herself back to her feet while swiping at her face with a sleeve. Shellie let loose a shuddering breath and reached for the dust cloth as her phone pinged a message.

Need me to pick up anything before I come home?

Just the thought of Ronan brought a weak smile to her lips. He was thinking of her. She quickly texted him, *milk,* and looked around the room. He had suffered so much more than she had, the least she could do was pull herself together and keep them moving in the right direction. With a firm mental shake, Shellie set to work cleaning and dusting. Blue stayed glued to her hip for a few more minutes and then returned to his pile of dirty curtains.

After lunch, Shellie set the alarm on her phone and snuggled up with Blue to nap. As she dozed off, she remembered she needed to pack up the curtains. At least being on nights there shouldn't be a problem doing laundry.

Shellie awoke to find Blue leaning tightly against her back, his steady breaths puffed into her ear, and one paw rested on her shoulder. Close up, she could see the parts of his toes and nails that were missing. She shuddered at the pain the dog had gone through to save his handler. She wasn't sure how many *people* would have been that dedicated. She rolled over and planted a kiss on Blue's wide forehead. "Thank you for saving him; he's one of the good ones, even if he doesn't believe it."

She was rewarded with a thumping tail.

Laughing, she sat up. "Okay, time to make dinner so I have a chance to hear how Ronan's day went."

Blue quickly rolled to the down position, his big triangular ears up and swiveling at the word 'dinner'. Shellie dressed for work and trotted over to the *Dining Cabin.* Blue tried another dive in the direction of Ronan's track, but came up short against the leash.

"No, you don't," Shellie scolded. Blue slinked to heel position and walked dejectedly beside her.

"It's been hours since Ronan left. How can you still find his foot prints?" She let the two of them into the *Dining Cabin* and went to work cooking. Earlier, she'd made a key lime pie out of yogurt, gelatin, and whipped topping, and decided on pasta for dinner. She was debating whether to bring Blue with her to collect the salad greens and risk them being trampled or trust him not to steal the meat sauce when Ronan strode through the door.

The sight of Ronan's grin and confident steps, lifted the doldrums, which had plagued her throughout the day. Her stomach did a happy little flip-flop. Blue launched all four feet off the ground. His front paws landed squarely on Ronan's chest while whiney yips and squeals filled the air. Ronan took a step backwards before collecting his balance. He wrapped his free hand around Blue in a hug. Shellie hurried forward to grab the gallon of milk. With both hands free, Ronan rubbed behind the dog's ears and up and down the furry neck. "I missed you too, boy. Did you take good care of Angel?"

Shellie glanced over her shoulder to find Ronan's eyes watching her. "He took great care of me. We even napped together. He's a great snuggler."

Ronan emitted a mock groan. "You let him sleep on the bed, didn't you?"

His suffering expression made her giggle. "I'm going to grab the salad while you two catch up."

Shellie shared her progress over dinner. She glanced at her phone as Ronan cleared the dishes. Time to go. "Are you moving your things into the *Manager's Cabin* tonight?"

"Yes. Do you mind?"

The thought of Ronan nearby made her feel both safe and at the same time unsettled. How could she explain to him what she didn't understand herself?

"It's fine. We agreed to it and it will make the hand-off of Blue easier in the morning." She hefted the backpack with the curtains and had to lean to keep her balance.

Ronan frowned. "What's in the pack?"

"Curtains."

Shellie headed for the door, but he reached her side in three long strides.

"We agreed when there was laundry, I'd carry it for you."

Shellie reveled in the idea of Ronan walking her to work. It felt like they had barely started to talk when it was time for her to leave. "I know, but you've been on your feet all day. It doesn't seem fair to have you walk all the way back into town. Besides, you need to move your things."

Ronan scooped the pack off her back and held the door open for her. "Not a problem."

Blue scooted out the door and danced circles around them as they walked.

"How did work go?"

"Fine. I'm getting better at recognizing the produce, so I don't have to bother Sally as much when the stickers are missing, and I finished the course on checking IDs. Tomorrow I'll be working in the deli."

Shellie looked up at him and cocked her head. She had a feeling he would be handsome without his beard. "Are you going to shave, tonight?"

"No, why?"

"If you don't, you'll have to wear one of those scratchy beard nets."

Ronan narrowed his eyes and looked away. "I've put up with worse."

Shellie reached out and rested her hand on his arm. The tension in his muscles made her hesitate. "What's wrong?"

Ronan let out a long breath and scrubbed his hand down his face. "I grew the beard this long to cover the scars. Without it my face scares people, or at least makes them uncomfortable."

The air left her lungs and Shellie saw black spots in front of her eyes. Until that moment she hadn't realized how badly Ronan had been injured. She reached out a trembling hand and stroked his face. "It bothers me to think you've been hurt and in pain."

Ronan trapped her hand with his and smiled his gentle smile. "It was a long time ago, Angel. Don't think about it."

He slipped the pack off his shoulder and handed it to her. "You better head in or you'll be late."

Unable to trust her voice, she nodded and walked away.

"I'll be here when you get out. If I'm not, wait for me where it's well lit."

Shellie turned. "You'll get no sleep if you walk me home."

"Angel, I'll get no sleep until you're safely home, whether I walk you or not."

Ronan disappeared down the street before she could reply.

Chapter 16

It didn't take Ronan long to wash the dishes, then return to his cabin to pack his things. He took a last look at the inside of *Loon Cabin*. It had been a haven when the bleak madness filled his mind. He had been able to shriek his pain and anger at the walls without fear of censor or judgment. While he'd been physically healed, the emotional wounds had been open sores. Only Blue and his faith that God walked with him in that dark valley, had kept him from taking his own life, although the thought had crossed his mind more than once.

Ronan shook his head, for better or worse, he couldn't hide any longer; not if he was going to be there for Shellie. The thought of her brought a smile to his lips. He could visualize her and Blue napping together. Now that he thought about it, she'd seemed a little sad this evening. Ronan couldn't quite put his finger on it, but some of her gaiety seemed forced. He needed to bring up the appointment with Dr. Parish again. No way was he letting her fall down the rabbit hole he was still trying to climb out.

The *Manager's Cabin* was neat and tidy. In the bathroom, Shellie had moved her cosmetics to one side of the sink and emptied a shelf in the medicine cabinet. Ronan dropped his shaving kit on the toilet tank and hauled his duffle into what would now be his room. He glanced over at the pillow and burst out laughing. Shellie had left a wrapped chocolate, a small card printed with "Enjoy your stay," and the key to the room.

Ronan sat, picking up her gifts. The chocolate and card looked suspiciously like they had come from *Lakeside Resort and Hotel*. He chewed the sweet treat and flipped the key from one hand to the other. How had she known the biggest loss of *Loon Cabin* was the loss of privacy? Somehow, she had understood and given it back to him. Anytime he wanted to be alone, all he had to do was lock his bedroom door.

After putting his things away Ronan settled into bed to catch a few hours of sleep before going to walk Shellie home.

Shellie hadn't realized how quiet the night shift was. A few guests wandered by on their way from the restaurant or bar to their rooms. Occasionally someone would arrive for a late check in or stop to ask a question, but this late there wasn't much to do. Shellie couldn't even run the checkout sheets until just before going home to make sure they had all the restaurant and bar charges.

Kelly cruised up to the desk. "Can you believe how quiet it is?"

"No. Does anyone ever get fired for sleeping on the job?" Shellie asked.

"It's happened to more than one person. Why do you think I'm walking around?" Kelly winked. "Did you get signed up for any classes?"

"Yes, Hospitality Futures."

"I took it last semester. In fact, I never returned the book for store credit. Do you want to borrow it?"

Shellie wanted to do a happy dance. She had been wondering how she would afford her textbooks. "Please."

The radio buzzed. Both women listened to the request for coverage of the hostess station for a few minutes. Kelly turned to Shellie. "I've got this. I'll bring you the book tomorrow."

Shellie watched her friend skip away and offered a small prayer of thanks. She moved to the computer and inserted her thumb drive. Grady had been clear that customers came first, but she had use of the computer to play games, do homework or whatever else would keep her awake and alert. Shellie started designing the *Pine Cone Motel* website. The travel sites were very clear on what they wanted for pictures and she quickly loaded shots of the interior of *Raccoon Cabin* and another of the exterior, carefully angled to hide the swimming pool and new boards. Even with the occasional interruptions of guests calling for service or someone checking in, she had it finished and uploaded by her lunch break.

Kelly took over the front desk at nine in the evening and Shellie helped herself to some pizza from the buffet. The lights in the employee lunch room had been dimmed and the food had spent too much time under the heat lamps, but she didn't want anything heavy to make her sleepy anyway. She dropped into a chair and glanced around the empty room.

Her phone rang. She didn't recognize the number. "Good evening, *Pine Cone Motel*, Shellie speaking."

"I saw your place on the horse show website and I had a few questions."

"How can I help?"

"Do you have any rooms available for the first week in July?"

Shellie grinned, boy did they have availability. "Yes, we do. However, we rent out cabins rather than individual rooms. We do have one, two and three-bedroom cabins available. Each cabin has one bathroom and a lovely front porch. The *Dining Cabin* has an area to relax and socialize."

"You called it the *Dining Cabin*, does that include a restaurant?"

"Unfortunately, not at this time. However, there are complimentary coffee and pastries available and guests are welcome to order food delivered or bring take-out orders in to eat."

"That's a bummer. Still - What's the parking like? I have a large truck and horse trailer. Would you be willing to let me park the trailer for the week, maybe for an extra fee?"

Shellie hadn't thought about charging to park the trailers. "There is plenty of parking and a large side lot. I'm sure we could work something out."

Now the caller sounded enthusiastic. "Really? When we stayed at the *Lakeside Resort and Hotel* last year, they wouldn't let us have the horse trailers anywhere near the place. We had to park in a lot far from the fairgrounds and our hotel and it was a real problem."

"I'm sorry to hear that." Shellie wondered how to bring up the subject to Mr. Grady.

"I'm going to talk to a couple of friends and see if any of them want to go in on a cabin with me. I'll call you back."

Bummer, Shellie had hoped to get a reservation. "If you would like to hold a cabin, we do take credit cards. I would hate to be booked up by the time you called back."

Shellie held her breath.

"I really need to talk to my friends and show them the brochure before I make a commitment. I won't see them until tomorrow night at the barn."

"I understand. If you would prefer, you can do a virtual tour on our website and make your reservation there." If she couldn't close the sale she could at least see if the website was working.

"Perfect! I was wondering how to get them the brochure quicker."

"If you have any problems or prefer to do things over the phone, please feel free to call back."

Shellie gave the caller the website address and disconnected. Picking up her now cold pizza she debated even bothering to eat it.

"I wouldn't feed that to my dog." The night chef smiled at Shellie and settled a plate of crab cake appetizers in front of her.

The man reminded her of her grandfather. Shellie laughed and motioned him into the chair across from her, quickly forking one of the round disks into her mouth. It practically melted on her tongue with just the right amount of spices to complement, not hide, the delicate crab flavor. She closed her eyes and savored the taste. "How is it I got this treat?"

"A customer ordered them, then changed the order. They were already cooking so I was going to put them on the employee buffet, but you're the only employee in the dining room."

"Their loss." She savored another mouthful. "I suppose all the lunch leftovers are gone."

"You'd be surprised. You're the only employee willing to take cooked food on a regular basis."

Shellie felt her face color. Was she taking too much? "I didn't mean to be greedy. The food is really good, and I hate the thought of it going to waste when people go hungry every day." She mentally added, like Ronan and me.

The chef patted her hand. "Shush, you aren't greedy, and it makes me feel better when someone appreciates my cooking."

He leaned back against the wall and closed his eyes. Shellie polished off the rest of the crab cakes and glanced at her watch. She had just enough time to switch the curtains to the dryer before heading back to the desk. She stood as quietly as possible, but her phone buzzed a call. She hit the ignore rather than let anyone know about her activities with the *Pine Cone Motel*.

The chef's eye popped open and he used the table and chair back to haul his rotund body out of his seat. "I'll drop by the front desk after the restaurant closes with the leftovers for you."

Shellie smiled and waved before hurrying off to the laundry. That was one more worry off her mind. She hadn't wanted to mention it to Ronan, but she had wondered if the food she got from the hotel might stop with the change of shifts. She hurried down the hall.

She watched the alerts coming in from the website as the cabins were booked and they got several more questions about trailer parking. At this rate they would have no problem filling the place for the two weeks of horse shows.

She would talk to Ronan and e-mail back the answer when they got home. Her stomach tingled with the realization she had a home. She would never again take for granted a roof over her head.

Remembering the call, she'd ignored, she played the message.

It started with a pause and she almost hit delete when she heard a man's voice. "This is Detective Evans with the Greenville Police Department. I am trying to reach a Miss Shellie Morgan. I was given this number to contact her. Please have her call me. If I -"

Shellie hit delete, without listening to the rest of the message. Her good mood evaporated, and she rubbed her arms to dispel the sudden chill to her body. Memories flooded back, and she fought the urge to cry.

She was still struggling to contain her chaotic emotions when Kelly came by. She reached for Shellie's arm asking, "What's wrong? Are you sick?"

Shellie forced herself not to jerk away and gave her best imitation of a smile. "I'm fine. I got a difficult call is all."

Kelly shook her head. "It must have been a doozy of a call. Do you need a break?"

The thought of hiding in the bathroom and crying was so tempting, but Shellie shook her head. "Tell you what, you take the desk for a bit and I'll walk the floors."

Kelly signed in and Shellie proceeded to walk the quiet first floor hallways, checking conference room doors and looking in on the exercise room. By the time she had regained control of her expression if not her feelings and returned to the desk, Kelly was engrossed in a book. Shellie switched the station over to games to finish out the evening.

Chapter 17

Shellie saw Ronan waiting for her in front of the hotel and stepped out into the cool night. Ronan smiled and handed her a jacket. "I thought you might need this."

As she slipped her arms into the warm fleece, her phone rang, and she answered it automatically. Getting a call at midnight had to be someone about a room. "*Pine Cone Motel*, how may I help you?"

"Miss Michelle Morgan, please."

Being doused with a bucket of ice water couldn't have chilled her more. "Who is this?"

"Detective Evans with the Greenville police department."

"I have nothing to say to you, please leave me alone."

"Miss Morgan, I need your help stopping a sexual predator. With your testimony and that of his other victims we can stop this from happening to anyone else."

"I tried that. His frat brothers lied, and I paid the price. I'm rebuilding my life and I'm not going to let Chad destroy it - again!"

The detective responded quickly, as if knowing she was about to disconnect the call. "But this time it isn't you alone. We have another victim and her story is exactly the same as yours, except she was able to get tested for roofies and it came back positive for flunitrazepam."

Shellie stifled the urge to throw her phone. "Then why do you need me?"

"With the suspect's political connections, expensive lawyer, and only one victim, he's liable to get off with only a slap on the wrist. With your testimony we can show a pattern covered up by his father's abuse of political power and try for the maximum sentence."

Would it be possible to bring Chad and his father to justice? The thought of being vindicated in her father's eyes made Shellie light-headed and she stumbled over a small rock. If Ronan hadn't caught her, she would have landed on her face in the gravel.

Even knowing Ronan had reacted simply to protect her, Shellie couldn't keep from flinching at his tight grip. Ronan gently loosened his hold while still being prepared to catch her. Shellie looked up expecting to see a hurt expression on his face. What she saw was genuine concern, and maybe something more.

"Miss Morgan?"

Shellie jerked her concentration back to the conversation. What did she want to do? A part of her wanted to hurt Chad and see him discredited. She wanted to be able to smirk at him the way he had at her expulsion hearing. She wanted to go to her dad and say, "See how wrong you were about me." But what would it cost?

"I'm sorry, Detective, I can't risk wrecking the new life I'm building. I would never be able to get the time off from work, and even if I could, it would cause too much of a financial strain. Good luck with your case."

"Please Miss Morgan, think about it. You can call me back any time, day or night."

Shellie disconnected the call.

Ronan's long stride easily kept up with Shellie's agitated march. "Will you tell me about it?"

Shellie sighed. She really needed some advice and there was no one she trusted more than Ronan. "That was a detective from back in Illinois. Chad hurt another girl, like he did me, but this time they have proof she was drugged."

Ronan's smile reminded her of a wolf about to dine on fresh caught rabbit. It was a small glimpse of the hardness left behind by his soldier days. "I hope they lock him up for a good long time. Slime-balls like him are an insult to men."

"The thing of it is, with only one woman testifying, his fancy lawyers, and his dad's connections, the detective thinks Chad may get off easy with something like probation." Shellie kicked a pebble. "He wants me to come testify to show a pattern, so the judge will give Chad a tougher sentence."

They walked along in silence for several steps. Shellie glanced up at Ronan's moonlit face trying to gauge his reaction.

His gentle voice was at odds with the stone-cold expression. "What do you want to do?"

Shellie shook her head, "I don't know."

"So, talk it through. Do you want to see Chad pay for what he's done?""

Her answer was instantaneous. "Yes."

"So, if you go back to Illinois do you think your name will be cleared?"

"I would hope so. It only seems fair, doesn't it?"

Ronan smiled sadly. "Angel, the world's not fair. It's fallen and run by men. But that being said, the possibility exists for your wish to happen. You do need to know, even if your name is cleared, some people will never believe you and will still attach a stigma to you."

Shellie felt like groaning. She was pretty sure her father would be one of those people.

There was a catch in Ronan's voice as he asked, "If you are cleared, do you want to go back to your old life?"

"That's the crux of the problem. I don't think I can." Shellie paused trying to form her thoughts into words. "I mean, after living on my own, I'm not sure I could go back to living with my parents and following the house rules. I'd always be afraid I would get set adrift, broke and without hope for some small infraction or perception of an infraction. I know my dad would be suspicious of everything I did and that would be a difficult way to live. I've had to take responsibility for myself, but I've acquired control of my life. I'm my own person, not an extension of my parents. I think that would be hard to give up."

They had reached the entrance to the *Pine Cone Motel* and Shellie stopped. "I was working on an English degree, not because I was interested in it, but because my father said it was what I should do. After all this," she gestured to encompass the motel, "I want a degree in Hospitality Management. This has been scary, but it's also been fun and challenging, and it makes me feel strong and capable and excited about my future, which is something I never felt about my other studies. I couldn't see my future then - I can now."

Ronan started walking toward the *Dining Cabin* and Shellie fell into step beside him. "So, it seems you would like to testify, but not go back to your old life."

"Yes," Shellie grabbed his arm and hugged it. He had voiced her exact sentiments. "But I don't have any vacation time coming so I would have to ask for unpaid time off and we can't afford that. As much as I want to see Chad pay, it isn't worth the cost to my future."

Ronan stopped and gripped her shoulders with both hands forcing her to look at his face. "Don't let the money stop you. If going back is truly what you want, we can find a way to make it happen. Your happiness is more important to me than anything else, and I don't want you to regret this decision a few years from now."

Shellie's stomach did some serious flip flopping and her whole body tingled. Ronan's expression was so open. He cared, no more than cared, he loved her more than himself. He hadn't said the words, but it was all there in his face. She reached up with her hands, tangling her fingers in the hair at his nape and brushed her lips to his, trying to say without words, how much she returned his feelings. Slowly, gently, Ronan drew her closer, giving her the freedom to pull away. His lips were warm and moved across hers like the brush of a butterfly. Their breath mingled softly. A part of Shellie marveled that she wasn't afraid, but this was Ronan and she knew he would never force her to do anything she didn't want to do.

A hard, fur-covered head and long snout shoved between them like a wedge. As Blue forced them farther apart, he sidled his body forward demanding their attention. Shellie stepped back and giggled.

Ronan ran a hand through his hair, an expression of amused frustration on his face. He closed his eyes for an instant then opened them, stepping forward to hold the door for Shellie while muttering dire consequences for his dog.

Shellie took a seat in the rocker and Ronan settled onto the sofa. Blue hopped up to stretch out with his head in Ronan's lap.

She watched Ronan pet the dog. "The problem isn't the money. I would have to miss class, which I don't want to do. I want that degree. But the real issue is I would have to tell Mr. Grady why I was expelled. I don't want him to look at me differently and wonder what kind of person I really am."

Shellie pulled her feet up onto the seat, wrapped her arms around her legs and rested her chin on her knees. "It's probably pretty shallow of me, but the people at *Lakeside Resort and Hotel* think highly of me and I'd like to keep it that way."

Ronan continued to pet Blue in slow strokes. "It's not shallow. You're trying to build a career and careers rest on reputation. Once a person's reputation is tarnished it's almost impossible to repair it."

"So, I guess my only choice is to let Chad get away with what he did to me?" Shellie's insides went cold at the realization. The world really wasn't fair.

"Not necessarily."

Shellie jerked her head up. "What are you saying?"

"Call the detective back and tell him the situation. Ask if he'll accept a deposition in place of personal testimony. But, Angel," Ronan paused, "you're going to have to tell whoever takes the deposition everything that happened in all its embarrassing detail."

Shudders wracked Shellie's frame, in her desire to make Chad pay, she hadn't thought about what it would cost her.

"Off you go to bed, Angel. I'll close up here and be over in a few minutes."

Ronan hoped his smile didn't give away his thoughts, because right now he was ripe for a little murder and mayhem. He had given his life to Christ, but he was also a trained soldier. The thought of the way Chad hurt Shellie put a fine edge on his temper and he knew a lot of ways to cause that boy a full measure of pain. He was going to have to pray for help forgiving and to not act if he and Chad ever came face to face.

Shellie gave him a tired smile and scurried off to the *Manager's Cabin*. Ronan waited until the lights from her room went out before pushing off the soft sofa and turning off the lights in the *Dining Cabin*. He slipped into his room. Blue followed only half awake, head hanging low, to land with a thump on the carpet. The dog's eyes were closed, and he snored softly before Ronan could climb into bed.

Tired as he was, he couldn't sleep. He cared about Shellie, deeply. He had thought he was in love with Andrea, but those feelings were nothing compared to his feelings for the woman sleeping down the hall from him. The question was, what was he going to do about it? Under normal circumstances he would be asking her out to candlelit dinners and presenting her with trinkets and other small gifts, so she would know she filled his thoughts. He would take her in his arms and ply her with kisses until they were both breathless. But nothing about their situation was normal.

Their candlelit dinners had a lot more to do with not running up the electric bill and little to do with romance. The closest he'd come to gifts was a stringer of fish. As to the kisses, so far, she'd treated him more like a brother than a lover avoiding physical contact. It would be a long time for her to accept a man's touch without flashbacks to being drugged, helpless and hurt.

Even if he had the wherewithal to really court her the way she deserved, was it fair to saddle her with damaged goods like him? His future and ability to provide for a family were in question as long as his PTSD stood in the way. And what would she think when she saw his scared and damaged body? Knowing her, she would say it didn't matter, but it mattered to him. It was vanity, but he wanted to see admiration in her eyes not horror.

The first time he'd looked in the mirror and seen the ugly red scars, he'd fought back the moisture in his eyes and manned up, but seeing how ugly he'd become made him realize no woman would ever want to spend her life with the mess that was his body. Much of his anger had been directed at the loss of having a normal life with a loving wife and children. It wasn't fair. He still felt the same. He still had the same desires and dreams, but they had burned up along with the rest of his team. In the early days he had railed against God for letting him live. He would have been better off dying with them than the half-life left to him. There hadn't been any hope or future beyond existing until Shellie came along. There shouldn't be any now; she deserved better.

Knowing he'd spend the night going around and round in his head, Ronan rolled over and purposely cleared his mind, using all the mental tricks he knew to relax. He'd barely drifted off to sleep when he heard Blue at his bedroom door. Ronan waited, listening, trying to identify what had awakened his dog. Whatever it was Blue clearly intended to deal with it himself. Ronan watched as Blue sat partway up on his haunches to grip the lever doorknob in his teeth. The dog dropped back to all fours unlatching the tongue from the receiver and allowing the door to open a few inches. A quick shove with his snout and he was in the hallway.

Ronan threw back the covers and followed on silent, bare feet just in-time to see Blue open Shellie's bedroom door in a similar fashion. Ronan tried to stop Blue with a series of hand commands, which the dog either didn't see or totally ignored.

Muttering threats under his breath, Ronan held the partially open door to hide his presence. The last thing in the world Shellie needed was to awaken and find a man in her room. He looked in expecting to see Blue stretched out on the bed, napping someplace softer than Ronan's rug. He heard a choked noise and then Shellie muttered a sharp, "No! Please don't. No, no."

Thinking she talked to Blue, Ronan was about to verbalize a stern recall, when she spoke again in a sleep slurred voice, "Please, Chad, don't." Recognizing she was having a nightmare, Ronan debated how to wake her without frightening her even more. Blue moved next to the thrashing woman and began licking and shoving her with hard thrusts of his muzzle. Shellie's sad cries stopped, and her hand came out from under the covers to pet Blue. The dog downed next to her and gave one more gentle slurp to Shellie's face. She sniffed and hugged the dog. Moonlight glittered in the tears on her face.

Within a few minutes her slow, steady breathing told Ronan she had gone back to sleep. He slipped back to his own room, leaving the door open. Twice more he was awakened by Shellie's pleading voice. By the time his alarm went off, he awoke exhausted and his thoughts darker than the rain-filled sky. He sat up and rested his head in his hands, praying for guidance. After dressing quietly, he headed for the *Dining Cabin* hoping a cup of hot coffee would clear his brain.

He sat savoring the fragrance of the strong brew when Shellie appeared, a raincoat over her sweats. Try as he might, he couldn't muster a smile for her. "I'm sorry, I didn't mean to wake you."

She hung the coat and reached for a cup. "You didn't. I couldn't sleep anymore."

The words he'd prayed to find popped into his head. "Nightmares will do that to a person."

She spun to stare at him, sloshing hot coffee onto her hand. Distracted by the pain, she shook the injured appendage while looking for a rag to clean up the spill. Bitterness laced her voice. "How did you know?"

"Blue opened the doors and I heard you."

Shellie closed her eyes, but not before Ronan spotted the sheen of tears. "I'm sorry. I'll lock my door tonight."

Ronan set his cup aside and gave her a half smile. "Do you really think that will stop him? He's a trained military working dog. He'll chew through the door to get to you if need be."

Shellie hung her head, defeated. "I hadn't thought of that. Maybe it would be better if the two of you moved back into *Loon Cabin,* so I don't disturb your sleep."

"That's a band aid solution if I ever heard one." Ronan grimaced. "No, it's not even that because it doesn't even give a partial fix to the problem. You need help, Angel. You need to keep that appointment with Dr. Parish."

Shellie's dejected expression tugged at his heart. He ended more softly than he had started. "Please?"

Shellie stared into her cup for a long moment before giving a small nod.

Ronan went lightheaded from the combination of relief and hope. "Good, girl. You're brave to do this and I'm proud of you."

Shellie finally met his gaze, her expression showing her surprise. "Why would you be proud of me?"

"Because you're doing what I was too stubborn, stupid, and proud to do myself."

Chapter 18

Tom Carter, the store manager, waved Ronan over to the office. "Ronan, I need you in the deli, again."

"Gunny, are you sure you don't need me on clean up detail someplace else?" This was not Ronan's favorite duty, only slightly better than digging latrines in the desert. In the last week and a half, Ronan was assigned to the deli five times and spent the days in a hair and beard net. Shellie had been right - it was scratchy.

"I'm not wasting your talent with a broom. As a matter of fact, Harold suggested you be trained as his assistant deli manager." Tom grinned and scrubbed his own chin. "You can always shave, Lieutenant."

Ronan clocked in and headed over to his assignment. Using sharp slicers, he would have to stay focused and today that would be hard. Shellie had her first appointment with Dr. Parish and had promised to text him when she was done. If it wasn't too late, she had promised to meet him for his lunch break. Until she got there, Ronan wasn't sure he could concentrate. He checked his phone for texts one last time, did some deep breathing exercises to hone his focus, and donned the nets and plastic gloves. Stepping up to the counter, Ronan faked a smile and asked the first customer, "How may I help you?"

Shellie sat in the outer office filling out forms, checking the "single" marital status and listed no meds. She sighed. This was such a monumental waste of time she didn't have. No one could help her; she needed to tough it out and let time heal her. The horse show guests were arriving tomorrow, and she had a million last minute things to get done along with plenty of homework, but Ronan kept pestering her and finally said they would have to pay for the appointment if she went or not. If she had to pay this kind of money she was at least going to show up.

A middle-aged woman with chin length blonde hair, friendly blue eyes, and casually dressed in a short-sleeved blouse, capris, and running shoes opened the office door. "Miss Morgan?"

Shellie stood and held out the form. "Do I give this to you or your receptionist?"

The woman smiled, "I'll take it. Come on in. Can I get you some coffee or tea or water?"

"Water, please."

The woman headed for a small refrigerator. "Take a seat anywhere you feel comfortable."

Shellie looked around the office. Translucent fabric shades blocked the view, but not the bright sunshine. A pale blue sculpted carpet covered the pine floor and comfortable looking stuffed chairs were arranged around a coffee table. A desk was off to one side, but it was partially screened by plants and the walls were lined with bookcases filled with books, magazines, and knick-knacks. The place welcomed her and felt more like Dr. Parish's living room than an office.

Shellie settled on the edge of one of the comfy chairs, fighting the urge to scream and bolt from the room. A young golden retriever trotted over and bumped up against her hand, demanding to be petted. The tension left Shellie's body so swiftly, she felt limp. Ronan had taken Blue this morning and she would pick up the dog after her appointment. Shellie hadn't realized how much she missed Blue until this moment.

Dr. Parish handed Shellie a water and dropped into a nearby chair. "Sorry about that, Chelsea is young and doesn't know to wait until she's invited to come greet people. I hope she doesn't get you all covered in dog hair."

Shellie laughed. "No problem, I live with a German Shedder."

"What's her name?"

"Blue and he used to be a military working dog. His feet were badly injured rescuing his handler from a burning vehicle, so they were both discharged."

"Is that Mr. Flanagan?"

"Yes. Ronan insisted I come, but I don't see how anyone can help me. I don't see how talking about what happened is going to be effective in changing anything. I need to move forward with my life and leave this in the past." Shellie took a gulp of water and continued. "I'm working two jobs and going to school. You seem like a nice person, but I don't see this helping. Frankly, if it weren't for Ronan insisting, I come, I wouldn't be here."

Dr. Parish smiled. She didn't seem the slightest upset or put off by Shellie's tirade. "Your feelings are quite common, Miss Morgan, and with all you are doing, I can understand your reservations."

"You can call me Shellie."

"Thank you. How about I give you a quick overview of the process and then you can ask questions. We'll take about an hour and we're not going to solve anything in one session, but it will give us a starting point. Please understand everyone processes traumatic events differently so no two paths are the same. Absolutely everything is on the table here for discussion. I am here for you and to listen to what is happening in your life. I can't

SHERRI S. GALLAGHER

change the past, but I can help you deal with the here and now."

A lump filled Shellie's throat. She knew it was silly, but she wanted to burst into tears. Not trusting her voice, she swallowed and nodded. Since the incident with Chad, she'd turned into a real watering pot.

Dr. Parish reached down to pet Chelsea. The dog looked at her and they seemed to communicate on a non-verbal level, then Chelsea shifted her weight to lean against Shellie's leg even harder. For some reason it helped Shellie collect her emotions.

Dr. Parish sat back again. "I want you to know how truly sorry I am you have had this terrible experience. You can tell me as much or as little as you want about what happened, and if the details are too much right now, you can add them at any time you feel up to it."

Shellie gulped water. The doctor seemed nice, but would she look at Shellie strangely after she knew what happened? Her father's angry voice floated up from her memory. "You've embarrassed your family, our friends, and yourself with your actions. When people find out how truly shameless, deceitful, and promiscuous you are, they will look at you and treat you like the dregs of the sewer. If you're smart, you'll keep your mouth shut and never speak of this to anyone again."

No way could she risk opening up. She shrugged noncommittally.

Dr. Parish sipped her water. "Why do you think Ronan has been so insistent you see me?"

"At first, memories started coming back and the littlest thing would leave me shaking and in tears."

"Has that changed?"

Shellie hesitated. "I guess it hasn't, I think I hide it better, but the nightmares are getting worse." She sighed. "I wish I could solve that part, at least. To make ends meet, Ronan had to move into the same cabin and the noise I make wakes him up. I feel really bad about that. I mean, the nightmares are what I deserve, but he shouldn't have to suffer along with me."

"Why do you think you deserve the nightmares?"

Shellie stopped. Is that what she really thought? "I-I don't know. I think if I had been smarter and maybe dressed more conservatively, I wouldn't have attracted Chad's attention. Certainly, my dad told me this was my fault."

"Your dad is entitled to his opinion, but what really matters is what you think. Do you think your clothing was more alluring than your peers'?"

Shellie visualized herself with her friends walking across campus, laughing and joking. "Not really. When I think about it, I never had a bare midriff or low-cut top. I have kind of chicken legs, so I wore jeans, even in the summer when everyone else was in short shorts and halters. My friends used to tease me and say I dressed like a nun."

Dr. Parish waited. Shellie panned through memories, not seeing her surroundings, but herself on campus. She turned to Dr. Parish. "I didn't do anything wrong. Is it really possible this isn't my fault? I mean, I always thought he put something in my soda, but I can't prove he drugged me."

She really wanted to believe, but it had to have been her fault.

"It's not only possible, it is probable. A woman has a right to say no and expect to be listened to. If you don't want to have sex, it's not okay for them to force you."

Shellie stared at her hands. She couldn't hold back the tears. "I couldn't move. I couldn't speak. All I could do was lay there. In my head I was screaming no, but no sound came out."

"So, you were helpless. This man took away your voice and ability to protest?"

Shellie's could only manage a whisper, "Yes."

"That is rape. A man needs your consent. Drugging you so you can't protest, or act indicates he knew you would not consent if given a choice. It would also indicate he clearly understood you were not trying to attract his attention."

"I'm not sure that's true. I mean, he was handsome, and he seemed to want to hear what I had to say. As the chancellor's son, his social status was much higher than mine and yet he treated me like an equal. The other guys at the party laughed when I asked for a soda, but Chad told them to leave me alone and got me a can of diet cola. I kind of liked him and I wanted to get to know him better."

Dr. Parish sipped her water. "Were you planning on a physical relationship with him?"

Shellie's water bottle slipped from her numb fingers. She caught it before it hit the soft carpet. "No! At least not that night. I mean, if we married, well, you know —"

"So, you thought he could be a friend?"

"Yes." Shellie gave up and sobbed.

Dr. Parish handed her some tissues. "So, what kind of signals did Chad give you?"

Shellie wiped her eyes and blew her nose. "What do you mean?"

"Did he kiss you or hold your hand or hold you close to his body?"

Shellie shuddered. "No. He smiled a friendly smile and he'd winked sometimes. I didn't know him that well. I wanted to get to know him better and see if we could be more, but I wasn't ready for more at the party."

"What do you think your actions told him? Did you try and touch him in more than a friendly way?"

"No."

"Then why do you think your actions were communicating a desire for physical attraction?"

Shellie's voice was a whisper, "They weren't." She lifted her head so swiftly her neck hurt. "I didn't do anything wrong, did I?"

"No, you didn't. This wasn't your fault. Sometimes bad things happen to good people and this is one of those times."

"Somehow that seems hard to believe."

Dr. Parish smiled. "So, we have something we can work on."

By the time Shellie left Dr. Parish's office she was so tear-weary all she wanted to do was sleep. The bright sunlight hurt her tired eyes. Slowly the crisp mountain air revived her, so she was able to smile naturally when she got to the store and texted Ronan, but her eyes were a bloodshot mess. Blue wagged his tail as she approached, and she sat close, petting and hugging him. Of course, he had to sniff her pants and hands and seemed a little miffed that she had been around another dog.

Ronan appeared a few minutes later, still wearing the hair net. She watched him scan the parking lot. There was a precision in his moves and actions. He homed in on her location swiftly. A smile spread across his lips and he hurried over to them. "How did it go?"

"I really didn't want to be there at first, but I think it helped."

Relief showed on his face. "Are you going back?"

"Yes, I made another appointment. I'm not sure this will make the nightmares go away, but I feel better about myself."

"How so?"

"I didn't realize I was holding myself responsible for what happened. I mean, I said it was Chad's fault, but I still blamed myself. The doctor said I was innocent. My head knows it now, but a little voice keeps telling me it was my fault."

Ronan reached out and squeezed Shellie's hand. "Angel, you didn't cause any of this, but you stepped up and kept going. That's an amazing kind of courage."

Shellie's face heated to her hairline.

He released her hand gently and glanced away. "So, what are you going to do now?"

Shellie flopped back on the grass. "I'd like to take a nap, but I want to do one last damp mop of the cabins and check the towels and soap, and such are all set."

"Take a nap. You deserve a break. I'll take care of it when I get home." Ronan glanced at his watch. "I need to get back. Pamper yourself a little."

Shellie sat up and watched until Ronan was out of sight. Turning, she picked up Blue's leash. "Come on Blue, let's go home."

Walking up the driveway, she spotted a high-end rental car in front of the *Manager's Cabin*. Two men stood in the shade of the porch; one leaned on the railing, the other seemed to be peering in the front window. Something about them was familiar, but Shellie couldn't see them clearly. She hesitated, not liking the fact that she was alone with two men between her and the safety of the cabin.

Still, this was a motel, open for business, and maybe these two needed a place for the night. Of course, that was all she could offer them since *The Pine Cone* was sold out tomorrow night but renting a cabin or two for a night would help meet the expenses Mrs. McClelland's grandson had sent them.

Blue bumped her leg. Shellie glanced down and realized the happy go-lucky shepherd she knew had morphed into a military working dog, all focus and business. If these two meant trouble, clearly Blue would be happy to accommodate them. Her confidence restored, Shellie drew herself fully upright, threw her shoulders back, and marched forward.

Both men turned toward her, watching her approach.

"Good afternoon, are you gentlemen looking for a—Dad?"

Her father looked her up and down. "At least you had the courtesy to move to the middle of nowhere. So, are you renting out the cabins by the hour or half hour?"

Shellie's whole body flushed with heat. She hadn't seen him in three months, and this was how he greeted her? "I'm doing fine, Dad, thanks for asking."

Her father flushed at her words. "Mind your manners, young lady. Both Chancellor Meyer and I will be treated with respect or else."

Not only her father, but Chad's was there as well? Had they brought Chad along, too? The angry heat left in a flash, leaving her chilled. She glanced around wildly;

half afraid Chad was sneaking up behind her. Her breath caught in her chest and she couldn't empty her lungs. Black dots danced in front of her eyes. Blue let loose a rumbling growl, his focus fixed on the two men, and he moved between Shellie and them.

The ability to breath returned. No one would sneak up on her with Blue's sharp senses on guard. She stepped to heel position. "*Sitz*."

Blue slowly lowered his rear to the ground. Clearly, he didn't like being called off. Her fear contained if not abated, Shellie thought about how Ronan would react in her position. The answer was instantaneous, he'd go on the offensive. She made a show of crossing her arms and tapping her toe. "Or else what, Dad? Will you throw me out with no money, no job, and no place to go? Oh wait, you already did that. You have two minutes to tell me what you want. While you're doing that I'm going to be deciding if I should call the police or turn my dog loose."

Her father opened his mouth, but Chancellor Meyer spoke up. "Miss Morgan, I'm sorry. We seem to have gotten off on the wrong foot here. Could we let tempers cool a little and sit down to talk for a few minutes?"

Shellie surveyed the man. He exuded confidence that she would go along with anything he said even as he gave her a conciliatory smile. Funny how a few months ago, she never would have realized how he manipulated people. Kelly had labeled a guest with the exact word to describe the Chancellor, *smarmy*. He was so sure she would go along with him that he took a step toward her and held out his hand as if to guide her up the steps. Big mistake. Blue exploded into a snarling, barking mass of fur and teeth. Both men jumped backwards, scrambling to put the porch rockers between them and the dog as the Blue stalked forward.

"*Hier fuss.*"

Blue backed into heel position, growling and staring.

Shellie put on a show of bravado. "Ninety seconds."

Her dad's voice squeaked. "Is that dog under control?"

"He is under complete control and doing his job, protecting me."

Her dad wiped sweat from his forehead. "Your mother told us a detective wanted to talk with you. You are not to have anything to do with him. Do you understand?"

Shellie made her voice super sweet. "You mean that nice Detective Evans? We've already had a long conversation. He wants me to come testify about what Chad did to me."

Chancellor Meyer lost his friendly expression. "I would advise against it, Miss Morgan. There is no evidence to support your unfounded charges against my son. Were you to state them under oath I will sue you for slander and press to have you charged and jailed for perjury."

Could he do that? Anything was possible, but if that was the case, why had they made the long trip here? Ronan would tell her it was time to push back. "Detective Evans didn't think that would be a problem."

"Be reasonable, Shellie," her father said. "Do you want to go through the same pain as last time and have our name dragged through the mud? Think of your mother and brother and sister. Don't you care what this would do to them?" He gripped the back of the rocker so tightly his knuckles were white. "I'm up for tenure. If you offend Chancellor Meyer, I have no hope of providing for my family. After all the years of moving and dreadful rentals, we now have a nice house and are comfortable. How can you take that away from your brother and sister?"

Shellie hesitated. She didn't want her mom and siblings to go through what she had, but was it right to let Chad and his father use their power to destroy the people around them? "I am thinking of my sister. I don't want a predator doing to her what Chad did to me. And as for providing for your family, if you'd gotten an advanced degree and were easier on your female students you wouldn't have such a poor work history that you can't keep a job."

Chancellor Meyer waved at the dilapidated pool, a derisive expression on his face. "What if I make it worth your while?"

Shellie jerked her head toward him. "What do you mean?"

"Surely you can't be happy working as what, a maid, in this place. In my position I could allow you to return to school on probation, of course, provided you never speak of this matter to anyone again."

Wow. Shellie was so glad she'd talked all this through with Ronan. It made her answer easier.

"No, thanks."

Her father stepped out from behind the chair. "Are you insane? How can you pass up an opportunity to have your old life back?"

"Because Chad stole that life from me when he raped me. There's no such thing as going back, and I certainly wouldn't do it with the threat of expulsion hanging over my head. As for being a maid," she gave a fake chuckle. "Think what you want, you've been wrong about everything else. Your time is up. Leave."

The Chancellor held his hands out in supplication. "Please, Miss Morgan. Is there anything that will change your mind?"

"Actually, you have managed to do just that."

Hope flashed across the man's face. "You won't testify, then?"

"I told Detective Evans I wouldn't testify; I didn't think it would make a difference. After this conversation, I'm going to call and tell him I've changed my mind. You wouldn't have come all this way, if that was the case."

"Please, I beg you. Don't ruin my son's life. He shouldn't have his life destroyed by one little mistake."

"This was not one little mistake. How many women's lives have your son destroyed by raping them? I think it's well past time he paid."

Shellie strode confidently up the stairs and into the cabin. Blue stared malevolently, lips curled and dripping saliva, staying between her and the men while she unlocked and opened the door. She swiftly flipped the deadbolt and hurried to her room to collapse on the bed, shaking. Car doors slammed, and the spurt and crunch of gravel told her they had left in an angry hurry. Blue leapt on the bed to lick her face, tail wagging, back to acting like a puppy. Leaning against his furry shoulder, Shellie pulled out her cell phone and thumbed through her call history selecting a number. "Detective Evans? This is Shellie Morgan. What if I gave you a sworn statement?"

Chapter 19

Ronan stepped out of the deli area and removed the hair and beard nets and white coat. Harold followed him, clapping Ronan on the shoulder. Instantly adrenaline flooded his system. Muscles tensed, senses on full alert, Ronan was more than halfway to a wristlock and takedown before he even registered what he was doing. Thankfully Harold didn't notice, but Ronan's knees felt wobbly after the close call. When would he stop reacting? How could he think about a long-term relationship with Shellie if he over-reacted at a simple pat on the back?

"You do a great job, son. I really would like to have you as my assistant full time at the deli, but you need to shave."

Ronan gave him a weak grin. "I don't think that's going to happen any time soon."

Tom stood outside the office, a concerned expression on his face. As soon as he saw Ronan, his face lit up with a smile. "Ronan, you may be the help I was praying for."

Happy to have any reason to avoid explaining why he wore a beard, Ronan hurried over to the store manager. "What can I do for you, Gunny?"

"You have a degree in accounting, right?"

"Yes."

"Good, come with me." Tom led him into the small office. "I cannot get the receipts from yesterday to balance. This is the third day this month the columns don't add up to the receipts. I've never been a numbers guy and now corporate is breathing down my neck because of errors. They said if I can't get the books straight and keep them that way they'll send in a new manager. Can you try and figure out what I'm doing wrong?"

Ronan nodded and sat at the crowded desk covered in piles of paper. It had been a long time since he'd used his degree, so he could only hope he remembered enough to help. He didn't want Tom in trouble with the home office. So much of what made the store a success was Tom's personality and understanding of human nature, he cared about the staff and his customers.

It took the rest of the afternoon for Ronan to unravel the daily receipts and find the error. When he waved Tom over, the man's grim face demonstrated the worry and strain he was under. "No luck?"

"I got it. Everything balances, you're good to go."

The relief on Tom's face warmed Ronan's insides. He owed the store manager for giving him a chance and it boosted his confidence to solve Tom's problem. If only his own were as simple as balancing a column of numbers.

"How did you fix it?"

Ronan moved to the desk. "Here, let me show you."

Twenty minutes later, Tom shook his head. "I never would have found that. Thanks."

Ronan grinned. "All in a day's work, Gunny." Ronan glanced at his watch, surprised to see how late it was. He would have to hurry to even be able to walk Shellie to work.

Tom made a shooing motion. "Go. Get out of here. I saw that pretty, young lady you took break with, go spend some time with her. Don't worry about the overtime, it was worth every penny."

Ronan quickly clocked out and jogged to *The Pine Cone Motel,* arriving as Shellie attempted to slide out the cabin door without Blue. She smiled and waved to him before opening the door wide enough for Blue to burst into the open. The dog raced to Ronan, leaping and air snapping in a circle around his master. As she came down the steps her face seemed pale and deep lines framed her mouth. Her smile was definitely strained.

"You're working too hard, Angel. Did you get any rest?"

Shellie started to walk out the driveway and Ronan fell into step with her. "Yes, it only took a few minutes to do a last run-through of the cabins."

"I told you I would take care of that. If you get too worn down, you're going to get sick. I'm worried, you're so pale."

Shellie looked away and kicked a pebble. "It isn't about sleep. I had some very unwelcome visitors. My dad and Chancellor Meyer showed up to try and talk me out of testify." She met his eyes. "I was really nasty to them and let Blue scare them, then I called Detective Evans. He'll be here between the horse show people and the rugby players to take my statement."

No wonder she was exhausted. Ronan reached out to draw her into a one-armed hug, something she could easily escape if she felt uncomfortable. "You poor thing. I should have been there to take care of it for you."

It pleased him more than a little when instead of pulling away, she leaned into him and wrapped one arm around him.

Her voice was muffled against his side, but her words came through clearly and with a hint of laughter.

"Blue did an awesome job and had them cowering behind the rockers."

Ronan reached down with his other hand to rub Blue's ears. "Good boy!"

Shellie continued to lean against him. "Enough about me, how did your day go?"

Ronan deliberately made his day in the deli and helping Tom with accounting into a humorous story, so she was laughing, and her color was better by the time they made it to the revolving door of the resort. He opened his mouth, but Shellie cut him off.

"I know, wait in the lighted area if you're late. Ronan, you're never late." She reached up to peck him on the cheek above his beard and hurried inside.

Warmth pooled in his belly and it took every ounce of restraint not to reach out and draw her into a real kiss, one that would let her know how he felt. But he couldn't do that. She was the kind of woman who would stand by him no matter what and his problems would likely sink her along with him. Things had been good for too long, something bad would happen, it always did.

He stood there trying to regulate his breathing for a minute before turning back to *The Pine Cone Motel*. Blue bumped Ronan's leg, a happy light in the dog's eye challenged Ronan to play.

"Yeah, me too. Race you back and then how's about some protection work? I want you tuned up if any more unwelcome visitors appear."

Ronan took off jogging, Blue bouncing along at his side. Rowdy marching calls, setting the cadence of his steps.

The marching tunes were called "Jodies" after "Jody," a recurring figure who tried to steal a soldier's girlfriend. A vision of Shellie appeared in Ronan's mind;

would she be true to her boyfriend? No question about it. He could count on Angel if she became his girl, but was he ready for that kind of relationship? When they first met, he'd tried to think of her as a kid sister, but even then, his heart had wanted more. Nope, Shellie would never fall for a Jody, but could he become the kind of man worthy of a woman like her?

Maybe it was time he took steps to fix his broken life. Shellie had started counseling, even though she didn't want to, so what was his excuse?

Kelly stood near the door as Shellie entered the lobby.

"Are you crazy, kissing that scuzzy bum?"

Shellie jerked back. Heat boiled through her that Kelly could think of Ronan that way. "Ronan is my friend, he's not a bum."

Kelly dropped into step with Shellie. "I've seen him around town, and he's worked here cleaning up trash occasionally for leftover meals. He looks so scraggly and he always has that skinny dog around. You be careful around him. He might drag you into an alley some night and hurt you."

No way was Shellie going to let this pass. She swung around and blocked Kelly's path. "That bum shared his food with me when there wasn't enough for one person, much less two, and he found a way to put a roof over my head when no one else cared. That bum served with honor as an officer in the military. That bum and his skinny dog almost died fighting for this country and to give people the freedom to express their opinions. When they came home injured, they were thrown out like yesterday's trash, but instead of being mean or

looking for handouts they worked in the most unpleasant
conditions, doing the jobs nobody wanted to provide for
themselves."

Shellie dragged air into her lungs. "We've become friends and I'd like it to stay that way, but the only
way that will happen is if you either speak of Ronan with
respect or at least keep your negative opinions to yourself."

Kelly hung her head and whispered, "I'm sorry. I
had no idea. I assumed from his appearance that he was
crazy, and that was wrong. Friends?"

Shellie's anger washed away in a cooling wave,
but along with it came a fear as to what she had revealed
about her life. Could she trust Kelly not to say anything?
At least while they were on nights, there really wasn't
any one for Kelly to tell, but what would happen if Kelly
went back on days? She'd have to deal with that situation
if it happened. Shellie forced a big smile. "Friends. I
have to admit; Ronan's fashion sense can be a bit deceiving."

Ronan plugged in the dryer and hit the start button. He gave it a few minutes and then checked the interior. Warm air wafted out to him. It was fixed. The mice
had done a number on both the washer and the dryer.
He'd had to give them a thorough cleaning and ordered
several replacement parts. This was the last of the repairs, so when guests arrived tomorrow, he and Shellie
had a way to wash linens without Shellie hauling them
into work. He was thankful they'd been able to do all the
cleaning of curtains using *Lakeside* machines otherwise
they never would have gotten the place open in time for

the horse shows, but they had been pushing the limit that said only personal laundry.

After a relaxing hot shower and a big bowl of the stew Shellie had left simmering, Ronan sat down at the computer and pulled up the closest VA hospital. The one in Saranac Lake held a group meeting on Tuesday nights and best of all it was free, but could he make himself go? Ronan gripped the mouse so hard the plastic flexed. It was easier searching for IEDs than opening up about his problems. Still, if he wanted a future with Shellie, he had to do it. He had to try being as brave as she was.

Shellie stepped out into the warm sunshine and walked over to the horse trailer that was the last one for the day. She'd been checking in people since late morning. Water dripped from the tailgate. She climbed in through the front passage door and verified the interior had been emptied of manure and hosed down. Nodding, she put a check mark on the check-in form and climbed back out of the horse hauler.

The owner stood nearby wearing a worried expression.

Shellie smiled and walked over. "It looks great. Thank you for following our directions to clean the trailer before you arrived. Do you have some fly spray?"

The women relaxed and held up the big spray bottle. "So, this is all you need?"

"Yes. I contacted *Lakeside Resort and Hotel* to see why they wouldn't let you park there. They gave two reasons; one was space and the other was the horse fly problem." Shellie waved in the direction of the side lot."

We have the space and hopefully cleaned and sprayed trailers will prevent a fly issue."

The woman hopped up and quickly spritzed the inside of the trailer. Shellie guided her as she backed into the parking spot parallel to the five other trailers and fifth wheel rigs, handed her the key to *Bear Cabin* and hurried to the *Dining Cabin*. Blue had finally accepted his job was to watch over Shellie during the day and trotted alongside her. She suspected the fact that she fed him his meals might have something to do with his loyalty to her.

Shellie smiled and washed her hands. For once everything seemed to be working fine. She had turned in her on-line exam last night and was pretty sure she had aced the course and had been able to save enough money to pay for the last one she needed. The professor had already agreed to let her count her work at *Lakeside* as half the internship, so she would have her degree a few weeks before the taxes came due. She chewed her lip. The power and payments to Henry for the insurance bills had used up the deposits from the horse show. Even with that gouge to their budget, they were on track to cover all the motel expenses by the end of the summer. Barring a disaster, they would be able to keep *The Pine Cone Motel* open.

She'd checked on the regulations for bed and breakfasts and found out they didn't need to open as a restaurant if they provided breakfasts as part of the room rental. Strawberries were in season and Ronan had been able to buy heavy whipping cream at cost from the store. She planned on providing pancakes with strawberries and whipped cream for breakfasts, so she set about cleaning and hulling the berries.

Ronan sat in the office working on the receipts from yesterday. Tom was due back from the local Chamber of Commerce meeting and Emily had the customer service window. He liked this setup. His back was to a wall, the desk and computer were a protective barrier in front of him and the music and general ambient noise covered loud bangs or things that could have him diving for cover.

A woman walked up to the customer service window. "Did you know you have a big spill on aisle five?"

Emily smiled at the woman. "No. Thanks for letting me know."

As the woman walked away, Emily made eye contact with Ronan. "How much you want to bet the kid she had in tow created the spill?"

Ronan laughed. "No bet."

He glanced at the computer, checking staff locations. "No one is available to do the clean up. Let me grab a broom and mop and take care of it."

"Are you sure?" Emily asked.

"Yup, no problem."

Ronan hurried to collect the cleaning supplies and headed for the baking aisle. The closer he got the stronger the smell of spices: cinnamon, clove, and paprika. The fragrance brought back memories of patrolling the local market in Bagdad. Ronan's breath came in short gasps. He became hyper-sensitive to the people moving around him, automatically gauging each for potential threats. Muscles tensed, he kept close to the displays, using them as cover from a sniper. As he turned the corner into the aisle, a loud bang went off somewhere up ahead. Ronan dropped and covered.

"What are you doing, Mister?" A dirty five-year-old boy with curly black hair and dark eyes regarded Ronan solemnly.

Ronan pushed the boy back behind him, using his body to protect the child. "Hide. Sniper." He growled at the boy in Arabic.

The child's eyes got huge and he ran away, crying.

This didn't make sense. Where was Blue? Where was his team? He reached up to key his shoulder mic only to find it gone. Where was his weapon? Why was he in civvies and carrying a broom?

Movement started from the other end of the aisle. A woman. Ronan shouted a warning and she retreated. More people gathered behind him. This didn't make sense. What was going on?

Shellie was three-quarters of the way through hulling the strawberries when her phone rang. She looked down at her stained, wet hands and debated ignoring the call. Still, it might be someone looking for a reservation, so she dried her hands and answered, "*Pine Cone Motel*, Shellie speaking. How may I help you?"

"Are you the Shellie Morgan that Ronan Flanagan listed as his emergency number?" A woman asked, barely controlled panic in her voice. Shellie couldn't breathe for a second. Ronan was in trouble.

"Yes. What's happened? Is Ronan okay?"

"Tom the manager said to have you get here ASAP. Ronan's hunched up in an aisle and shouting at people in gibberish and he looks really scary."

"Tell the manager Ronan may think he is in combat in Iraq, give him space. I'm on my way with a dog that can help." Shellie snapped her phone closed as she sprinted out the door. "Blue, *fuss.*"

Blue racing alongside his long, powerful strides pushing Shellie to go even greater speed. She gasped for air racing faster than she could ever remember doing in her life, yet it seemed to take forever to get anywhere. A stitch knotted her side. She ignored it and pushed on, racing across the road to the blare of car horns and screeching brakes as she darted toward the store door, Blue still glued to her side. She had to get to Ronan. She had to.

Ronan crouched in his position weighing his options, when Gunnery Sergeant Tom Carter, scurried in and dropped down beside him.

"What have we got, Lieutenant?"

Ronan wiped sweat from his brow. "I'm not sure. I thought I heard a report up ahead and I seem to have lost my weapon."

"Sounds like we need to withdraw, sir, and regroup where it's a little safer."

"My MWD is missing. I'm not leaving him for the insurgents to torture. Loan me a weapon and I'll meet you back two klicks as soon as I've recovered him."

"Not necessary, sir. We already picked him up. Let's retreat. Follow me."

Blue was okay. Relief eased some of Ronan's tension and he turned to crab walk behind the Gunnery Sergeant.

Moving swift and low, the Gunny lead him to a short door and quickly keyed in a code. They swept in and the sergeant motioned for a female non-com to leave and handed Ronan a bottle. "Have some water, sir."

The cold drink was a real treat. In the desert, mostly, you were happy if it was drinkable, not like the Adirondacks of home where water dripped off the trees and rain was called Adirondack sunshine.

Ronan glanced around the small area. It looked familiar, but it didn't fit with what was in his head. "Where are we? And where is Blue?"

The Gunny nodded and motioned for Ronan to take another drink. "We're safe. You're safe."

Shellie charged through the entry door and had to skid to a stop to wait for the interior door to open. Her breath sawed through her lungs and her limbs trembled from the exertion. Blue stuck his nose into the initial slice of space and shouldered through, Shellie a half a step behind, ignoring the shouts of "No dogs allowed." Blue took a hard left, head up scenting the air and headed straight to the office.

Why wasn't the man telling him what he wanted to know? Had it been a trick to get him out of danger at the sacrifice of Blue? Tension returned. Ronan opened his mouth to order the truth out of the Gunny and head back to find his MWD when a quick knock caused the man to open the door. Blue was through in one flying leap and into Ronan's lap, swiftly licking his face with his soggy tongue, Shellie one step behind.

Shellie.

He wasn't in Iraq - he was at work in the grocery store. He looked around and everything made sense and he realized he'd ruined everything.

Chapter 20

Shellie crept forward and rested her hand on Ronan's knee. "Ronan?"

The store manager's voice was gentle, "Easy, Miss. Give him enough time to assimilate where he is. Flashbacks suck the life out of you."

Shellie glanced at the man. "How do you know that?"

"The usual, been there, done that."

Ronan lowered his hands. "I'm sorry, Angel. I ruined everything. Just like before."

The store manager swallowed some more water. "This isn't your first flashback, Ronan?"

Ronan turned to face him. "They happened a lot when I first got back, but I haven't had one for months, so I thought I could rejoin the civilized world. My mistake. I'm sorry, I know this can't do much for the store's reputation and I understand that you have to let me go."

"Maybe, maybe not."

Ronan refused to hope. "What do you mean?"

"If you're willing to check into the V.A. Hospital and get some help, I'm willing to keep your job open and make sure your insurance is covered."

Ronan looked at Shellie, who appeared about to explode with excitement.

"Angel, it will mean you have to handle the *Pine Cone Motel* by yourself. Can you do that?"

She gave him her sweet, innocent smile. "You made me go to counseling and much as I fought it, it's helped. I want you to have the same chance."

"You realize without my paycheck there won't be enough money for you to go see Dr. Parish."

"We'll find a way. And if you don't go, you'll still be out of work." She turned to Tom. "Right?"

He met her eyes and stared for a second like they were silently communicating. "That's pretty much it."

"I guess that answers that. Looks like I'm headed for the V.A."

Ronan watched the sunset from a chair in the hospital break room. How was Shellie doing? Would she be okay walking home alone tonight? How was Blue handling the separation? German Shepherds weren't known for liking change and having his handler go missing was going to make for one very unhappy dog. Ronan hadn't crated Blue since they moved into *Loon Cabin* a year and a half ago, he wasn't sure how long it would take for the dog to go to work freeing himself.

The V.A. room wasn't bad. It was minuscule with only enough room for a bed and one chair. He shared the bath with another man, but at least he wasn't bunking in with a crowd. Ronan wasn't sure he could handle that.

Movement in the doorway brought him around from the window, hands chambered to protect himself. He recognized Dr. Walters. Ronan attempted to hide his response by opening his hands and pretending his intention was rubbing his nose.

The Doctor leaned against the door jamb. "Sorry, I didn't mean to startle you. You're supposed to be in your room."

"I wanted to watch the sunset."

Walters walked in and sat at the table. "The view of it is better from in here."

Ronan nodded and turned back toward the window. Was Shellie watching it, too? She should be clocking in at work about now.

"Have you settled in?"

Ronan nodded again, trying to figure out what answers would get him out the fastest. He needed to get back to Shellie. She was too vulnerable without him.

Doctor Walters sat quietly for a moment. "Are you worried about your young lady?"

Ronan whirled back to face the man. Was he a mind-reader? "Why do you ask?"

The Doctor wore a big grin. "She called a little while ago to see how you were doing and asking when she and your dog could come visit. She finished up with several admonitions about our care of you and some not so veiled threats, if she didn't like our treatments."

Ronan had to grin. He could visualize her and Blue clearing a path to his room, ready to rescue him. Some of the battle tension left him. There was a reason he was doing this.

"The lady is not fond of sedatives. She made it clear they were a course of last resort."

"She has reason not to like them. Are you going to sedate me?"

"Do you think we need to?"

Ronan thought for a moment. "No. I need to find a way through this without chemical crutches."

"Good. We start therapy tomorrow." Doctor Walters stood and headed for the door.

Shellie arrived at *Lakeside* only three minutes before her shift was to start and clocked in. She stopped in the lobby to even out her breathing from her jog. The sun set in a glorious display of reds, oranges and purples. At least it wouldn't be raining when she walked home tonight. She inhaled one more deep breath and formed a fake smile. Knowing Ronan wouldn't be there to walk her home made it hard to be positive.

The night dragged by with agonizing slowness. They were full up, so she didn't have the distraction of checking someone in. An occasional guest stopped by with a question and a loud round of laughter could be heard now and then from the bar. Guests wandered in loaded down with shopping bags of mountain memorabilia until the shops closed. An hour later there was an influx of people streaming through the doors after the last movie of the night finished, but it quickly dribbled away leaving silence behind.

Shellie watched the cleaning staff perform a final scrubbing of the marble entry floor and wondered for the umpteenth time how Ronan was doing. What was he doing? Had he watched the sunset from his hospital bed, or had they sedated him into oblivion? She shuddered at the thought of chemicals making him helpless, like the drugs Chad slipped into her drink had done to her. Ronan would hate having to depend on others and the loss of privacy.

Kelly was on vacation, taking advantage of the short break between the two summer semesters. Her substitute was a quiet young man who waved shyly but didn't have much to say. When he took over the reception desk for Shellie's break, he quickly buried his nose in his phone, thumbs flying over the letters.

By the time Shellie clocked out her shoulders ached and her skin itched. Her stomach knotted until she thought she would lose her dinner. She stood for a second in the bright lights of the entry, half expecting

Ronan to appear out of the darkness. His admonition to wait in the lighted area if he wasn't there was as clear in her mind as if he stood beside her and spoke.

She closed her eyes and shook her head. How silly. Flipping on her flashlight, she stepped out into the dark night. Even with the cool air caressing her skin, sweat beaded her forehead. As soon as she was around the corner civilization disappeared in a shroud of darkness and her world narrowed to the slender beam of her LED light.

A few yards ahead the bushes rustled, and twigs snapped under the weight of an animal. Shellie immediately envisioned a bear, its eyes flashing red and saliva dripping from its teeth. She let out a small shriek and dove to the side, landing on a granite boulder the size of a big dog. The light flew from her fingers, smacking the gravel shoulder with a metallic clink as a fat raccoon waddled out of the brush and scampered across the pavement.

Shellie shifted to sit on the rock while her heart slowly stopped pounding. Shaking, she stood only to have a shooting pain in her knee sending her gasping and slumped back onto the rock. Her hands burned where they had contacted the rough granite surface and she could feel liquid warmth seeping down her shin. She struggled to her feet, taking most of her weight on her uninjured leg. A hobbling step got her to the flashlight. She grasped it gingerly, shining it to see the damage.

Her stocking was ripped and run almost the width of her leg from her hem line to her ankle and blood welled up from a gash and dripped like a ruby river from her knee. Carefully Shellie transferred weight to the injured leg and while it burned, it supported her. Slowly she started walking, gradually increasing her speed as the pain settled into a dull, but livable ache. The bright sign announcing *Pine Cone Motel, No Vacancy* lit up the night. She quickened her pace, knowing safety waited a few yards away.

Blue bolted out into the night as soon as she opened the door only to whirl around and rush back in barking and jumping then rushing out into the darkness to return once more.

Shellie put her hands on her hips, regretting the action as soon as her damaged skin contacted her skirt. "How did you get out of your crate?"

Ronan had warned her to crate Blue before leaving for work or he would most likely chew through the door before she got back. Shellie turned to what had once been a large wire box. Blue had reduced the door and front panel to a pile of bent and mangled metal. Turning, she saw the dog had done significant damage to the door with his claws and teeth.

"Now what am I going to do with you?"

Blue came back and sniffed her injured leg. His big tongue lapped out and with surprising gentleness the dog began cleaning her wound.

"Oh, that's hygienic."

Shellie pushed him away once again noticing the burning pain in the heels of her hands as they contacted Blue's fur. She stalked to the bathroom and flipped on a light. Slipping out of her shoes and stockings, she moistened a wash cloth in warm, soapy water and began the painful task of cleaning her injuries. Blue made the task twice as hard by sticking his nose in the way as soon as she removed the cloth to rinse it. Her knee had a wide patch of missing skin and a lovely shade of purple spread down the front of her leg. The heels of her hands were abraded. While painful, the injuries were minor.

She applied bandages and readied herself for bed, but Blue wasn't having it. He kept grabbing her pajamas and dragging her out of bed. She tried to ignore him. Blue placed both front feet on the bed and grabbed her sleeve, tugging sharply. Each tug jerked Shellie several inches. Tightening her muscles, she attempted to stay in place, figuring Blue would give up. Instead the sound of ripping fabric and the cool night air on her warm skin bolted her upright.

Blue stepped back, tail wagging and staring intently. Shellie examined her ruined sleeve and turned to the dog. "Just stop it!"

Blue wagged his tail and gave a high-pitched bark.

"I know Ronan isn't here and he should be, but I can't change that. Now let me sleep."

Shellie flopped back on the bed. Blue closed back in and reached for the ruined sleeve once more. She groaned and threw the covers off. Her feet hit the wood floor and she rose pointing toward the door. "Show me."

Blue darted out of the room and down the hall to Ronan's. Shellie limped to the doorway and switched on a light. Blue kept nosing the bed and turning to look at Shellie then ran to the door only to return and repeat the routine.

Shellie sat on Ronan's bed and grabbed Blue's collar. She drew the dog close and hugged him, resting her cheek on his warm forehead. The dog struggled for an instant and then settled to lean against her as if drawing solace from her.

"I miss him, too."

Shellie laid down on Ronan's bed, drawing Blue with her. The pillow smelled of Ronan, soap and wood smoke. Blue settled into her arms and she drifted off to sleep.

Chapter 21

Shellie heard the alarm in the dark stillness of early morning. She rose from Ronan's bed after only four hours sleep, smoothed the quilt, and plumped the pillow. She ached from her tumble the night before and her limbs weighed a ton.

Blue leapt to the floor, leaning against her leg as she moved. Clearly the dog was afraid she would disappear, too. She dressed quickly and hurried to the *Dining Cabin* to start the coffee and pancakes for the horse show people. Two hours later she began cleaning cabins and doing laundry. Shellie barely finished in time to dress for work.

She looked down at Blue as he sat beside her. "What am I going to do with you?"

Blue wagged his tail and stared up at her with a pleading gaze. She could try putting him on a down in the cabin, but that still left her walking home in the dark. Alone. She hesitated. How much trouble would she be in at work if she brought Blue along with her? If she could hide him for a couple of hours all the managers would go home, and no one would know she had a dog with her.

"I hope you're as good for me at a long down as you are for Ronan."

At the mention of his handler's name, Blue glanced around as if to spot Ronan returning.

Shellie opened the door. "Come on."

She managed a quick stop at the butcher shop by jogging the whole way to *Lakeside Resort and Hotel.* She took Blue off to the side and behind some of the bigger bushes. "*Platz.*"

Blue dropped to the sphinx position.

"Settle."

The dog responded by relaxing his position and rolling a hip. Shellie unwrapped the bone and placed it between Blue's paws, giving him the quick hand motion to eat. She placed a small bowl beside him with water and walked inside. After clocking in, she accessed the security feeds on the hotel exterior until she found one that allowed her to watch Blue.

A guest approached the desk. "Excuse me, could you print out the bill to my room? I want to check the restaurant charges."

"Certainly, Mr.?" Shellie let the pause ask the man his name.

"McCarthy. Tom McCarthy in 408. I'm a diamond club member."

Shellie nodded. The fourth floor was for diamond club members and the information matched the hotel records. She hit print and handed the man the bill. "Is everything alright?"

He scanned the papers and smiled. "Yes. There was some confusion when we split the bill last night and I see the restaurant got things straightened out."

"Is there anything else I can help you with?"

Nelson shook his head and walked away.

Shellie felt a presence behind her and turned to see Mr. Grady wearing a frown as he looked at the security monitor, she had open. "Whose dog is that?"

She wished she could sink through the floor and disappear. "Mine, sir."

Grady crossed his arms and tapped his toe. "What is it doing in our lilac bushes?"

"He's a retired military working dog. His handler is a friend and checked into the V.A. suddenly and there was no one else to watch him."

"You should have left him home. Do you really think he will stay in that one spot for eight hours?"

Shellie issued a quick mental prayer for guidance. "I left him last night and he did what he was trained to do, attempt to escape and find his handler. I am confident he won't move from the down for my shift and I can go out and let him exercise on my breaks."

Grady leaned on the desk and observed Blue. "I heard about an incident of a veteran having a flashback episode yesterday." He turned to look at Shellie. "Was that your friend?"

Her throat closed so she nodded.

Grady pinned her with a sharp look. "You think you can handle the dog? A trained military working dog?"

"Yes, sir."

Grady thought for a moment and then gave a slight nod, as if coming to a decision. "I prefer to give special treatment to veterans and that dog is a veteran, all be it a four footed one. I don't normally do this, but I think we could technically claim the animal is a service dog, so he can enter the hotel. Keep him behind the desk and out of sight. I don't want to regret this decision later."

Shellie thought she would collapse, her body felt so weak. "Yes, sir. Thank you, sir."

She hurried around the desk to collect Blue.

Ronan had been here for a week and sat with a half a dozen other veterans in chairs arranged in a circle. Each man shared his experiences. Today was Ronan's turn. Sweat rolled down his back and he fought the urge to run. They had been completely honest, even with the hard stuff, so he knew he could do no less.

Ronan cleared his throat. "I don't know why I survived when the rest of my unit didn't. Corporal Ansley was supposed to ship out the next day and go home to his pregnant wife. If anyone should have gotten out of that fire ball it should have been him, not me. I was the second in command, an officer. It was my responsibility to keep my team safe."

"Did you set the IED? " Andrew asked.

"No."

"Then the insurgent who did is responsible, not you."

Ronan closed his eyes. He knew what Andrew said was true, but he felt guilt riding his shoulder. "I still feel responsible. How do I face their families?"

Silence filled the room like an oppressive black cloud. Until Larry spoke. "Is that why you've been hiding?"

Ronan felt like his heart had stopped beating. "I have flashbacks, so I try and stay away from people. I don't want to hurt anyone."

Larry spoke again. "That's an excuse. We all have them at various levels. Watch for your triggers and break the cycle. But you're hiding, man, look at that beard and hair. Your appearance is guaranteed to drive people away. What girl would want to kiss you and get a mouthful of fur?"

A vision of Shellie popped into his head. Who did Larry think he was, anyway? "Any girl who saw the scars under the beard would run away screaming."

Larry leaned forward. "Prove it. Shave and show us what you're hiding. If I'm wrong, you can always grow the beard again. But you need to open up. You're not being honest with yourself, so how can you be honest with anyone else? Until you do that you don't have a chance of talking to the families of your men."

The other men in the room nodded.

"Some of our injuries are physical." Andrew rapped his knuckles on his prosthetic leg. "Some are emotional. If we don't accept the physical, how can we ever deal with the emotional?"

Ronan's palms were sweating. "There is a woman I like. We're good friends. She doesn't mind my beard."

The group hooted and laughed.

Ronan could feel heat crawling up his neck. "We just kissed, guys."

More snickers and a muttered, "Yeah, sure."

Ronan narrowed his eyes and started to gage who would need the first silencing punch. "She has reason to be afraid of guys, so knock it off."

Silence filled the room. The men there had a strong protective instinct and Ronan knew each man immediately wanted a piece of whoever had hurt Shellie even though they had never met her.

Ronan exhaled. "She's the first good thing to happen to me since I came back. I don't want to lose her over some scars. Cut my hair, yeah, I'm good with that, but shave? I don't know if I can do it?"

Silence.

Andrew uncrossed his legs and leaned forward. "Tell us about her."

The man had already talked about his fiancée leaving him because of his missing leg. If anyone would understand Ronan's fear it was Andrew. Still Ronan hesitated. He didn't want to violate Shellie's trust.

Andrew apparently understood Ronan's hesitation. "No names or what happened to her, but her personality. Why do you think you're friends and why do you want to take things further?"

A vision of Shellie came to Ronan and immediately peace filled him. He smiled. "She's indomitable. She lost everything, home, family, everything. Most people would be bitter and most women I know would have sat down and cried, begging for someone to save them. Not her. She got a job and we've been working together to open an abandoned motel. We get a problem and she sees an opportunity. She has a smile and a kind word for everyone."

"How did you meet?" Larry asked.

"I got stiffed out of a meal I'd worked for. She was the next person in line. She had less than twenty dollars and no roof over her head or a job to earn more, but she bought a meal and gave it to me. That's the kind of person she is."

Andrew shook his head. "She's not going to care about the scars. She's not that shallow. She's not like my former fiancée."

The risk was so great. No way did Ronan want to jeopardize what he had with Shellie. "How can you be sure?"

"Look, the signs were all there with my girl, but if your lady accepted, you looking like a bum and kissed you, she's not going to run from a few scars. Either she's strong enough to take you as you are, or you need to find out before your heart is anymore committed."

Ronan shook his head. Life couldn't have been much worse than where they started, and Shellie had stuck it out. Andrew was right, he had to trust her or know they were wasting each other's time.

After the session Ronan returned to his room and stepped into the small bathroom. He stared at his reflection. Was he hiding? He remembered the first time the bandages came off and his lower face glowed red and painful. He thought he would lose his lunch. He hadn't shaved since. Had he been in denial? There was only one way to find out. Ronan dug the scissors out of his shaving kit and started clipping chin hair.

Shellie watched the last of the horse show people loading up. Mary had been a nice guest, never complaining or making extra demands. The equestrian slammed the truck door and walked over to where Shellie stood in the shade of the *Dining Cabin* porch.

"I'll bet you'll be glad to see the last of us horse people for a while."

Shellie smiled tiredly at the woman. "You guys were great. I've dealt with some very demanding guests in my career and you guys are at the opposite end of the scale."

Mary smiled.

"Before you go, do you have any suggestions on how to make your stay here better?"

Mary hesitated and avoided Shellie's eyes for a few seconds before looking back. "To be honest the appearance of this place had me a little scared. I mean the cabins are great and everything is spotless, but when I pulled in and saw that pool, I almost turned around and left. I knew I couldn't find reservations elsewhere or I wouldn't have stopped. After staying here, I'll be back next year, but if you want more business, you better do something about the pool."

"Thanks." Shellie thought about the comment as Mary headed down the road. She went inside and poured coffee and pulled out the application to have *Pine Cone*

Motel included on the *Lakeside Resort and Hotel* alternate list. The requirements were specific; the facilities inside and out must be in top working order to qualify. There was no way to get on the list until the pool was fixed.

Shellie glanced at her watch. There were zero reservations for today; she could afford some office time. Picking up her coffee, she headed for the computer in the *Manager's Cabin*. She had heard Mr. Grady and Mrs. Anderson exchanging anxious comments. New York State had developed a grant program to help people re-open the small motels and cottages that dotted the Adirondacks and Catskill Mountains. The two had been worried it would take business from the hotel.

Shellie typed in the search parameters and a page on the State website opened. She read through the requirements and clicked on the grant application form. She printed it and began filling in the boxes. It took three drafts to create the explanation narrative the way she wanted it and then she did one more run through for punctuation and spelling. Satisfied, Shellie typed everything into the form and hit print. She still needed a cost estimate for the repairs, but who should she trust? She checked on-line for listings and service ratings. There was only one company in the tri-lakes area building pools and it belonged to Ronan's father.

After what Ronan had said about his father, she hesitated. Should she check with Ronan? After a lot of thought she decided against bothering him. His focus had to be on getting well and if he thought she needed help he'd check out and be at the *Pine Cone Motel* before she could hang up the phone. Besides, his father's company was pretty big. It wasn't likely the man would be the one to look at a little pool job.

Shellie's fingers shook a little as she dialed. She hoped she wasn't being disloyal to Ronan.

"Tri-Lakes Construction." A woman answered.

"I need an estimate to repair a swimming pool."

"Is this a private or commercial pool, ma'am?"

"Commercial. I don't know if you remember the *Pine Cone Motel*. I want to see if the pool can be fixed."

The pause on the other end surprised Shellie. There was enough background noise to know the line was still connected.

"Yes, ma'am. Excuse me for asking, but your voice sounds a lot younger than the last time I talked to the owner."

"Mrs. McClelland already got an estimate?"

"Two years ago. But estimates are only good for ninety days. What is your relationship to Mrs. McClelland?"

"A friend and I have opened and are operating the motel for her. You can call her for verification. I'm Shellie Morgan."

"Miss Morgan, the last estimate was several thousand dollars. A new one will be higher. Mrs. McClelland said the income couldn't support the investment."

"I need the estimate to apply for a state grant. If the grant comes through it must be spent on the motel and I can hire you to do the work. If it doesn't, I can't afford the repairs."

"I understand. I'll have an estimator come out around two tomorrow. Will that work for you?"

"Yes. Thanks."

Shellie hung up the phone and went to work cleaning cabins. She turned on some music and danced and sang while she worked. She kept telling herself there were no guarantees they'd get the grant, but her heart wasn't listening.

Her telephone rang and Shellie recognized Detective Evan's number. "Hello, Detective, are you calling to tell me Chad confessed, and you don't need my deposition?"

A girl could hope.

"Don't I wish. No, things are still moving forward, and I'll be there as planned. There has been one change, though."

Shellie held her phone with her shoulder so she could haul dirty sheets to the laundry cart. "What's that?"

"The defendant's lawyer wants to question you as part of the deposition."

Shellie dropped the sheets into the laundry bin and collapsed into the porch rocker as deflated as a popped balloon. "You mean Chad will be there?"

"No, there will be me, the prosecuting attorney and the defendant's attorney and the stenographer, of course."

Shellie's voice broke and she swallowed back tears. "Why?"

"It's part of the process." The detective's tone was gentle.

"I'm not sure I can still do this. It was hard enough knowing I would have to tell what happened to complete strangers, at least I knew you were sympathetic. Now someone who supports Chad being there makes this almost impossible."

"That's exactly what they want. They're hoping to intimidate you into not giving a statement. I know it will be hard, Miss Morgan, but you can do this. You're one tough lady." There was a slight pause and then his voice came through softer, like he was trying not to let people around him hear what he was saying. "I can tell you this, their attorney is worried, or he wouldn't be trying to cut deals. With any luck, they'll resolve this before we get there, and your statement won't be needed. I have to plan for the worst, so I wanted to give you enough time to understand their strategy and counteract it. Do you have someone you trust who could be there to support you?"

"I don't know. The one person I trust is in the hospital and even so, he's protective of me which, if Chad's attorney is mean could turn into a bad situation. I guess I can call my psychologist and see if she'll advise me on what to do. I wish I could have her there, but I can't afford to pay her right now and she's probably busy."

"You know what, I'll get my department to cover her fee as a medical necessity. I'll see you in two days at your motel."

Shellie closed the phone and fought the shakes. She needed Ronan. Now. Blue chose that moment to plop his front feet in her lap and give her a face and ear washing. Shellie shoved him away groaning, "Blue!"

She would not call Ronan. She would not derail his progress with her problems.

Shellie scrolled to the contact number for Dr. Parish.

"Doctor Parish's office."

"Hi Bonnie, this is Shellie Morgan. Could you have the doctor call me when she gets a minute?"

"You're in luck. She's between patients and has a few minutes."

The doctor's calm voice flowed through the phone. "Hi Shellie. You wanted to speak to me?"

Shellie quickly brought the doctor up to date. "I was okay with this when it was just the detective but having Chad's attorney ask me questions worries me. Things are still foggy and disjointed and from what I've seen on TV dramas, his job will be to make me out as a liar."

"You have reason to be concerned, particularly with two attorneys asking questions. I think you would be better with someone you trust there to support you."

"The only other person who knows about what happened is Ronan and he's not in a position to come help. The doctors won't even let me visit him until next week."

Shellie sucked in a deep breath. *Here goes.* "The detective said he could have his department pay your fee if you could be there. I know you probably have patients already scheduled and this would be impossible, but could you come to the motel for the deposition?"

Shellie waited, trying to steel herself to accept a 'sorry, no'."

"Actually, I block Wednesday afternoons to up-date patient files and notes, so I am available."

Shellie felt lightheaded. She wouldn't be alone. "Thank you."

"Shellie, I have a recommendation to make."

"What's that?"

"The motel has been your haven and right now it is a bit of a crutch you need until we work through all of this. Giving the deposition some unhappy feelings are going to attach to your home. See if the meeting can take place here in my office. You've been able to open up here and it will give you the opportunity to go home and leave the unhappy association behind."

Shellie heard a vehicle pull in, the sound of tires on gravel floating through the screen door of the *Manager's Cabin* along with road dust. A quick glance at the clock on the computer screen told her the Tri-Lakes estimator was punctual. That was a good sign. A tall, middle-aged man stepped down from the pickup truck. The bright sunshine glinted off his dark red hair. He closed the truck door and stepped closer. Shellie's heart started to pound. He was an older version of Ronan; this had to be Ronan's father.

She glanced down at Blue, wondering if she could get the dog back inside before Mr. Flanagan recognized him. Too late. Blue trotted down the porch steps to greet the man with a friendly tail-wag.

"Hello, Blue." The man petted the dog and looked around. "Where's your handler?"

Shellie approached and held out her hand. "Hello, Mr. Flanagan. I was expecting an employee, not the owner of Tri-Lakes Construction."

"Are you Miss Morgan?"

It was on the tip of Shellie's tongue to offer her given name, but something made her hold back. "Yes."

He shook her hand and looked around some more and asked, "Where's my son hiding? I'd hoped to see him and find out how he's doing. He was a good man and a good worker before he went off to the war."

Shellie yanked her hand back and crossed her arms over her chest. "I'll tell Ronan you asked for him. Now if you would care to go to work on the estimate, I have things to do and places to go."

The man looked her up and down. "Where is my son?"

Shellie ground her teeth. "Ronan is not here right now and frankly if there was anyone else in the area that did pools, I would have called them to prevent a confrontation. I need a written estimate from a construction company to apply for a grant. If the grant is approved, I will hire your company. If it isn't our business ends with this estimate."

"If Ronan isn't here, why is Blue? The dog never left his side. Ever."

"Ronan does not take Blue to meetings. He leaves him with me." To emphasize the point, she gave the hand signal and Blue came to heel.

The man hefted his clipboard. "I'm glad to see my son is making progress at rejoining the world. If he's managing to take business meetings than he is starting to be the man I can be proud of once again and I'd like him to visit his mother and me when he gets a chance."

Shellie had the option of enlightening Ronan's father as to where Ronan was, but considering his attitude, she decided to leave him in the dark. "I'll have to consider whether I tell him you were here or not. I am not fond of your attitude toward him."

Flanagan looked taken aback and laughed. "I see Ronan's taste in women has improved, too."

He strode off to the pool and started taking notes.

Thirty minutes later Shellie held the single page estimate as she watched the pickup truck pull onto the road. She looked down at Blue. "I'm glad that's over, aren't you?"

Blue wagged his tail and followed her back inside. Shellie almost didn't want to submit the grant application if it meant having Ronan's father come back. Still, for the long-term good of the *Pine Cone Motel* she needed to get the eyesore of a pool cleaned up.

Only one more box needed completion: the owner's signature.

She chewed her lip. Did she ask Mrs. McClelland to sign it or her grandson, Henry?

She picked up the phone. "Hi, Mrs. McClelland, I need your signature on a grant application. Have you got a minute while I explain?"

Chapter 22

Shellie entered Dr. Parish's office with Blue on a leash. Detective Evans was due to arrive any minute with a court stenographer and the attorneys to take her statement. Her phone vibrated with a text message. It was from Ronan. *I can be there in ten minutes if you've changed your mind.*

She exhaled a breath; she hadn't realized she'd been holding. It helped knowing Ronan was there with her in spirit. She thumbed back, *Thanks no, I'm okay.* She was glad he hadn't called; they'd probably burned though a good chunk of their minutes over the last couple of days as she worked to convince him he needed to stay in the hospital. Ronan growled threats against Chad's attorney and floated plans to sneak out of the hospital to be at the deposition. If he heard her speak a single word, he'd know how stressed she was and ignore her pleas to stay in the V.A.

Blue stuck to Shellie's leg like he'd been attached with Velcro. He wasn't exactly in protection mode, but he clearly recognized Shellie was nervous and like most German Shepherds he was doing his canine best to offer comfort.

Dr. Parish nodded at the dog. "So, this is Blue."

At the sound of his name Blue glanced her way. Dr. Parish squatted down and waited. Blue glanced up at Shellie and she gave the release hand motion. He walked over to the doctor and gave a detailed sniff of her clothes, hands and face.

"You smell Chelsea. I left her home today so you could have the run of the place. Please don't bite the defense attorney."

Blue butted her hand gently and Dr. Parish gently stroked his head while Shellie giggled. After a few pats and a tail wag, Blue returned to her side.

Two men and two women followed the receptionist into the inner office. She handed the doctor several business cards. "Dr. Parish, Miss Morgan, this is Detective Evans, Ms. Fellows is a stenographer, Assistant District Attorney Green, and Ms. Hall, also an attorney." She pointed to each person as she said their names.

Dr. Parish motioned to the sitting area. "Shall we sit down? Ms. Fellows, you can use the side table, if you like."

After everyone was seated, Dr. Parish continued. "Miss Morgan is my patient and her well-being is my primary concern. If I deem it necessary, I will stop the proceedings and give her time to compose herself before we continue."

Shellie noted Detective Evans' grin as he gave the thumbs up gesture. She got the feeling he was going to support Dr. Parish in protecting her. He wasn't imposing; average height and build with thinning hair and weary blue eyes that seemed to say he'd seen a lot of the bad, but still had hope. He wore an inexpensive, well-used suit, shirt, and tie.

Ms. Hall was quite the opposite. Shellie figured the dress she wore would cost a month's salary and it looked like she was wearing Jimmy Choo shoes or excellent knockoffs. She settled gracefully into a chair and frowned at Dr. Parish. "My purpose in being here is to get to the truth and prevent a vindictive young woman from destroying the life of a promising young man. So, don't be surprised if I ignore your interruptions."

"I see we've drawn our lines in the sand. Shall we get started?" The Assistant District Attorney grinned.

Two hours later, Shellie watched as the visitors left the office. Ms. Hall didn't look happy and Detective Evans gave Shellie a wink and a grin as he exited last. Dr. Parish pulled two bottles of water from the mini-fridge and handed one to Shellie. Exhaustion weighed Shellie's limbs to a point she could barely reach for the beverage.

"You did a good job. I had reservations about putting you through this, but you handled it well." Dr. Parish said.

"I'm glad you were here. I don't think I could have kept it together much longer with Ms. Hall's rapid-fire questions and twisting my words. You stepped in and gave me the break I needed. She wasn't happy."

"No, she wasn't, but that is for her to deal with. I think Blue's chattering teeth helped her agree. What does the rest of your day look like?"

Shellie glanced at her phone for the time. "I need to head back to the motel and eat, get changed, and head to work in a couple of hours."

Dr. Parish recapped her water. "Do you want to talk about today?"

Shellie stilled. Even collecting her thoughts was exhausting. "Ms. Hall made me wonder if this really was my fault. I felt like I did when I talked to my dad. But Mr. Green's question helped turn that around a little. I'm glad his questions came after hers. Talking through what happened again, makes it feel more –" she struggled for the words, "distant, like a story. I know it happened, but so much has changed in my life, it doesn't feel completely real."

Dr. Parish nodded.

Shellie sat up straighter and took a drink of water. "I do know, I'm glad this is over and behind me. I'm glad I did give a statement. It makes me feel less helpless, but I want to move on with my life. Chad has stolen enough of it without stealing my future."

"That's a good place to be, but don't be surprised or beat yourself up if you still have the occasional nightmare or blue mood. I am here for you and there are some things we haven't resolved."

"Like what?"

"Believing one hundred percent that you were not responsible for what happened."

Shellie slumped back in the chair. "For right now, believing ninety percent is going to have to do."

The hospital barber whipped the haircutting cape away with a snap and stepped back. "You're all done, soldier."

Ronan looked at his image in the mirror and grimaced. The guys were right, no matter what direction you gave to the barber, you could expect a standard military, high, and tight haircut. Add that to the fine white lines crisscrossing his closely cropped beard and he looked nothing like the guy he'd seen in the mirror for the last few years, but was that an improvement?

Ronan stood and dropped some cash into the jar next to the combs. Time to go to group.

Ronan had barely dropped into his chair when Larry started in on him.

"Still hiding I see."

"Take a good look." Ronan pointed to the gaps in his beard. "Are you sure you want to see more?"

Andrew picked up the gauntlet. "Yes. Besides, with your red hair the scars are probably more prominent than if you finished shaving."

Ronan's guts knotted. He could not do it.

Larry leaned forward, passed Ronan a bottle of water and waited while Ronan drank. When Larry spoke, there was compassion in his voice. "Think of this as the mental form of basic training. We've got to strip down to the base man and build up from there. If we don't, the chances are things will fall apart when trouble comes, and trouble always comes."

Ronan struggled to talk around the lump choking his throat. "Shellie is supposed to visit tomorrow."

The group fidgeted and exchanged glances.

Andrew offered an understanding smile. "At least you'll know."

Sunlight streaked through the sliding glass door of Shellie's room and tickled her eyelids. She rolled over and stretched. She had today off, from *Lakeside* at least. Normally she would have had a session with Dr. Parish, but the money wasn't there. Without Ronan's paycheck every penny she earned went to motel expenses.

Provided nothing went wrong, the final payments from the horse show people would go a long way toward meeting the tax bill. The next step was to prepare for the rugby players, but first she needed to get both Blue and herself cleaned up. Today they would visit Ronan for the first time in two weeks. She was looking forward to seeing him, but for some reason she was depressed and out of sorts. Dr. Parish had been right, she still had a way to go.

Shellie slipped on some sweats and ordered Blue into the tub. She carefully adjusted the water temperature and started on his bath. Blue's ears drooped, and he looked up at her with sad eyes.

Shellie felt about how the dog looked. It seemed like all she did was work. Days at *The Pine Cone Motel* and nights at the *Lakeside Resort and Hotel.* Her time off was spent going to classes. When did she get a chance to rest and goof off? Was life always going to be this difficult? What if Ronan realized he couldn't handle the world outside the V.A. and never came back? She shook her head; Ronan had promised to take care of her. If there was one person she could trust not to abandon her it was Ronan.

She straightened her spine and tried for an upbeat tone. Maybe she could force some joy into her soul. One thing was certain, whining and crying didn't help. Shellie applied some shampoo to the dog. "Don't give me that look. You're the one who rolled in the dead fish."

Blue issued a deep sigh and sat dejectedly through the scrub and rinse until it came time for drying. As soon as Shellie wrapped the towel around him the dog went into a full play mode. In one smooth leap he was over the side of the tub and grabbing at the towel to play tug. Even in the small space it took Shellie several minutes to corral the rambunctious canine and get him remotely dry.

The buzzer from the front desk went off. "Hello? Is anybody here?"

Blue dropped the towel and started barking and clawing at the bathroom door.

Shellie closed her eyes and reached down deep inside for patience. Whoever was out there would probably look at her and Blue and sprint for their vehicle.

"I'll be right there." She wasn't sure her shout could be heard over Blue's barking. She hurried to the front desk. A quick glance over her shoulder told her she was leaving soggy footprints.

A man, about the age of her father, leaned on the desk, a look of mild confusion on his face. "I'm sorry, this is an open motel and not a private residence, isn't it?"

Her heart skipped a beat, realizing she was alone with a stranger, a male stranger. Shellie smiled to hide her anxiety and pretended she was dressed in her uniform, carefully groomed, and surrounded by additional hotel staff. "I'm sorry to keep you waiting Mr.-?"

"White. Ernie White."

Shellie went through the task of checking the computer even though she knew there were no reservations for today. "I'm sorry to keep you waiting Mr. White. I don't show a reservation under that name, but we do have available cabins."

She slid a card and pen toward him. "If you could fill out our registration card, we can get you settled in a jiffy."

Pretending it was an afterthought, she added, "We take all major credit cards."

"So, you really do rent cabins? I wasn't sure, what with the pool and all." He looked her and Blue up and down, making it clear what "all" meant.

Shellie gathered the slender threads of her patience and tried to weave them into a rope strong enough to keep her from exploding in a tirade. This was her day off, her one time to not have to be nice to anyone and say and do what she wanted. Here was this man treating her like dirt under his fingernails. "I'm sorry this looks so unprofessional, Mr. White. My friend and I live on site to provide twenty-four-hour management. Today is normally my day off and since we didn't have any new reservations, I took the opportunity to bathe my dog."

"Then you do have reservations?"

"Yes." Shellie didn't see any reason to tell him the next guests weren't scheduled to arrive for several days when the ruggers were expected. "How many people are in your party and how long would you like to stay?"

White stood up straighter and looked out through the screen door. "Just one and I'll need the cabin for two weeks."

Shellie paused in the act of starting the reservation. "I'm sorry. I have a cabin available for the next four days, but we are booked solid for the following three weeks. I do apologize."

"Really?" White drew out the word, emphasizing his incredulity.

"I'm afraid so. There's the largest rugby match in North America starting Friday followed immediately by a lacrosse tournament. After that, a major country artist is performing."

Shellie tried to visualize the computer screen at *Lakeside*. "If you would like, I can check with some of the larger chain hotels. I don't believe they are booked up during the rugby tournament. You can stay here for four days and if I get a cancellation, I can give you first priority to stay or I can try and get you a reservation with another establishment once our current reserved guests start to arrive."

"I'll stay the four days. Are you sure you can't get me in someplace other than the chains?"

"You know there is one B&B that probably isn't booked up. It's a very quiet place and they were talking about refusing to rent to the ruggers and lacrosse players. If you would like, I can check with them while you get settled in."

White handed over his credit card and filled in the registration card. He handed it back and pointed to Blue. "So, you accept pets?"

"Yes, as long as they are under control and not left unattended in the cabins."

Shellie turned and selected the key to *Loon Cabin*. "Are you traveling with a pet?"

"No, for future reference."

"Let me show you to your cabin." Shellie slipped on a pair of loafers she had left under the desk, ignoring the water that squished out of her socks and pooled in the toes of her shoes. She led the way out the door, signaling Blue to her side. White followed.

Having a stranger so much bigger and stronger walking behind her made Shellie's skin crawl. She couldn't help glancing over her shoulder repeatedly. Blue must have sensed her disquiet and slipped into guardian mode. He flipped his position, so he was still beside Shellie, but facing White and walked backwards, watching the man's every movement.

White stutter stepped. Blue moved a half step toward the man, but as soon as he continued forward, the dog resumed his position beside Shellie.

"What is your dog doing? I have to say he's a little scary."

Shellie exhaled some of her disquiet. Blue wouldn't let anything happen to her. "He's a retired military canine. He doesn't know you, so he is guarding me against attack. If I am safe, so are you."

"Isn't he a danger to have around, especially the children of guests?"

"He is fine with children and keeps them away from the river out back. They love playing with him. He's very gentle, even when they aren't."

Shellie pointed as they walked. "That's the *Dining Cabin*. We have a simple complimentary breakfast starting at six in the morning and there is always coffee or ice water flavored with ginger and oranges. We do lock it up around ten pm."

"Do you serve other meals?"

"No, but guests are welcome to order delivery or eat take out there or simply relax by the fire in the evening."

Shellie unlocked the door to *Loon Cabin*. The pleasant smells of lavender and lemon oil wafted to them. "This is a one-bedroom unit. Extra linens and blankets are in the closet here by the door. If you need anything, please feel free to call the office."

White looked around and glanced in the bathroom. "No, this will be fine."

Shellie turned to leave but paused. "I'll have to go out a bit later, so the office will be locked up, but I'll leave the *Dining Cabin* open for your convenience."

"What about your friend that helps run the motel?"

Shellie debated lying that Ronan was expected home soon for an instant. She would be caught out almost immediately and didn't want White to regard everything she said from then on with suspicion. Blue would have to do as a deterrent. "He's been ill and is hospitalized. I hope he can come home soon."

"Thanks."

Shellie returned to the *Manager's Cabin* and looked around at the soggy mess. "Good thing we're going to see Ronan and not him coming home to this mess."

She quickly mopped up the water and collected a clean rug which Blue promptly commandeered by flopping across the fluffy surface. Stripping off her wet clothes, Shellie sniffed her hands and grimaced. "Yuck. I smell like wet dog."

Blue thumped his tail and wrapped his paws around the towel he'd dropped earlier. Shellie rolled her eyes and climbed into the shower.

Knowing they had at least one cabin occupied to help raise the tax money brightened her mood. Clean and dressed in jeans, a pink tee-shirt and a light blazer, Shellie clipped a leash onto Blue's collar and started walking. It took almost an hour to get to the V.A. The bright sunshine and cool breeze dried Blue and kept Shellie refreshed. She checked in at the desk and was directed to the visiting area.

Shellie glanced around looking for Ronan's distinctive hair and beard. Blue jerked the leash from her hand and galloped toward a clean-shaven soldier sitting off on a side with a neat, short, military haircut. The dog jumped into the man's lap, whining and yipping while licking at the man's face frantically. Realization flashed across her brain. She raced to greet Ronan.

Ronan collected Blue in his arms and rose to his feet, hoping the energetic dog would disguise how badly he was shaking. Shellie hadn't recognized him; definitely a bad sign. He watched her approach, working to keep his face impassive as he waited for her smile to slip once she was close enough to see the scars.

She raced up to him and flung her arms around both him and Blue. "Oh my, Ronan, I didn't recognize you. You look so handsome."

Ronan let Blue drop and wrapped Shellie in a bear hug. He knew he wasn't handsome like she claimed, but she hadn't run away in disgust. His whole body shook, and he was so lightheaded, he thought he might pass out. Shellie stiffened for an instant as his hug engulfed and held her prisoner. Annoyed with his self-centeredness at not remembering Shellie's fears, he loosened his hold and let Blue wiggle in between them. She emerged flushed and grinning like a five-year-old on Christmas morning.

"Man, the other girls at church are going to be so jealous when I walk in with you. They'll kick themselves for not beating me to you."

Ronan laughed as he felt a blush climb his face, the downside of being a redhead. Shellie looked up and he saw fleeting sadness enter her eyes. She reached up and gently stroked his cheek.

Ronan's heart sank. She had noticed the scars. It had taken a little longer, but now, thanks to that stupid blush that still heated his face, she realized how ugly he was. He stepped back, trying to rein in the pain and find an easy way for them to walk away.

"I'm sorry. Did I hurt you?" she asked.

Did she *hurt* him? She'd smashed his heart into a thousand pieces and thrown it in the trash. "I'm fine."

He took a step back trying to gain some space, but she moved with him and reached for his arm. "I didn't think your face would still be sore. It must have hurt like the dickens to shave." She looked down at the floor.

"I didn't mean to be so insensitive. You're handsome with the beard, too."

Why would she think it hurt to shave? Was this her way of getting him to cover up the scars, or something else? The Shellie he knew didn't have an ounce of guile. He had to know what she was thinking. "The only painful part of shaving is looking in the mirror and seeing the scars."

"So, I didn't hurt you when I touched your face?"

"Weren't you exploring the scars?"

Her utter confusion started to glue his shattered heart back together. She looked down, did her own blushing and shook her head.

"Shellie, talk to me."

Her voice came out in a soft whisper. "I missed you so much I wanted to kiss you, but I was afraid."

Ronan wrapped an arm around her shoulders. "Why were you afraid?"

"Be-because I didn't want to give you the wrong impression, like I did with Chad." She looked up through those long lashes of hers. "I miss you so much. I wish I could wrap my arms around you and smuggle you out in my purse."

Ronan guided her to a chair and knelt in front of her. "Please, Shellie, I have to know. Please, please tell me the truth. I can deal with it, so don't lie to spare my feelings. That would be worse. Do the scars bother you?"

She gave him that warm, sweet smile and captured his hand in both of hers. She scanned his face carefully, then looked him in the eyes. "It bothers me, you suffered the kind of pain caused by the injuries that left those scars. But when I look at you, I see Ronan, the man I care about. A man I respect and trust, not the scars.

With the beard or without it, visible scars or not, it's a little piece of the man who matters to me. The man I see."

Ronan closed his eyes and swallowed hard. He
should have known. He should have trusted Shellie.
"Thank you."

He rose to his feet. "Would you like some coffee?"

"That would be great, as long as you remember
lots of cream and sugar."

Ronan nodded, understanding what she was saying. Shellie trusted him. She knew he wouldn't slip
something into her coffee or do anything else to hurt her.
She saw the man, not the scars. He had been such a fool
these last couple of weeks worrying about her reaction.

They sipped coffee and shared their news. Ronan
did his best to hide his feelings toward Chad's lawyer.
Shellie's giggling description or the interaction between
Ms. Hall and Blue did much to alleviate his anger.

Blue grabbed Ronan's pant cuff and tugged. Ronan surrendered. "Let's go out to the lawn so I can play
with Blue."

Shellie followed in his wake, Blue offering the
prettiest heeling Ronan had ever seen him do. A canine
handler stopped to watch and agreed to put on a bite suit
while a small crowd quickly gathered. Ronan knew he
was showing off a little, but wasn't that what guys did for
their special girl?

The sun had slipped low on the horizon when
Shellie and Blue left for home. Andrew joined Ronan as
he stood there watching until they disappeared around
the curve in the road then glanced at his friend.

"I've got something for you." Andrew handed
Ronan a package of razor blades and walked away.

Chapter 23

Shellie tripped on a tree root as she stepped off the road onto the *Pine Cone Motel* driveway. She was so tired from the long walk and the emotionally draining afternoon. All she wanted to do was crawl into bed. Instead, she flipped on the office lights and signed into her email. First, she scanned for any motel questions or potential reservations. There was a depressing lack of the latter. An email from one of the rugby players asked about the policy for alcohol use. Shellie chewed a fingernail. Here was another time she wished for Ronan's wise advice.

Visions of the frat party that had changed her life danced through her head. It took her a moment to realize there were tears streaming down her face. What in the world was wrong with her? She wished she could call her mom; but that was a waste of time. Her dad supported Chad and her mom wouldn't contradict her husband.

Her grandmother had a bad heart, there was no way Shellie was going to bother her. She thought for a moment. There was one person with a lifetime of experience managing a motel she could call. A quick glance at the clock told her it wasn't too late. She picked up her phone and speed-dialed Mrs. McClelland.

"Hello, Shellie, how is Ronan doing?"

Shellie gave a quick synopsis of her visit and shared the hope Ronan would be back soon.

"I loved the pictures you sent. The place looks like it did in its heyday."

Shellie could hear the smile in the older woman's voice. Her happiness was contagious and lit some of the dark places inside Shellie. "I'm glad you think so. If we can get the pool fixed, I think we'll be in really good shape and can get on the overflow lists from the big chains. That will make a difference in making a profit versus scrambling to cover expenses."

"Have you heard anything about the grant? I couldn't believe it when you told me about it and Henry was very excited at the prospect."

Shellie bit back a cynical comment about Henry and avarice and reminded herself for the hundredth time the man was simply trying to protect his grandmother.

"Nothing yet. I'll let you know as soon as I hear anything. There is another reason I called. I need your advice."

"I'll do my best."

"Did you ever rent to the rugby players?"

"Oh yes. Very good-hearted people with lots of laughter echoing around the place. They did tend to use some strong language, particularly in their rowdy songs, but all together they were nice people enjoying a simple vacation. We seldom had any issues with them and no damage beyond normal wear. The last few years we were open, some of the young men would rush over and help my husband if they saw him trying to lift something heavy."

"I got an email asking me about our alcohol policy. What did you do?"

Mrs. McClelland paused. "We allowed quiet indulgence and while the players seemed to consume significant quantities of beer and wine, we never saw any issues. We were very upfront about the repercussions from drunken behavior. One of the things that helped is we didn't have rival teams staying with us."

Shellie huffed a deep breath. She hadn't thought to ask about team affiliations. Even if she had, she had no idea what the rivalries between teams were. "I don't know who is staying here and what teams they represent. Did I make a big mistake?"

"Don't worry, dear. I found that if one member of a team made reservations, the rest of the place filled quickly with other members of the same team. I never organized it, but they like to socialize with each other and try to get into the same place, so they could drink together and not be concerned about driving."

Shellie worried her nail some more. With her luck two rival teams would have equal numbers of cabins rented and there would be fist fights in the parking lot. She sat lost in thought, visualizing the disaster.

"Shellie? Are you still there?"

Shellie returned to the present. "Sorry. I'm still worried I messed up."

Mrs. McClelland chuckled. "I remember feeling that way. Trust in the Lord, and you'll be okay."

"Yes, ma'am."

"Why don't you send a polite note to everyone with reservations, stating the policy of quiet enjoyment of alcoholic beverages within the boundaries of the law. If you look in the desk drawer in the office there are pre-printed notes, we used to send to everyone when they made a reservation."

"Do you think that will offend anyone and have them cancel?"

"Very few people cancelled on us. We figured if someone did cancel, we were avoiding trouble."

Shellie opened the desk drawer and spotted the creamy, white cards with the motel logo of a forest green pine cone. It would be easy to design an electronic card that mimicked the physical one. She would have to think about how to link it up, so it went out automatically when someone made a reservation. For now, she could send it out manually, since they didn't have a lot of reservations. The thought was not comforting. The idea someone would cancel was even less appealing, but at least she had Mr. White to help them over the gap if that did happen.

"Thank you. Your advice is a huge help."

"Anytime, it's wonderful to be useful. Sometimes it seems like people discount us seniors simply because we're old."

Shellie hung up and made a mental note to call Mrs. McClelland more often for advice. Without Ronan around it helped having someone with whom she could discuss problems or concerns. Certainly, Shellie couldn't think of anyone who had more experience running a motel.

Skipping down the list of unopened emails, Shellie spotted one from her professor with an attachment. She had been expecting Dr. Sampson to return the draft of her paper with comments. Since the students' grades rested on a single paper, the professor insisted on reviewing their drafts at intervals and making recommendations. This was her first draft and she was looking forward to her input. Shellie normally got A's and expected simple tweaks.

I found this paper profoundly disappointing. In order to get a degree in hotel management you need to actually do some managing! This is a report from a night clerk with little to no

*evidence of handling more than a late-night
check in. Without serious changes showing decision making, this will not result in a passing
grade.*

Shellie bolted out of her chair. "Who does she
think she is?"

Shellie pounded on the desk and then threw herself into a corner. She drew her knees up to her chest and
sobbed into her hands. Somewhere in the back of her
mind, she knew she was over-reacting, but couldn't help
herself. Dr. Parish had warned her excessive emotional
outbursts were a common response of rape victims. Even
knowing she was over the top and why didn't help. She
couldn't stop crying.

Blue silently shoved his nose against her hands,
using his powerful neck muscles to force his muzzle
passed her defenses and gain access to her face. He gently swabbed her eyes with his big, warm tongue. Shellie
wrapped her arms around him and simply wept.

She wasn't sure how long it took for her tears to
run out. She wiped her irritated eyes with her sleeve and
whispered hoarsely, "Will anything ever go right?
Doesn't Dr. Sampson understand *Lakeside Resort and
Hotel* doesn't let us be anything more than clerks? They
can't afford to let us make decisions. As part of a big
chain, everything has to be the same in all locations."

Shellie gently shoved Blue out of her lap and
used the wall to help her climb to her feet. Neither she
nor Blue had eaten since early morning. Maybe she
would feel better if she ate something. Shellie dragged
herself over to the *Dining Cabin.* She placed her hand on
the knob. A movement behind her caused her to shriek
and jump away. Blue immediately launched barking and

snarling between her and the man that had been approaching from behind.

White froze, the blood draining from his face.

Shellie's whole body quivered. She could barely breathe. Her first, *"hier fuss"* was inaudible. Gulping air into her lungs, she issued the command as forcefully as possible. Blue quieted and backed into position, never taking his eyes off White.

The silence that followed was thick and uncomfortable.

Shellie rested her hand on Blue's head. "Was there something you wanted, Mr. White?"

The man's voice came out shaky, "I was going to open the door for you."

"Thank you, but I'll open my own doors. I don't care for strange men within grabbing distance. Neither does Blue."

The dog glanced at Shellie and then back to watching White.

Mr. White looked her up and down and nodded. "I don't believe in hurting women, Miss Morgan, especially when they remind me of my daughter."

Shellie felt heat flood her face and squirmed. Was she ever going to be able to act like a normal person? "I'm sorry. I was going to have some hot chocolate and a sandwich. It's only a PBJ, but you're welcome to join me."

White glanced at Blue and hesitated.

"I'll direct him to stand down."

"I wouldn't mind a snack."

Shellie led the way inside and poured out a bowl of kibble for Blue. Blue stood at his bowl gobbling up his food all the while wagging his tail as he ate. Shellie poured milk into a pan and put it to heat on the gas stove.

White eased into Ronan's chair, all the while watching Blue. The dog ignored him. Shellie stirred the chocolate powder into the milk and poured it into two cups. She served White his food and then brought hers over to the table.

They ate in silence. The simple food and quiet eased some of Shellie's anxiety.

Finished with his food, White played with the handle of his mug. "Have you had much trouble with rowdy guests?"

"Why would you think that?"

"I scared you earlier. I didn't mean to, but I did. Your reaction gave me the impression not everyone you've met has been – polite."

Shellie hesitated. She didn't want to discuss something so personal with a stranger, but she did owe him some explanation. "You're correct in that I had an experience in college, which has made me a bit mistrustful. I am truly sorry I overreacted, which set Blue in protection mode."

White watched her closely. "You aren't afraid of your friend?"

Shellie smiled, and a wave of homesickness swept over her. She missed Ronan so much. "Ronan would never allow anything bad to happen to me. I really hope he can come home soon."

White smiled. "I'm glad you have someone besides Blue. If I hear or see anything the dog can't handle, you can trust that I will weigh in and protect you, too."

Shellie's voice came out as a whisper, "Thank you."

White rose.

"Mr. White, what time would you like breakfast?"

"Does 7:30 work for you?"

"Sounds good."

Shellie sat quietly. Her mind went back to her paper. About the only management thing she had done was work on finding accommodations for the overflow guests. She rinsed their cups, put them in the dishwasher and headed back to the *Manager's Cabin*. It took almost four hours to re-write the paper, emphasizing her decision-making in negotiating with the B&Bs and small motels. She sent it off without much hope that it would be enough.

Shellie sat at the small table near the stove and sipped coffee. She had watched for the lights to come on in *Loon Cabin* before preparing food and setting it in the warming trays. Mr. White arrived dressed in slacks, a dress shirt, and sport jacket. After loading his plate, he looked over at Shellie. "Mind if I join you?"

Shellie waved him into Ronan's chair and provided him with coffee.

"This food is great. These are real eggs, and everything is fresh, not warmed over; and fresh berries? Wow."

What did the man think, this was some kind of sleazy place? "Why wouldn't it be fresh and real?"

White waved his fork and swallowed. "You have no idea the kind of food I've been offered at some of the places I stayed. This is a real treat."

Mollified, Shellie asked, "What do you do that you travel so much?"

Her guest hesitated for an instant before answering. "I work for the State of New York. It involves a lot of travel."

Shellie warmed up her coffee and refilled White's cup. "We may be small, but we want to provide excellent service. "

"How long have you been open?"

"*The Pine Cone Motel* was built in the 1950s. The original owners had to close it about five years ago. My friend and I got permission to re-open it a few months back and we're looking to rebuild our clientele."

White nodded and continued to eat. "How are you going about increasing business?"

"Repeat business and a strong internet presence. The horse show people loved us, and we're already booked up for next year's horse shows. I'm hoping to have the same result with the Ironman contestants, rugby and lacrosse players and snowmobile riders."

"You're not looking for guests from people driving by?"

Shellie waved at the front window. "Not with the current situation with the pool. People take one look and keep going. Besides, most people make reservations online before travelling nowadays."

After cleaning his plate, he settled back in his chair and sipped his coffee, a slight smile on his face. White drained the last few drops waving away Shellie's gesture with the pot offering a refill. "I better get on the road. Did you happen to find a place that will be available later this week?"

Shellie stood, too. "Yes, *The Rambling Rose B&B* is holding a room for you. They're on Old Military Road if you want to stop by and check them out."

Shellie cleaned up the kitchen and then took care of *Loon Cabin*. She collected her reusable grocery bags. "Blue. Let's go to the farmer's market and see what we can find to feed hungry rugby players."

Chapter 24

Ronan hurried to join the group session. He was late. He knew he was grinning like the Cheshire Cat and he didn't care. Life was good.

As soon as he dropped into a chair, Andrew piped up, "I told you so."

A chorus of male laughter echoed off the walls and Ronan joined in.

"So, when are you going home?" Andrew asked.

" I'm late because I was packing and lost track of time. I'm ready to go home."

Joe spoke. "So, the only issue was whether your girlfriend would dump you because of your scars?"

Ronan inhaled sharply. "No. I never really doubted Shellie. She's been a rock of stability through everything."

Joe gave Ronan the look he'd come to expect from commanding officers. "Then why are you here?"

It felt like Ronan's heart had stopped beating. Chills ran up and down his spine. Ronan dropped his head into his hands and closed his eyes. "You're right. Nothing has changed."

"Hey, don't give up," Andrew growled. "That dog of yours is your ticket to a real life."

Ronan looked at him. "What has Blue got to do with this?"

"Here, look at this website." Andrew passed over his phone. "They train veteran-owned dogs to be service dogs and help guys like us to live around other people."

Joe grinned. "Didn't you say your dog would wake you out of nightmares and pull you back when you had a flashback?"

Ronan's hands shook. He nodded.

"Go ahead and make the call, but put it on speaker. We all want a piece of this."

Ronan pressed the dial button. "Good morning, this is 'Help a Vet'."

Ronan cleared his throat. "I'm a veteran and I have my retired MWD. I have PTSD and my dog has helped me a lot. I'd like to train and certify him as a service dog."

"First, let me say, I applaud your efforts to help yourself, I must tell you a Military Working Dog has a much different skill set than a service dog and would not be suitable for this kind of work. In addition, since the dog is retired, it would be too old to bring into the program."

"The dog is young, only four years old. He was injured pulling me from a burning Humvee. He's helped me since I left the service."

"Since the dog was released due to injuries, it's most likely the dog has his own version of PTSD and is not a viable candidate for a service dog."

Ronan closed his eyes and shook his head. So much for hope.

Andrew brought Ronan back to the present with a hiss. "Ask if she has suggestions for what you should do."

"Okay, if you won't train my dog, what do you suggest I do?"

"If you really like your old canine partner I would suggest you get a puppy from his breeder. Send it to us and we will train it for you."

All the guys smiled and gave Ronan the thumbs up sign.

"How long is the training?"

"It takes about two years."

"What am I supposed to do in the mean time?"

"Keep working with the local doctors and psychologists. It should give you the time you need to place your MWD in a new home."

Ronan looked at the phone like it was the serpent of Eden. Place Blue? Not happening. "Why can't I keep both dogs?"

"The older canine may bully the younger service dog. Even if it doesn't, the service dog will be torn between helping you and helping the military working dog through its PTSD."

Ronan inhaled and exhaled deeply a few times to level his emotions and steady his voice. "Thank you for your time." He couldn't keep the sarcasm out of his voice as he added, " You've been a wealth of information."

Ronan disconnected the call and handed the phone back to Andrew. No one would meet his eyes and the guys shuffled their feet and shifted in their chairs.

Joe broke the silence. "Well, that bites."

Andrew shook his head. "I don't get it. You see all these things about people listing their pets as support dogs, even though they have no training and don't really do anything. You've got a dog that helps you and it can't be certified. It doesn't make sense."

The guys in the circle growled their agreement and nodded.

Joe looked at Ronan. "There must be some way around this. Let me do some research."

"Okay, but I have to start thinking about going home and getting back to work. I can't heap everything on Shellie while I sit around with my thumb in my ear, especially not for two years."

Shellie looked at her emails and clicked down the list. Only one of the rugby reservations had been cancelled, but three of the lacrosse had as well, at no charge, after being informed of the alcohol policy. If she couldn't fill them, it was distinctly possible they would miss the income requirements Henry had placed on them.

She had made the email chatty and added the alcohol policy as an, "oh by the way" attachment. One of the questions she asked was which teams they were representing and what were the team colors. Mrs. McClelland was right; all the rugby reservations were from the same team. Shellie made a mental note to get blue and yellow crepe paper streamers and balloons to decorate the *Dining Cabin* in the team colors. She pulled up the match information from the event website and set up a whiteboard from the craft room to list match times and scores. She would hang it over the fireplace before the guests started to arrive.

Shellie quickly changed the hotel status from "booked up" to space available on the booking sites for the lacrosse tournament and changed into her uniform. As she walked down the driveway, Mr. White pulled in and she flagged him down. He rolled down the window and smiled, but he looked tired.

"Mr. White, you're in luck. We had a cancelation so if you would like to stay for the whole two weeks, *Loon Cabin* is available."

White puffed out a deep breath and closed his eyes for an instant. "That's the first good news I've had today. I much prefer the cabin and your breakfasts to the B&B. I stopped over there, and they were serving powdered eggs and instant coffee."

Shellie smiled. Now if she could get two more lacrosse reservations they would be back to full.

White scanned her outfit. "Where are you off to? That looks like a hotel uniform. I thought you worked here, or does that mean you're on duty now?"

"I work nights at *Lakeside Resort and Hotel*. I'll be back a little after midnight. If you need anything, feel free to call the main line. It will ring on my cell phone."

White's concerned expression gave Shellie a warm feeling. "I don't like the idea of a young lady walking home at that hour. If you would like me to pick you up, I don't mind. I promise to be a gentleman."

Childhood warnings about riding with strangers strobed across Shellie's mind. "Thank you. I'll be fine. Blue goes with me."

Shellie stepped back while White continued and parked. He really was a nice man, and she probably would have been safe, but she couldn't bring herself to accept his offer.

She clocked in and Blue took up his position under the registration desk. His sable coat blended with the shadows, making him almost invisible. There was a quick flurry exchanging information with the shift workers going off duty and then the evening settled into the normal, quiet routine. Shellie had the rugby team roster open when Kelly walked up.

"Hey, lady. How was your vacation?" Shellie asked.

"Absolute heaven. At least it was until I got Dr. Sampson's comments on my paper."

Shellie rolled her eyes. "I so understand. She bombed my paper, too."

Another employee, Joel, hurried over to them. He gave Kelly a big smile and stared into her eyes. "Hi, Kelly. I'm glad you're back. We really missed you."

Shelley looked down at the keyboard to hide her smile as the two people looked with longing at each other. Both had confided in Shellie that they had a crush on the other. They were so sweet together, it made Shellie ache. Had she ever been that innocent and in love? The answer came crashing in on her; just a few months ago she had looked at Chad the way Kelly looked at Joel. At least Joel gave the look back to Kelly. Still, she would have to pull the boy aside and have a discussion with him. She didn't want Kelly to end up like her.

She must have been frowning because when Joel looked her way, his expression seemed startled and he took a slight step back. "What were you guys talking about?"

Kelly did a theatrical eye roll and heavy sigh. "Our emails from Dr. Sampson."

"Yuck. She's a professor you'd love to miss, but her internship class is a requirement. I hope you signed up to include the classroom portion instead of just the paper."

"I did," Kelly answered. "Why?"

Joel looked around and then lowered his voice. "The college is small, and students liked to go home over the summer and work locally instead of staying in the Adirondacks and trying to find someplace they can afford to live. The administration realized that and wanted to accommodate the students, so they gave them the option of classroom time and a paper or a write in paper with weekly updates."

Shellie leaned closer. She had opted out of the classroom portion, so she could have more time for the *Pine Cone Motel*.

Joel continued. "The word around campus is Sampson was furious and went to the administration claiming they were undermining her authority and ability to teach. When she got vetoed, she began failing any student that opted out of classroom time and making them take the class twice as payback."

Kelly shuddered. "I didn't know that. I thought I'd made a mistake signing up for the classroom time because she's always in such a bad mood and ranting about things like politics and stuff that have nothing to do with hotel management."

Joel nodded. "Keep your head down and agree with her opinions or she'll single you out and spend the rest of the semester picking on you."

Kelly leaned on the desk. "I think it's too late for that. She bombed the first draft of my paper. I don't know what she wants. She works with *Lakeside* employees all the time. She has to know we don't have much authority to make decisions."

Joel patted Kelly's shoulder comfortingly. "She does that to everyone on the first draft. You'll get through."

Their radios crackled. "Can someone come to the restaurant and help set up for a large party arriving in ten minutes?"

Joel spoke into his microphone. "This is Joel. On my way."

He waved as he hurried toward the restaurant.

"What are you going to do?" Shellie asked.

Kelly turned back from watching Joel. "I said I would do an analysis of the corporate procedures against the special conditions of a small resort town hotel. She told me to give her a rough draft and if it contained what I would do as a manager to address the issues it might be enough to get a passing grade."

Shellie patted Kelly's arm. "That's a great idea."

"What are you going to do?"

A flash on the screen indicated Shellie had an email from Dr. Sampson. "Speak of the devil. I rewrote my paper talking about negotiating with the smaller places for our overflow guests. Dr. Sampson just replied."

Shellie opened the email and fought to keep her expression pleasant.

Kelly stood up on tiptoe, trying to see the monitor. "What did she say?"

Shellie swallowed hard. "She said it's not enough."

Kelly's face looked as stricken as Shellie felt. "What are you going to do?"

"I don't know."

Kelly went back to walking the floor. Shellie fought back tears. Couldn't anything ever work for her? She wished she could call Ronan or someone who would understand.

By the time her shift was over, she still hadn't come up with a solution. She walked into the motel driveway and paused to admire the sign. While the cost of all that neon was exorbitant, it gave her a good feeling knowing she and Ronan had brought the old place life, at least for a little while. They still had to come up with enough money to prevent Henry from bulldozing all of it.

Shellie continued walking and gave herself a mental shake. When had she become such a Debbie downer? A couple of lacrosse reservations and a concert or two and they would make it.

Mr. White sat in one of the rockers on his porch. He waved. "I couldn't sleep."

His concern eased some of Shellie's tension. "Would you like to join me for hot chocolate?"

"Love to." White waited until she had entered the *Dining Cabin* before leaving his chair.

As they sipped cocoa, Shellie asked, "You looked tired when you came in. I hope watching for me won't make tomorrow more difficult."

White smiled. "No, not at all. I just finished talking to my daughter when I pulled in and she informed me she wanted to change her major, again. I love her dearly and I want her to be happy, but this is the third time she's changed majors. I don't think this will give her any better chance of getting a decent job than the other two. I don't know what to do. Is it unfair of me to expect her to get a degree with a good potential for a decent paying job?"

Shellie thought for a moment trying to put herself in the other girl's shoes. The answer came immediately. "Tell her your concerns."

"I don't want to discourage her from following her dreams."

"How different is this major?"

"The first was bio-tech, but the chemistry courses were too much for her to handle. The second one was photography. I had my suspicions she took that to be in the same classes as her boyfriend. She recently broke up with him and now she wants a degree in literature. Am I a bad dad to think this change is because she is dating a guy who writes poetry?"

Shellie fought back a giggle. Many of her friends changed majors to take classes with their "true love" only to break up with him halfway through the semester. She might have done the same if her dad hadn't insisted on selecting her major. "I think you might try addressing her as an adult."

White frowned. "What do you mean?"

"Until I was out on my own, I never thought about college as a means to a career, or for that matter a job. All I focused on was getting through as fast as possible with the best grades I could get. Suddenly I had to support myself and my college skills were no help in getting a job."

"So, I tell her it's a mean world out here? I've already done that. I don't think she heard me or understands what I am trying to tell her."

"She wants to switch to literature, you said? Ask her what kind of job she will get when she finishes her degree. Can she live on that income? Is it something she would want to do for the rest of her life?" Shellie paused to catch her breath. "Suggest she do some interning. It wasn't until I started working that I realized how much I liked hospitality management. It was a career I never imagined."

"And that will change her mind?"

"I don't know her, so I can't give you any guarantees. But do you think it will hurt your relationship?"

"Is this the speech your dad gave you?"

"No. I wish he had. Now I'm stuck and my whole college career depends on a course I can't find a way to pass."

"What's the course?"

"Hotel Management. I must write a paper based on my experience as an employee of the *Lakeside Resort and Hotel*. The problem is as a night clerk I'm not part of management and can't make management decisions. The professor said, unless I can show my ability to manage I'll get a failing grade."

"Why does it have to be about *Lakeside Resort and Hotel*?"

"What else could it be?"

"How about *Pine Cone Motel*? From what I've seen, you make the management decisions here. Reopening a facility after it's been closed several years, drawing in clientele and making policies that create repeat business, creating a marketing plan and applying for a grant to fix the pool are all management activities."

Shellie's brain froze for an instant, then started firing on all cylinders. "How did you know about the grant for the pool?"

White smiled at her. "I wasn't going to say anything because I didn't want you to give me special treatment. I've already learned what I needed to know; your application for the grant is real and it will make a difference in your business." He looked down and played with his mug, then looked back up at her. "You see, I'm the person who approves the grants. The reason I'm here is to verify they will go to the right places. I submitted the approval for *Pine Cone Motel* and rejected two other places today. You should get the official letter in a few days, but I can tell you, the money is as good as in the bank."

A million questions flashed across Shellie's mind. She latched onto one to stop her brain from spinning. "Why did you approve us and not the others?"

"They weren't real businesses."

"What do you mean?"

"The purpose of the grant is to get the small, abandoned hotels and motels back up and running. It creates business and jobs in a depressed area. The ones I rejected were closed motels with no intention of re-opening. The owners were looking for money to bulldoze the sites and sell them. The places were run down and infested with bugs and mice and would take a small fortune to get back into operation."

"What if they got the money and didn't use it to re-open?"

White expression became grim. "We would track them down and require repayment plus interest and a penalty. This isn't a game to waste taxpayers' money. We're trying to revitalize the Adirondacks."

"I didn't think I made a very good first impression."

White grinned. "It was memorable. Finding out you were booked up told me you were in business. Hearing your plans to create repeat business told me you intend to stay in business. It didn't take a genius to recognize the positive impact fixing your pool would make. *Pine Cone Motel* is exactly the kind of business we want to help."

White stood. "I better get some sleep; I need to check on three other applicants tomorrow."

Shellie sat staring into her empty mug. Tomorrow she would call Mrs. McClelland and tell her they had gotten the grant. She debated telling Ronan and decided against it. Maybe she could get the work done before Ronan came back, so he wouldn't have to run into his father. He'd seemed so much better when she visited, she didn't want to derail his progress.

Shellie rubbed her tired eyes. She needed to consider what to do about her paper. She had made a point of keeping her job at the *Pine Cone* secret from the staff of *Lakeside* out of fear she would be fired for conflict of interest or that they would worry she would be too exhausted to perform properly. Dr. Sampson clearly had close associations with Mrs. Anderson. What would happen if the professor mentioned Shellie's second job? Still part of the reason to get the pool fixed was to get on the chain hotels overflow list. When that happened, they would find out she worked here.

If she didn't take White's suggestion, she would fail the class and not be able to complete her degree—again. That would keep her in low paying jobs and back where she started; always one step away from homelessness and hunger. There really wasn't a choice. She would have to take the risk. If *Lakeside Resort and Hotel* did fire her, at least if she had her degree, her options at better, future jobs would be improved.

Chapter 25

Ronan rolled out of his rack and scrubbed his face with his hands. Sitting here with little or nothing to do made his skin crawl and his nerves vibrate. He wanted to go fishing or hunting or move a bunch of stock or pull weeds. Well, maybe not pull weeds. He wasn't that desperate, yet.

Twice-a-day group sessions and conforming to the cleanliness requirements for his room and person killed time, but didn't take the kind of physical energy he usually expended. He'd taken to spending hours in the weight room to fill the time.

He smiled to himself. He missed Shellie and Blue and the freedom living at the *Pine Cone Motel* gave them. Right now, if he was home, they would be having breakfast and planning the week. The rugby players should be checked in and Shellie would have her hands full. He didn't like dumping everything to do with the motel on Shellie. That wasn't fair.

What if the players got too friendly and scared her? She had been making great strides under the guidance of Dr. Parish. That bothered him, too. Without his salary Shellie had to do without the help she needed while he was stuck here sitting on his hands.

Then there was Henry and his plan for the motel. He and Shellie included using part of Ronan's salary to cover expenses. The plan had been tight before, not having his salary could make the difference of keeping the place open or both of them being homeless again. He needed to get out of here.

Ronan reached for his phone. Maybe talking to Shellie would help.

"*Pine Cone Motel*, this is Shellie, may I help you?"

"You already did, Angel. Hearing your voice makes my whole day."

Shellie laughed. "It's eight in the morning, there's a lot of day left."

"How are things going?"

"Wonderful and a little scary."

Ronan tensed, focusing in on her voice, trying to read if she was holding back. "Scary how?"

Silence.

He didn't like her hesitation. "Don't hold out on me. I don't need protecting. I'm not that crazy."

"Ronan, you've never been crazy. Flashbacks, yes. Crazy, no."

The exasperation in her voice made him smile. She wasn't handling him with kid gloves. His Angel made him feel like a whole man, not a shadow of the one he had been. "So, what's scary?"

"I got a grant to fix the pool. Now I'm afraid of what will happen if we don't meet Henry's demands, but I spend the money to make the repairs."

Ronan jumped to his feet. "What? When? How?"

"The horse show people said the pool was a real drawback and made them hesitate to plan on staying here in the future. After they left, I went on-line and found an application for a state grant for capital improvements of small motels. I didn't mention it because I didn't think we would get it. We passed the inspection and I got a letter saying we were approved and the funds would be transferred shortly."

"Have you chosen a contractor?"

Silence again.

"Shellie?"

Her breath rattled through the phone. "Should I spend the money or return the grant until we're sure Henry isn't going to shut us back down?"

"If you return the grant will it be there when we know for sure where we stand?"

"Probably not."

"With the pool fixed we would have a real chance at the drive-by reservations and we could develop a relationship with the big hotels for the overflow. I think it's worth the risk."

"You're right, but it's still scary."

Ronan's heart thumped in his chest like he'd sprinted a couple of miles. He had the same fears, but if they held back they would fail and Shellie had made a huge step forward in making it possible to meet Henry's demands. "I don't think we have a choice in the matter. You need to hire a contractor."

Ronan wished he was there. He was comfortable dealing with contractors. There were too many of them that would take advantage of Shellie.

"Your dad's company is the only one who does that work in this area. I got the estimate for the grant through him. He—he asked about you."

"Yeah, I'll bet." Ronan ran his hand through his hair. "I was going to suggest you hire him. His guys do good work and he stands behind what he builds."

"I didn't want to, on principle."

Her attitude made him laugh. Trust his Angel to champion him. "Oh Angel, I miss you."

He heard her sniff. "I miss you, too. You really don't mind if I hire your dad?"

"I don't mind at all. Are the rugby players behaving?"

It was Shellie's turn to laugh. "*Pine Cone Motel* has turned into a New Jersey team's command center and all it took was a few balloons, and streamers in the team colors and the use of a white board for game notices. I have to say their songs make me blush, but they are very polite and not at all pushy like I was expecting. The only arguments are other teams trying to hire us for next year. We're already booked up for the coming year's tournament."

Relief flowed over Ronan. Shellie was safe. "You've got your hands full. How about I call and get my dad's company started on the pool?"

"That would be a huge help. Between both jobs, and completely rewriting my paper, I feel like I'm pulled in a hundred different directions. But are you sure you want to talk to your dad?"

"Why are you rewriting your paper?"

"Long story, mostly it's because the professor enjoys making students sweat and grovel for a passing grade. It won't be a problem for me to call your dad. You need to focus on getting well."

Ronan would be just as happy to keep his distance from his family, but for Shellie he'd face them. "Not a problem. I'll take care of it."

Ronan took a minute to settle himself before dialing the number he knew by heart. It wasn't the office number. It was his dad's private line. "Hello, Dad."

"Ronan. How are you doing?"

Was that excitement in his dad's voice?

"I'm doing a lot better. How's Mom?"

"She misses you."

Ronan opened his mouth, but before he could get a word out his dad continued. "I miss you, too."

That comment took out Ronan's knees. He dropped to his bed. "It had to be that way. I wasn't safe to be around."

"I met your young lady, she's quite the firecracker. I like her."

"Shellie's an angel, with a temper."

His dad laughed with him. It was a phrase Dad used to describe Ronan's mom.

"Dad, we got the grant for the pool repairs to the motel. I'd like you to start working on it as soon as you can get it into the schedule."

"Hang on while I pull up the estimate." Ronan heard keys clicking. "I have the basic materials in stock. I'll authorize the purchase of the specialty items. We're getting into the high season, so the lead times are getting out there. Let me see if I can expedite them."

"We don't have the funds for expedited charges. Much as I want the thing fixed fast, we're going to have to wait. There's no room in the budget."

"I'll tell you what. If you can supervise the job, I'll absorb the rush charges on any parts."

Ronan hesitated. The sooner they were done the better. He didn't know how much longer he would be in the hospital and once he got out, he needed to get back to his old job. "When were you looking to start it?"

"Jamie's wife had a baby so I have his whole crew he supervises available. I was going to spread them out on other jobs until he came back, but if you can supervise, I can have them over there on Monday morning. Your project should be finished about the time he's ready to come back."

Monday? Today was Thursday. Still, they needed this. "I'll be there."

Chapter 26

Friday morning Shellie sat in the office updating the accounting program Ronan had installed before he went into the V.A. The rugby players had left. She had two days before the lacrosse players started to arrive. She finished making the transfer of funds to Henry's account for the motel and switched over to check her emails. There were some additional queries about reservations from families of ice skaters looking to train at the Olympic Arena. Shellie answered quickly and chewed her fingernail as she considered how to make the *Pine Cone Motel* desirable to the skating crowd. She'd have to spend some time over at the arena.

A new email popped up from Dr Sampson and she clicked on it. *The purpose of this class is to use actual experience as a measure of hotel management ability, not fantasy. The idea of re-opening one of the many abandoned motels is ludicrous. Claiming to be part of the management of such an enterprise when I am well aware of your current position with Lakeside Resort and Hotel indicates a problem with veracity and good judgement on your part. We are rapidly coming to the end of the semester and I do not see any potential for you to achieve a passing grade. Frankly, I am considering contacting the hotel to review your employment with them.*

Air caught in Shellie's lungs and choked in her throat until her vision disappeared in a black and red haze. She never would have expected Doctor Sampson to give her such a mean-spirited, arrogant comment. Blue jumped in her lap and frantically licked her face. Shellie coughed and inhaled deeply. Her vision returned and with it an anger more intense than she had ever known. Without hesitation, she hit the reply button and hammered out her reply.

Dr. Sampson, your assumption this paper is fiction provides me with a view of just how out of touch you are with the reality of life as a hotel clerk in a resort town. We are not paid a living wage. Even sharing lodging with several other people, a night clerk's salary barely covers the rent. Unlike most of my co-workers I do not have parents helping with my financial support, so I had to become creative to put a roof over my head as well as food on my table. That meant opening the closed and shuttered Pine Cone Motel for business. I invite you to contact Mrs. McClelland in Florida who owns the property or Mr. Ernest White at the NYS Business Development Center to verify that indeed I am responsible for the management of this facility. Or if you prefer, you are welcome to stop by anytime during the day and see for yourself how real my paper is at presenting my management skills. Unfortunately, I work a second job nights at the Lakeside Resort and Hotel and am not available to provide a tour during those hours.

Shellie knew she should wait and not hit send, but she'd had enough. If she was going to fail, it might as well be in a blaze of glory. Her hands shook as she reached for her empty glass, knocking it over. She quickly righted it, stood, and headed for the *Dining Cabin*. Maybe a cool drink would steady her nerves.

She collected her phone, her fingers itched to call Ronan. He was so good at making her believe everything would be all right and she needed someone to talk her off the ledge. After hesitating, she slipped the device into her pocket and headed for the door. She was not going to bother Ronan with her petty problems.

Shellie stepped off the porch as a strange car pulled into the parking lot. She paused to see if she needed to return to the *Manager's Cabin* or if it was a driver who needed a place to turn around. A man stepped out and pulled a duffle bag from the back seat before waving as the car drove off with a quick beep of the horn. He looked at her and grinned.

Shellie dropped the glass and flew into Ronan's arms, hugging and sobbing into his neck. Ronan gave her a squeeze and kissed the top of her head. Blue danced around them, his tail wagging so fast it made circles in the air while he barked and tugged at Ronan's pant leg and jumped up on both of them.

Gently, Ronan disengaged from Shellie's hug, but kept one arm on her shoulder. Blue took the opportunity to leap into the air, landing with his front paws on Ronan's shoulder. Ronan used his free arm to support the excited canine which was a slight tactical error. With both arms full, he couldn't defend himself against the big, wet tongue slobbering over his face and into his ear.

"Blue! Enough!" Ronan laughed as he tried without success to dodge dog kisses.

Shellie laughed and sidestepped so Ronan had a hand free. Ronan dropped Blue to the ground and recaptured Shellie's hand, swinging it back and forth as they walked to the *Manager's Cabin*.

"What are you doing back?"

Ronan slipped the duffle onto his shoulder. "I talked to my dad and they can start on the pool on Monday if I supervise the construction, so here I am."

Shellie stopped. What risks was Ronan taking for their sake? "Is that wise? Getting you back to one hundred percent is more important than getting the pool finished."

Ronan leaned on the counter. "I don't know if it's wise, but I have to try. I felt I had hit the limit of what would help me at the hospital. In the controlled environment, there weren't any triggers so there was no testing to figure out if the skills I learned would help diffuse a flashback."

He looked around the office and Shellie could see him visibly relax.

"I was getting tense and uncomfortable sitting around the hospital with nothing to do. Being here, I feel like I can sleep and eat and be myself. I need physical work. I wasn't getting that there."

Shellie watched him closely, trying to determine if he was putting on a show for her or if he meant the words. There was no one in the world she trusted more than Ronan. "Have you had breakfast?"

Ronan laughed. "Nothing as good as your cooking. Let me drop my gear and I'll meet you in the *Dining Cabin.*"

An hour later they lingered over their flavored water, quiet, after the flurry of conversation sharing their news. Ronan took the opportunity to study Shellie. He had an almost overwhelming desire to lean closer and kiss those luscious pink lips. Knowing what she had gone through and the fear any form of intimacy brought kept him glued to the back of his chair.

When she came to the hospital, she'd been dressed up and wearing makeup. Today, though Shellie relaxed in shorts and tee shirt and no cosmetics, she still looked beautiful, but he could see the dark circles under her eyes and the pallor of her skin. The toll on Shellie of handling everything confirmed his decision to come home and help. Clearly, she was exhausted.

After she had told him about her paper a dozen ideas ran through his head to help her, including grabbing her supercilious professor by the neck and dragging her out to see what Shellie had created at the motel. Of course, he wouldn't act on his thoughts, but the fantasy helped. The fact of the matter was Shellie had good reason to be stressed and not sleeping well. The real question was how to get her to relax and let him help.

"If the crew is going to be here on Monday, I better get a hold of Henry to transfer the first half of the project cost. That was the agreed deposit."

"What does Henry have to do with this?"

"The check had to be made out to the motel owner, which is Mrs. McClelland. The State would only direct deposit into an account either in Mrs. McClelland's name or listed to *Pine Cone Motel,* so I gave the motel account number Henry used while the motel was closed -- the same one we've been paying into for the taxes."

Ronan nodded. The thought of trusting Henry made him nervous, but he couldn't explain why.

Shellie stood. "Let's head over to the office. I have the paperwork there and I'll need to give Henry the exact amount."

Ronan refilled his glass and followed Shellie. She put her phone on speaker and dialed Henry. It rolled to voice mail. "That's funny. I've tried to call him the past couple of days and he never answers. Do you think he's avoiding my calls?"

Ronan shrugged to indicate his uncertainty. "Give Mrs. McClelland a call."

Keeping the phone on speaker, Shellie quickly dialed.

"Hello, Shellie, dear. How are things up north?"

"Sunny and warm, but probably not as warm as Florida right now."

"Oh my, don't you know it. You have no idea what I wouldn't give to be able to sit on the motel patio and enjoy a cool breeze. There's no point in going outside here; we're hunkered down in the air conditioning and waiting for the cooler weather to come."

The older woman's comment made Ronan laugh. "You know you're always welcome to come back, but then you'll have the opposite problem of waiting through the winter for the weather to warm up."

"Ronan, are you there, too? It's so good to hear your voice."

Ronan smiled at the genuine warmth in Mrs. McClelland's words. "Yes ma'am, it's good to talk to you, too."

Shellie and Ronan exchanged smiles. She raised her eyebrow and pointed to her chest. Ronan nodded and gestured for her to continue.

"Mrs. McClelland, do you know where Henry is? I called him the last few days and I haven't been able to reach him."

"He left a couple of days ago on a golf junket. They're going to travel to several places in Europe, ending at St. Andrews in Scotland. I don't think he's going to be reachable for another week or more. He didn't want to spend the fees for his phone to work in Europe. Is it something I can do?"

Shellie hesitated, then spoke. "The construction to fix the pool is starting on Monday. We need a check for half of the project cost to give to the construction company when they start."

"I'll tell you what, I have a checkbook for the motel account. Henry doesn't want me writing checks, but under the circumstances, I don't see any alternative."

Shellie thanked Mrs. McClelland, gave her the information for the check and hung up. She closed her eyes and rubbed her temples like she had a headache.

"Why don't you take a nap?"

She hesitated, but clearly the idea sounded appealing. "I was going to catch up on washing the linens and start getting the cabins ready for the lacrosse guests, so it wouldn't be a rush."

Ronan gently cupped her elbow, helped her to stand, and turned her toward her room. "I can do that. I need some physical work and that's the perfect recipe."

Shellie still hesitated.

"Shellie, let me feel like I belong and have value. You don't have to do it all."

She nodded and shuffled off to her room. The door closed with a soft click of the latch. Ronan was alone, he'd rather have been with Shellie, but clearly, she was dead on her feet.

Silence wrapped him in loving arms and he took a few minutes to savor his memories of the woman in the next room. He stepped out onto the porch and leaned on the railing, listening to the bird songs and the soft hum of insects. The smell of pines underlaid with the linseed oil on the log walls filled his nostrils. Sheltered from the sun by the porch roof, the warm rays reflecting off the gravel parking lot heated the air around him.

He glanced down the row of buildings. A sense of pride filled him. Was it only a few months ago the cabins had been slowly disintegrating? Now they gleamed, the logs clean and freshly stained, the porches dressed in new paint and sporting rocking chairs begging for someone to 'sit a spell'.

From the looks of the linen bin, Shellie had started at *Loon Cabin* and was working her way toward the *Manager's Cabin*. She'd finished about half the cabins already. Ronan pushed off the railing and headed to work whistling, Blue glued to his side. He was home.

Shellie awoke and stretched. She had needed the rest, but her happy mood couldn't be entirely attributed to the extra sleep. She had missed Ronan sitting across the table and really listening to her and her ideas. While they sat there she'd had an almost overwhelming urge to lean over and press her lips to his. She shook her head, more evidence of her wanton nature. Her dad was right, she was shameless, at least when it came to Ronan.

Groggily, she rolled over to check the time. One look and she jerked to a sitting position. "That can't be right."

A second look at her phone confirmed she'd slept for four hours. She threw the covers back, yanked on her clothes and raced out the sliding glass door. Her cleaning supplies and the linen bin were no-where in sight and the parking lot was empty.

Where was Ronan? Had she dreamed his return?

No sign of Blue, either. That had to mean Ronan was back. The dog wouldn't have left her side otherwise.

Shellie walked over to the *Dining Cabin*. The back door stood open, letting a cool breeze waft through the screen. She stepped onto the patio. Ronan had made significant headway weeding the vegetable garden, something Shellie hadn't had time to do. A movement by the river drew her attention. Ronan stood on the dock casting a fishing rod while Blue dozed nearby in the sun. Ronan smiled quietly at her as he reeled in line. "Feel better?"

"Much, but you shouldn't have let me sleep so long. There's too much work to do."

Ronan cast again. "Like what?"

"Clean the cabins."

"Done."

"Do the laundry."

"Done."

Shellie couldn't come up with more chores.

Ronan grinned and set the pole aside. "How about making dinner? Grilled fish and a salad?"

Shellie shook her head. He had her. "I'll go make the salad."

"It's already in the refrigerator. How about you pour the ice tea while I fire up the grill?"

Shellie hurried to set the table. It was good to have Ronan home.

As they lingered over the delicately grilled trout, she had an irresistible urge to touch Ronan, to feel his warmth physically as well as emotionally. His hand rested on the table and she covered it with hers. It startled him so much he stopped mid-sentence and stared into her eyes, then flipped his hand over to clasp her fingers. Electricity sparked between them. She couldn't have said if Ronan drew her closer or she moved of her own volition. All she knew was she was milliseconds from being clasped in his strong arms and she wanted it very much.

"Hello? Anybody in there? Shellie?"

Getting tossed into the river couldn't have chilled her more. Shellie dropped back into her seat while

Ronan stood, his chest rising and falling rapidly as his hands curled into fists and he faced the screen door.

"Out here, Mr. White." She looked over at Ronan wondering if he was having a flashback. The fact he made eye contact with her and raised an eyebrow with his unspoken question gave her the impression his agitation probably had more to do with the interruption than a trip into a nightmare world. "Mr. White is the person who approved our grant. He's staying in *Loon Cabin* while he evaluates other applicants."

The older man appeared in the doorway and hesitated. "I'm sorry, I didn't realize you had company."

Shellie stood and smiled at him. "Mr. White, I'd like to introduce you to Ronan Flanagan, my partner. We were celebrating his homecoming."

The older man looked Ronan up and down as if evaluating him, then smiled. "I'm sorry I interrupted, then. I'll head back to my cabin."

"No need. Why don't you sit and have some ice tea? I need to get changed for work."

Shellie opened the screen door and motioned White out. As she escaped to her room, she glanced over her shoulder to see both men sitting back and Ronan pouring tea. She told herself she was thankful for the interruption. Maybe if she told herself that enough times, she would come to believe it.

Chapter 27

Ronan and Blue walked Shellie to work.

"Wait for me in the lighted area, if I'm not here when you get out." Ronan reminded her.

Shellie gave him a big hug. "I'm so glad you're home. I missed you."

She practically danced through the doors to clock in. It felt like someone had lifted a two-hundred-pound weight from her shoulders. She didn't think she could stop smiling if her life depended on it.

Mr. Grady stepped into her path. "Miss Morgan. I would like a word with you."

Shellie followed him down the hall, her heart thumping double time. Was it possible she could be getting a raise? She'd been with the hotel almost six months and since she'd been on nights, she'd ended up acting as the manager, solving problems. If her income increased it might be the difference they needed to save the motel.

She stepped through the door and stopped. Mrs. Anderson sat beside Mr. Grady. She handled the human resources concerns. Yup, she was definitely getting a raise. Shellie gave the older woman a big smile. She got a frown in response.

Mr. Grady sat behind his desk and motioned Shellie into a chair facing the two managers. He turned and indicated Mrs. Anderson should speak.

"I understand you have some complaints about your salary and working conditions. If that is the case, you should have brought them to me or Mr. Grady, not aired them with an outsider. Do you have any idea how damaging your comments are to this facility?"

Shellie's mouth went dry. She opened her lips, but no sound came out. She swallowed and tried again.

So much for a raise. "I am assuming Dr. Sampson contacted you. I wrote a paper utilizing the management decisions I have been making for a small motel where I live. Dr. Sampson accused me of making it up and said no one working here would have a second job. The truth of the matter is, without the second job, my salary here would not pay for a place to rent. This is a resort area and the rents are exorbitant. I did not say I was underpaid, only that I could not live on my salary."

"You're working at another hotel?" exclaimed Grady. "How much of our confidential information are you sharing? Which of our competitors is this?"

Shelley realized her words had upset the man. She should have kept her mouth shut and left it with an apology.

"Well?" Grady demanded when Shellie remained silent.

"I'm not working at a hotel. A friend and I reopened one of the small cabin rentals on the way into town. It's *Pine Cone Motel*. There isn't anyone to share confidential information with even if I knew any."

Mrs. Anderson leaned back in her chair, arms folded over her chest. "So, you aren't using our procedures to manage the housekeeping and kitchen staff?"

"I am the housekeeping staff, and the accounting staff, and the reception staff. As for the kitchen staff, we only provide breakfast like the B&Bs this facility shifts overflow clients to and I do the cooking, mostly on a wood stove. So, there is no way to use the *Lakeside Resort and Hotel* systems and procedures if there was anyone besides me working."

"And what about this 'friend'?"

"Ronan does the repairs, cares for the garden and lawns and provides part of the expenses. Since he has an accounting degree, he also does most of the government reporting and transfers of funds to the owner of the motel."

"You're telling me you don't share any of our procedures with the owner?" Mrs. Anderson pressed.

"Mrs. McClelland is in her late eighties and living in a retirement facility in Florida. When I talk to her, she's sharing her decades of experience working in the hospitality business with me, not the other way around."

Grady looked down at his desk and then at Mrs. Anderson. He spoke to her in a low voice that Shellie had a feeling she wasn't supposed to hear. "I told you Sampson's comments needed to be taken with a grain of salt. This is not the first time she has made damaging comments about our employees taking her class."

Grady looked back at Shellie. When he spoke, his voice was much calmer. "I know Mrs. McClelland. You could share our bank account access and she wouldn't take advantage of the information."

Silence filled the room.

Grady looked at her. "I remember the *Pine Cone Motel* when it was one of the jewels of the Adirondacks. People returned year after year. It was their summer home. As the couple got older and people started taking shorter Adirondack vacations, they tended to stay at larger full-service facilities like ours. I wasn't totally surprised when the *Pine Cone Motel* closed, but I was saddened by its demise. I had seen that the sign was lit when I drove by, but I didn't realize the place was open. I seldom see cars there. If you are running it as you described, why haven't you approached me to get on the overflow list? I would imagine you need the business."

"*Lakeside Resort and Hotel* has very strict and specific requirements for the overflow list. The pool at

the *Pine Cone Motel* does not meet those requirements.
We have been awarded a grant and the repairs will start
next week. I wouldn't dream of asking to be on the overflow list until we are the kind of facility this hotel's
guests expect."

Mr. Grady nodded and looked down at a paper on
his desk. The silence grew. Shellie wondered if she
should ask to be excused. What was the proper protocol
for exiting this kind of interview?

Mrs. Anderson shifted in her chair and glanced at
Mr. Grady. He gave a negative head shake which seemed
to make her even more annoyed. "While we may be satisfied, you aren't spreading gossip or disseminating confidential information, I for one am concerned as to how
well you are able to function for us when you work a difficult and tiring second job. Tell me, how often do you
sleep here when you are supposed to be working?"

"I have never slept on the job or been anything
other than professional. Ask Kelly or the chef or anyone
else on nights."

Mrs. Anderson tilted her head and looked over
her glasses. "Well, that is the problem, isn't it? We don't
have anyone on nights other than your coworkers to really determine if you are doing your job or not."

"I am not a liar or a shirker."

Mr. Grady and Mrs. Andersons exchanged looks.
Shellie got the impression they weren't in agreement.

Mrs. Anderson shifted in her chair and focused
her gaze on Shellie. "Under the circumstances I feel it is
necessary to put you on probation and move you to the
day shift, so we can observe first hand how much or how
little you are doing for the very reasonable salary we are
paying you."

Mrs. Anderson's emphasis on the word 'reasonable' was not lost on Shellie. If Ronan went back to work in the store, that meant neither of them could be at the motel during the primary time when people checked in. Their ability to run the motel would be seriously impacted, but without both of their salaries they wouldn't be able to raise the funds Henry required to keep him from bulldozing the place. She'd have to handle one disaster at a time. The first task was to stay employed.

One look told Shellie they'd made the decision before she ever entered the room. She got the feeling Mr. Grady might have changed his mind, but wouldn't stand up to Mrs. Anderson, at least not in front of Shellie. Score one more for Dr. Sampson messing with her life.

"When do you want me to switch?"

"You get off at midnight. Shift workers must have eight hours between shifts so be back here at eight o'clock tomorrow morning." Mr. Grady made a shooing motion with his hand to indicate she was dismissed.

Shellie scuffed her way to the reception desk. She arrived as Kelly finished checking in a new guest.

"Where have you been? Grady will have your head for being late."

"I was in Grady's office. They put me on probation and shifted me to days."

"Why?"

"Good old Dr. Sampson told them I was working a second job. Now they think I'm goofing off and sleeping here at night."

Kelly stomped her foot. "That's so unfair! You never do anything like that. The rest of us hide out sometimes and play video games, but you're always on the desk smiling and helping guests. When we don't know what to do we come to you at night instead of calling

Grady. For all intents and purposes, you're the night manager."

"I'm learning the hard way life isn't fair."

"I've a mind to go in there and tell them how wrong they are."

"Don't," Shellie warned. "Sampson made them think I was gossiping and complaining. If you go in there, it will prove her point."

"It's still not fair," Kelly grumbled.

Shellie agreed with her one hundred percent.

Saturday morning, Shellie left for work. It bothered Ronan she had to do such a quick turnaround, but he kept his thoughts to himself so she wouldn't be even more upset. Ronan began prepping for the lacrosse players, whistling a country tune. He could feel the tension leaving his muscles. It was easier to breathe because he was home. Home. It was something he dreamed about while deployed, and yet when he came home his childhood house ceased to be a refuge and became a different kind of battlefield. When he and Blue had moved into *Loon Cabin,* it had been enough shelter to survive. The lack of running water and electricity made the place barely livable. Their existence had been a daily struggle against longer and longer odds.

He glanced around at the sparkling clean room. Shellie had changed all of that. Who would have thought the half-drowned waif he'd decided to let take shelter from the rain could make such a difference? She'd brought with her hope and the spark of a dream that he might be able to have some semblance of a normal life. She looked at him with trust not fear, despite all that had happened to her and was an amazing combination of energy, dreams and practicality that made him want to be a better man.

He and Shellie might have breathed life into the old motel, but it had become a haven for the two of them. This was home and hope and the glimmer of light in the darkness that whispered he did have a future. The thought of the *Pine Cone Motel* being bulldozed was intolerable. They had to find a way to get Henry the tax money.

A nudge to his thigh brought Ronan out of his reverie. Blue wouldn't let Ronan out of his sight. Every time Ronan tried to take a step he tripped over the dog until he finally ordered Blue into the corner. The dog hung his head and slowly shuffled over to his blanket, settling with a thump and a deep sigh. Ronan softened the time out command with a soup bone. Blue happily set to chewing, but Ronan noticed the dog still watched his every movement. If Ronan stepped toward the door, Blue dropped the bone to stare, coming to a sit ready to follow his handler.

Ronan cleaned the fruit Shellie had purchased at the farmer's market in Saranac Lake and mixed up a compote to put on the breakfast buffet. He wondered if the raspberries were really local since the bushes along the river bank were far from ripe. The compote was barely into the refrigerator when he had to take delivery of several dozen eggs.

As he stowed them on a shelf of the frig, ideas for building a chicken coop out back floated across his brain. Of course, paying Henry took precedence and Ronan would have to calculate if the savings justified the purchase of the birds. He'd have to do some research, too, into how chickens survived an Adirondack winter.

The first players arrived around three and from then until close to six in the evening Ronan was kept busy checking people in.

Shellie arrived home with several slabs of prime rib and three huge baked potatoes. "It was too warm today, so most people were opting for lighter fare or something grilled. If you caught fish, put them away for tomorrow. This stuff is still warm."

Mr. White pulled in as they walked to the *Dining Cabin*.

"Do we have enough for three?" Ronan asked softly.

Shellie nodded.

White got out and looked around at the activity. Lights were showing in most of the cabins, laughing and cheers could be heard through the screen door of the *Dining Cabin* as a few families gathered to play board games. Nelson grinned and turned to them. "Wow, this is the kind of change we were hoping to generate. This old place is really alive tonight."

Ronan smiled back. "We start the pool repairs on Monday. That should make a big difference in keeping the place this lively all summer long."

White nodded and started to walk away.

"Mr. White, have you had dinner yet?" Ronan asked.

"No, I was going to change and then run into Saranac Lake."

Shellie held up the doggy bag. "We have some prime rib and baked potatoes to share."

"If you're sure you have enough, I'd be delighted."

The three of them settled on the patio, finishing the meal with cups of coffee as the sunset turned the western horizon into a giant palette of reds and oranges and purples. Ronan had the same view from the hospital, but out here as the air began to chill and he could smell the woodsmoke from the fire, the vista was so much prettier. Sipping hot coffee with Shellie nearby and Blue at his feet made him realize how homesick he'd been for the simple pleasures his life offered.

"I'm going to miss this coffee when I check out. I don't suppose you would share the secret?"

Shellie smiled. "It's no secret. It's making it on the wood stove. You have to be patient and give it time to perk."

Nelson laughed. "Guess I'll have to settle for swinging by occasionally then. I don't see packing up that iron behemoth anytime soon, or that you'd let it go."

Shellie and Ronan laughed with him and wished him, "Goodnight."

Shellie covered her mouth as she yawned. "At least I have tomorrow off so I get to be at church when all the other girls see the handsome man that bushy beard of yours was hiding. Boy, are they going to be jealous."

Ronan smiled and tried to hide his fears about going to church in the morning. Shellie might not mind his scars, but he wasn't sure if he was ready for the stares and the shock he expected from the rest of the congregation. A few of the guests had clearly been uncomfortable when he checked them in. Just thinking about what he would face tomorrow had his heart pounding like he'd been running in full pack and gear. Still, he'd promised Mrs. McClelland he would go to church in return for staying here. Ronan wasn't about to go back on his word.

Shellie looked at him inquisitively, apparently waiting to see if he was going to bed, too. Ronan needed time to get his emotions under control or he wouldn't be able to rest. "Why don't you head over to the cabin and get some sleep? I'll wait up until ten and then close the *Dining Cabin.*"

Shellie nodded and headed out the door. "Come on Blue, I need a few minutes of cuddling before you abandon me for Ronan for the rest of the night."

Blue rose slowly to his feet and trotted over to Ronan. Ronan petted the dog and looked into the creature's big brown eyes. Blue gave some gentle kisses and bumped his head against Ronan's hand. It was the reminder he needed to bleed the tension from his system. Blue would still be with him at church and Shellie would be there, too. He wasn't facing a crowd alone. The church had always been a friendly place, even when he wasn't a friendly person. Ronan gave Blue a quick hug and motioned him to go with Shellie.

It took Shellie's eyes a few seconds to adjust to the dimly lit porch after the bright lights of the *Dining Hall.* A racket at *Raccoon Cabin* drew her attention. Four college age players sat on the porch railing, laughing, and talking in loud voices. Shellie immediately remembered the frat party and started to back away from the noise. She fought the urge to run to the *Manager's Cabin* and hide. Chills raced up and down her spine.

While she watched, one of them crushed the can in his hand and tossed it over the railing into the parking lot. Moonlight gleamed off several other empty containers scattered in the gravel. The young man opened a cooler, grabbed another can and quickly guzzled the contents to chants of "chug". That can landed with a metallic sound in the gravel as well. Shellie had almost made it to the edge of the porch away from the group, her breath uneven and her hands like ice.

"A few more steps and I'll be safe," she whispered to herself, ready to turn and bolt down the steps to the safety of the *Manager's Cabin*.

One of the group started bouncing on the railing and the others joined in, bouncing in rhythm until the board let loose from the support post amid loud cheers. Another of them grabbed the post supporting the porch roof and started to yank, "Come on guys, let's wreck this place."

Shellie froze in place for an instant. Her chills were replaced with heat and she ran toward the boys shouting, "Hey! Stop that! You have no right to destroy motel property."

As she got closer she could smell the stale beer. Another memory of the frat party flashed up from her subconscious, but she ruthlessly shoved it aside to focus on the present situation. "You were sent a notice that alcohol would not be allowed here. This is a family place not a frat house."

One of the players let out a loud belch and all the others laughed. "So, what are you going to do about it, Sweetie?"

"Evict you."

"Huh?"

Shellie shook her head and assumed it was the alcohol making the guy stupid. "Pack your things. You are no longer welcome here."

"You can't do that." another member of the group yelled. "We gave you a deposit."

"Actually, as manager here, yes I can. You have ten minutes to pack your things and leave. Your deposit is forfeit to pay for the damages."

One of the group sauntered forward with a smarmy smile that reminded her of Chad. He glanced over his shoulder. "Chill out guys, let me handle this."

The group quieted a little, but Shellie didn't like the way they exchanged glances and smirked. She put a hand on Blue's collar and felt the tension in the dog's muscles. He didn't seem to like things either.

"I'm sorry. Joey got a little carried away. We'll pay for the repairs. Here's a beer, why don't you join us and relax a little. A sweet little thing like you shouldn't be so wound up." He reached toward her, holding out the can.

The swift movement was all the excuse Blue needed. He exploded in a snarling, barking mass of fur, his momentum dragging Shellie slowly forward as she fought to hold him back. Mister Confident dropped the can and retreated quickly.

A deep male voice came from behind her and commanded, "Sitz."

Shellie glanced over her shoulder to see Ronan approaching. Blue obeyed his command, but watched the now quiet group on the porch, his head following their slightest movement. Shellie noticed Mr. White approaching the group from the other side and several guests looked out their doors.

Ronan stopped next to Shellie and Blue, feet planted shoulder width apart, arms loosely crossed over his chest. "What's going on here?"

The young man regained some of his confidence and moved forward again. A low growl rumbling from Blue's chest stopped him. "We were just hanging out and this drama queen came over making a fuss. We invited her to join us and that dog tried to attack us. I'm tempted to report you have a dangerous animal on the place and see if animal control will take him away."

Ronan's expression made it clear to Shellie what he thought of the story. His head turned to take in the broken railing and crushed beer cans littering the parking lot. "You were told when you checked in, no rowdy use of alcohol would be allowed on the premises. You said it would be no problem. Clearly, it is a problem. Pack your things. You are no longer welcome here."

"You can't do that. Where are we supposed to stay? We have a game tomorrow."

"You should have thought of that before you violated motel policy and damaged property."

"We didn't know about the policy. You can't throw us out."

Shellie spoke quietly. "You were sent a written notice at the time of reservation and clearly warned. You signed an acceptance when you made the reservation."

Ronan's voice was calm. "And I warned you verbally, so pack."

The guest's expression was clearly angry. "I'm going to sue you for this and see that dog gets destroyed."

Ronan turned to Shellie, his voice calm, his expression relaxed. "Can you call Able at the Sheriff's office and ask him to send someone out? We'll need the police report to collect damages."

Shellie nodded and made the call.

Ronan turned back to the young men on the porch. "Pack."

Within minutes a sheriff's car pulled into the parking lot and Able strolled up to Ronan. "Ronan. Glad you're home. Will I see you and Shellie at church tomorrow?"

Ronan smiled and shook the sheriff's hand. "Count on it."

The way the young men were exchanging worried looks and shuffling their feet told Shellie they were getting shocked into sobering up and their confidence had taken a hit. It made her realize the difference when she had made a complaint to campus security. Chad and his friends had known they were safe. How different would her life be if the police had believed her?

Able surveyed the area. "Dispatch said you have some rowdy guests?"

Ronan nodded to the group. "This bunch has been drinking and destroyed the railing. We've told them to leave multiple times and they have refused."

"That's not true. The railing on this dump was broken when we got here. I want you to impound that dog; it tried to bite me," Mr. Confident demanded, indignation in his voice.

Mr. White stepped around the group. "I can testify to that being a lie. The railing was fine when I walked down to my cabin a short time ago. I work for the state evaluating motels and the railing was not weak or damaged in anyway, prior to these men renting the cabin."

Able nodded. "I'll get your statement for the report in a minute."

He turned to the group. "I drove by the motel a few hours ago and I saw the railings were intact. As for Blue trying to bite you, if that was his intent you'd be on the ground screaming and bleeding. He's a well-trained, retired veteran. My guess is he gave you a loud and scary warning. So, you can pack your things and leave quietly, or I can arrest you for vandalism and disturbing the peace. Your choice."

The spokesman for the group flushed a deep red. "Crappy, inbred, small towns. You'll be hearing from my lawyer."

He turned to his buddies, "Let's go."

Able grinned at Ronan. "This is a nice turn around. It used to be you I was threatening to arrest if you didn't leave."

Ronan laughed. "It's amazing how things change. Would you like some coffee?"

"Love some."

Shellie ran back to the *Dining Cabin* and brought back a tray for all of them. Her hands shook, but she was pleased to see none of the liquid spilled. Able took Mr. White's statement, then Ronan's while Shellie snapped pictures with her cell phone and emailed them to Able. By the time Able got to her, the young men were loading their car. Able and Ronan walked through the cabin with one of the group.

Shellie waited outside. She couldn't stand still, not knowing if the cabin was damaged. *Raccoon Cabin* was special to her. It had been the catalyst to reopening the *Pine Cone Motel*. She grabbed a recycle bin and picked up the cans to stay busy. The flowers she'd planted in front of the cabin had been trampled, but they were annuals and easily replaced. It really could have been worse, but what would she have done if Ronan hadn't been here? It never crossed her mind to call Able. She had been getting ready to dial 9-1-1. Calling a friend had made a difference. Would she have been as lucky dialing the emergency number?

Able and Ronan returned, and Ronan gave her a reassuring smile. They watched together as the guests drove off in a cloud of dust and sprayed gravel. Mr.

White returned to his cabin and Able walked back to the *Dining Cabin* with them.

Able settled his cup in the sink and turned to Ronan. "I'm a little surprised to see you back so soon."

"I'd made about all the progress I could in a cocoon. Now I have to work on handling the real world."

"They give you any tools to help?"

Ronan ran his hand through his hair. "The recommendation was to get a service dog, but they won't let me have one and keep Blue."

This was news to Shellie. "Why?"

"They thought Blue would interfere with the service dog and I'm not placing Blue. He's here to stay."

"Of course, he is," Shellie rinsed the cups and loaded them in the dishwasher. "So why not use Blue as the service dog?"

Ronan nodded. "I wanted to do that, but they won't train MWDs for service work because of their protection training so I can't get him certified as a service dog."

Able leaned on the half wall. "You don't need him certified."

Shellie and Ronan exchanged glances, then turned to look at him.

"Can you explain?" Ronan asked.

Able straightened. "When emotional support dogs became more common and I started to get more complaints, I took a training course on the legalities of when and where they were allowed. If you have a letter from a medical professional stating you have a condition requiring an emotional support dog, the dog doesn't need training or certification."

"So, I can take Blue with me into work?"

Able smiled. "Yup. I need to get going. See you two and Blue at church tomorrow."

Sometimes Shellie's beauty took Ronan's breath away. He carried a picture of her in his mind to mentally caress and marvel that she would have any interest in someone like him. In it, she wore blue jeans, a flannel shirt and little makeup while a smile lit her whole face with joy and her laughter made him feel warm. That image was his link to sanity and gave him the strength to keep going even when he was dog tired or worried. Today she was drop dead gorgeous. Gone was the timid young woman clinging to his arm in fear. Dressed in a simple sheath dress of navy and a brightly colored scarf, she looked like a model off the pages of a magazine. She linked her arm in his and smiled that big trusting smile he loved.

They walked along quietly, laughing when Blue started after a chipmunk and corrected himself to walk alongside Ronan. As they passed the grocery store, Ronan felt a pang of guilt that he hadn't reported back to work. He would need to call in on Monday. The closer they got to the church the harder it was to move forward. Shellie gave him an inquisitive look. He opened his mouth to respond to her silent question when he heard a male voice behind them call out a greeting. Ronan and Shellie turned.

""Hi Shellie, Ronan is that you? I like the haircut." Sophie McCollum strolled up to them, a significant baby bump in evidence. Her husband Patrick carried their two-year-old son, Randall.

"Hi, Sophie. How are you feeling?" Shellie asked.

"Like I ate an elephant," she laughed.

They all joined in the merriment, even Randall. The toddler leaned far out of his father's arms and Ronan reacted, afraid the child would fall. The little boy latched onto Ronan's shirt and Patrick released his son to Ronan with a smile.

Ronan felt stunned that anyone would trust him with their child and even more amazed the little boy wasn't terrified of the scar tissue lining Ronan's face. Randall pursed his lips, made a smacking sound and patted Ronan's mouth.

Ronan looked to Patrick. "Is he afraid of the scars?"

Patrick grinned. "He wants you to kiss him."

Ronan looked to see if the other man was joking.

"Make smacking sounds when you do," Sophie added.

These people wanted a scarred monster like him to kiss their child?

Randall patted Ronan's mouth again and started to screw up his face.

Shellie spoke up. "Uh oh, I remember that expression from my little sister. You better kiss him soon or he's going to cry."

Ronan moved his head to brush his lips on the baby's soft cheek. The child tilted his head clearly confused.

"You forgot the smacking noise," Sophie admonished.

Ronan tried again providing suitable sound effects. Randall giggled and leaned against Ronan's chest. Shellie laid a hand on Ronan's arm and he glanced down into her eyes. Was it possible she had similar thoughts to his? What would it be like to carry their child in his arms as they walked to church? It was a possibility Ronan had thought impossible when he had returned, and his girl-friend had walked away. Maybe the impossible was pos-sible, if he had Shellie at his side.

The rest of the walk was lost in the joy of holding the warm little boy against his shoulder. Reluctantly, he relinquished the child at the door, so Patrick could take him to the nursery. Dominick, an Italian-American man in his eighties, was a greeter and warmly shook Ronan's hand and patted Blue's broad head.

Walking to their seats, several people called out happy greetings and pleasant comments about his hair-cut. Millie waved as they walked by and stood to give both of them big hugs. "I'm so glad you're back. We missed you."

Shellie grinned and winked at him. Ronan could feel the heat of a blush rise in his face. He had so many nice friends, why had he been worried?

"Have you heard about Tom Ross?" Millie asked.

At their negative head shakes she continued.

"It seems he left the restaurant last night and never made it home. His wife is worried sick."

The organist started to play, and they separated to their seats. Several people gave him a quick hello. Ronan noticed when a pretty girl said hello, Shellie placed a possessive hand on his arm. He wanted to shout with laughter, settling for a big grin. Once again, his fears had been unfounded. He opened the bulletin rejoicing in be-ing in the house of the Lord.

Chapter 28

The rumble of diesel engines and the beep of equipment backing up drew Ronan onto the porch, mug in hand. Shellie had left for work and he was enjoying one more cup of coffee after finishing the dishes.

Al Hanson jumped down from the dump truck hauling a backhoe, a big grin on his face. "You finally decide to get a real job, Ronan?"

"And get my hands dirty? I don't think so."

Al sprang up the stairs and the men exchanged bear hugs. Several other men climbed out of pickup trucks.

Ronan waved for them to come over and led the way into the *Dining Cabin.*

"Help yourselves to coffee, then come over here." Ronan had the plans spread on the table.

Once everyone was gathered around, Ronan spoke. "It looks like the pump was not properly winterized, broke and the water drained out. In subsequent years, a few feet of water were left in the pool instead of completely draining or completely filling it. The ice expansion cracked the pool walls, so the first part of this project is to remove all the concrete. We need it done by Thursday when the fiberglass replacement pool arrives, and the crane is scheduled."

He glanced around the group. Most of the men nodded.

"Al, put the concrete hammer on the backhoe. Max, set up the compressor on the far side of the pool so we can run the jackhammers on the end walls. Owen, you have the trucking of the rubble." Ronan rolled up the drawings. "Let's get to work, we're burning daylight."

Late Monday afternoon during the day and night shift overlap, Shellie walked through the public areas of *the Lakeside Resort and Hotel*. It was almost time for her shift to end and she wanted to make sure everything was shipshape before she left for home. A young family hurried in from the beach trailing sand across the polished floors. Shellie keyed her radio and notified housekeeping to send someone to clean it up.

She turned back to the reception desk and saw Anna, one of the night shift people motioning her over.

"Shellie, I'm not sure how to help this guest. Can you take over?"

"Certainly," she offered the man a smile, "how may I help you?"

His exasperation was evident on his face. "As I told the last two people, I'm in room five-oh-eight and I need a late check out tomorrow. I don't understand why that is such a big problem."

Shellie quickly keyed in the bookings and saw a specific request for that room with check in tomorrow. "How late were you looking to leave, sir?"

"By three."

Normal check out time was eleven with check in time at three-thirty. "I'm sure we can accommodate you as long as you can be out by three. It looks like a couple has reserved the room for tomorrow. There is a note it is their anniversary and they had your room for their honeymoon. If you can guarantee to be out by three, we'll have enough time to clean the room and prep it for them."

The man nodded. "Now I understand why they called over a manager. I'll do my best to be out a little before three and I'll notify the desk when I leave."

"I'm not a manager sir, but I'm glad I was able to help." Shellie pulled a coupon out of the drawer. "Please have a complimentary beverage on us. I'm sorry we took so long getting you an answer."

The man took the paper and walked away smiling.

Shellie turned to Anna. "Why didn't you call Mr. Grady immediately instead of making the guest wait?"

Anna twisted her fingers. "Grady scares me and you were always so good at handling things, it's easier to come to you. I wish you were back on nights, so we didn't have to call Mr. Grady with this kind of stuff."

Shellie took a deep breath. "Okay, I understand, but I'm not a manager. All you must do is remember we are a service business and the best way to accomplish that is to accommodate the guest whenever possible. When you have a question or situation, ask yourself how you can make this benefit the guest. If you do that, you'll usually be right."

"You make it sound so easy."

Shellie smiled. "It is. Now in this situation you have to give housekeeping the heads up that they will have to respond as soon as the guest checks out."

She clicked the mouse and changed screens. "Remember to always put that information here. This will keep the desk attendants aware they have to notify housekeeping and informs housekeeping to keep staff over."

Anna gave Shellie a hug. "Thank you."

"No problem." Shellie glanced at her watch and turned to clock out, almost bumping into Mr. Grady. He nodded to her and walked away. Shellie watched him go, wondering if she was in trouble again.

Ronan watched the crane lift the pool shell off the flatbed and swing it toward the hole. Three of the guys grabbed the guide lines and stopped the rotation. Satisfied the alignment was correct, Ronan raised his arm and made a circling motion in the air. The crane operator responded by lowering the blue fiberglass shell. Ronan monitored the location of the pool, his guys, and the lines running to the crane hook. Gradually, the pool dropped from overhead to eye level to ground level, the guys pulling on the lines as needed to get the pool exactly aligned with the hole. As soon as the support lines went slack, Ronan clasped both hands together over his head signaling the crane operator to stop. Quickly, he walked around the pool checking for level and location.

Ronan gave a quick nod and the guys began removing the rigging. As he watched the crane move out of the way, a sedan pulled into the motel driveway and parked near the *Manager's Cabin*. Several of the young lacrosse players stood around wide-eyed watching the heavy equipment working. Ronan shouted over the equipment noise. "Make sure all the safety barriers are back up and keep an eye on the spectators while the crane is loaded."

Ronan approached the slender middle-aged man climbing out of the car. He was a bit surprised when Blue rose from his position on the manager's porch to advance with a wagging tail.

"Can I help you, sir?"

"Thank you, but I wanted to speak to the day manager."

Ronan gave a friendly smile. "This is a small operation, among other things I am the day manager. How can I help you? We do have one cabin available immediately."

The man held out his hand, "I'm Benjamin Grady. I remember when the McClelland's ran the place and I was happy to see it re-open. I understand you would like to be on the *Lakeside Resort and Hotel* overflow list and I wanted to see the operation."

So, this was Shellie's boss. Interesting after all that had happened for him to show up here when he knew Shellie was at work. Ronan also knew Shellie hadn't asked to have them on the overflow list yet. So, what was Grady's real purpose in being here?

Ronan pulled off his glove and shook the man's hand. "Give me a minute to get the crew back to work and I'll be glad to show you around."

Ronan walked back to the workmen, noting Blue sat calmly next to Grady and after a quick glance around as if to make sure he was not being observed, Grady gently petted Blue's head. It earned the man a quick slurp of Blue's tongue.

"Al, you get to climb in the hole and start on the plumbing connections. Owen, give him a hand. Max, you and the rest of the guys start building the forms for the outside of the pool."

Ronan removed his hard hat as he returned to Grady. "Would you like something to drink? We keep flavored ice water available for the guests all day."

"Maybe after the tour."

Ronan led the way to *Raccoon Cabin*. "This is typical of most of the units having three bedrooms and one bath. We also have two cabins with one bedroom and bath."

Grady walked around, carefully examining the linens and bathroom. He peered into the linen closet. "You leave linens in the cabins? Are you seeing much loss to theft?"

"So far, it hasn't been a problem. A few extra bars of soap and bottles of shampoo are missing, but not much else."

Grady led the way out onto the porch and paused to examine the screen door and test the hinges, then he stepped back, taking in the general view of the porch. Ronan was glad he'd fixed the railing and touched up the paint.

"Your flowers look a bit worse for wear."

Ronan nodded toward a tray of flowers he'd picked up that morning at the farmer's market. "The replacements are there. A few of our guests aren't too careful where they walk. It's a cost of doing business."

Grady sniffed and spoke stiffly. "Please show me your laundry facilities."

Ronan took the man out to the back work area and pointed to the two big washers and dryers.

Grady grinned. "I haven't seen that model in years."

"They still work just fine."

Grady turned to Ronan. "Between you and me, they last better than the new models and cost less to fix."

Ronan lead the way back to the *Manager's Cabin*. Grady asked a number of questions about the check in process, the accounting methods, and their ability to take credit cards. Ronan brought up the various hotel rental websites listing the *Pine Cone Motel*. They finished in the *Dining Cabin* where Ronan served up cucumber and ginger flavored ice water.

Grady looked at the big woodstove. "When I was a teenager, any time I was on the outs with my parents, I would come over here. Mrs. McClelland would sit me down at that table near the stove and make up hot chocolate while I spun my tale of woe. About the time I finished my drink she had me talked around to understanding maybe my parents weren't so bad and I probably should go home and give them a chance. I have many good memories of this place."

Ronan scrubbed his hand over his chin. "Mr. Grady, I know you're Shellie's boss. I also know she hasn't made the request to get us on the overflow list, yet. We've gone over the requirements and we both know we aren't ready. So why are you really here?"

Grady inhaled sharply and narrowed his eyes. He carefully set his empty water glass on the nearby table and finally turned back to Ronan. Ronan waited and watched. The man's body language said he was weighing his answer. "When Miss Morgan told me you had reopened the *Pine Cone Motel* it brought up so many memories I had to see for myself if it was possible to return the old girl to her glory. So many of these places have disappeared and been consumed by the forest."

Ronan found it interesting that the man wouldn't meet his eyes. Nope, he wasn't letting this drop. "Respectfully, sir, I don't think you are telling me the whole reason you're here. You live in Lake Placid, you could have stopped anytime in the last three months if that was the whole story."

Grady drew himself up sharply and attempted to stare Ronan down like he was an impertinent clerk. The silence filled the room as thick as a cloud. It didn't bother Ronan. This man had a significant impact on Shellie's life. If his intention was to cause her more grief, Grady would have to deal with Ronan first. He'd be more than happy to switch into predator mode and intimidate the heck out of the older man if it gave Shellie some protection.

Grady finally interrupted the silence. "Miss Morgan has excelled in her position at the hotel. She has excellent natural instincts. I was pleased by her dedication and performance when she joined our staff and delighted she decided to obtain a degree in hospitality management. I was shocked to hear she was complaining and making negative comments about the hotel. It didn't fit the character of the young woman I hired." Grady collected his glass and refilled it from the dispenser. "I've had several other employees, excellent workers, whom Dr. Sampson failed. Having her place a cloud of doubt over Miss Morgan was something of the last straw."

Ronan assessed what he'd been told, doing his best to read all the non-verbal signals. Grady was telling the truth or else he was an excellent liar.

Grady downed his water. "I acquired a copy of Miss Morgan's paper and decided to see if Dr. Sampson's analysis was accurate or character assassination. Your tour proved the point -- it was the latter."

Ronan relaxed his stance. "Is there anything you can do to help her? She doesn't deserve to fail."

"No, she doesn't. And it will not help my plans if she does." Grady headed for the door, pausing before leaving, "I would appreciate it if you would not mention my visit to Miss Morgan. I'm not sure my aid will be effective, and I would hate to give her false hope."

Chapter 29

Shellie heard the bang of nail guns and masculine shouts long before she could see any sign of the motel. She remembered Ronan's comment about nail guns putting him into flashbacks and hurried forward. Worry the crew would call his father instead of her added wings to her feet. She turned into the driveway to see Ronan standing talking to another man. The other man said something, and Ronan leaned back laughing. The picture he made brought a smile to her lips, his relaxed stance telling her more than anything he was in control. He spotted her and headed her way, his long, ground-eating strides carrying him quickly to her side.

Ronan pointed at the pool. "So, what do you think?"

The small tanker truck blocking her view pulled away. Crystal clear water lapped in the bright blue pool, sparkling in the sunlight. The crew moved in to finish driving wooden stakes and nailing boards in place in the space the truck had occupied.

"It's amazing. It makes me want to jump in."

"Better not. The water needs to gain some solar heat and we still have to add the chemicals." Ronan cautioned.

"I wasn't expecting it to be filled until everything was in place."

"If it was a cement pool, that would have been the case, but with fiberglass it needs to be filled immediately to balance the pressure from the surrounding ground. We'll pour the walkways and set the safety fence tomorrow. Dad threw in a slide, so we'll install it at the same time. In another couple of days, we can set out chaises and open the pool for use."

Shellie grinned. "I'll start the paperwork to get us on the overflow list."

She wondered at the strange expression crossing Ronan's face, but it was gone almost instantaneously, so she decided to let it go. "You look really happy. I have to admit I was worried when I heard the nail guns."

"Working with the crew has been fun. Some of the issues I faced before aren't bothering me and the methods I learned are helping with the ones that still start to set me off. I'm spotting the triggers and dealing with them."

They walked toward the *Manager's Cabin.* Shellie asked, "Do you want to go back to work for your dad?"

"I'll have to think about that one. In some ways yes and in others no. I owe Tom, the store manager, and I need to go back for a while since they covered my insurance and benefits all this time. Besides, while construction pays more, it's seasonal and sunny days make it a great job, but most of the time we don't have such nice weather. Can I deal with long days in the soaking wet? Yes, but working inside is a lot nicer."

Shellie nodded.

"So how was your day?"

"It was okay. Days are a lot busier than nights. Mr. Grady left for the afternoon which surprised everyone. I ended up fielding a lot of questions he normally handles. I don't know why people have such a hard time making decisions, the answers are usually obvious."

"Obvious to you may not be obvious to others."

One of the crew motioned to Ronan. He nodded and turned to Shellie. "Excuse me for a minute."

She made a shooing motion. "Go."

She made a quick stop in the *Dining Cabin* to drop the grilled chicken she'd brought home and then hurried to change into shorts. She saw Ronan had collected the laundry and apparently found the time to clean the cabins, but hadn't started the wash. She'd be up late to get it done and available for tomorrow.

Shellie checked her emails. Dr. Sampson had not responded with any further comments about her paper and she was at a loss as to what to do.

While Ronan had managed to clean the guest cabins, the *Dining Cabin* was showing the lack of attention. Shellie spent the next hour straightening up and moving furniture to sweep and mop. Several of the lacrosse players wandered in and out, a few mutterings about the lack of television and video games. It was another need they were going to have to address.

Ronan joined her, and they relaxed on the patio after dinner with ice tea and watched the sunset. As the evening chill settled in they moved inside, lighting the woodstove and brewing a pot of coffee.

"Hello? Ronan?"

They turned to the screen door.

Ronan waved. "Come on in, Dad. Would you like some coffee?"

The older man walked toward them. "That would be great."

Shellie poured the hot liquid while Ronan moved another chair to the table.

"What do you think of our progress?" Ronan asked.

Ronan's dad nodded his thanks to Shellie and sat down. "I'm thinking you have the guys moving a lot more efficiently than I expected and I'd like you to take the crew and supervise the next job. It would help us with the schedule and might help solve a problem with this job."

Shellie's stomach did a flip flop. Now what was wrong? Ronan spoke before she could ask.

"What problem?"

"The check from Mrs. McClelland bounced."

"What?" Shellie and Ronan asked in unison.

"The bank called and said the check had been returned for insufficient funds."

Shellie pulled out her phone and scrolled through her saved emails. "That makes no sense. I received confirmation from the state the funds had been deposited."

"Maybe Mrs. McClelland wrote the check from the wrong account," Ronan offered.

Shellie exhale. "You're probably right. She did say Henry didn't like her writing checks, maybe she has an old checkbook and he didn't give her a new one. Let me call her."

She put the phone on speaker and set it in the middle of the table.

"Hello, Shellie. How is the pool going?"

"It's almost done. The pool itself is in and full. Everything should be finished by tomorrow."

"That's wonderful news. I can't wait to see pictures."

Shellie glanced at Ronan and continued. "I've got you on speaker phone and Ronan and his dad are here. We've run into a bit of a glitch."

"What can I do to help?"

"It seems the check you wrote was returned for insufficient funds. I thought maybe it was for a different account than the one the state used to deposit the money."

"Oh dear. I'm sorry. Can you hang on while I get the checkbook?"

"Sure."

It didn't take long for the older woman to return. "Here is the account number."

Shellie opened the email and verified the account. The numbers were the same. She looked up at Ronan, not sure what to say.

"Did I use the wrong account?" Mrs. McClelland asked.

Shellie shook her head. "No. That is the account number I gave to the state and they confirmed they used."

Ronan leaned toward the phone. "Mrs. McClelland, is Henry back yet?"

"As a matter of fact, he is. He got back last night."

"Okay, we'll give him a call."

"Ronan, please call me back and let me know what is going on."

Shellie disconnected the call and dialed Henry. "Hi, Henry, this is Shellie from the motel. Ronan and Mr. Flanagan, the contractor for the pool, are with me."

"What do you want?"

Shellie looked at Ronan. She didn't like Henry's tone of voice. "We have a small problem with the payment for the pool installation. The check was returned."

"That's your problem."

"What do you mean?"

"You signed the contract for the repairs, not me. It's on you to come up with the funds to pay for it. Our agreement was for you to cover expenses and pay enough to cover the taxes. If you put extra money in that account from motel profits it belongs to Gram, she owns the place not you."

"We had the money for the pool deposited in the motel account to cover the expense of repairs. The State deposited the money in that account. The account the check was drawn on. The account without enough money to cover even half of the cost."

"I already transferred that money into Gram's stock account. You'll have to come up with what you need some other way. Look at it this way, at least the Fall taxes and insurance are paid."

Ronan spoke. "Transfer it back. Those funds were specifically for the repairs to the pool. It was from a government grant."

"I repeat. That is your problem, not mine. I didn't sign the grant application, you did."

Shellie struggled to keep her voice even. "No, your grandmother signed the application."

"Gram's signature means nothing. She isn't mentally capable anymore, so I have power of attorney. I control her finances. You should have talked to me, not her. You didn't, so it's your problem."

Shellie was too stunned to speak.

Ronan narrowed his eyes. "You're the one who utilized the funds. That's fraud. If you didn't intend to use the grant according to the agreement, it needed to be returned to the state."

"I repeat, I was not signatory to any grant application. I don't need to follow any contract commitments you made. It's up to you to deal with the situation and come up with the funds. It's my job to invest funds from the motel to benefit my grandmother. It's your problem, not mine."

The line went dead.

The three of them exchanged looks.

Shellie clutched her coffee cup with ice cold fingers. "What do we do now?"

Ronan shook his head. "I don't know. I really don't want to sue Mrs. McClelland, but that seems to be our only option."

Mr. Flanagan cleared his throat. "You want to bring me up to date on what is going on here?"

Ronan drew in a deep breath. "Henry has a buyer for the motel land and wants to bulldoze the place. Mrs. McClelland was thrilled to have us reopen and run it. Henry agreed to let us run things as long as we came up with the running expenses and paid the taxes."

"Since he took the pool money, I'd have to say you've more than covered what you owed him."

Ronan nodded. "True, but it doesn't cover what you've spent for the repairs."

"So, I'll lien the job."

Ronan's grim expression was not encouraging. "What does that mean?" Shellie asked.

Mr. Flanagan turned to face her. "It prevents Henry from selling the place until I get paid. Any contractor big enough to knock this place down is going to check for liens before going to work. That means they'll call me. Trust me when I say that will be the end of Henry hiring a demolition contractor."

Ronan's voice was gravelly. "That still leaves you holding the bills for the repairs."

Ronan's dad leaned back in his chair. "True, but it will buy you some time to work things out and keep a roof over your heads."

Shellie looked at the man with new appreciation. He might not have understood Ronan's issues with PTSD, but he did love his son. "If we call Henry back and insist we have paid the expenses through next year by the grant money, we could take the money we were setting aside and use it to make payments to you against the cost of the pool."

Mr. Flanagan smiled at her. "Think carefully about that. Once I'm paid off, I have to remove the lien and that gives Henry the option of shutting you down."

Shellie could see the love in Ronan's face as he looked at his father.

"So, we pay all of your costs, but not the profit, you leave the lien in place, but aren't stuck for what you actually spent." Ronan shook his head. "I don't like it. You'll still take a hit. We're going to be making small monthly payments for a long time. It's going to take a while even only paying for the actual material and labor costs to recoup what you've laid out."

Mr. Flanagan grinned. "I'm not worried, especially if it means I get you running crews for me."

"There's one problem with that. If I run a crew, no one is here during the day to take care of guests or do the cleaning."

Mr. Flanagan turned to Shellie. "I thought you were here during the day."

"I was. I got shifted to days at my other job."

Mr. Flanagan shook his head. "That won't work then. Guess I'll have to work with what you two can pay over time."

He stood and rested a hand on Ronan's shoulder. "Don't worry, son. It's a small price to pay to have you back."

Shellie watched the man walk out the door. She glanced at Ronan's glum expression. "I know this whole situation isn't what we wanted, but at least you've gotten back your dad."

SHERRI S. GALLAGHER

Ronan glanced up at her. "True. I don't like what this will do to his business. He's going to have to pay interest on the money he spent to buy the materials."

Shellie's phone rang. "Hi, Mrs. McClelland. It's getting late, I didn't think you'd still be up."

"I couldn't sleep worrying about what happened to all that money. Were you able to clear things up with Henry?"

"He told us where the money went."

Shellie could hear the relief in the older woman's voice. "Oh good. So, you'll be able to pay the contractor?"

"In a manner of speaking."

"What aren't you telling me, dear?"

"Henry used the money elsewhere. Ronan and I are going to have to make payments to the contractor over time."

"That's not right. What did he do with the grant?"

"He invested it in stocks."

"Posh. I'll tell him to transfer it back right now."

Shellie exchanged looks with Ronan. He shrugged.

"I hope you have more luck than we did."

"That boy has gotten too full of himself. I'll get this straightened out, you wait and see."

Chapter 30

Ronan evaluated the cloudy sky while the cement truck backed up to the forms. They needed to get the concrete poured and covered in case it rained. He watched the three cabins empty as lacrosse players and their parents headed off to the fields. Rain wouldn't stop the tournament unless lightning occurred. He had to get to cleaning those cabins soon.

The loud splash of the pebbly mix sliding down the trough brought his attention back to the construction. He signaled the truck forward as the individual forms filled and the guys went to work leveling the piles. They were about halfway through when a small SUV pulled in and parked. Ronan glanced at the woman climbing out and did a double-take. She strolled over to him and he engulfed her in a bear hug. "Hi, mom."

She returned the hug with interest until he gently released her.

"What are you doing here?"

She grinned. "Your dad told me what was going on and the problem of leaving the motel unattended. I decided to help."

Ronan glanced at the forms and signaled the truck to move forward.

"What needs to be done?"

"I can't ask that of you, Mom. How many times did you tell me as a teenager that you weren't a maid service?"

She laughed. "And here I thought you weren't listening."

Ronan signaled the truck again.

"So, let me guess, the cabins need to be cleaned. Where do I get the keys and the cleaning equipment?"

"The keys are behind the reception desk and the maid cart is in the back area near the dryer."

She glanced up at the sky. "Got it. Take care of your concrete before it rains."

He signaled the truck to move as she disappeared behind the buildings. With the last of the cement in place the truck pulled away and Ronan hurried to help the guys insert the fence posts as he heard his mom knocking on a cabin door and announce "housekeeping."

Shellie's phone vibrated in her pocket. She finished checking in a guest at *Lakeside* and made a grab to answer it before it rolled to voice mail.

"Miss Morgan. This is Detective Evans."

His voice jolted her system. It had been more than a month since she'd given him her deposition. She glanced around to make sure no one could over hear her end of the conversation. "Please tell me you don't need something else. I'd like to put my past behind me."

"I called to give you an update. Between your deposition and the other young lady's testimony, Chad was given the maximum sentence. It's over."

Shellie felt so light headed she grabbed for a chair. "You're sure?"

"I'm sure. You did a very brave thing and because of you and the other young woman a predator is off the street. I wanted to say thank you. Your deposition made a difference."

Shellie closed her phone. What did she feel? She'd expected to be elated. Instead, her body and brain felt numb. So, Chad would go to jail. Why didn't it feel like a victory?

They got the tarps strung in place as the first big rain drops pelted down. Ronan herded the grinning crew into the *Dining Cabin*. They'd done it. Once the concrete hardened, they could string the fencing and the pool would be finished. For now, the job was done. Shellie had left a big pot of vegetable soup on the woodstove. Ronan started some grilled cheese sandwiches and passed out bowls to the guys.

"Man, you need to come to work for your dad fulltime," Al said. "I'll volunteer for your crew any day if it means you feed us."

The rest of the guys voiced their agreement around mouthfuls of toasted bread and warm cheese. Once they finished eating, the crew left, and Ronan went in search of his mother. He found her loading the washing machine.

Ronan quickly moved in to lift the heavy linens and start the cleaning cycle. "Can I interest you in some lunch?"

"That depends?" she answered with a grin.

"On what?"

"Who did the cooking?"

"Shellie."

"In that case, yes, and I expect you to tell me all about her."

They hurried through the back door of the D*ining Cabin*. Ronan settled in with coffee while his mom ate.

"This is great."

"Shellie's a wonderful cook. She made a chocolate cake that's insanely good."

"How did you meet?"

Ronan hesitated. How did he explain Shellie's situation? "She got upset when I wasn't given a meal I had worked for and bought one for me."

His mom paused in spooning up soup. "I think I like her already."

"Wait until you meet her. You'll love her."

His mom paused and watched him silently until he wanted to squirm. "What?"

"So, when are you going to ask her to marry you?"

Ronan froze. "She deserves better than me."

"But does she want better than you?" Mom watched him for a few seconds and then went back to eating her soup.

"Our situation is too precarious right now to be talking about weddings. We still don't know if we'll have a roof over our heads in a month or be back to being homeless."

"Think about it." She finished her soup. "Now dish me up some of that cake and then show me how to run the motel office."

Ronan showed his mother how to check people in and out and she promised to be back first thing in the morning. He needed to make some decisions. After tomorrow, the pool work at the motel would be done. Did he go back to the grocery store or run a crew for his dad?

He dialed the grocery store and waited for Tom to come on the line. "Hey, Ronan, how are things going?"

"Going well. I'm out of the hospital and back home."

"Are you ready to come back to work? I could really use your accounting skills."

Guilt ate at Ronan. "I would like to, but I'm not sure it'll work."

"Why not?"

"I have a service dog and that doesn't fit with a grocery store."

The silence on the line told him what he needed to know.

"You're right. The board of health would never agree to a service dog being here."

"I really appreciate all you did for me, Tom. You made a difference and I feel bad not coming back. Is there anything I can do to make it up to you?" Ronan didn't expect anything, but a trite answer.

"Actually, there is. We can't have the dog in the store, but the biggest help you provided was with the accounting. Would you be willing to work part-time balancing the daily receipts and maintaining the books? You could pick up the information each afternoon and work from home."

Ronan grinned. He could run a crew and still help at the store. When construction shutdown for the winter he could still bring in some income. Maybe he could start a small accounting practice on the side. "I think that would be a possibility."

Chapter 31

Shellie stood at the reception desk. The other staff members were on lunch break when Mr. Grady approached her. "Miss Morgan, a word, please."

Chills ran up and down Shellie's spine at Grady's serious expression. Now what had she done? "Yes, sir?"

"There is a search being mounted for a local man who went missing a few days ago. The Lake Placid fire chief called and asked if we had any open rooms for the searchers and their dogs."

Mr. Grady was going to allow dogs on site?

"As you know, our home office has a strict policy on the subject. Before I turn them away, I was wondering if you had any availability at *Pine Cone Motel*?"

Shellie exhaled a breath she didn't realize she'd been holding. "We have two, three-bedroom cabins and one, one-bedroom cabin available."

"What is your room rate?"

Shellie thought for a second. They could certainly use the income, but was it right to charge volunteers? "Under the circumstances, no charge."

Shellie watched as the fifth SUV pulled into the Motel drive and parked. It was a big red Excursion. The man driving got out and waited for the pretty, petite passenger to come around to him. He gave her a laughing hug and then limped to the *Manager's Cabin*.

"Hi, we're Conor and Sloane McCollum. Nick said you had rooms available for searchers?" the man said.

Shellie smiled and handed over the key to *Loon Cabin*. "Glad you could make it. I hope you can find Tommy."

"My wife's dog, Orex, will, if anyone can. Provided a pregnant handler doesn't slow him down too much."

Sloane glared at her smirking husband. "Even pregnant, I can walk you into the ground."

Conor laughed and hugged his wife. "Ain't it the truth."

Sloane filled out the registration card. "What is the rental per night?"

"No charge."

The couple exchanged looks. "We don't understand."

Shellie smiled at the. "We didn't have reservations. Rather than have the cabins empty, we'd like to support the search and the community, so we are donating the use of the cabins. We'd like to think if we needed someone to look for us, people like you would be available."

The couple exchanged looks. All joviality gone, Conor responded, "We would. It's what we do."

Chapter 32

Shellie had been on days for a month and it was getting old. She had submitted weekly updates to Dr. Sampson and received an automatic reply that Dr. Sampson was out of the office and would respond when she returned. Ronan's mom handled most of the work Shellie had done before returning to day shift. In the evenings, Shellie made cookies and other treats to leave out for the guests and she and Ronan shared their experiences with each other.

Having the search team there was an educational experience. They had found Tommy in a ravine within two days. He'd fallen down the sharp drop off in the dark and hit his head on a rock. Falling debris, brush and leaves hid him until one of the dogs made the discovery. He was suffering from the fall and exposure, but thanks to the dogs and the searchers he was alive.

The searchers had been fun and funny, always joking with each other and complimenting Shellie and Ronan on the meals they prepared for the group. When they left, every single cabin had the normal cabin rental left in cash on the night stands.

Shellie had been particularly taken with the all-black German Shepherd Sloane McCollum worked. He'd reminded Shellie of a black lion. He'd been polite around Blue even though he was twice Blue's size. He didn't approach Blue, but averted his gaze and maintained a distance, not engaging, but not bowing. Blue also maintained an aloof distance. It was enlightening to see the two together; both strong, dominant, males focused on doing a job, no tail wagging or sniffing. Each dog gave the other his space. It made Shellie wonder if someday she could get another German Shepherd and learn how to do canine search and rescue.

Ronan and Blue ran crews while his mom handled the *Pine Cone Motel*. She was glad he'd been able to mend his relationship with his parents.

Shellie used the lull in checking out guests to sign on to the college portal. She'd submitted the final draft of her paper a week earlier. The silence from Dr. Sampson was deafening. She fully expected a big, fat "F". All grades had to be in by today, so students could sign up for the next semester.

Since she was on days indefinitely, she wouldn't be able to attend the classroom part of Dr. Sampson's course, so there was no point trying for a second attempt to pass. Besides, nothing had changed in her work at *Lakeside*. If anything, her opportunity to make decisions was worse. Mr. Grady made decisions on days that she had made on nights. Her job was to handle the reception desk and nothing more.

The screen opened and blinked notifying her, she had a message from Mr. Pataki. Shellie clicked on it and had to read it twice.

Ms. Morgan, Congratulations! You have completed the requirements for a bachelor's degree in hospitality management. Please contact this office to arrange for your diploma and to tell us if you will be walking in the graduation ceremony at the end of the Fall semester.

Shellie clicked on her grades. Dr. Sampson had given her a "B". A squeal snuck passed her lips and she danced in place.

"Miss Morgan, A little more decorum please." Mr. Grady scolded.

Shellie turned to him covering her lips with both fists as her whole body shook. "Mr. Grady. I passed. I've earned my degree."

"Really?"

Shellie pointed to the screen and flipped to the message.

Grady read it and smiled. "Congratulations. Now if you please, we have guests that need assistance."

"Yes, sir." Shellie switched back to the hotel system and beamed at the customer at her station. "How may I help you?"

Shellie was in the middle of briefing Kelly, when Tom tapped her on the shoulder. "Hey Shellie, Mr. Grady wants to see you in his office before you leave."

Shellie's stomach clenched. Was she in trouble for celebrating too much? "Why?"

"I don't know. You'll have to ask him and Mrs. Anderson. They're waiting for you."

Shellie and Kelly exchanged worried glances.

Shellie hurried to Mr. Grady's office. Both managers sat in the same place as the last time. She couldn't prevent the tremor from entering her voice. "You wanted to see me?"

"Please come in and sit down." Mr. Grady pointed to a chair.

Shellie forced her shaking legs to carry her forward. She perched on the front edge of the chair and waited.

"Mrs. Anderson and I have discussed at some length your actions on the night shift. It has become very clear much of the staff feels comfortable taking direction from you and considers you their manager."

Shellie swallowed. "I'm sorry, sir. I've told them I'm not a manager."

Grady cut her off. "Please allow me to finish."

Shellie nodded.

"The hotel has clear policies and job descriptions for managers and a key requirement is a four-year degree. Since we have verified with your advisor that you have in fact completed the requirements, we would like to offer you the position and salary of night manager."

Shellie clamped her jaws together to keep her mouth from dropping open. This had to be a dream.

"Well, Miss Morgan, are you interested in the position?" Mr. Grady was clearly fighting a smile.

"Yes, sir. I would like that very much."

"Good. You start tomorrow night. Mrs. Anderson and I will draft the announcement." They stood.

Shellie rose to her feet and Mr. Grady reached out to shake her hand. "Congratulations."

Shellie's hand trembled. She clocked out in a daze and headed out the door, walking toward the motel.

A horn beeped, and she turned to see Ronan behind the wheel of the company truck he now drove. He pulled alongside of her and pushed open the passenger door, a worried expression on his face. "What's wrong, Angel?"

She smiled at him and climbed in. "Sorry. I'm kind of in shock. This has been the most awesome day. I passed my course and earned my diploma and Mr. Grady made me the night manager and gave me a raise."

Ronan shifted into park and pulled her close for a celebratory kiss. As soon as his lips touched her, fire raced through her bloodstream. She kissed him holding nothing back. There was no better way to celebrate than to be held in Ronan's arms.

They finally came up for air and Ronan gently brushed a long strand of hair behind her ear. His beautiful eyes flashed a deep blue, his happy smile matching hers. He spoke softly. "I am so proud of you."

Ronan held her for a few seconds more then gently released her. She latched her seatbelt and he accelerated out of the hotel driveway. Instead of turning toward the motel, he turned back toward downtown Saranac Lake.

"Where are you going?"

"To take my girl out for a celebratory dinner at the *Downhill Grill*."

"We can't afford that." Shellie protested.

"Yes, we can. This is too important a day not to mark it with a special celebration."

Shellie smiled and handed the key to *Raccoon Cabin* to Mr. Witherspoon, the early September sunshine spilling through the windows. "Welcome back."

He took the key. "Same cabin as last time?"

"I held it for you. Your staff has all checked in and I informed them breakfast will be at eight. The vans to take you to the ski jumps will be in the parking lot at nine-thirty." Shellie walked out onto the porch with him.

Mr. Witherspoon paused and looked around. "You've made amazing improvements in a few months."

She nodded and looked around as well. The *Pine Cone Motel* was alive with activity. Several families unloaded luggage and people were shouting back and forth between cabins. A middle-aged couple sat on the porch of *Loon Cabin* sipping ice water and watching their coworkers. "Yes, we have."

"I guess I better get unpacked and check in with everyone."

Shellie spotted Ronan pulling into the driveway and waved. He had barely parked and joined her on the porch when a dusty sedan pulled in. The car stopped next to Ronan's truck and an elderly woman probably in her eighties or nineties slowly exited the vehicle.

"I don't believe it," Ronan muttered and hurried down the steps to assist her. A woman in her sixties and with similar build and facial features to her passenger exited the driver's seat, a legal folder in her hand. Shellie wondered if it might be Ronan's grandmother and aunt.

Ronan offered his arm and gently helped the older woman to get her balance. "Mrs. McClelland, why didn't you tell us you were coming?"

Shellie froze for an instant. Mrs. McClelland looked so different from what Shellie had imagined. She hurried to Ronan's side.

Mrs. McClelland stood for a minute, looking around, a smile on her lips. "You really did it. You've brought our old girl back to life."

Mrs. McClelland leaned on Ronan and used a cane with the other hand. Her daughter walked beside her to the *Dining Cabin.* Once they had her inside and seated by the wood stove, Shellie poured everyone large glasses of flavored water.

After taking a deep swallow, Mrs. McClelland put aside her drink. "I had to see it once more. The pictures are wonderful, but to hear the laughter and see the lights on in all the cabins ---. I had to see it one more time."

She nodded to her daughter and the woman opened the folder, drawing out some legal documents.

"I was very upset after talking to Henry."

Shellie's heart skipped a beat. Had Henry sent Mrs. McClelland on a troublemaking mission? She and

Ronan didn't have any money in reserve. Every dime they brought in, they were giving to Ronan's dad to pay for the pool. If Henry had sent her to collect income from the motel, they didn't have any.

"I knew he didn't value the *Pine Cone Motel* the way I did, but that he intended to bulldoze it and sell the land hurt." She paused and took a sip of water. "When I found out the awful thing he did to you two young people I was embarrassed and angry. I decided right then and there not to let him have ownership. What I didn't realize is he had a doctor declare me incompetent. It's taken quite a bit of time to turn that around."

Mrs. McClelland looked at her daughter who nodded encouragingly. "Now that it has, I had a long discussion with my daughter, Daisy, so my family understands or at least accepts my decisions. I had my attorney draw up the papers to transfer the deed of the motel to the two of you, provided you will promise to keep it open for at least five more years."

Mrs. McClelland pushed the papers toward them. Ronan picked them up and Shellie could see the title "Deed" on the top.

"Are you willing to agree to that?"

Ronan and Shellie exchanged looks. He looked as stunned as Shellie felt. She nodded, and Ronan spoke. "We would be more than happy to make that agreement."

"Of course, there is also the money Henry stole from you for me."

Daisy whispered a drawn out, "Mom."

Mrs. McClelland looked over at her. "All right, appropriated."

She turned back to Shellie and Ronan and passed them an envelope. "Since you will now own the motel, you need the tax money you sent to Henry and the funds from the state to repair the pool. I'm afraid some of it was spent as part of the brokerage fees and the commission paid to Henry was spent on his European golf trip, so it isn't all here, but it is the bulk of the grant and the other funds you paid."

Shellie opened the envelope and withdrew a check. The amount staggered her. The check was made out to the *Pine Cone Motel*. Tears clogged her throat and she spoke around them. "I – I don't know what to say, Mrs. McClelland. This place has been a haven for us when it seemed like the rest of the world had thrown us away."

Shellie's throat closed. She looked at Ronan and shook her head. He continued for her. "It seemed like no one wanted us or the *Pine Cone Motel,* but with your blessing we were able to come together and become something of value once more. Thank you. Without you and your love and support, none of this would have happened."

"I think it's important you understand how the *Pine Cone Motel* came into existence, so you can carry on for us. Angus, my husband, and I were working in a small, local diner trying to save up enough money to open our own restaurant. Late one night, not long before closing, a bedraggled old man came in. It was raining cats and dogs and as far as we could see he'd walked to the diner. The poor man was soaked to the skin. I poured him some coffee and asked if he wanted something to eat. He shook his head, said he'd run out of gas and forgot his wallet at home. He'd come in to get warm and would only stay a minute if we didn't mind. We gave him a bowl of homemade stew and fresh corn bread and told him to eat his fill. Angus gave him a ride to the gas station, paid for five gallons of fuel, took the man to his car and in general made sure he was safely on his way before coming to pick me up to go home.

"We didn't think a thing of it. It was simply the Christian thing to do. Six months later some fancy lawyer in a really expensive suit and driving a big foreign car pulled up to the diner. He said that the old man had died and left us this piece of land and the money to build a restaurant. All he asked was we continue to live Matthew 25:40."

Shellie knew tears were streaming down her face as she quoted, *"Truly I tell you, whatever you did for one of the least of these brothers and sisters of mine, you did for me."*

Mrs. McClelland looked around the *Dining Cabin*. "My husband and I built this place from a small patch of forest. It was a labor of love and we valued it for the symbol of the love we shared. We did just as our benefactor asked and tried to help the people in need who crossed our paths. I think it means the same to the two of you and I'm happy to know it will continue for an additional lifetime. I think as long as it exists my husband and I won't be forgotten. I would ask that you honor the original promise and continue to help those in need."

Shellie rose and hugged Mrs. McClelland and whispered, "Thank you, we will."

Ronan was misty-eyed as well as he took his turn at sharing a hug. "You touched so many lives here. I can't even begin to tell you the number of people who have stopped by to share memories and talk about how you helped them while they were growing up. We'll try our best to continue the tradition."

Mrs. McClelland rose. "Walk me around here one last time so I can say goodbye."

Shellie wiped at her streaming eyes. "You know you are always welcome here."

The older woman nodded and leaned on Ronan. It was a slow procession down the length of the cabins with Mrs. McClelland explaining why each cabin got its name. "We built the *Dining Cabin* first and lived in the back section that became the laundry and workshop. We started out as the *Pine Cone Restaurant*. I worked days as an assistant to an attorney and Angus worked nights doing maintenance at the *North Pole* amusement park, working at the restaurant in our off hours. When we saved enough money, we built *Raccoon Cabin* to rent to fisherman and I would cook up their catch for them. We added cabins as we saved the money, finally building the *Manager's Cabin*. Angus laid the slate for it and the patio himself. He said no one else would take the time to build it so it lasted."

Ronan smiled. "He was right. I've never seen slate stand up to our freeze-thaw cycles the way this has."

She pointed to the peony plants in front of the *Manager's Cabin*. "Those came from my grandmother's garden. Once my babies started to come along, I quit to be here full-time and focus on my children. Without both our salaries, there wasn't enough money to add more cabins, but that was all right with us."

Mrs. McClelland looked at the neat garden, her eyes watering and pointed to the various herb plants, telling where the garden's original stock had come from.

As Ronan helped her out to the front, Shellie tugged on Daisy's arm. The woman looked at her with a questioning expression. Shellie led her back into the craft room and pulled down the picture albums. "These are about your family and they should be with your mom."

Daisy opened the one about herself and smiled. When she opened the one about her brother, she drew in a shaky breath. "This was my brother, Benjamin. I think Mom will be happy to have these."

They reached the front of the building where Mrs. McClelland and Ronan waited. As the two visitors move to the car, Shellie asked, "Aren't you going to stay the night?"

Mrs. McClelland smiled. "No, dear, we need to go home."

Ronan and Shellie watched the two women drive away until they could no longer see the tail lights. They returned to the *Dining Cabin* and Shellie lit the wood-stove to make a pot of coffee. Ronan looked through the paperwork.

Once Shellie sat across from him, he spoke. "We have to pay the property taxes out of this, but between what we already paid Dad and the balance of what will be left from this, we should be able to pay off what we owe for the pool. Dad can remove the lien and get a normal profit."

Shellie looked around. "I can't believe this is ours. Five months ago we were homeless and alone. Now we have each other and all of this."

Ronan looked at her, a gentle smile on his face. "You hit the nail on the head, Angel. We have each other and that's what made all of this possible. I know I'm not the greatest prize in the world, but I promise to love you with all my heart for the rest of my life. Will you marry me and stay with me forever?"

Shellie flew into his arms. "You are my world and I would be honored to be your wife and spend the rest of our lives together."

Ronan smiled and claimed her lips.

Chapter 33

Shellie had the lunch room to herself. She pulled out her phone and took a deep breath before dialing. Her mom answered as she had hoped. "Hi Mom, how are you?"

"Shellie, I can't believe it. I was just telling your dad, he should call you."

That piqued Shellie's curiosity. "What's going on?"

"The chancellor was investigated for abusing his position and your father is no longer on probation."

"Why was Dad on probation?"

"Ostensibly for being late and missing classes, but the Chancellor told him privately the whole thing would go away if he could keep you from helping the detective investigating Chad. Now Chad is in jail, the board lifted your Dad's probation and your expulsion, and we're waiting for the announcement that the chancellor has stepped down."

Shellie had trouble breathing. When her dad had visited the threat to his livelihood was real, not made up to get her to change her mind. Realizing her family could have ended up as homeless as she had been turned her stomach.

"Shellie? Are you still there?"

"Yes. I'm a little in shock. I didn't know this was going on."

"I'll put your father on the phone." She was gone before Shellie could protest.

"So how is life as a maid going for you? Your mother wants you to come home, but you'll have to live under my rules, and expect to be grounded until you graduate."

The guilt that had been drowning her evaporated. "Hello to you too, Dad. I am sorry about what was done to you. It wasn't fair, just like what Chad did to me wasn't fair."

There was a short pause before he spoke. "Things here were pretty difficult after what you did to Chad."

"What I did to Chad? What about what he did to me?"

"I can't believe the judge allowed that piece of fiction that was your deposition. I know you feel he forced you, but are you sure you didn't play the tease, even a little bit?"

Shellie's stomach clenched and memories of the party before she was drugged flashed through her mind. Thankfully, with their increases in salary, she'd been able to go back to seeing Dr. Parish. Before she could tumble back down that dark hole she remembered Dr. Parish's words. Her breathing evened out.

"Dad, no is no, and every woman has the right to say no. Chad drugged me and took away my ability to speak and that was wrong. I'm not the only woman he abused. What about them? Are all those women teases and responsible for whatever Chad decided to do to them? A man has the responsibility to respect a woman; and a woman has a right to control who does or doesn't touch her."

"I can't speak for the other women who testified, only my daughter and you caused this family a lot of embarrassment and put all of us at serious financial risk. What would have happened to your brother and sister if the Chancellor had carried out his threats and fired me? Your brother is enrolled to start here in the fall, your selfish need for petty revenge could have cost him his future."

"I didn't expect the Chancellor to act on his threats. And once the case was decided, I thought you would be safe from repercussions. If you want to blame anyone for petty revenge, the chancellor is a lot better candidate than I am, but then I've always been your preferred whipping boy."

A sigh rattled through the phone. Shellie had a feeling her dad was really exasperated that she hadn't given in and accepted his view of the situation.

"Fine. I see you're as stubborn as ever. You better get over it, I won't accept that behavior once you move back. The fall semester starts in two weeks. I can get you enrolled, but you need to get your behind back here ASAP."

Heat flashed through Shellie. This should take her dad back a step or two, not the most Christian of attitudes she knew, so she used her sweetest tone of voice. "Actually, I called to invite you to my college graduation ceremony. I finished up over the summer and will walk across the stage in December. I'm holding a cabin for the four of you, so you don't have to pay for a hotel. If you want to stay the week, you could watch me marry Ronan the following Saturday."

The silence on her dad's end brought a smile to her lips.

"What did you get a degree in, maid service?"

Shellie cringed. Couldn't he be a little happy for her? "My degree is in hospitality management and I have been promoted to a manager at the resort where I work."

"I would hardly call those cabins a resort."
Shellie could hear the sneer in his voice.

"Dad, I've worked hard at two jobs and finished my bachelor's degree. Sneer all you want. I've made something of myself when you abandoned me."

Silence.

"So, does this -- what's his name -- Roman, know you're damaged goods?"

Shellie almost threw the phone. "His name is Ronan, not Roman, and he's stood by me through all the difficulties I've faced, including getting counselling to understand why what happened wasn't my fault."

Shellie gulped down her rising anger. "You've shown more loyalty to your boss than you have to your own daughter. I thought my parents would want to share my joy. Obviously, that was a foolish dream. Let me know if you're going to show up or not."

She hit the disconnect before he could respond further. Her body shook, and she fought to keep her emotions in check. How could he still think so poorly of her after everything that happened to Chad and the chancellor vindicated her?

Shellie gulped in deep breaths, trying for a calm demeanor. She was a manager and needed to appear cool and collected at all times. She had a good life and she needed to be grateful for it. She had Ronan, the image of him laughing, and Blue dancing around him, gave her the perspective she needed. It would take a while to get over the schism between her and her parents, but with the bright future ahead of her it was possible. If they ever changed their minds she would welcome them back into her life, well at least her mom, it would take a lot of prayer to forgive her dad.

Shellie stood and exhaled hard, shooting the sleeves of her uniform jacket and tugging it into place at her waist. She squared her shoulders and prepared to walk back to the reception area when her phone rang. She cautiously looked at the caller ID and recognized her brother's number.

"Man, Shellie, what kind of bombshell did you drop on Dad?" The laughter in her brother's voice made her smile. "Mom and Dad are having quite the shouting match. She told Dad, she's going to her daughter's graduation and wedding if she has to walk to get there. Did you really graduate? Are you really getting married?"

Shellie sat back down, letting her excitement bubble to the surface. This was the kind of response she'd expected when she made the phone call. "Yes, and yes. I got a degree in hospitality management and I met a great man. His name is Ronan."

"Awesome! Will I like him? He better be nice to you."

"You'll have a blast with him. He was a canine handler in the military and he's a supervisor for a construction company and he's started a side accounting business. He loves to hunt and fish and garden and make things."

"I want to meet him. Can I come to the wedding?"

"I invited all of you. If Leslie wants to come, too, she can be a bridesmaid, as long as it doesn't make Dad mad at her."

"Cool. I've been working at the local coffee shop. Even if Dad won't pay for us to come, I think I can swing tickets for the three of us. Mom's going to have to help with a hotel."

"Don't worry about that. Ronan and I own a small motel and I have a cabin blocked for you guys."

"You own a motel? How did you manage that?"

"Long story. I'll tell you when you get here. Look, if you need help with the cost of travel, call me. I can help."

"That's okay. You must have a lot of expenses and I don't imagine you earn a lot as a maid."

"Why would you think I'm a maid?"

"When Dad came back from seeing you earlier this summer, he said you were working as a maid at a dump of a motel. He figured when you'd had enough of that you'd come back and be a better, humbler person, and appreciate what he and Mom were giving you."

Before Shellie could articulate her thoughts, her brother chuckled and continued. "I'm glad you made good and things are going better for you. Did you tell Dad you own a motel? Why'd you get a degree in hospitality management instead of literature?"

"I didn't get a chance to tell him about the motel. For the record, it's not a dump and it's the place Ronan and I own. I work nights at an upscale resort, they reimbursed my tuition, and I was able to transfer my other courses. Once I got my degree they made me a manager."

"So, it was a matter of economics?"

"A little, but once I started working at the hotel it was a fun career and I felt like I had more options for a job. I'm not professor material."

"Okay, I've got some thinking to do."

Shellie felt a chill. Her kid brother often followed her lead with disastrous consequences. "What kind of thinking? A lot of amazingly good things happened for me to survive, not the least of which was meeting Ronan. Don't get yourself in trouble because things worked out for me."

"Chill, Sis. I'm not teacher material either. I want to travel and see the world, not be stuck in some backwater town never traveling more than twenty miles from home. Sometimes I think Dad is so controlling because that's the only way he can feel important. His literature degree doesn't seem to give him much security or happiness."

"A part of Dad's problem is not getting a higher degree. It limited the places that would hire him and gave them a lot of leverage against him. If I hadn't come along, he could have continued his education." Just because she and her dad didn't get along, Shellie didn't want to poison the relationship between her siblings and their parents.

"Isn't that part of the issue with me getting a literature degree? I'll have to get a PhD and I don't want to spend that kind of time to get a 'piled higher and deeper'. Dad needs to let me choose my own career."

Shellie silently agreed with her brother, but didn't want her brother to feel the same pain of estrangement she felt. "Think long and hard before you rock the boat. Not having Mom to talk to hurts, a lot."

"Okay, makes sense. You've got my cell number, right?"

Shellie smiled. "Yup, and you have mine. Look, if things get dicey, call me. I'm here for you and Leslie if you need it."

"Thanks. Hey, it's starting to sound like Mom is winning the argument. Expect us for your graduation and wedding."

Chapter 34

Shellie watched her brother through the sliding glass door of the *Manager's Cabin*. He was playing tag with Blue in the ankle-deep snow. She laughed when Matt tried to duck around the dog to the right only to be tripped by a fast paw. Ronan was working in the office on the grocery store books while she and her mother adjusted the hem of her sister's bridesmaid dress. A stray shaft of sunlight shattered into a rainbow of colored reflections from the diamond engagement ring on her finger.

Ronan had insisted on taking a portion of the funds from Henry to buy Shellie an engagement ring. Shellie looked down and rubbed the diamond with her thumb. It was by no means the largest stone available. It was, however, imbued with Ronan's love and that made it more valuable to her than the Hope Diamond.

Her father stepped out of *Raccoon Cabin* and made some kind of sharp comment to Matt. Shellie grinned when Blue moved protectively between the two of them, facing her father. Matt's face lost its smile and calling the dog he hurried into the *Manager's Cabin* followed by her father.

Blue waited for the two men to shed their coats before shaking ice and snow from his heavy winter fur. The shouts of outrage were too much, she dropped to the floor laughing. The next thing she knew, Ronan had scooped her into his arms, holding her close as he spun in a circle.

Her father frowned at them, his expression reminding Shellie of the less than pleasant comments he made about Ronan and her sharing a cabin. "You aren't married, yet, keep your hands to yourself, young man."

Ronan grinned, hugged her close, and whispered in Shellie's ear, "Don't worry, Angel, he needs something to complain about."

Shellie smiled up into Ronan's face. "You better put me down. I need to make supper, so I can get to work on time."

Ronan slowly lowered her to her feet, holding her against him as he did. Shellie blushed despite herself.

"So, how's the dress going?"

"All done," Mom said.

Leslie twirled in a circle. "This makes me feel like a princess."

Shellie understood. When she had tried on the simple satin sheath wedding gown and the fingertip length veil in *Cinderella's* in Saranac Lake, she'd had the same feeling. "Go look in the full-length mirror. You look like a princess."

Her mom had tears in her eyes as Shellie's fifteen-year-old sister skipped out the door and down the hall. "In another few years it will be her wedding dress. I can't believe my girls are all grown up."

"Now if only their brother would grow up and use his brain, life might be tolerable."

Matt scowled at his father. "Funny, it seems the only time you think I'm using my brain is when I blindly follow your direction."

"I want you to take advantage of my experience, not suffer from making the same mistakes I did. Educators get tenure and are given a level of security other fields don't have. That's why I want you to teach literature."

"You didn't have an easy time of finding a job and that made you an easy mark for the chancellor to bully you. If I got a degree in hospitality management, like Shellie, if the boss is a jerk, I can find another job and I can travel like I want to and still find work."

Dad scowled at Matt. "I'm not paying for your education or your living expenses unless you follow my direction."

"Fine. I'll make my own way, like Shellie did. She and Ronan seem a lot happier with their lives than you do with yours." Matt stomped to the entry, grabbing his coat on the way out and slamming the heavy pine door behind him.

Leslie appeared in the hallway, an anxious expression on her face. She scurried to hide behind her mother. Shellie's heart ached for her younger sister. She and Matt had defied their father on more than one occasion, but her younger sister was the peacemaker, trying hard to pacify angry parents. It worried Shellie that her little sister tried too hard to be perfect, as if she could prevent the anger, hurt, and arguments if she was only good enough. Shellie had tried to do the same, but it was never enough and made the hurt of being abandoned, that much worse. "Hey, Leslie, why don't you get changed and you can help me with dinner. I'll show you how to cook on a woodstove."

"Like that'll be a benefit to her." Dad muttered.

Ronan watched Shellie and her sister hurry to the *Dining Cabin*. He smiled grimly when Matt ambushed them with a barrage of snowballs. Shellie quickly returned fire, encouraging Leslie to join in while Blue snapped the icy missiles out of the air. His heart did a funny flip flop when he spotted Shellie blocking Matt's snowballs from hitting Leslie. Eventually the three ran laughing into the *Dining Cabin*. How had his sweet Angel turned out so well growing up in such an unpleasant environment?

He nodded to himself. Shellie was with him and safe from further abuse, but her siblings weren't and knowing his soft-hearted Angel, she'd be hurt by Matt's and Leslie's troubles. Time for a little man to man talk with his future father-in-law.

Ronan slipped on his coat and handed Mr. Morgan his garment. "Let's take a wander down by the river. The view suggests Victor Hugo's poem, *Tomorrow, At Dawn*."

Shellie's father jerked around, as if surprised Ronan knew anything about literature and poetry. He seemed about to protest, but Ronan wrapped an arm around Morgan's shoulders, propelling him out the door. As they approached the river, Ronan let go with a slight shove and stepped out onto the snow-covered dock.

"I'm assuming this is your way of saying you want a private discussion?" Shellie's father huffed. "Bringing up a poem where Hugo remembers his dead daughter lacks subtly. My daughter isn't dead."

Ronan looked at the man. "I want to understand how you can be so abusive to your children? Right now, your oldest daughter could indeed be dead, if things had been even the slightest bit different."

Shellie's father shouted explosively. "How dare you make such an accusation? I want what is best for my children. That means being the bad guy sometimes. I'm their father, not their friend. If I was an abusive parent, I'd have taken my belt to them like my father did to me.

I never once struck my babies. Even the one that ruined my life with her existence. I am not abusive."

Ronan had a hunch he'd been given a key to the source of the issue. "Tell me about your father. From what Shellie has said, he died fairly young."

The older man sighed and moved to lean against the railing. "I'm nothing like my father, thank God. He was a big, brash man who loved sports and the outdoors and working with his hands. He also loved to drink and always had a beer or two at lunch time. He worked construction. One afternoon he fell off some steel girders. His safety harness was attached incorrectly, and it disconnected. He died on impact."

Ronan gave the man some time to collect himself. "That had to be hard on the family. How old were you?"

"I was twelve. Dad's life insurance didn't pay out because he had alcohol in his blood. Suddenly it was just my mother and me and a house with a huge mortgage. Mom was a school teacher and had tenure, so we had some income, but not enough. We sold the house, moved into a small place and Mom encouraged me to follow an academic career. I was already a bookworm and my lack of sports prowess was always a disappointment to my dad, but after he was gone, I didn't have to be afraid he'd hit me, throw my books, and grab my collar to throw me outside because he saw me reading. Books became my friends. Literature was so easy for me, it was natural to go into that field."

"Why didn't you get higher degrees or teach at the high school level?"

"I always wanted the life I saw my professors have instead of living on the tight income of a school teacher. I would've had it too, if Shellie hadn't come along. As soon as she was born I had her mother quit working so she could be home with the baby, but it meant I couldn't get additional degrees."

Ronan compressed snow from the railing into a snowball. "Couldn't you have gone to night school and worked days?"

"How would I pay for it? And besides, after working all day I was too tired to study at night."

Ronan turned to face Shellie's dad. "Don't you realize Shellie worked two jobs and went to school? Why can't you compliment her on what she's achieved?"

"If I do, Matt will follow in her footsteps and I can't allow that."

Ronan considered his next words carefully. "I get the feeling Matt's interest in sports and outside activities reminds you of your father."

Shellie's dad nodded. "Shellie is my dad in a skirt, but Matt reminds me of my father, too. It terrifies me that he'll make the same kinds of mistakes. He has always pushed the boundaries, but now that he thinks Shellie is a success he refuses to listen to what I have to say about his future. I'm afraid he'll end up homeless on the street with a useless degree and a huge debt."

Ronan's temper flared. "Funny, making Shellie homeless didn't seem to bother you at all."

"What was I to do? It was either send her out on her own or have my whole family without a roof over our heads. I tried to get her to compromise and accept responsibility, so she could stay, but no, she had to fight until I had to make a choice between her or the rest of the family."

"Why do you still believe Shellie was at fault?"

"Have you looked at her lifestyle? She's living in sin with you."

"We live in the same building, but in different rooms. It isn't any different than living in co-ed dorms."

"She had multiple chances to accept that she was at least a contributor to what happened and get her old life back. But would she do it? No. She had to put all the blame on that poor, young man."

Ronan could feel angry heat climbing his face. Only his military training allowed him to speak in a normal tone. "What did she do that makes you exonerate that creep and blame her?"

"You should have seen the way she dressed. Tight tee-shirts and jeans, short, tight skirts. Look at the length of her uniform skirt if you want an idea of how she looked. She was a huge tease, getting young men with raging hormones all excited and no way to relieve their stress. It's up to the women to comport themselves so they don't drive young men mad with lust."

Ronan practiced some breathing exercises to calm his rage. He had been an officer. He needed to handle himself with that level of dignity and rise above the emotions and tempers. It had never been this difficult before, but then, it had never been about a woman he loved and would protect with his life. "In discussions with Shellie's therapist, we went over things where she felt she contributed to the situation, like her appearance. She felt horribly guilty because you held her responsible, but what we learned, going through pictures, was Shellie was more conservatively dressed than her peers."

"So what? College girls' wardrobes are designed to drive men beyond their limits of control. She could have worn looser clothing and less makeup. And I saw her making eyes at Chad. What was the poor boy to do?"

"Not drug her, for one thing," Ronan snapped. He ran his hand through his hair trying to find the right words. "In the military we're dealing with healthy young men and women, living and working in close quarters. While rape isn't unknown, it is not common. It comes from respecting and taking responsibility for your own actions. We did a lot of training, so everyone understood. Most colleges have similar sensitivity training."

"That nonsense. Now that the chancellor is gone, the new man has insisted the staff take all that feel-good training where no one is to blame. I wanted to teach at this college because they had some old-fashioned values. Those left with the chancellor, and it's all because my daughter couldn't resist flirting."

Ronan collected some snow and crushed it into another icy ball. "Even if Shellie flirted with Chad, he had to know she wasn't interested in a physical relationship with him or he wouldn't have had a date rape drug on hand."

"Date rape drug," Shellie's father scoffed. "She knew want was happening, so she had to have been able to protest. It was her excuse."

"That comment makes me want to roofy you and see if you still believe that in the morning."

Morgan's eyes widened, and he took a step back.

Ronan kept packing the snowball. It was that or strangle the man next to him. "You believe in education, right?"

Shellie's father swallowed and nodded.

Ronan slipped into drill instructor mode. "Right? I can't hear you."

"Right." Morgan croaked.

"Then educate yourself, because your ignorance is showing. Look up the drugs your daughter was given and while you're at it, look up verbal and emotional abuse. Your father was a physical abuser. You abuse with words, and you of all people should know that words have the power to hurt. Do you understand me?"

"Y-yes."

"Good boy. Now here is what else you are going to do: you're going to bite your tongue and never again say Shellie is responsible for what happened."

"Or what?" Morgan sneered.

"Your words are hurting someone I value more than my life. When I see her cry, or her eyes fill with self-doubt I get a purely unholy desire to hurt the source of her pain. So far, I've exercised a heroic level of self-control, mostly because she isn't my wife, yet. Once I vow before God to love, honor, and protect her I'll be a whole lot more likely to slip the leash on that control. You really don't want to be on the receiving end when that happens."

Shellie's dad met Ronan's eyes and swallowed hard. Sometimes the only way to get through to a bully was to be a bigger bully. "Since we're on the subject of what upsets my future wife, let's talk about Matt and Leslie. You are not going to stand in their way of following the career of their dreams, even if it is not a role in academia. You pursued your dream. Let them pursue theirs. As for not having a roof over their heads, well, the *Pine Cone Motel* will always have space available for them."

"Are you threatening me?"

"I'm promising. There is a difference."

Shellie's father finally looked away. "Fine."

Epilogue

Shellie stood in her black robe and mortar board hat and scanned the crowd. It didn't take her long to find Blue and Ronan, who grinned and snapped pictures. Her grandmother sat on one side of him. Her brother and sister were sandwiched between her parents on his other side. Things were starting to get better. Her dad had stopped making comments about her being responsible for what happened with Chad and had even talked civilly to Matt about getting career testing. A week without raised voices had done wonders for Leslie. She laughed and roughhoused with Blue and giggled over toasted marshmallows and hot chocolate through more than one board game.

The director came through and shooed Shellie back behind the curtain. It was hard to keep her mind on the graduation ceremony when there was so much still to be done before the wedding. They would host a small reception at the *Pine Cone Motel* and then leave for a short three-day honeymoon in New York City. Ronan's parents had already agreed to move into the motel and take care of the snowmobile guests while they were gone. Although, Shellie's mother had become adept at checking guests in and out and kept hinting she wanted to stay longer.

Ronan's dad had only accepted the material and labor costs for the pool repairs and returned the rest of the money. Shellie had invested most of it in a modern Wi-Fi system, large screen television, and high-speed internet at the motel. Remembering the stories Ronan and finally Mr. Grady had told her, she promised herself that the *Pine Cone Motel* would be a haven where the next generation of teens could come for a sympathetic and supportive ear. In Mrs. McClelland's generation that meant books and board games, now it meant video games. Of course, she would still buy the latest games from *Goody Goody's* and books from the *Book Nook*.

She promised herself she would carry on the same kind of investment as Mrs. McClelland and hoped and prayed she would make the kind of difference in a young life that her mentor had done. Thanks to Mrs. McClelland, she and Ronan had been able to turn their lives around. Now it was their turn, as they had promised.

The band struck up Pomp and Circumstance and the graduates filed in. As she listened to the speeches, Shellie reflected on the changes in her life. Her relationship with her parents was still strained, but they were at least communicating. She glanced up and smiled at Ronan. It really didn't matter because above all else she had him. A man who loved and respected her and encouraged her to dream. And the haven of the *Pine Cone Motel* where so many dreams became the reality of love.

Author's note

First, let me apologize, this book does not center around a search and rescue dog, but is more of a romance. The original intent was to convert Blue into a SAR dog, but like many characters, Ronan, Shellie and Blue refused to cooperate with the author and took her down a completely unplanned path. *Out of the Storm* was wrapped around a search and the next book in the series, *Labrador Tea,* will take place almost entirely on a search for a missing person so I hope my readers will forgive the slight break and accept a military working dog/service dog character instead.

Blue is loosely based on my son's dog, Boomer. Very loosely as Boomer is a family pet and has never been trained as a MWD or a service animal. The photo of the dog on the cover was provided by the breeder of my current sport puppy, Chet.

A note about service dogs. Emotional service dogs require no training. There have been a number of reports of this fact being abused with unruly pets. Military Working Dogs (MWD) have a great deal of training which includes protection work and when I contacted institutions training service dogs, they said they would not train MWDs for service work because of their protection training. They also pointed out some MWDs return with the canine version of PTSD. Real service dogs, including those providing emotional support to individuals with PTSD, have an extensive personality testing and training to make them effective. Please consider carefully before you claim your pet is a service dog so it may enter a public facility. If the abuse continues, restrictions will be put into place that will hinder access for these wonderful animals, providing a life changing service to their handlers.

I would also like to mention there is not a youth hostel in Saranac Lake. I am sure the youth hostel near Lake Placid is much nicer than the hostel in this book. However, if things had worked out for Shellie at the hostel, there wouldn't have been a need to rehabilitate the Pine Cone Motel and this wouldn't have been much of a story.

One of the questions my beta readers asked is why Shellie didn't apply for education loans and why she and Ronan didn't apply for public assistance. Many people in their situation don't know what is available to them. Many people consider it a point of pride they didn't take what they consider as charity. Most people I know give generously with no expectation of receiving anything in return. It is much harder, sometimes, to accept help than to give it. There was enough going on in this story not to delve into this point of the characters' psyche.

Those who read the previous books will recognize their main character cameos and may pick up on the fact that Ruby's husband was promoted to Pastor, from youth pastor, of his church in Saranac Lake.

Pine Cone Motel is the third in a four book series set in the Adirondack Mountains. *Sophie's Search* was set in Lake Placid. *Out of the Storm* took place near Keene and had some of the geographic characteristics of Au Sable Chasm. *Pine Cone Motel* features Saranac Lake. The shops and restaurants mentioned in this book exist and are great places for coffee, dining and shopping. The author has done her best to contact them and send them advanced copies for approval to include them on these pages. Please drop in and patronize them, you might run into the author sipping a Lavender Latte or chowing down on a Reuben sandwich.

Made in the USA
Lexington, KY
16 July 2019